Mary Earnshaw was born in Lancash
read history at Oxford. Her career be
then rambled through consultancy
rectorship with a regional utility company.

She has always managed to fit in some freelance writing for newspapers, magazines and businesses and now runs a small academic publishing venture which allows her to drop everything whenever Africa beckons.

Mary caught the Africa bug on a working trip to Zimbabwe and South Africa. She met her husband, Professor Larry Barham, in Swaziland where they worked together for several seasons on archaeological digs. Thanks to Larry, who lets her tag along on his adventures, she has now been visiting Zambia for 18 years and has never been bored. To misquote Pliny the Elder, there is always something new in Africa.

A Wake of Vultures

Mary Earnshaw

Cosi & Veyn, Liverpool
MMXII

First published in England in 2012 by Cosi & Veyn, an imprint of the Western Academic & Specialist Press Ltd, PO Box 191, Liverpool L23 3WZ

ISBN 978-0-9535418-3-6

A catalogue record for this book is available from the British Library.

Typeset in Leawood Book and Baskerville Old Face by Password Publishing Services, Burnham Deepdale, Norfolk, PE31 8DD http://www.passwordpublish.co.uk

Printed by Oriel Studios Digital Ltd, Orrell Mount, Hawthorne Road, Bootle, L20 6NS

Dedication

To all the peoples of the Luangwa Valley, Zambia

Humans of one species or another have lived in this remote and fabulous rift valley for nearly two million years, but now their cultural heritage is under threat. In a place where wild animals so often come first, the people who made way for the National Park in which they thrive surely deserve a showcase of their own. Twenty-five per cent of the profit from the sales of this book will therefore go to the University of Liverpool Africa Endowment Fund, set up by Professor Larry Barham, to help achieve his goal of building a heritage centre in the Luangwa Valley.

Acknowledgements

There are so many game scouts, guides and lodge staff in the Luangwa Valley and elsewhere in Zambia who have helped create this book that I can't mention them all by name. At Wildlife Camp in particular, where I have spent so much time over the last 10 years, there must be hundreds of people who have contributed in one way or another to this tale – and to my comfort and enjoyment – so, thank you all most sincerely for your hospitality, kindness and tolerance.

Officials – colleagues – from the National Heritage Conservation Commission have been excellent advisers, hosts and friends over the years. Scouts (and their bosses) from the Zambia Wildlife Authority, ZAWA, have taught us much, kept us safe and been great conversationalists to boot.

Pioneer Camp, Lusaka, deserves a mention for its intergalactic bar (not really, it just feels like it) where I have not only met countless interesting people whose idiosyncrasies have fed into my fictional characters but eaten some great steaks and chips.

I am deeply indebted to Margaret Melitsiotis, Patsy Hahn, Rebecca Wilson and Stephen Robinson for taking the time to read and comment upon this book in draft form. I am also very grateful to Patsy for all her encouragement and help over the last few years and during some difficult times. Professional readers from Hilary Johnson's Authors' Advisory Service were kindly constructive - it's all my fault if it's still not right!

I am doubly grateful to Stephen Robinson, not just for reading the draft, for his encouragement and for all the knowledge he has shared but for the photograph used on the cover of this book (which he designed). To see more visit *Spirit of the Land* http://www.spirit-of-the-land.com/ which is a not-for-profit project highlighting the importance of Zambia's natural environment to the welfare of human populations.

Peter and Penny Simmons of Password Publishing have been more than just helpful and professional with words and fonts and meanings, so has Pete Copple at Oriel Studios - may print never die. Thank you all for your advice, moral support - and good deals!

AND FINALLY. Thank you, Larry, for more than that.

Chapter 1

Dry grass, shoulder high, rustled and crackled as they walked in line. Isaiah, a skinny man in a game scout's dark green uniform, led them through the scrubby vegetation with cautious steps, his eyes alert to any sign of life. He stopped and listened. Turning, he made a sign to the young woman walking a few paces behind him. Birgit, the guide from their camp, stretched out her arm, signalled the six walkers to keep still, then moved forward, alone, as if in slow motion.

Tension rose in stifling waves through the watching clutch of tourists.

Birgit edged closer to their scout.

Centuries passed, or so it seemed to Lizzie, bringing up the rear and feeling vulnerable, the sun scorching her shoulders through the faded green of an army surplus shirt.

Isaiah raised his rifle.

Lizzie felt warm sweat trickle through the knot of hair coiled under her hat.

Birgit was level with Isaiah now. The two leant together and stared in the direction of a tree trunk burnt in the last bush fires. With a snarl and a shriek the leopard streaked across their vision like a demon – and was gone. Birgit turned around, her voice low, but firm.

'Sorry folks, I was hoping we'd see him in action. Isaiah thought he hadn't spotted us. But not bad for the first cat sighting of the day. Isaiah, thanks for that, perhaps you could start us off again. Remember, everyone – quiet, careful, just like the wildlife.'

They resumed their stealthy patrol.

The early morning cool had mutated into a dry, almost opaque heat. Sweat was seeping through everyone's clothing, the silence becoming oppressive.

After a few minutes' stalking Isaiah stopped again, turned to Birgit, then pointed straight ahead.

'Ah, yes. I can see them. Up ahead folks, a few hundred metres away – can you see the vultures circling? Looks like there may be some kind of kill nearby, possibly very recent since they've just started appearing. We'll take it steady in case there's something big there.'

On they stepped, tall grass blades drawing the occasional gasp of pain as they inflicted tiny wounds, sudden and sharp as paper cuts.

The grass up ahead was beginning to look disturbed. At each step it became more tangled, more matted, till at last it was clear that a struggle had taken place. Isaiah stopped again, looked around and then signalled to Birgit to stop. He raised his rifle and this time they all heard the click of its cocking.

'Stay quiet, take it slowly,' mouthed Birgit. 'If anything comes at you just stand still, don't run. OK, let's move.'

They strode forward over the crumpled stems.

A woman in the middle of the line was the first to cry out. Everyone else was reduced to a groan or a gasp. In front of them was a fresh kill, oozing blood. The vultures hesitated, distracted for the briefest of moments, then resumed their feast, pecking at the body, pulling at juicy chunks of flesh. Isaiah ran forward, waving his gun, shouting at the birds to go. The dark shapes took wing, landing just a few metres further away. But then they hopped back, tenacious, irreverent. Isaiah grabbed a handful of stones and threw them at the creatures. As they hit their marks the birds flapped off to circle overhead, but all too soon they began the descent to resume their sinister feast.

Birgit turned to Isaiah, even paler than usual.

'What are we going to do? I don't know what to do. I ...'

It was as if the voice had drained from her body, not just the colour.

Isaiah took charge.

'I must radio for help, madam. This man, he must be carried home. These people cannot do this. You and I cannot do this. They will come with a vehicle. Do not worry.'

Birgit turned to look at the gory mess before them. Lizzie turned too, willing herself to be wrong, but she was not. The vultures had been pecking at the body of a man, a white man. She had a horrible feeling she knew who it was, that distinctive, long pale hair in disarray, the Hawaiian shirt and baggy shorts. Birgit's one time lover

– Jake, the Valley's Lothario – would not be stringing her along any more. Whatever, whoever, was there before the vultures had made sure of that. Birgit turned and ran a few paces before throwing up into the grass. Lizzie ran after her and clasped her by the shoulders.

'Come on, sit down. We can't go back yet, Isaiah's right, we have to stay here and wait for help. Come on.' She helped Birgit slump into a sitting position and then turned and walked over to the rest of the group, accidental voyeurs, torn between the two dramas unfolding before them: the kill and the aftermath.

'Does anyone by any chance have a hip flask? Our guide knew this man very well, he was the local vet – she's obviously shocked. I think a slug of spirits might help.'

A portly man of middle height and uncertain years – hard to tell if he was nearer thirty or fifty beneath the safari gear of the wealthy American – reached into one of the many pockets in his hunting waistcoat and pulled out a flask covered in puckered ostrich skin. It came with its own little silver cup. Lizzie smiled her thanks and took the offering. She turned to find Birgit standing, looking towards the bloody mess that everyone else was avoiding. Stepping nearer to the body, with some reluctance, she proffered the tiny goblet. Birgit gulped down the brandy.

'Oh, God, Lizzie, I thought it was Jake – that hair, the clothes – but it's not. Thank God. It's not him.'

Shocked by the joy that now transfigured her friend's face, but wary of upsetting her, Lizzie said nothing. She touched the young woman's arm in an expression of silent solidarity, then forced herself to look at the obscenity to which everyone else had turned their backs. Isaiah alone was scrutinising the body. Lizzie turned a puzzled face towards him.

'It's not Jake Deacon, is it?'

'No, Professor. This man, I think he is the new guest who hunts for bones. The man who has been trying to find you and Doctor Alex when you do not wish to be found.'

A big grin flashed over his face and was gone almost before she saw it. She kept her own amusement in check, it was hardly the time for mirth. But the game scout was right, ever since he arrived, she and her husband, Alex, had been evading the man who now lay before her. Harvey Miller: university professor, fossil hunter and absolute bastard. Dead absolute bastard.

Chapter 2

The body, wrapped in a grey groundsheet, was hoisted onto the shoulders of two strong men and dumped in the back of a battered pick-up truck. No weeping, no reverence, just a job that had to be done. They were taking the corpse to Elephant Camp – the base where Lizzie, her husband Alex and his crew of student archaeologists were spending the digging season. The Camp's old brick-built cold store had long been superseded by an array of battered chest freezers, heavily insulated against the erratic public power supply – and the Camp's own temperamental Chinese generator. The not-so-cold room was now used as a generic store and, on very rare occasions, such as this, as a makeshift mortuary. In its cool and private sanctuary a cursory post-mortem examination would be conducted by the closest thing to experts the Valley could muster.

Staff in red aprons from the next-door kitchen were still clearing space for the body when it arrived, removing tins, pots and bottles to leave just a large wooden table. The mortal remains of Harvey Miller had no choice but to wait. At last the corpse was laid out in the chapel-like cool of the dark and otherwise empty interior.

The rest of the place was deserted. Lunch had come and gone, the zinc-roofed kitchen was abandoned, door locked, windows shuttered.

A solitary Lizzie stood deep in thought under a flamboyant tamarind tree that shaded both the kitchen and the cold store. Its fruits, brown pods rich with a fleshy pulp, were a favourite of the monkeys skittering through the branches. The occasional sticky pawful dropped to the ground as she waited for Jake – vet, amateur pathologist and still very much alive – to join her for their semi-expert examination of the body.

With a roar his boneshaker of a pick-up truck rounded the bend in the dirt road and shuddered to a halt. Observing him as he approached, Lizzie could see that his grey-blonde hair was much longer than Harvey Miller's, long enough to be tied back in a surprisingly neat plait today. But otherwise, the shorts were similarly baggy, the shirt equally loud and the skin tanned to pretty much the same tobacco shade. It had been an understandable mistake.

Jake slopped over on leather sandals that were old enough to be collectors' items.

'Hey, Professor, how you doing? Long time no see a body, eh? More than a year since the last one. God, was that a case of the blind leading the blind. Brushed up on your techniques since then, by any chance?'

'Yeah, I did a forensics update in our anatomy department, but it's all about equipment now – so unless you've got a mass spectrometer tucked in the back of your pick-up it won't make a blind bit of difference.'

'Well that's a relief, I hate getting upstaged by pretty chicks. Where is the little bugger?'

'You have such a lovely turn of phrase, Jake. The little bugger's in the cold room. They've set up a table for us. And Thomas Nkhoma's on his way from Parks HQ.'

'Why? Oh, I get it, the death happened in the Park. So that means we don't need to bother with the police, does it, Professor? Please tell me we don't.'

'If we're lucky. Thomas will have to schmooze around the local sergeant – but as long as he keeps them informed and there's no evidence of hanky-panky it's his Park, his authority and he gets to sort it out. Should be pretty straightforward. It looked to me like he left his vehicle by the side of the road, stopped for a pee – or to take a picture or something – got dragged off by some vicious beast and died in the long grass.'

'Vicious beast, eh? That's a handy term. See a lot of those around here. Can we narrow it down any further d'you suppose, Professor?'

'Stop calling me Professor! If I knew what kind of animal it was, I'd say.'

Lizzie gritted her teeth. She hated showing nerves, especially to someone like Jake, but the prospect of the post-mortem was making her tense. Fresh bones, caked with flesh, crusty with dried blood – that was not her thing. Ancient fossils, caked with dirt, crusty with age – especially the bones of *Theropithecus darti,* a rather special and long-extinct baboon – now that most definitely was her thing.

'Let's get this over with before the rot sets in, shall we?' Lizzie squinted up at the cloudless blue sky. It was winter in the southern hemisphere, but the sun was searing. 'This is the tropics, after all.'

'No, really? Aren't you clever? I just thought it was jolly warm and the trees were a pretty shade of green. I'll get my bag of tricks.'

He winked at her.

She seethed.

That man always wound her up. She took a deep breath, stepped into the sombre chill of the room with its baleful guest and pulled on her latex gloves. The light was not great, but there was little she could do about that.

The door swung open and a whistling Jake Deacon breezed in.

'Got a head torch? Jolly useful. I've got a spare if you want.'

Annoyed at herself – it was an obvious solution to the problem – she took the torch from the vet without so much as a thank you and pulled it on.

Both experts – neither in the field of pathology – stood, staring at the mess before them as if mesmerised. They both spoke at once.

'I think –'

'You know –'

'You first, green eyes.' Jake's grin was eerie in the half light.

Lizzie sighed in exasperation.

'I was just going to say, it doesn't really look like an animal kill to me, in fact . . . '

She bent forward and peered at the neck. Her tone changed.

'Jake, take a look at the neck.'

'Bloody hell, the guy's been garrotted, or I'm a Dutchman. Looks just like the animals I find in poachers' snares.'

'I think you're right, it's certainly some kind of strangulation. Oh, bugger, you realise that makes it murder? That means we have to get the police involved.'

Jake groaned, but before he could speak there was a knock on the door. It opened with a creak, revealing Isaiah, the scout who had been guarding the guests on the walking safari which had happened across the unfortunate Professor Miller.

'Professor, I have spoken to madam Maggie, she says I should speak to you about this man who is dead.'

Somewhere in the background Lizzie could hear Maggie, one half of the couple who ran Elephant Camp, shouting into the bush radio, and wondered, irritated at the interruption, why she had not come herself.

'Is it urgent, Isaiah?'

'Madam said to tell you right away.'

'Tell me what?' Lizzie bit back her impatience. Then it dawned on her: the poor man was standing in a dark room containing a dead body with two searchlights shining in his face.

'I'm sorry, just give us a second, Isaiah. Wait outside, we'll come and talk to you there.'

The relief was visible on his face as they stepped out into the welcoming warmth of the sun.

Jake pulled off his gloves and slapped Isaiah on the back.

'So, big man, what's the story?'

Isaiah, a slip of a man, ignored the joke. He was in the presence of death.

'Sir,' he pronounced it the local way, 'seh', 'this man did not just walk from his car. I am looking around this place where he died. I see the grass is very broken. I follow this grass and see it is like this all the way back to where his car it is parked. By his car I see marks of feet, to me they say one person has dragged this other person away from this vehicle.'

'My, my. That *is* helpful, Isaiah. Thank you. The good Professor and I are just looking at the man's body to see how he died.' Jake paused. 'Dragged, hmm? That figures. Well done.'

Jake held out his hand and shook that of the 'big man', who disappeared into the bushes, at a trot.

'Where's he going?' asked Jake.

'To the staff quarters, they're hidden in the scrub. I walk past them to get to the campsite if there are elephants on the riverbank path. But you never know what's lurking in the bushes either – so it's a bit of a gamble.'

Elephant Camp was divided into three sections that hugged a bend in the Luangwa river: on the side where Lizzie and Jake now stood was a small, basic office, a thatched 'dining room' or restaurant and a handful of thatched chalets; the strategic centre location was reserved for the owners' house and staff quarters; the third, budget site was a large campground dotted with trees which straggled off into the bush on the far side.

The Luangwa, a tributary of the Zambezi and itself one of Zambia's three most impressive rivers, formed a visible – but permeable – boundary for the South Luangwa National Park. This vast expanse of unpopulated bush boasted some of the best wildlife in Africa which, with no fence to keep it in, roamed freely to and fro, day and night. Elephants, hippos, giraffes, lions, buffalos – and battalions of baboons – passed through the Camp on a regular basis. Only the rhinos, poached to extinction, were absent. Outside the Park, but in plain view of its treasures, Elephant Camp was the perfect spot for travellers with limited means, such as archaeologists and fossil baboon-bone experts.

An important local official was approaching the baboon-bone expert now: Thomas Nkhoma, the man with the almost impossible task of running the South Luangwa National Park for Zambia's parks authority. With a slew of academic qualifications, including an MSc from Cambridge and a PhD from Berkeley, Thomas was a formidable critic, a great conversationalist – and not a little eccentric.

He stopped now, spread his arms wide and burst into song.

Jake, for the first time, looked at a loss.

'I wish I had a picture of your face right now!' laughed Lizzie.

Thomas mopped his brow. The outburst of song had been an effort.

'Dr Deacon, I have disconcerted you! This charming song was from the film, "My Fair Lady" and referred to the delightful Miss Eliza Dolittle.' Thomas frowned, 'But I see you are still confused, maybe you did not know that Eliza is the Professor's real name? Remind me, Professor, who was it played her in that film?'

'Audrey Hepburn. And no, I don't look at all like her before you say anything rude, Jake. Thomas, it's lovely to see you, how are you – and Jane and the girls?'

Lizzie looked down at her hands and realised she was in no fit state to perform the usual polite handshake routine.

'I'm sorry, we're just in the middle . . . '

'Don't worry, we shall have many chances to shake hands again, God willing. Me – I am fine and my girls are fine and my wife is fine. And I am pleased to say I have seen your husband already this week. The great Alexander came to see me for my most valuable signature on his permit. Which of course I have given him with no fuss or bother, as usual. This is not Lusaka.'

As regional Parks boss, the man whose word was law across

the river, Thomas Nkhoma could easily have made life very difficult for the two researchers. His predecessor had been a nightmare, but for three years Thomas had been an ally. His conspicuous lack of interest in Alex's archaeological research, or Lizzie's fossil baboon-bone quest, was offset by his genuine delight in studying wildlife – and people.

Thomas was rarely to be seen without a smile on his face, but now it was eclipsed as he considered what lay within the old cold store.

'My good people, tell me, have you had a chance to examine the body?'

Lizzie looked at Jake and raised her eyebrows as if to say, 'Go on, you're the official one here.'

'Bad news, I'm afraid,' Jake shrugged. 'We've only just started and the vultures have made a pretty mess, but it's already obvious the guy's been garrotted – it's definitely murder. Your scout Isaiah was there when they found him – he's just told us the grass was beaten down between the victim's car and the spot where he was found, so we were just going to look and see if there are any signs he's been dragged.'

Thomas frowned and tapped one foot in its polished, nut-brown shoe, raising a puff of orange dust. He took a deep breath and exhaled like a sighing wind.

'I have come by some information which suggests that he was not all that he seemed. I know he was not your favourite man, Professor,' she looked surprised and Thomas's smile returned, 'a certain Doctor Alexander Sommers mentioned to me that you did not have the profoundest admiration for Professor Miller. I have done a little digging of my own – not the archaeological kind of course – and I can see why that might be. But I am detaining you – please, carry on with your sad task, we may talk when you are done. I will see if I can find Maggie, she and I have a little project we must discuss – and I feel a rumbling coming from the depths of my slender belly. Perhaps she will assuage my pangs of hunger with a morsel of cake and a cup of tea.'

Thomas walked away patting his large round belly in its pristine, but rather tightly fitting white shirt.

Lizzie shook her head, amused and amazed.

'How does he keep so clean? I'm covered in orange dust the

minute I step out of the door.'

'And very lovely it is too, goes with your hair. Come on, let's get this over with.'

The two returned to their labours, to the chill, the dark and the dead.

Chapter 3

Humming, Thomas made his way to the small thatched hut which served Maggie as an office. Here the all-important bush radio crackled and whined, here the hefty safe sat brooding in one corner and here sat Maggie, cigarette in hand. Stolidly middle-aged, tough as old boots but twice as soft, her round face was the perennial pale of the white Zambian, framed by faded blond hair tinged with nicotine. As Thomas drew near he could hear her berating a young woman for mixing up a guest's laundry.

'Just look at the size of the thing, does it look like it belongs with the others? Never mind, I'll post it on to her. Let's hope she had another one! Off you go.' She swivelled in her chair and threw a skinny black and white cat off her lap.

'Thomas, how the devil are you?'

She stood and shook hands with the National Park Chief in the traditional Zambian way, a pattern of three rapid clasps.

'I am fine, my dear Maggie, how are you?'

'I am fine.'

The rites duly performed, Maggie went straight to Thomas's heart.

'Chef's just made date and peanut cake – can I offer you a slice with some tea?'

His stomach growled in appreciation.

They wandered over to the dining room, a thatched canopy supported by hefty tree trunks on a concrete base, and sank into heavy chairs of local wood. Beyond them, the ground dropped steeply and after about fifty metres the flat, parched grass and desiccated bushes gave way to the sandy borders of the glistening river. The homeward-heading sun was already seeking the high escarpment on the edge of the Valley. In two hours' time it would sink there for the night, leaving darkness to the wildlife. Even now the braver, or more foolish, animals were venturing out. A small herd of nervous impalas grazed around a nearby clump of bushes. A family of elephants began wading in line across the river, seeking ripe tamarinds from the Camp's many trees.

'What a lovely view.' Thomas turned to Maggie. 'And what a shame we humans have to spoil God's natural order.'

'You say that, but it's not as if the animals are nice to each other, is it? I saw a leopard kill right out here the other night – made my blood run cold. The strength of those shoulders as it dragged the impala away. Frightening. I sometimes worry about the children we get staying here, they're pretty vulnerable really and you can't always be keeping an eye . . .'

Her words tailed off. She was talking to a man whose first-born, a son, had been killed by an elephant. Just nine years old, he had been collecting wood with his school-friend, a weekly boarder who had to make his own fires to cook his own food, or starve.

'I'm sorry, Thomas. I didn't mean to upset you. How is the school kitchen area coming along – and what about the latrines? Have they started yet?'

Thomas shook his head.

'I fear I am becoming impatient with this headmaster. The money has been transferred from England, as you know, but there is not a single sign of progress. He says the supplies are on order, but no one seems to be able to tell me when they will arrive. We are going to have a meeting and press him for some answers.' He fell silent.

'You can press us all you like but we've not got a whole heap of answers.'

They turned to see Jake and Lizzie approaching from the direction of the makeshift morgue.

Jake threw himself into one of the big chairs.

Lizzie shook her head. With two older brothers she was used to fending for herself but it still rankled.

'Thanks Jake, I'll just get myself a chair, you make yourself at home.'

She dragged one over. It made a complaining squeal on the concrete floor.

'Tea, you two?' Maggie asked.

They both nodded. Even Jake was subdued by their confrontation with violent death. He sighed before he spoke.

'We checked his back. We reckon he was dragged, like Isaiah

said, probably by the feet. Definitely murder.' He shrugged and sighed. 'So that means the police. Sorry, Thomas.'

Thomas cleared his throat.

'I will deal with them tomorrow. They will be in no hurry, as we know. The vehicle left by the victim has been taken to Parks HQ, we can do no more for the moment. So, perhaps now is the time to tell you what I have discovered about our dear Professor Miller.'

A snort came from Maggie.

'Dear? That man? He was a total creep. You should have seen some of the guys who came looking for him. Terrifying.'

Everyone turned to stare at her.

'What? I'm just speaking the truth. You weren't here. The day he arrived and pretended to be one of Alex's mates, I knew then he was a wrong 'un. "Professor Miller, *the* Professor Miller, from the USA." Ha! The cheek of the guy. Tried to convince me he was the top man in Alex's field and that he was doing him a big favour coming out here to advise him. I should have known someone that snooty was no friend of Alex.'

'Did he really say he was *advising* Alex?' Lizzie was blazing. 'How dare he, why—'

Maggie interrupted.

'Forget it, Lizzie, he's not worth getting upset about. Now his dubious friends, on the other hand . . .'

Thomas leant forward and put his empty plate on the table before speaking.

'This is all very interesting. We have here a man whose word could not be trusted, who had dubious friends – to which we shall return – and whose ego was out of all proportion to the reality.'

'That's putting it mildly.' Lizzie had calmed down, a little, 'I knew the guy – he was nasty, devious, cunning and a total hypocrite.'

'Professor Lamb, you are being too kind, you have not mentioned that this man was a liar and a cheat.'

Lizzie looked in surprise at Thomas. He rarely spoke ill of anyone other than criminals or poachers.

'Yes, my friends,' Thomas nodded as he spoke, 'he lied and cheated with me, too. I suppose since I had been playing my charade of being a corrupt, lazy African official, delaying his permit, foiling his plans for locating the site where Lizzie's famous bone was found, he was somewhat justified, hmm?'

'Nice one, Thomas. Respect, man,' Jake grinned.

'But I have been checking up on Professor Miller,' Thomas continued. 'I asked him for references from his work in Tanzania – all part of my delaying tactics. He gave me some names and email addresses, but I did not follow them up. Today I sent two emails which came back, so I checked on the internet and he had given me incorrect addresses. Now, my clever young daughter, who is only eight,' he beamed around at the assembled group, 'has installed that free telephone service called Skype on our computer in the office. It has satellite internet access – when the electricity is working. My own antennae were picking up worrying signals, so I thought I would phone one of these gentlemen.'

Jake interrupted with a noisy yawn.

'To cut this long story short,' Thomas responded, 'the man in Tanzania made you look like Miller's most devoted fan, Lizzie. He told me Professor Miller caused nothing but trouble and they revoked his work permit more than three years ago.'

'You can't be serious?' Lizzie's astonishment was plain. 'He's been working there for years, I was at one of his presentations just a couple of months ago in Atlanta. He showed pictures of the excavations and everything.'

'He has been very clever. He has been forcing young researchers to put his name on their articles, even passing some off as his own. He has bribed young Africans to hand over their research findings, telling them he will obtain money for them to do further degrees in America, telling them this is the normal way, that everyone does it. The first one he exploited received funding, so the others all believed him, but you will not be surprised when I tell you that this first one was a rather attractive young woman and the others were young men and they were not so successful.'

He stopped briefly for a sip of sweet tea.

'There have been many complaints, but the man has been most careful to put things in writing, he even has copies of the failed grant applications for their courses. My new friend in Dar es Salaam – a professor at the university – has lost his best archaeologist, because this young woman has now been hired in America. He is incandescent with rage. I must ask him to come to visit, he will find it interesting here professionally – and he sounds like a good egg.'

Lizzie hid her amusement. Thomas had a vast repertoire of English sayings, ancient, modern – and quaint.

If Thomas had planned to say more he was stopped by a rattle and a roar as the main expedition vehicle swung into view.

'Ah!' he exclaimed as the engine fell silent. 'I see the trusty Bucephalus is back from battle.'

For a moment no one said a word. Then Jake spoke for them all.

'Thomas, what on earth are you talking about?'

'The war horse of Alexander the Great, Bucephalus. Our own great Alexander's trusty Land Rover is surely just a modern reincarnation?'

There was nothing much anyone could say to that.

Soon the air reverberated with the clash of buckets, shovels and surveying equipment as the students unloaded the digging kit. News of the murder had reached the digging crew in one of the radio's rare working moments and Alex was plainly concerned about Lizzie. He strode straight to her side, put one arm round her shoulder and held the other out for the obligatory handshakes. Thomas, Jake and Maggie made tactful excuses to head for the bar, leaving the couple alone. But tact was not a student virtue. It was only a matter of moments before one of the noisy gaggle, Zach, came bounding over like a foal up on his legs for the first time.

'Hey, Lizzie, hear you've been splicing a corpse. Man, what a boss job. Can I look?'

'Zach,' Alex's voice strained at the borders of anger, 'this is neither the time nor the place. Bodies are not fun. Lizzie will tell you more when she's ready. Now go and get yourself a drink and give us a few minutes' peace and quiet.'

The youth looked vaguely disgusted and walked off without saying a word.

'What is it with that lad?' asked Lizzie. 'I had him down as a potential PhD before we came out here, but he's being such a pain I'm not sure we'd want him.'

An eruption of noise at the bar diverted Alex. He craned around to see what was going on.

'Ah. Leah's back. Hmm. Doesn't look like she's been crawling over rocks today, does it?'

Leah, a PhD student surveying local caves for rock art, stood out among the other dusty scruffs at the bar – she was the one with the skin-tight white trousers, skimpy t-shirt and short, spiky black hair. The couple watched, spellbound, as Jake sidled up beside her, one hand stroking the peachy contour of her bottom as the other raised a beer to his lips. Lizzie raised her eyebrows and looked at her husband.

'Oh boy,' Alex muttered, 'I think we're in for an interesting season.'

Chapter 4

Jake's presence had upset the group dynamics. The students seemed unusually subdued and as soon as dinner was out of the way Alex drove them over to the campsite where they dispersed, rather than congregating at the bar as usual. Driving back to their chalet he and Lizzie succumbed to the general dampening of spirits and well before ten o'clock the pair was asleep.

As midnight approached, even the sounds of the bush seemed muted: the distant whoop of a hyena, the cough of the night watchman standing over his little fire – it was as if a cloth had been flung over the cage of night.

Inside Chalet five the witching hour came and went.

A restless yet slumbering Lizzie was finding it hard to breathe. Her legs kicked out. She struggled to open her mouth but it was as if someone had taped it shut. She tried to scream but nothing came from her lips except a strangled moan. Gasping free at last, she woke to find Alex looking down on her as she surfaced from a nightmare.

'It's OK, Lizzie. You're all right.' He reached under the mosquito netting, took a glass of water from the bedside table and placed it in Lizzie's hot hands. 'What is it, what were you dreaming about?'

Lizzie looked at the glass as if it were a strange and unwelcome creature, then raised it to her lips and gulped down a great mouthful of water.

'Oh, God, it was horrible. I was standing on the river bank with Birgit watching a huge crocodile drag Jake into the water. There was blood everywhere, he was screaming and screaming but Birgit just stood there laughing like a demon. There was all this thrashing around as the crocodile shook him in his jaws and I knew I shouldn't but I ran into the water. I knew they'd get me too. I could hear the tails beating the water, then my feet started slipping and I realised I couldn't get back, I couldn't get out, I could see you running towards me and I couldn't stop sliding. I knew I was going to die, no one could save me and you were there, you were crying out. Oh, Alex, it was awful.'

One fat tear rolled down her cheek. Alex wiped it away with his finger.

'Sweetheart, I know you had an awful day, but this isn't *just* about the murder, is it?'

More tears escaped.

'I suppose not. No. It's that bone.'

'I thought so. Damn fossil hunters. They're like a pack of bloody hyenas.' He shuffled closer and put his arm around her. 'Look, we knew they'd all pile in once you published the article about the jaw. But they can't just walk in and take over.'

'There's nothing to stop them, is there? They've got more money than we have. They'll just buy their way in. That lot are like sharks with blood when there's a decent fossil find.'

'It's not as bad as all that. I had a chat with Thomas when I was getting our permits. He can't stop them working here, but he won't give them permits for anywhere we're already working. And he's following official procedure to the letter.' Alex stroked her back as he spoke, as if she were a frightened animal. 'You know how long it takes to get permits if you don't know the ropes. They need at least two lots before they can even think about starting work.' Alex paused and wiped her wet face with a tissue. 'They may have east Africa sussed, but they don't know Zambia like we do.'

'That's not the point though, is it?' she sniffed, taking the damp tissue from him. 'Harvey Miller was just the first of many – and probably not even as horrible as some of them. They'll be crawling all over the place before we know it and probably bribing officials in Lusaka to get round Thomas. *Why* did I have to find a jaw with teeth still in it?'

'Yeah, that really did get Harvey Molar-man excited. You know, I won't miss the sight of him blowing his nose in his napkin while we're eating dinner.'

Lizzie almost smiled. She sniffed.

'The other thing is,' she sniffed again, 'they make me feel as if I had no right to find the bone – and even if I had found it, I had no right to publish it. They drop sly hints that maybe I should have stuck to baboon bones, that I don't know enough about *Homo rudolfensis* – or any human ancestors come to that – to publish in *Nature*.'

'Well, you're *not* the world authority – but you had one of the biggest as co-author – and anyway, it was reviewed by lots of other experts. They're just jealous, they're determined to find bigger and better bits before anyone else, but they don't know where we found it, do they? You can just smile serenely, tell them you're not really interested in early humans and you're hot on the trail of some more *Theropithecus darti* which you find *much* more interesting. They're vain – they'll probably believe you. A young woman, out here with her husband – can't be serious. They'll run around hunting for needles in this huge haystack while we apply our little grey cells to the task.'

'You're right. I know. I'll try and keep my cool. It's just that it's been such a big deal, finding a really key bit of such a rare species, it's kind of got to me.' She wriggled down in the bed and pulled up the white sheet. 'I'm sorry I woke you up – but I feel lots better for talking about it.'

'I'm glad. Come on. Let's try and get some sleep before the fish eagles start.'

Alex turned out his torch, bent over and kissed her. Moonlight slid through the wire mesh windows turning their mosquito nets a ghostly white.

A hundred paces away, down an orange dirt track, the night watchman saw the light go out in Chalet five. As the British couple slept, he turned his face in the direction of the kitchen, ears straining for the sound of footsteps. There was nothing. Maybe the new man from the kitchen had not been able to slip away tonight with the flask. Lucky he had brought his own tea again. He looked at the sky and reckoned it would be light in about four hours – a long time still to go. He sat, laid his head on the wall and then he, too, slept. No one was there to watch the night watchman, after all.

Chapter 5

Dawn was running late. The cry of the fish eagle, plaintive as a lost soul, was muffled beneath a thick blanket of cloud that had slipped in under cover of dark. Lizzie frowned as she padded away from the mesh window of the thatched hut. This weather was all wrong. Africa should be sunny, winter or no winter. Strange things happened when the clouds rolled in, everyone behaving out of character, including the animals, and frankly, she had enough on her plate already. Standing naked in the near-dark, she turned the shower's metal handle and squealed as it gave her a small electric shock. Warm brown water began to trickle out through the ancient shower head, scenting the air with the tang of wet iron as she picked up her shampoo from the rough concrete floor.

'This hole in the floor's blocking up again, I bet it's my conditioner. Maybe it'll keep the snakes out.'

In the adjoining section of the thatched hut, screened by a head-height wall, Alex yawned. He poked his head around the corner.

'Are you coming out with me today? Only I really need to get a move on.'

'Of course I am! Give me a break, it's not even six yet.'

Alex smiled and kept his peace. Mornings did not become Eliza.

He stopped, head cocked, listening.

'Lizzie, do we have any neighbours at the moment?'

'Nope, the chalets are all empty. That's why we got such a good deal. Why?' She paused and listened. Turning off the water she stepped into the bedroom.

'Is that a vehicle?' Lizzie asked as she padded, dripping, round to the other side of the room to fetch her hairbrush from the bedside table.

'Yeah, a noisy one. Looks like two people, man and a woman. Oh great. Jake Deacon. Are you fit?'

Alex's intruder alert was too late. Jake had already jumped from his pick-up truck and was at the door, the open door. Lizzie shrieked and ran back to the sanctuary of the shower.

'Jake, I'm not dressed.'

'Doesn't bother me, sweetheart, seen it all before.'

'You've not seen all *me* before. Just get out and stay out till I've got some bloody clothes on.'

'Yes, sir, ma'am, Professor Lamb.'

Alex and Jake stepped outside. Jake lit a thin black cigar that looked battered, as if it had been smoked in instalments between heavy-duty action sequences. The two stood in silence watching one baboon diligently grooming another as the rest of the troupe rummaged for breakfast beneath the trees.

Lizzie stomped out to join them, tugging a brush through the tangled mass of her long copper hair.

'Right, Jake, what's all this about and why couldn't it wait till breakfast – and who's she?'

'Poachers and urgent – and Vickie.'

'Start again, slowly.'

'Poaching incident, nasty one. Buffalo caught in a snare but he's got it out of the ground and is limping around, mad and mean, near a village. I've got this kid staying with me at the moment, name of Vickie, Vickie Monk. Wondered if I could dump her with your lot for the day, Alex, keep her amused, keep her out of danger. She's a bright kid, postgrad from your uni, in fact.'

Jake dropped the last of his cigar on the concrete floor of the verandah and ground it into oblivion.

Alex shook his head.

'How do you do it, Jake? OK. I'll take her. But warn her she's got to go with the flow, we've got a tight timetable this season, lots of digging to do and not enough time to do it.'

'Good man, I owe you one. I'll go turn the jalopy round and get Vickie. I took her to the bar at Wild-Dogs last night after I left here, we bumped into that PhD student of yours, Leah. She'd brought some young lad with her – Zach is it? I thought she and Vickie might get on but – what do you know – women, eh?' He lowered his voice. 'She's a great kid, but a bit clingy, if you know what I mean, do her good to get a change of scenery. See someone else besides a grumpy old geezer from Zim'.'

His grin had Alex raising his eyebrows and Lizzie shaking her head as he sauntered off to his vehicle.

'"Grumpy old geezer from Zim" my foot,' muttered Lizzie. 'He's from Milton bloody Keynes.' Then, exasperated, 'Oh great! Check that out.'

'What?' Alex frowned in puzzlement.

'Slim, blonde, long legs, short shorts, that's what. Way taller than me – or you for that matter,' Lizzie regarded herself as tall at five feet eight – Alex convinced himself he was really six feet when the reality was an inch less, 'looks like a model.' She shook her head. 'Dear old Jake's running true to form. Let's hope Birgit's not around today to see her.'

'Don't tell me Birgit's still carrying a torch for that old roué?'

'Oh yes. And how. Shush.' Lizzie smiled broadly at the new arrival. Jake had driven off with a wave and without so much as an introduction. 'Vickie? I'm Lizzie, this is Alex – we'll be about five minutes – then you're welcome to join us for breakfast.'

Lizzie was surprised to see a blush accompany Vickie's polite thank you. Unusual for Jake to go for a shrinking violet. But she was definitely gorgeous.

Lizzie and Alex finished their ablutions and packed for the day in silence. The presence of the startlingly attractive young woman on the porch was disconcerting.

Alex locked the flimsy door of the hut behind them and Lizzie jumped the big step to the ground. The sun was peeking timidly through the clouds, much to Lizzie's relief – the day was getting better. They scanned the bushes for elephants then drove over to the main buildings for breakfast, waving at the departing night-watchman in his thick black coat and woolly hat.

Vickie and Lizzie settled themselves at a large table while Alex foraged for tea. The students were just arriving, ambling along the river bank in clothes that looked like they had never seen soap and water, hands dangling with books and cameras, iPods and cigarettes and other early morning essentials. Lizzie liked this year's arrangement, sleeping on a real bed under a thatched roof with her husband while the students pitched in the campground on the other side of the site. Mornings were difficult enough without having to face students in the shower block.

'So, what are you up to here, Vickie?' Lizzie asked, more out of politeness than interest.

'I'm researching the impact of tourism on local attitudes to dangerous or disruptive wildlife. You know the sort of thing – elephants ruining subsistence farmers' crops, destroying small villages, killing people.'

'Interesting topic. Is it a PhD, did Jake say?'

'That's right. I'm at the vet school in Liverpool – I wish I'd known about you two, it would have really helped knowing someone here.'

'How long are you here for?' asked Alex.

'I've been here a month, so maybe just a few more weeks, it's flexible. I might spend some time with my dad later – he works here some of the time – but you never know with him, a bit of a maverick.'

'What does he do?'

'I'm not totally sure, something to do with mining I think – he always used to be visiting dangerous places like Chad or Sudan – mum's really pleased he's got involved in Zambia instead. That's kind of why I chose it – that and the wildlife.'

'Is your study just in South Luangwa?'

'Um, no, I was supposed to be in Lower Zambezi by now, but – well, I have a few more things to do. And Jake's been really helpful – I don't know what I would have done without him.' Another blush suffused her face.

Lizzie gently kicked Alex's ankle and went boldly in for the kill.

'So, are you staying with Jake – or have you got a bolthole somewhere else?'

Alex grinned into his tea mug as an innocent Vickie replied.

'I was staying at Wild-Dogs, but then Jake said I could stay with him – it's saved me quite a bit of money. I'm on a grant, it's not exactly generous – and he's been so kind, feeding me and everything. But I have to leave sometime. He said he might be off on a long trek with an anti-poaching squad any day, could be gone a while, so …'

Vickie lapsed into a glum silence.

'Well, if ever you need a change of scenery,' Lizzie offered, 'you're welcome to come over here – if Jake's not around just radio for me or Alex to pick you up – or Leah – she's got her own transport, she's hiring a vehicle from Gus.'

'Gus?'

'Mechanical genius, loves fiddling with machinery and mending things – runs this place with Maggie. Sorry, I'm going on a bit, aren't I?'

'Not at all.' Vickie squirmed in her chair. 'Listen, it's really kind of you to offer to take me out today but, to be honest, I'd really like some time to myself. Jake doesn't ask me what I want to do – just kind of herds me around like a bossy sheepdog. Do you think I could just chill by the pool with my laptop and catch up on some stuff – would Maggie and Gus mind?'

'Of course not – but are you *sure* you wouldn't rather spend a day getting hot and tired scraping around in the dirt with us?' Alex sounded genuinely welcoming, but Lizzie knew he would be relieved.

'No, honestly, I really need to get some work done and I could do with a snooze too. I haven't been getting much sleep lately. I mean, I've been worrying, you know, about the project, it's been keeping me awake.'

This time Vickie's blush surpassed all the others as she realised what 'not been getting much sleep,' implied. Lizzie mastered a strong impulse to smirk.

'Right, I'll have a word with Maggie,' she said, 'then we have to dash. The students will be heading over to the campsite to get ready so why don't you go with them – we pick them up once we've got the lunches on board, then it's Parks HQ to pick up our armed scout before we finally hit the road. It's quite a palaver – and we're running late today, so we'll love you and leave you.'

Lizzie slipped off to the office and as she got there turned to see Vickie walking down the riverbank with two of the students, en route to the campsite with its panoramic views and its puddle of a pool. For a moment she envied Vickie her day of idleness, then remembered what it felt like to be insecure in love and shuddered.

Maggie was bustling around, sorting out the latest mini-crisis. Seeing Lizzie she immediately stopped moving and began chatting, hands firmly on her solid hips.

'You know, it may be bad news for you Lizzie, all these fossil hunters traipsing around the place, but it's great for our bookings – we've just got another one – three doctors, moving over here from Beacon Ridge, French names – they have to be after your bone.'

Lizzie groaned and hid her face in her hands.

Maggie continued as if she had not noticed.

'You know, you'll look back on all this with a smile, I bet you. I can see it now – *'Lizzie's bone* – a drama in six parts starring – who'd you fancy – Scarlett Johansson? Or someone more mature and brainy looking, like Susan Sarandon? Too old? No, I know, Julianne Moore – she's got the nearest to your hair colour.' She stopped a moment and squinted at Lizzie through the sunlight. 'Are you sure you don't dye it?'

By the time Alex had returned from the kitchen with the lunches, looking impatient, Lizzie and Maggie were discussing eyebrow plucking. Lizzie sighed.

'I'd best be off. Alex is desperate to get going. Try and keep those fossil hunters off my trail, hey?'

'I'm sure this is a stupid question, but why don't you just take them out and show them the place and then ignore them – won't they go away when they realise it's your patch?'

Lizzie snorted.

'You have *got* to be joking! They're not archaeologists, they're treasure hunters. They've ruined really important sites in their hurry to find the next big thing, that's why I've kept the location quiet. Alex spent years working his socks off to find that site. We're not about to hand it over to plunderers.'

'Just a thought.' Maggie shrugged.

Alex slammed the door of the Land Rover and started the engine. Jumping in, Lizzie pulled off her hat and tucked her duffel bag under the seat. It would be cosy, soon, when the scout and his AK47 joined her up front.

They swung by the campsite, stopping just long enough to pick up the students and wave at a lounging Vickie, then on to Parks HQ where their scout Isaiah was waiting, gun in hand, metallic shades gleaming in the now-bright sunshine. Finally, at 9.15 – nearly an hour late – they hit the dirt road to the pontoon bridge, shadowed by the usual billowing cloud of terracotta dust. They had gone about three miles when Lizzie noticed a vehicle a fair distance behind them.

'Alex, that vehicle behind us, I swear it passed us going the other way a few minutes ago, I think it's three fossil hunters that Maggie's just booked in.' She leaned over and whispered into Alex's ear so no one else could hear. 'When we get to the pontoon, why don't you ask the guys to be really slow about bringing the bridge back. That way we can throw them off the trail.'

Alex grinned.

'Nice idea – they'll spend the day driving round in circles if they haven't been out here before.' He stared into the rear view mirror.

'I can't see over the stacks of kit in the back, are you sure it's them?'

'No. But there's a black driver and three white people – can't make out more than that. Mags said they were three doctors and they'd been staying at Beacon Ridge, that's the direction they were coming from when I saw them go past.'

'Let's take evasive action anyway, it won't harm anyone, just hold them up a bit.'

They slowed to a halt in front of the pontoon. Alex frowned in concentration as he aligned the front wheels with two rows of sandbags sitting beneath the tea-coloured water at the river's edge. He drove forward until the wheels, now totally immersed, made contact with a wooden ramp then eased the front upwards, onto the small wooden platform that made up the pontoon. Alex, Lizzie and the scout climbed down first, then the four students edged out of the back. There was just enough standing room for them all.

Two muscular men now sat and heaved the pontoon across the river with notched wooden pick handles, pulling on the strong wire ropes to which the platform for the vehicle was attached. The snorts of basking hippo accompanied them, their bottoms sticking up like steamed chocolate puddings in the tawny water.

When they reached the other side Lizzie turned to see a man emerging from the passenger seat of the four-wheel-drive behind them, his hat rather more elegant than the usual tourist's bush attire. A woman appeared next, from a rear seat. Lizzie nudged Alex. He took one of the pontoon operators to one side. They exchanged a few words, then Alex slipped him a couple of grubby 10,000 Kwacha notes from his fat roll of local currency. The man grinned and gave one to his friend. The two chatted for a moment, then walked away from the pontoon and started crouching, examining it from the bank as if something was amiss. Alex and the crew drove off at speed. The pontoon had still not moved by the time they reached the crest of the hill and passed out of view.

Chapter 6

The diggers reached their site, marked out with strings on the side of a small incline, and unloaded their equipment: buckets, trowels, plastic bags, picks, shovels and large wooden-framed sieves made from heavy metal mesh. Soon the air rang to the metallic scraping of the trowels on the hard ground as the students uncovered large lumps of stone that, to the untrained eye, looked just like broken river cobbles.

Lizzie was pacing around, frustrated. She wanted to head out for a recce on her own, but armed scouts were in short supply this season and she could not go anywhere without one.

'Alex, can we pack up early and go look at that bit of riverbank I was talking about last night?'

'Depends – I want to dig down another ten centimetres today and this stuff is like concrete.' He stood, put his drawing-board to one side. 'I'll see how they're getting on.'

They skirted two students sieving a bucket load of debris raising clouds of orange dust and peered into the pit.

'How's it going, Zach?'

The young man in filthy t-shirt, shorts and sneakers squinted up at him from his squat-legged perch on the side of the rectangular hole in the ground.

'Not too bad actually – should make it down ten centimetres before lunch anyway. Quite a bit of stuff coming up.'

'Great. OK, Lizzie, your trip's on if we make it down by lunchtime. Crack on everyone.'

Zach immediately stood, shot a furtive glance at Lizzie then wandered off to roll a cigarette, almost as if he knew she wanted him to keep on scraping. She shrugged and let it go. Paranoia. One to watch. All too easy to see demons everywhere when the fossil hunters were on her trail.

It was nearing midday. The sun shone fiercely through the paltry shade of the tree under which Lizzie sat helping Alex with his site plans. The pungent smell of insect repellent filled the air, but nothing stopped the voracious tsetse flies and they were biting clean through socks, trousers, shirts, no matter how thick the fabric. A tube of anti-histamine cream that sat on a handy rock was in frequent use.

'Sir,' Isaiah called. He pointed back down the track, the way they had come.

'Oh no!' Lizzie moaned. 'Not the fossil hunters?'

She flopped like a limp rag.

'Looks more like a Parks vehicle,' said Alex. 'Do you recognise it, Isaiah?'

'Yes, sir, I think this must be Dr Nkhoma.'

'Ah! This must be lunchtime,' Alex grinned.

As usual, Thomas stepped out of his rickety old Land Rover looking the picture of cleanliness and tidiness. He was wearing the same green overalls as his wildlife scouts, but his were pressed, the black leather belt around his ample waist was polished to a sheen and his leather boots shone like jet. Lizzie sighed, she just couldn't keep clean out here – and tidy was never her forte. She pushed a stray lock of tawny hair back under her hat.

'Professor Lamb,' Thomas advanced on Lizzie, 'I see this husband is exploiting your talents as usual. But perhaps you are stuck without a vehicle and a scout?'

'Got it in one. But I don't mind helping the poor man out now and again – and he's promised me a trip after lunch.'

'Ah, lunch, I wonder if you might have a little to spare – I neglected to bring anything with me and a rumbling is rising from the depths of my malnourished belly already.' Thomas patted his stomach. 'But first,' he put one hand on Alex's shoulder, 'tell me what you have been doing here – but not in too much detail – I have a report to write and need to compose a sentence or two about this season's work.'

'I can write that up for you,' Alex looked at Lizzie, they both knew that this was what Thomas had really meant, 'would a paragraph or so do?'

'That would be most kind. Now, Alex, Eliza, I have a little problem. Perhaps we can go and sit under that tree where I see your drawing-board, hmm?' A subtle way of moving away from possibly prying ears without being too obvious.

They all sat in the shade of the tree, Thomas switching his back with a leafy twig to keep away the flies.

'I am sorry to say that your less than pleasant colleagues – let us call them vultures – are becoming increasingly vociferous in their demand for assistance with their permits and also their demands for scouts. My inbox is bulging at the seams. Sadly it is now so full I cannot receive any more emails and I might miss some requests.'

An impish grin appeared for an instant and was gone.

'But these men – and women – will arrive regardless, indeed some are already here. They will need someone with local knowledge to assist them and while we really are short of scouts I cannot stop them hiring local guides. Considering the help you have given to us in the past, at great risk to yourselves, I am inclined to let you know what they are doing. But please, keep this under those nice, wide-brimmed hats of yours, eh?'

They both nodded.

'We're very grateful, Thomas,' said Lizzie, 'and you know, we really don't mind genuine academic researchers working here at all. It's just this lot, they're so . . . so . . . '.

'Such vultures. Yes, I agree.' He rubbed his hands together. 'So, my friends, here is what I can tell you. Some European doctors are trying to find out where you found the bone. I have told them it is being kept quiet for security reasons, because we poor, incompetent Zambians cannot guard the place. Once more I play the dumb, obstructive, possibly corrupt African official. They are gullible. They are also rich, so I must guard against temptation.' He grinned.

'I have scratched my head and thought about who else knows where you were working last year. One of them is in prison. They will not get to him, he is no longer in the Valley. Ah! I would never have believed that a scout of mine could be so bad.' He shook his head. 'The other scout who knows is Isaiah – we can trust him. But I am worried about those people who may not realise they are talking to a vulture, people who are too trusting or too greedy, who do not work for me or for you. We must cross our fingers – that is all we can do.'

'Have these Europeans – or any other *vultures* – applied for research permits anywhere else in the Valley?' Lizzie asked, not sure she really wanted to know the answer.

'So far, no. I have told them they can only have permissions to research when they have a particular area in mind. I have also told them,' here he winked, 'they need permission from the chief and headman wherever they work. I have told them to get this permission in writing for me. Strictly, this is not necessary, but it will do them no harm to have to talk to the chief and the *nduna* – his board of advisers – and maybe the district commissioner and the magistrate – and get their approval in writing, eh?'

'Thomas,' Lizzie exclaimed, 'that's wicked! The chief will demand all sorts of things they can't do, or expensive bottles of whisky they can't get here. Fantastic!'

'Worth a little crust for a hungry mite?'

'You can have *all* my sandwiches.'

Thomas's knack with humans even worked with students and in no time the diggers were laughing and joking with him over their cheese rolls and bananas. Lizzie was sure the students had no idea how important he was – without him they simply could not work here and she watched with interest as he drew out each one in turn. Then he turned to Zach.

'Tell me, what are your first impressions of our wild Valley?'

'Pretty dull. It's not really my scene. I miss the nightlife. Like, Liverpool's *really* buzzing after dark, here it's just mosquitoes.'

Lizzie stared at him, shocked at his tone.

'You've only been here a few days,' said Alex. 'You might find it a bit more exciting than you think after a few more.'

'Yeah, yeah, elephants walking through camp, hippos bumping into your tents, leopards killing local pets, you don't have to tell me, I've heard it all before, more than once. It may be your thing, but it's not exactly clubbing, is it?'

Thomas Nkhoma looked with raised eyebrows at his lunch hosts.

'I suspect this young man will enjoy the nightlife at Wild-Dogs more than the wildlife by night, eh? But, Alex, tell me, how is that nice young woman doing who is studying our rock art?'

Having moved the conversation on, Thomas reached down for another sandwich.

Lizzie took a slug from her water bottle and observed Zach. He was studying primate anatomy with her, archaeology with Alex and about to move into his final year. They had both earmarked him as a definite for an MSc and a potential PhD. He was hard-working, intelligent, sparky, ambitious – but she had never heard him talk like this back home. She shrugged off her concern and started to clear up her stuff.

Lunch over, they loaded up and drove off to the riverbank that Lizzie was keen to scrutinise. Her focus was a small, rugged cliff-face, rising from a dried-up sandy riverbed that looked like a miniature desert, with small peaks of sand rising above large, round depressions caused by large, grey feet attached to large, grey elephants.

Alex sniffed apprehensively. He always claimed he could smell if elephants were nearby. Lizzie teased him that his nose was designed for the task. Not really a big nose, it was just obvious, with a kink in the bone that wrongly suggested rugby. Today, though, they had Isaiah with his AK47 which was rather more reassuring than Alex's sense of smell.

Trowels at the ready, Lizzie and Alex headed straight for the eroded riverbank, leaving the students to top up their insect repellent, light cigarettes and lounge around gossiping. Kate alone, the quietest of the bunch, stood to one side, head cocked, watching Lizzie with a touch of adulation in her eyes.

It was the quiet, hot time of day when animals were in short supply. An occasional burst of laughter rose from the youngsters sitting on the baking sand. Isaiah climbed to the top of the steep sharp bank and stood surveying the landscape in both directions from under his green cloth cap, black boots hidden by the long dry grass. Thomas was humming a little tune to himself, just audible, but not identifiable. As if synchronised, he stopped and Isaiah stiffened. The game scout lifted his gun. Thomas whispered to Lizzie and Alex to stop scraping. Kate moved closer. The sitting group, alert now, looked up. Thomas raised his finger to his lips, indicating silence, then beckoned. They hurried over, pretending not to be alarmed but betrayed by their faces.

The first and second elephant were not so big, the third a mere baby, the fourth was built like a house. As the first two paced onwards the baby, suddenly frightened, squealed and began to run. The big one bringing up the rear stopped and lifted one foot from the ground. She started flapping her ears in anger, took a few paces back then ran straight towards them. Isaiah's gun clicked as he armed it. The elephant stopped, ears still flapping. Her family had passed into the distance now. She glanced their way, stood a moment more, then moved on, stately and unhurried, leaving the humans to heave a collective sigh of relief.

Soon the sound of giggling rose once more above the rasping of the trowels on hard earth. The heat of the day settled back down into silence.

The shrill trumpet of an angry elephant followed by a searing screech shattered the calm.

'What the hell was that? Isaiah, was that some kind of animal?'

Isaiah, tearing down the riverbank, ignored Alex.

'Go back to the vehicles,' he ordered, 'Mr Thomas, you are in charge.'

He ran across the grasping sands into the bushes – and was gone.

Chapter 7

Not knowing was the thing. Lizzie felt an urge to smoke, to deal with the stress, but instead bit the skin on the side of her thumb. They sat, Thomas, Lizzie and Alex, in the boss man's dilapidated Land Rover, while the students gossiped and smoked in the expedition four-by-four. Lizzie wriggled around on the back seat, scratching tsetse bites.

'We didn't hear any other vehicles, so it can't be someone out here legitimately, can it?' She sounded petulant, but was just frustrated at the inactivity. 'Even if it's a poaching accident they're still human beings and I'm a first-aider. We should have gone with him.'

'Professor Lamb,' Thomas took Lizzie's free hand in one of his and patted it, 'you are very learned, but we poor Zambians have some expertise here in the bush. Our scouts, also, are trained in first aid. If it is a poacher he may not be alone, in which case this is a very dangerous situation. Isaiah will know how to behave and will not be hampered by us sheltered town folk. Now, tell me, did you hear any other vehicles when we ourselves were driving to the riverbed?'

'No.' Lizzie admitted. 'And if there was one, of course I wouldn't have heard it over ours. Touché, Dr Nkhoma.'

He nodded acknowledgement.

'It is hard for someone active like you to stand by and do nothing. So, let us play a game while we wait. Tell me, of all the fossil hunters in the world, with whom would you least like to share a desert island?'

'Ooh, that's a tough one now Harvey Miller's dead. I'll plump for Fred Blackstone, he's a real creep. How many wives has he had, Alex? '

Alex held up a hand.

'Shh. I can hear something.'

Nature was still having her siesta so there was nothing to obscure the rustle of vegetation as Isaiah's green-clad figure emerged from the pale bush. He was no longer in a hurry. Thomas got out and went to meet him. The two men stood, heads close in quiet conversation, then both approached the vehicle.

'Isaiah has found signs of an unsuccessful poaching incident. There is a badly injured elephant somewhere nearby – as well as at least one badly injured human being, we guess. There are tyre tracks and footprints he could follow but we are concerned for your safety with this injured animal – and an armed poacher – on the loose, so, we will go with you back to Elephant Camp. I will first radio the GPS coordinates to Parks HQ – if you would be so kind as to lend me your technical expertise, my friends?'

'Of course we will,' said Lizzie, 'well, Alex will. But are you sure we can't help in any other way – driving after them with Isaiah, for example?'

'Poachers are dangerous men, my dear Eliza, more dangerous when wounded. You of all people should know that after your experiences last year with that treacherous scout – but we will not re-open that wound. I mention it simply to remind you how people can react when they are hurt. I suggest you concentrate on getting yourselves and your students home safely.'

'Yes sir.' She saluted him. 'I hear and obey.'

'That'll be a first, Thomas,' muttered Alex.

Lizzie swiped her husband.

'OK, smart Alex, you're the GPS wiz, get on with it.'

Alex checked his little yellow recorder, wrote down the coordinates and left Thomas in his vehicle reporting the incident. Soon they heard the crackle and buzz of the Valley's major artery of communication, bush radio. It had become the Cinderella service since the arrival of the cellphone masts two years ago, but it was always reliable in a crisis – especially in the many places where there was no signal.

'Parks HQ, Parks HQ, Parks HQ. Come in Parks HQ.'

A pause.

'Parks HQ, Parks HQ, Parks HQ, do you copy?'

'Parks HQ here, I copy you, Dr Nkhoma, I am hearing you.'

Thomas repeated his instructions and the GPS coordinates three times, then once more for good measure.

Isaiah climbed on board with the archaeologists and they drove off a reasonable distance behind Dr Nkhoma so as not to breathe too much of his billowing wake of dust, or the grey exhaust fumes of an elderly vehicle that needed some loving attention.

Clouds had come in again. It was as if a switch in the heavens had been turned off and all the brightness of the day had been transformed into gloom. The dulling of the light brought a dampening of the mood, even among the students. It was a pretty silent drive.

Alex must have spotted the empty vehicle at almost the same time as Thomas. The two vehicles bumped off the track in tandem. The sandy gravel of the dirt road gave way to a verge of sparse, knee-high grass, out of which arose a bald grey dome of rock, its rough, pock-marked slopes radiating heat. The once-white vehicle had been driven part way up the incline, its front doors were open and there was no sign of life, inside or out. Thomas jumped out and stood at the foot of the hill, surveying the scene, a frown on his face.

Alex switched off the engine and gave his orders.

'Isaiah, please come with me. The rest of you stay here.' Then Alex whispered to his wife, 'That includes you too, Lizzie Lamb.'

'But Alex—'

'No buts, stay here!'

Lizzie fumed. She had wanted to tell him something, but now her inner rebel kicked in and she was damned if she would try again.

Alex joined Thomas examining the exterior of the dirty white four-by-four with Zambian plates, while Isaiah began to survey the ground around it. Turning their attention to the inside, Lizzie watched in increasing frustration as she saw them stop, stand a few seconds with their heads together, looking grave, then set off to follow Isaiah. He was already on his way up the hill, AK47 in hand, scanning the ground and horizon by turns and stopping every few paces to listen. As they climbed further up the slope, onto the crest, Lizzie's anxiety grew, peaking when Alex's square frame in its dusty combats vanished from sight. She checked her watch and waited.

When they reappeared, nearly fifteen minutes later, Lizzie could tell straightaway that something was wrong. She hesitated, torn between wanting to know and staying put. In the end she realised if she left there would be no holding the students back. It was hot and cramped in the back and the tsetse flies were enjoying a banquet any vampire would have given his canines for.

Alex turned to look at her, then walked towards them leaving Isaiah and Thomas – delicate as a giraffe despite his bulk – examining the surroundings, presumably looking for tracks. Lizzie ventured to step outside of the vehicle. Alex drew up alongside her, facing the hillside, away from the students.

'It's a mess. Best not say anything to the crew, but it looks like whoever was driving this vehicle was involved in something pretty bad.' He sighed. 'And there's some stuff in the car—'

'Sorry, when you say a mess?' Lizzie interrupted.

'Someone's pretty badly injured, judging by the blood and the tracks, but he got as far as the river – looks like a man with a dugout canoe was waiting on the banks. You remember when we were looking through the binoculars from the camp and saw that fisherman with the dugout? I reckon that's roughly where we are.'

'OK, got it. Now, what stuff in the car?'

'Passports. Congolese, Libyan, Zimbabwean, different names, all the same picture. Left in the glove compartment. A small gun – with a silencer – not a gun for hunting.' He paused. 'And a piece of paper.'

'Paper? What do you mean? What was on it? Alex?'

He looked at his feet.

'Your article. The first page, with your contact details on it. And your address here, scribbled in pen.'

'Oh shit. You're joking?' She grabbed his arm. 'Alex, I was trying to tell you before – when you ran off all action hero – this is the same vehicle I saw earlier, the one with the three fossil hunters in it, I took the number at the pontoon. Those passports, were they for a white person or a black person?'

'A black person. A man. I'm guessing it was the driver. The glove compartment was locked – but whoever was driving left in such a hurry he left the keys in the ignition. And yes, I am assuming it's a man before you say anything – Isaiah showed me footprints by the river – one barefoot, one in trainers, one in boots. We're assuming it's linked to the poaching incident – maybe the guy with the canoe was the barefoot one – that would make sense – the driver was an outsider in trainers, the poacher in boots. But I'm just guessing.'

'So, if the false passports – I'm assuming you can't have triple nationality – if they're the driver's, and he's tied up with the poaching business, then whatever happened might not have anything to do with the vultures? I mean, he would have taken them back to Beacon Ridge after they lost our trail, don't you think?'

Alex hesitated.

'Yes, I guess so. But just because they weren't with him doesn't mean he has nothing to do with them. There is the paper with your address on it.'

'Alex, this is scary. What's going on? The paper, you're sure it was with the passports?'

'Yes. And the gun.'

Lizzie stared into space. Alex moved so that he was facing her. When he spoke his voice was quiet but firm.

'Lizzie. We have to go back to Camp. We need to get away from here. Get back in and I'll just sort things with Thomas. Please?'

She turned around and slipped back into the front seat, ignoring the chorus of interrogation coming from the back. Alex leant through the open door on the driver's side.

'We're heading back as soon as we can, there's been some kind of problem here and we need to report it, bear with us a few more minutes.' He turned to his wife. 'You OK?'

'Fine.'

She knew she could not look fine, so rather than face questioning, no matter how well-meaning, she sat firm in her resolve not to face the students. They soon got bored and started chatting amongst themselves again.

Staring into space, Lizzie gradually became aware that conversation in the back of the vehicle had become subdued, that Martin and Zach were having some kind of disagreement, one they obviously did not want her to overhear. She turned her head a fraction to the side, so as to hear better. They picked up the movement and conversation ceased. She turned. Everyone was looking at her. She was about to say something when Alex returned, looking tense.

'Thomas and Isaiah are staying here, they want to wait for help to arrive. They can't get a cellphone signal and his radio's packed up too, so we'll have to radio Parks HQ from the pontoon hut.'

Zach's voice piped up from the rear of the vehicle where he sat amid the buckets.

'So, is it a really big adventure, boss?'

'You could say that. Serious criminal activity, anyway.'

'What kind of stuff?'

'I said serious and that's what I meant. Look, just stop pestering me. I'd like to get us all back safe and sound before the sun sets and makes it twice as difficult and God knows how much more dangerous – if that's OK with all of you?'

The crew relapsed into silence, whether resentful or anxious it scarcely mattered. No matter how cool the students professed to be, they were not really that long out of school, far away from home and missing the false security of their umbilical mobile phones. Murder, a fright out on site and serious criminal activity were enough to put a strain even on youth's legendary resilience. Lizzie felt for them.

The sun was setting quickly now and as she watched Alex manoeuvring the vehicle onto the pontoon bridge the implications of the small gun finally sank in.

'Alex,' Lizzie whispered, 'they wouldn't want to kill *me*, would they? Not just for a bone?'

Chapter 8

It had been dark for almost an hour by the time the archaeologists made it back to base. Maggie ran to meet them, cigarette in hand. It was not like her to move so fast.

'Thank God you're home, I was getting ready to send out search parties.'

Alex reached out and gave her a big hug and a kiss on the cheek.

'Steady on, Alex, people are watching!'

'Boy am I glad to see you, Mags. It's been one hell of a day. Thank God Thomas was with us, he's still in the Park, waiting for help.' He stretched. 'I don't suppose there's any hot water left is there? The kids are desperate for a shower and a cold beer.'

'You may be in luck, I saw Gus fiddling with the timer. Get in there pronto, boys and girls – I'll rustle up some roasted groundnuts and chill down a few bottles of *Mosi*.'

'*Mosi*', the diggers' beer of choice, was named after Zambia's biggest tourist attraction, *Mosi oa Tunya*, 'the smoke that thunders' – Victoria Falls. At the end of a hot day out on site its golden, malty chill was the perfect medicine for a parched throat.

Alex shooed off the students and hung behind with a very subdued Lizzie till they were well out of sight.

'Have you heard what's been happening?' he asked Maggie.

'Nothing definite. There's been more activity than usual on the radio – that always means something's going on. Lots coming out of Parks HQ, some from Beacon Ridge Lodge, plenty of vehicles on the move – and a sense of urgency that's normally lacking amongst certain officials. So, come on, spill the beans.'

'We found a vehicle abandoned on that hill on the way to Beacon Ridge Lodge. Thomas is waiting there for some of his guys who are supposed to be bringing the police. Looks like there were two people in the vehicle and one of them's badly injured. They went up and over the ridge to the river and pushed off in a dugout. It might be just a poaching accident – but there could be more to it than that – for reasons I'd better not go into. We probably shouldn't have told you, so don't spread it around.'

Lizzie suddenly sat down with a bump, looking pale, tired and ready to cry.

'Lizzie!' Maggie exclaimed, 'Are you OK? You're not are you? Here's me blathering on – and you looking like a wraith. Oh my God,' she clasped her hand to her mouth, 'all that stress you had last year with those smugglers! That started with an abandoned vehicle too, didn't it? Then that *stupid* policeman, arresting you just because you were there. Well you're safe here – Gus wouldn't let anything happen to you. What you need is a nice hot bath at my house. Off you go, Alex, I'll deliver her back to the bar in time for beer and peanuts. You get showered and corral those kids into order before suppertime. I'll get chef to do some chips, that'll sort them out.'

Lizzie looked at Alex, and he nodded wearily back at her. They went their separate ways without a word.

An hour later the entire team, including the abandoned Vickie, was sitting at the bar, the great river invisible in the moonless night, stars scattered like diamond dust against the velvet darkness. Every hand held a *Mosi* except for Lizzie's and Maggie's which both held large glasses of red wine. A tin plate of freshly roasted groundnuts sat on the table and Alex was gorging himself.

Conversation, despite the day's events, took its usual course for the evening: news of celebrities garnered from five-day old newspapers, sports victories and defeats, pet hates on the iPod at the campsite bar, where music was allowed after dark. People were always shocked to see an iPod docking station on the rustic bar alongside the hand-carved wooden stools and benches. 'Remote, but not backward,' was Maggie's retort.

Dinner drifted by in waves of laughter and chatter. Harvey Miller, only one day into his journey through the Valley of Death, went un-mourned as any petty tyrant. Lizzie alone thought sad thoughts of his demise. Much as she loathed the man, he had done some good work before his fame got the better of him. So much he could have done, so much he did not.

'Well, Harvey Miller, I've learnt my lesson.'

Alex was used to such shorthand.

'You're not about to get murdered. You've got a good few years left to write the magnum opus.'

He slipped his arm around her shoulders and held her close.

'You never know,' she said. 'I'm going to knuckle down and start writing as soon as I get back to Liverpool.'

'I'm not going to stop you, but there are other things in life too, you know. There's an awful lot of money to be raised for that museum we've got planned – and the craft centre, and the clinic, and the school.'

'Stop! It's all too much. And there's still that big unanswered question to cap it all.'

'Oh yes. That one.' Alex looked uncomfortable. He always did when 'the procreation decision' as Lizzie called it, with an academic dispassion that she didn't feel, crept up on them. 'Do you want to talk about it now?'

It sounded like he did not.

'No. Not really. But do we ever?'

Lizzie stood abruptly. She walked over to the bar where Maggie and Gus sat working by the light of two candles. They were checking their orders for the next delivery of essential goods from Lusaka, twelve hours up the road.

'Hi, Lizzie, feeling a bit better?' Maggie asked.

'Much better, thanks. But I'd like to get an early night, I didn't sleep very well last night. Would you mind getting someone to run the kids back to the campsite? And sort out something for Vickie if Jake doesn't turn up?'

'No problem.' She paused as the sound of a vehicle emerged from the bush. 'Uh oh,' her tone changed, 'too late. Here comes trouble.'

The first vehicle's lights swung into view, followed swiftly by another set.

Gus piped up.

'That's an engine I'd recognise anywhere. Fixed it up myself. That's the Parks boss – and our vet's coming in fast behind him.'

Lizzie groaned.

'Well, at least Vickie will be happy. Is there anything left in that box of red wine, Mags?'

'And more. We've even got Thomas's favourite whisky.'

Jake and Thomas were looming into view now. They both looked weary.

'Hi there, campers,' Jake pulled off his baseball cap and scratched his head, 'any chance of a wash and scrub up for Adventure Vet?'

'Of course, Jake, come with me.'

Maggie bustled off with the vet and Thomas settled himself on her empty bar stool.

'Whisky, Thomas?'

He beamed at Gus.

'I don't suppose . . .'

'Yes you do, and yes we have. Gabriel, a double Bunnahabhain for Dr Nkhoma, my tab.'

'Why that particular unpronounceable scotch, Thomas?' Lizzie asked.

'Tut tut, Eliza. This is not just *scotch*, this is a single malt from Islay – fruity, malty, a touch of peat – aaah. My tutor at Cambridge bought me a bottle as a leaving present in ... well, a long time ago. I sipped a tiny drop every night and made it last nearly a year. Now my dear friends here have summoned up a magical supplier, no doubt somewhere out in the deepest forests of the night.'

Gus snorted.

'That's one way of describing Kinshasa. My cousin Artie brings it with him when he comes to call.'

'I'm surprised they have such a luxurious product on sale in the Congo,' said Alex.

'They don't, my cousin's a mining engineer, travels all over the place, often ends up in Amsterdam or London en route to some god-forsaken hellhole – Libya, Zimbabwe, Angola, the former Soviet 'stans' – and of course DRC – you get the general idea?'

Lizzie looked at Alex, wondering if he too was thinking about those passports, but he ignored her gaze.

They settled down to chat about the day's events, looking as unperturbed by their adventures as a clutch of farmers discussing the price of cattle.

'This vehicle,' Thomas told them, 'we have no idea where it came from or who was driving it. The police, of course, can raise no interest whatsoever in helping. We are almost certain there had been two men in this vehicle when it was abandoned, one injured, they left in a dugout and my scouts are sure they know where it has gone.'

Lizzie, for some reason, said nothing about the three white folks they had seen in it earlier, assuming Alex had told Thomas and that he was keeping it to himself for some reason. Maybe the same reason he did not mention the paper or the gun or the passports. Lizzie, weary and in imminent danger of falling asleep, roused herself to speak.

'You know, Thomas, I think you should ask for a transfer to the police, I mean, these guys haven't even sent anyone out about the murder yet, have they? You'd make a great divisional commander or whatever they have.'

'Hah! You think my current vehicle is bad? At least it has wheels. These police have no money, no vehicles, no computers, nothing. Well, the chief maybe has a camera and a computer – but how long they will last... There are *some* good men and women – but they struggle. The others, ayee! Me, I can do both jobs here in my nice park, answer for my conscience before God *and* enjoy the company of good friends.'

One of those silences fell, like angels passing over.

Jake breezed in like Lucifer falling.

'Shit, that was one hell of a day. Throw me a *Mosi* someone.'

He dragged a bar stool with a screech across the polished concrete floor.

'Easier dealing with a murder than a bloody buffalo on the rampage I can tell you. Mind you, I've never seen a garrotting before – the bugger who did it was pretty shit hot at it. Suggests it's not his first time. Maybe a smuggler or poacher. Or even a mercenary – you never know who you're dealing with out here do you? Not to put too fine a point on it.' He pointed his beer bottle at Lizzie. 'What do you reckon, Prof – was your Miller man a spy in disguise, or some other kind of American stooge? After Islamic terrorists maybe? There's plenty of the buggers in Chipata, you can bet your life. That bloody muezzin's always wailing when I'm up at Helga's place checking on her orphan bush babies.' He took another swig from his beer as his words sank, like pebbles in a still pond.

Jake laughed out loud.

'All a bit too real for you, lot, eh? God, this place sucks. The Valley. How bloody colonial. Sounds like something out of the 1940s, doesn't it? Full of fucking charlatans and wankers. Ah, Birgit, my lovely, come and join us, don't stand festering in the darkness.'

The young woman was indeed standing stock-still in a dark corner.

'Met my latest live-in lover, have you? Vickie, where the devil are you?'

Unfortunately for her, Vickie was sitting next to Leah. It was plain that Jake had been doing some serious drinking already. There was no polite way of stopping him.

'Vickie, my sweet, isn't it time you thought about heading off to Lower Zambezi, there's this rather nice young woman, oh my, she's sitting right next to you. I do get bored easily, don't I, Birgit? You see, Birgit knows me, she might be a bit tedious but she's a damn good fuck, that's more than—'

Gus forced his rugby player's bulk between the swaying Jake and the two young women, dragged the vet out of the bar and towards the office. The drunkard could be heard roaring with laughter as Gus shouted at him. Alex ran off to help Gus.

At the bar Maggie took charge.

'Gabriel, get Birgit a large white wine please. I'm sorry about that folks.'

She took Vickie to one side.

'We'll lend you a room for the night. Tomorrow someone can drive you to Jake's to pick up your things and take you to the airport, if that suits you. You don't have to decide now.' She patted the girl on her shoulder and left her to Zach, who had leapt to her side when Jake started throwing insults around.

Finally, Maggie sidled up to Thomas and whispered, 'How about a song – when things have settled down a bit, you know, settle the mood?'

He beamed by way of response.

It was some fifteen minutes later that his fine voice took on one of Tom Lehrer's sardonic songs – and several more before they could stop him.

It was after 11 when Thomas finally left.

'That man's a saint.' Maggie had put out her final cigarette of the day and was busy collecting glasses that the bar staff had neglected. Alex and Gus, who had put Jake to bed in one of the chalets, sat side-by-side on bar stools, like sad old men in an open-all-night American diner. Lizzie was picking up empty beer bottles.

'Well, we needed a saint tonight,' she agreed. 'Boy, was Jake drunk, have you ever seen him that nasty before?'

'He can be a bit in-your-face, but no, that was exceptional. I'll have a word with Birgit when she's calmed down. But you say Jake's been hitting on that PhD student of yours already?'

'Yeah, looks like it. I was only saying to Alex yesterday, I bet Leah's going to be a focal point for trouble, she's just too good looking. She's got something, you know that expression "come hither"? I thought she might toy with Zach first, but Jake spotted her right off. I just don't understand that guy. He's practically old enough to be their father – you'd think he'd behave a bit more like a grown up.'

'Come on, Lizzie, he's a man – not to mention the fact that he's on the rundown to his fortieth. Probably feeling a bit insecure.'

'Don't talk about birthdays. My next one's my thirty-sixth.'

Lizzie looked around to make sure no-one was within hearing distance.

'We were just avoiding talking about the baby thing – again – when Thomas and Jake arrived. It's pretty much now or never for me, but I still don't feel ready for it. Then, I'm not sure I ever will be. There's so much to consider – the kind of lives we lead, travelling, our work and everything. But then I look around at some of the women here – loads of kids, dumped by their husbands, left to cope with the family *and* subsistence farming *and* jobs if they can get them. Makes me feel utterly pathetic – I'd have it easy by comparison. I just don't know what to do.'

'Poor thing, I do feel for you. We simply decided not to. Gus was in two minds but I never really fancied the whole painful labour thing and the clucking mums. He had the snip and that was that. I have to say I do sometimes regret it, but they're the rare occasions. When we get a camp full of spoilt South African brats, I could cheerfully strangle the lot of them.'

'There,' Lizzie clanked half a dozen empty *Mosi* bottles onto the bar, 'that's all the empties as far as I can see. Well, it won't be resolved tonight that's for sure.' She yawned loudly. 'I'm dog tired.' She turned to call her husband. 'Alex? Are you about ready?'

Good nights said, they all jumped into their vehicles to drive to bed through the elephant-infested shrubbery. An owl screeched as Alex locked their chalet door behind them.

Lizzie propped her laptop up against the wall, before lighting a mosquito coil. She peeled off her dusty combats and t-shirt ready for bed. Alex was setting out his bags by the door, making ready for a swift departure come morning. He stopped a moment and watched his wife slip behind the mosquito netting.

'Thomas was in fine voice tonight,' she said as she wriggled her legs under the sheet.

'I don't know how he does it – I can't imagine anyone turning the group mood around like that,' Alex agreed, as he resumed his own, more extensive bedtime routine.

Lizzie sighed.

'I know, I'm deeply envious, – he's just too charismatic. Maybe he's got a horrible secret we don't know about – turns mad and grows fangs at midnight or something. But, did you notice, it was like Zach was totally immune? I just don't understand him.'

'I did notice he was hanging on Vickie's every word, what was that about?'

Lizzie waved her arms around a bit and went on as if he had not spoken.

'I mean, everyone else just loved that song about poisoning pigeons in the park – for goodness' sake, Thomas is in charge of animal conservation!'

Alex was still packing up their dirty laundry.

'I was talking to Gus,' he said, casually.

'I know, I saw you. Two sad gits ranting over their whisky.'

'Excuse me! Before you jump to conclusions you might like to hear what I learnt tonight.'

'Sorry. What did I miss?'

'Jake's been having anonymous letters. Threatening letters. Warning him to leave the Valley or leave it in a box. That's why Gus didn't thump him, says the guy's seriously spooked, he'd been to Wild-Dogs' bar on the way back here – he's been drinking even more than usual because basically he's scared.'

Lizzie was alert now, sleep forgotten.

'Do you know how long he's been getting them – does he have any idea who . . .'

Her words tailed off as her brain caught up.

'Oh dear, not Birgit?'

'That's who he suspects, but there are others. It's no secret he's broken hearts all over the place – I mean, it's not exactly a humming metropolis, is it? Even if you just take the unmarried white folk, there can't be more than a couple of single women living here full time – but there are at least five or six seasonal temps spread around the lodges. So there's a nicely defined little pool of potential writers.'

'What about men, I bet he's pissed off a few husbands.'

'Absolutely. Apparently he tried it on with Maggie once – Gus was up in Lusaka at the time. Can you believe it? She said it was pretty half-hearted, laughed it off and told Gus – they all joke about it now – but I can't imagine everyone being quite so sanguine about the local vet attempting to cuckold them.'

'What a sweet old fashioned word.'

'Thank you, glad you like it.' Alex paused amid brushing his teeth to spit out toothpaste. 'And then there's the local community, he's apparently become a regular at Osca's bar, you know, that sleazy dive just past God Only Knows investments.'

'Oh, yuk. I'm going right off him. I always thought he was a little bit naughty and lots of fun at a party, but that's bad news. Once you get into somewhere like Osca's it's only a matter of time. I just hope the man's taking sensible precautions.'

'He should know all about it, enough people dying around here to be an awful warning to anyone, especially someone who doubles as a pathologist.' Alex pushed back the mosquito net and sat on the edge of the bed to take off his socks. 'But back to this death-threat business. Gus said Jake was taking it seriously. He showed him one of the letters. It was very neatly typed, printed out on white paper, obviously done on a word processor, no chance of identifying handwriting or anything like that. Very good English. Knew lots about his home life so definitely someone who knew his routines. Threatening to kidnap him and torture him and so on, nasty stuff.'

'Hmm. I wonder. Love interest's the obvious angle, but you know he does have staff – not just his clinic, he's got some domestics now. He said he wouldn't when he first came here, but I know for a fact he had a cook last year and someone who does his washing and cleaning. You never know, it could be one of them. And he could have had relationships outside the European community. There are lots of very moral people around here who might not like it – that's another possibility. I can imagine a few devout Christians getting steamed up about his behaviour – I mean even his language tonight was a bit extreme for some people – I found myself wondering if Thomas would be offended.'

'I think he's used it to it, but it's sweet of you to care.'

Alex crawled across his wife to get to the far side of the bed. They both switched off their torches and tucked them under their pillows. The ragged-edged curtains were open as usual and they sat, backs to the wall, staring out at the night until their eyes became accustomed to the darkness. As they listened, a munching sound filtered through the wire-mesh windows.

'Hippo. Probably the same one I saw last night when I got up to pee.'

'You know,' said Lizzie, 'a thought has just occurred to me. If you were to take out a contract on someone – let's say, for the sake of argument, a middle-aged white man, and your hit man was – let's say a black Congolese or Zimbabwean, how would you describe Jake to your killer?'

'I'd say he was a white man to start off with, bit of a scruffy dresser, usually wears long shorts and sandals, long greyish blonde hair, wrinkled tanned face, piercing blue eyes. Go on, now give me the blinding revelation.'

'No, don't be so lazy, do it yourself. Describe Harvey Miller for me.'

'OK, badly dressed, usually wears long shorts, long grey hair, wrinkled olive-skinned face, bloodshot ... what colour were his eyes?'

'Blue.'

'Are you serious?'

'Very serious. So take the differences – you said badly dressed for Harvey because he had no style, but Jake is scruffy – he's got style – now if you're using your second language for this the difference is going to be virtually unnoticeable. Both have blue eyes, both have long hair – set aside the fact Jake's is much longer – and Jake's got those hot-climate smoker's wrinkles and a tan whereas Harvey basically was much older and had naturally darker skin.'

'Lizzie, I don't know where you're going with this and I'm sure it's very interesting, but can you please save the rest for morning? This has been a very long and very disturbing day. I have to get on with my work tomorrow come what may, we've only got five more weeks left.'

'I know, I'm sorry, it's just that I've been thinking—'

'Well stop it!'

'I can't.'

'You can and you will, come on, think about a giraffe. Count the spots.'

'Thomas would understand.'

'Well you can tell him in the morning.'

'I will.'

There was a brief spell of silence.

'But Alex, what if it was a big mistake? What if it was meant to be Jake?'

'Lizzie, Jake is well known around here, his vehicle is well known around here, why would someone local hire a foreign contract killer just to get it all wrong and kill the wrong "geezer"? Please, give it a rest.'

'Sorry. But Alex? Alex?'

He had adopted his best defence: sleep.

Lizzie rolled over grumpily and tried to visualise a giraffe.

Outside the hippos had moved on. The beam of a strong torch swept past their chalet and into the bushes. Someone, somewhere was out and about. But it was not the night watchman. His eyes were closed in the soundest of sleeps, twitching as he dreamed of glistening bunches of freshly caught fish.

Footsteps approached the golden couple's chalet and hesitated. A figure stood outside their door and listened. He had been plenty patient with the night watchman and was not about to ruin his hard work by moving too soon. He checked his watch with its little illuminated dial and gave it twenty minutes, they should be fast asleep by then. He sat on the wooden chair and waited.

When the time was up he slid the thick rubber mat from the front of his vehicle through the yawning gap under the door. Then he took a slender piece of metal from his pocket and gently wiggled it until the key on the other side dropped, with a very gentle thud, onto the absorbent rubber. He listened a little longer. Slowly he turned his own key in the door. The habitual squeak had gone, he had made sure of that earlier. He tiptoed on his crepe-soled desert boots into the couple's room and stood a moment watching the sleeping Eliza. Her pale face with its dainty dusting of freckles, the tawny hair golden in the moonlight, the slender arm flung outside the sheet and the fragile form barely concealed beneath. She looked so vulnerable. Pulling himself together, he made his way swiftly to the bags leaning against the wall. He sought out the laptop, slung it over his shoulder in its protective bag and left the chalet as silently as he had come. He picked up the rubber mat and locked the door behind himself.

Five minutes later as Alex turned in his sleep he woke up just enough to imagine he heard the sound of a car engine, far enough away not to concern him. Then he slid back into a deep sleep. Outside the hippo returned to its solitary munching under cover of the restored darkness, a witness, but to what?

Chapter 9

It was just before breakfast when Lizzie discovered something was missing.

'Alex, did I leave my laptop in the vehicle last night?'

'Don't think so, I brought everything in. Is it not with your other stuff?'

'No. I could have sworn I left it here, leaning against the wall. Where's yours?'

'Charging up in the office – thought I'd check emails this morning if the satellite link's working.'

'Alex, I'm worried. Please would you go check the vehicle. Pretty please?'

He kissed her by way of reply and slipped on his shoes. He looked around.

'Have you seen the key?'

She scanned the room and noticed it lying in the dark corner behind the door, on the floor. Alex picked it up and left, checking all round for elephants before he abandoned the relative safety of the porch.

It was ten minutes before he came back with a worried look on his face.

'It's not in the Land Rover. So I thought I'd get you a cup of tea and check the bar, just in case. I started walking over there and noticed old Moses the night watchman was fast asleep – he's usually packing up his bicycle by now.'

He just stood there.

'Alex, what is it? Is there something else?'

He sighed.

'Footsteps.'

'Where?'

'Outside. In the grass and on the porch outside our chalet. Coming and going. They had the hose out yesterday watering the grass. Male feet in proper shoes, not flip flops or wellies, and quite large.'

'So it wasn't one of the staff. Great. But . . .'

They both looked at the ground near the door where the big chunks of mud lay. They knew they had taken their own shoes off last night as they always did to spare the cleaner.

Someone had sneaked into their chalet by dead of night and sneaked out again, leaving the door locked, without even disturbing their slumber. Alex hesitated before he spoke again.

'Is anything else missing?'

'Oh my God. He could have murdered us.'

'But he didn't, he took your laptop. Which brings me to the point. Why?'

'The bone. That's the only thing I've got that's at all important. I'm not prospecting for diamonds, I don't have the next great blockbuster on there or a secret patent. It's that bloody bone. I wish I had never set eyes on the wretched thing!'

'Silly question, I know, but have you got it backed up?'

'It's all on my data stick. I updated it yesterday after I did my notes. It's in my pocket.'

'Well that's one small mercy.'

They sat glumly, side-by-side on the bed.

Eventually Lizzie spoke.

'I've had enough of this. As far as I'm concerned they want war, they get war. I'm calling the police myself this time and I'll be banging heads together if they don't do anything.'

She swung her legs off the bed and tugged on her socks.

'First, though, I'm getting hold of Thomas. He may be short of scouts, but if it kills me I am going to protect that site.'

Alex made no attempt to argue. There was a time for everything and now was not the time for getting in Lizzie's way.

They drove quickly down the dirt track and stopped beside the night watchman's post to rouse their sleeping Cerberus and make sure he was not ill or injured. Moses was groggy and had no memory of the previous night. There was no smell of alcohol around him, no empty bottles or containers, nothing to explain his obvious bewilderment. They agreed he must have been drugged.

Alex stood a moment looking out over the dry grass towards the river. Lizzie took his hand.

'Alex, we could both have been killed, couldn't we? This is serious. Why? That's what I don't get? It's just a bone for God's sake.'

'There has to be more to it than that. Come on, this isn't helping, let's go tell Gus and Maggie, we're too close to it, we need some outside opinion – and I need some breakfast.'

Back in the Land Rover and bumping along to breakfast now, Lizzie was thinking aloud.

'Gus. You're right, he's the man I want. He's got the scaffolding we brought in for that big river section you dug. Instead of setting it upright he could turn it into a fence around the site. It won't make it secure but we can stick up signs and make it absolutely bloody obvious that you have to have a permit to dig there. It'll be better than nothing.'

'Um, don't you think Gus might have a few other things to do?' ventured Alex.

'Of course he will! I'm not that stupid. But if I offer to pay his guys overtime – I reckon the ones due to go home today would do it. Don't you?'

'Try it and see.'

If Alex had doubts about whether men who had been at work, leaving their wives and families for two or three weeks at a time, would forgo their hard-earned home leave for the sake of Lizzie's bone, he said nothing. She could be very persuasive.

The sleepy morning rituals went by the board for once. Lizzie jumped straight out of the vehicle and ran over to Gus's garage.

Alex wandered over to where the students were sitting over toast and tea.

'Morning, guys, everything OK? Good. We'll join you in a minute – er – we lost a laptop in the night – don't suppose any of you saw it after we got back yesterday? No? Oh well, worth a try.'

Head down and looking serious, he pounded across the dusty yard to the reception office where Maggie sat checking her morning emails.

She turned, about to venture a cheery greeting, but one look at Alex's face and it died at the source.

'Oh dear, what's happened now, or dare I ask?'

'We've had a burglar. At least I'm almost sure we have, he was very careful. Footprints in the muddy grass, a man in shoes or light boots. Your night watchman was out like a light – I'm not telling tales out of school, I reckon he was drugged. I've never seen him there after seven and he was still sound asleep when we drove over just now, we had to wake him up and believe me it took some doing. Anyway, Lizzie's laptop was stolen – it's got all her work on it – she's got it backed up on a data stick but the details of the bone are somewhere in there – it's the only thing we can think of that anyone might want enough to steal it for.'

'I'm not sure I want to know the answer to this question, but, did you lock your door last night?'

'We did, we always do.'

'Oh, far out.'

'More or less my feelings.'

'You could have been killed.'

'It had occurred to us.' Alex's tone was light, but his face was grim.

'I'll have to call the police, but you know it won't do any good, don't you? They haven't even taken that wretched man's body yet.' Maggie tapped her pencil on the counter.

'I know. Look, I'll leave you to it – need a cup of tea before it's too late. I don't expect the police'll be rushing out here so we'll just head out as normal.'

'Alex, I am so sorry.'

'It's not your fault. I'm beginning to think that bone has been cursed. It's caused nothing but trouble.' Alex looked unusually sombre.

'Are you sure it couldn't be anything else?'

'Such as? We just don't have valuable information – for goodness' sake Maggie, we're academics!'

She snorted. 'Wasn't it you who told me that great quote – the reason academic disputes are so bitter is because the stakes are so low? Maybe it was more accurate than you knew.'

She directed a rueful glance at Alex's back as he walked away.

The scene in the yard was one of bustling activity. The biggest of Gus's vehicles was being loaded up with metal poles and braces and bits of rope and twine. Alex laughed out loud.

'Lizzie Lamb, where are you?'

A head framed in frizzy copper hair popped out from the shed.

'We got it, the scaffolding – it'll be perfect for security fencing!'

'Have you persuaded them to drive you out there as well?'

The big smile said it all.

'You don't mind if I don't come out on site today, do you? Gus has asked a couple of his guys to come out with me – one of them is painting up some signs too – "Protected site, no digging, by order of Zambia parks authority". I feel so much better just knowing we're doing something.'

'If it would help, you could take one of the students,' Alex offered. 'I can manage for one day – what do you think?'

'Hmm. That might be quite useful – who were you thinking of?'

'How about Zach? You can maybe find out what's eating him?'

Lizzie frowned.

'I guess that's a no, how about Martin, then, if you don't feel up to child psychology?'

'That'd be great – I'm too stressed to cope with Zach.'

'Fine – I'll let Martin know and then we'll be off.'

They both stood awkwardly for a moment before hugging as if for the last time.

When Alex drove by, a couple of minutes later, leaning from the window and waving madly, Lizzie grinned and waved back. They were both pretty good at putting a brave face on things. Then again, they had to be.

Chapter 10

At the same time that Maggie was sending the archaeologists on their way, Thomas was trying – and failing – to download his emails in the Parks office. The electricity had gone off. He sat, frustrated, tapping his fingers on the old wooden desk and staring out of the window to where the groundsman stood watering the grass. He was pondering how to tackle the school's headmaster about the lack of progress on the kitchen-building scheme when the door to the main office swung open, as if to admit a ghost. No one entered, but the office radio suddenly crackled into life. He smiled as Maggie's voice spoke out on the public channel, but when he heard what she was saying the smile vanished.

'Mfuwe police, Mfuwe police, Mfuwe police. Elephant Camp calling. Come in please, Mfuwe police.'

A lot of crackling and nothing happening.

She tried again.

And again.

And again.

Finally a languid voice took to the airwaves.

'Elephant Camp, police here, over.'

Maggie chose her words with care – Thomas was familiar with the technique.

'Good morning, officer, we have a burglary to report. Any chance you could send someone up to us today? We are still waiting for someone to deal with the other matter. Over.'

Thomas applauded her expert performance – she had done well not to broadcast the news of the murder with the rest of the world listening.

'Ah, madam, we have no vehicle. If you can arrange a lift for us.'

The statement hung in the air a moment.

'I will see what I can do, officer. Will someone be available if I find you a lift? Over.'

'Eh. It is very possible. I might come myself even. Can you give me lunch?'

'We will see. I will contact you when I have found you a lift. Over and out.'

He could picture Maggie fuming. He picked up the landline phone and, to his surprise, reached her at his first attempt.

'Good morning, Elephant Camp. Thomas here, can I give a lift to anyone for you – I might be going towards the airport, if that helps?'

'That would be fantastic. You obviously heard that nincompoop?'

'You said a burglary – was it from the office or one of the guests?'

'Someone broke into Lizzie's chalet last night – took her laptop and slipped out again – the bugger even locked up after himself – frightening as hell. They could have been murdered in their beds. I can't help thinking that bone of Lizzie's is at the root of it all. The poor thing must be beside herself with worry – I would be. Can't see the police are going to help much but you have to try, so if you really don't mind ...'

A few minutes later, Thomas was on his way to the police post to pick up the 'officer' who wanted lunch.

It was Saturday, you could tell by the hubbub on the road. Children in tattered rags or pretty dresses ran free, out of school and already home from working in the fields. Music spilled out from the concrete-box shops, ranged like Lego bricks alongside the thin strip of tarmac. Women brushed orange dust from the compacted earth in front of their huts, or sat on the dried-up riverbed digging holes for water, or carried vast bundles of heavy firewood on heads swathed in brightly coloured cloth, their world an endless succession of menial tasks that came around time and time again.

Thomas liked to present a buoyant face to the world, but he was not always the stereotypical, jolly, fat man that he knew people saw in him. No, there were times when Valley life depressed him – and this was one of them.

For many years he had lived in Zambia's Copperbelt, putting his environmental qualifications to work in the mining industry, juggling deadlines and managing international connections. Sometimes the Luangwa Valley felt like a torpid backwater. But that was also its strength. For the time being it was a good place for his young children. When they were a bit older he might consider a transfer, but for now its slow pace suited him, even if its petty irritations did not. One of those irritations was the state of the police. The only time they swung into action was when they needed money. Just last week they had stopped a vehicle owned by the electricity company and fined them for some trumped up 'offence' – because they had no money to pay their electricity bill. An amusing story for the westerners, but it was corruption – nothing more, nothing less – and it was embarrassing.

The crudely painted sign for the school his little son had attended – and to which his two daughters now went – came into view down the road. His vague feeling of dissatisfaction grew into a fully-fledged fit of anger at the sight. Only three months ago it would have made him happy – the thought that soon they would have a kitchen built of baked-mud bricks. It would not look like much to the people who raised the money back in the UK, but it would make so much difference. The current tiny, open-sided thatched shelter barely provided enough cover for one cooking pot and the ground turned to mud in the rainy season. Even more important, for Thomas, was the specially designed clay oven that would run on charcoal bought from roadside traders, meaning the little ones would no longer need to gather wood from the dangerous haunts of wild animals. But it was three months now since the headmaster had said they were ready to start work on it – and so far, there was not one single sign of progress.

Thomas simply could not understand the head, he had seemed so dynamic when he arrived and now it was interminable meeting after interminable meeting, supposedly pursuing 'community empowerment'.

The anger was beginning to show in his speed. Raising his foot from the accelerator he applied the brakes to cope with the shambolic bridge ahead. The vehicle bumped sharply down into a pot hole which covered the full width of the road. Across the bridge, the whine of the gears changing up sounded loud amid the dense swathes of tall reeds that had crept right up to the very edges of the road.

It was not far now.

Thomas tooted his horn as he drew near to the white-painted concrete block of the police station, not expecting – and not eliciting – any response. The chances were not high that his passenger would be ready. He drove into the yard and parked next to the husk of a Toyota Land Cruiser sitting on bricks where its wheels should have been. That was the police vehicle. Finally he edged out of his seat and carefully wound up all his windows and locked all the doors of his vehicle before venturing towards the entrance. A small man scuttled out.

'Ah, Dr Nkhoma, good morning. How are you? Sergeant Ezekiel, he says he is most sorry but he cannot come with you now. He says he can come tomorrow.'

'Ah, that is most unfortunate. I am going to Elephant Camp now, I cannot come back for him tomorrow. Tell the good sergeant not to worry, I will see what I can do to find out who did this new crime and report back to him when I can. Maybe he can find someone to bring him out to investigate this murder soon though, eh?'

Shaking his head, Thomas climbed back on board his aged Land Rover and headed back the way he came, an hour poorer, but richer in official goodwill. It was the perennial trade-off and there was nothing he could do about it.

Maggie was glad to see him. Moses, the night watchman was sitting in her office, his large black torch in his lap, his blue-overalled legs squashed into ill-fitting black Wellington boots – Dunlops, he called them.

'Madam, I do not know where this night it has gone. One minute I see this small hippo with fast legs and I am afraid for safety for our guests, next minute Dr Alex he is shaking me by the shoulder and the sun is here once more. This I cannot explain, madam. Where has this time gone?'

'Are you sure you didn't have any beer last night, Moses?'

'Madam, no! I had not one taste of beer. I have my flask with tea, this is all.'

Thomas interrupted, his tone reassuring.

'Mr Moses, my friend, did you drink some of this tea?'

'I did, Dr Nkhoma.'

'Do you have some left?'

'I have. Each night I drink it every hour, one small cup, until there is not more, but this night I have plenty still.'

Poor Moses was beside himself. As a watchman, being found asleep at his post was about the worst thing that could happen to him. The old man was just shuffling his way out of the office when Thomas asked him one last question.

'Mr Moses, forgive me, I have forgotten to ask you, who made this tea for you, was this your wife?'

'No, not last night. Our daughter's firstborn is ill with malaria and she was visiting her. I asked the new cook to do this for me.'

Maggie broke in.

'New cook? What new cook?'

'The tall one with the strange hair – he is not from this region, maybe from Congo or Angola. He stops to talk to me most evenings this week, I am thinking maybe he is lonely. Always he asks me do I want tea or food and always I say no, but last night my wife has not made me my food or my tea and I say yes. He was most polite.'

Thomas looked at 'madam' Maggie and raised his eyebrows.

'Maggie, can you take Moses to the kitchen on his way out and see if this new man is there?'

There was, of course, no new chef. It was plain that someone very, very patient had planned this theft down to every last detail.

'I think,' said Thomas when Maggie had returned with the answer they both knew she would get, 'that we must now take what Professor Lamb says more seriously. I do not think I really believed that these people could be so wicked in their pursuit of mere bones, but it very much looks as if someone has hired some criminals to do these things.'

'I hear what you're saying, Dr Nkhoma, but I really can't believe it still. It doesn't take a genius to see that Moses has been doped, but what a performance, why not just hijack Lizzie and Alex one day?'

'Aren't they usually with an armed scout?'

'Duh. Yes, of course.' As she frowned, deep ridges bit into her tanned skin. She had been a smoker from an early age and it showed. 'But surely there would be some other way of getting that information without spending days trying to drug a poor old night watchman and then break into a chalet by dead of night? Not to mention risking life and limb with our nimble hippo.'

'Our labour comes cheap to Europeans and Americans. It could be very inexpensive for them to hire such criminals for days upon end. It is too much of a coincidence that these fossil-hunting vultures are descending at the same time this is happening – and that our academic couple is the only target in this clever crime. But was it Professor Miller who arranged this, before he met his untimely end, or was it some other vulture entirely, I wonder? There are plenty more on the way, to judge by the requests in my in-tray.'

'Not to mention the ones who are already here in Mfuwe. Three of them were staying out at Beacon Ridge Lodge but they're moving over here – checking in later today. They're booked in for a week with an option to extend.'

'These are the French ones?'

'Yep. Two by name of Delfosse, one Gilles. Two men, one woman.'

'If this is something to do with these people, then there is something even more serious that worries me – I don't know if you know exactly where we found the abandoned vehicle?'

Maggie shook her head. 'I know it was somewhere over the other side of the pontoon, on the way to Beacon Ridge Lodge.'

'The vehicle was found parked on the slope of a small hill just off the last big bend in the dirt road before you get to the Beacon Ridge turn-off, almost within sight of the lodge. It could only have been hidden by a couple of trees.'

'That's close. It's a bit of a coincidence, isn't it? I thought–'

A crackle of radio static exploded into the still air inside the humid little office.

'Elephant Camp, Elephant Camp, Elephant Camp, Maggie, are you there?'

'Excuse me, Thomas.' Maggie reached for the radio.

'Elephant Camp, I copy you, Lizzie, what is it?'

'Mags, we're putting up the fence now, but it looks like someone has been here already this morning. Tyre tracks, signs of a small amount of digging and damn me if it isn't spot on the GPS coordinates where the bone was found. They must have heard us coming, there are very fresh tyre tracks and a couple of cigarette stubs they forgot to hide. We'll be heading back soon. Over.'

Maggie handed the receiver to Thomas, first warning him in a whisper that Lizzie was using the open frequency that the whole Valley could hear.

'Professor, this is Thomas Nkhoma, have you looked at those cigarette stubs? I would like you to pick them up and bring them back. Do not tell us anything more now, *les petits cochons ont de grandes oreilles, tu sais*. Over.'

'We should be back in about two hours, so why don't you stay for lunch, my treat, we can chat then, over?'

'An excellent plan. I shall wait here, over.'

He handed the handset back to Maggie.

'OK, Lizzie, we'll expect you for lunch between one and two. Tell Gus the new part for his tractor has arrived and I'm betting it's the wrong one – actually don't tell him that bit – let him live in hope. And for God's sake take care. Over and out now.'

Chapter 11

Gus parked the ancient Land Rover in the garage. Lizzie, making her way towards the office, could see Thomas sitting in the bar, chatting to one of the Camp's guides, and made a diversion to the loo for a perfunctory clean up. Martin had gone off with her packed lunch as well as his to spend the afternoon washing his clothes and lazing around the little pool. It was plain that something had happened between him and Zach but whatever it was, she had no better idea now than when she set out in the morning. A combination of an open vehicle and Gus's presence had put paid to that.

As she faced the mirror and despaired over her own quite gentle sprinkling of freckles she felt a surge of sympathy for the lad. Martin's densely freckled face combined with almost white eyebrows and eyelashes gave him an odd vulnerable look which she quite liked, but then she was not a potential mate. He was not a big hit with females, he dressed badly and to top it all he was painfully shy. Zach was just the reverse, golden skinned with glossy dark hair, mischievous eyes, a charming grin, perfect teeth – plus a wardrobe that was not just unusual for a student but wasted on a dig in the African bush. Dragging a comb through her unruly hair, Lizzie wondered. Something about Zach had definitely changed and she could not put her finger on it. She pulled out her spot concealer and applied it to the red bump a tsetse fly had added to her chin, then jogged over to the bar.

'Hiya, Thomas, how are you?'

Without waiting for an answer she threw herself down next to him and dangled a small, sealed plastic bag in front of him.

'Cigarette stubs, as requested. Now tell me, why?'

'Did you look at them – any clue as to what type they are?'

'No filters, quite dark, sort of nicotine-yellow-plus. Very smelly, so I'm guessing they're pretty strong. No name, but in my vast experience of the weed I would hazard, I don't know – Gauloises or Camel, or Turkish or something – not that I have any idea what Turkish cigarettes are like, but they're supposed to be quite strong, aren't they?'

Thomas took the bag from her.

'I am no expert either, but I know a man who is. We shall see what we shall see. Meanwhile I will try a little experiment on you – what does the name Delfosse mean to you? Or Gilles?'

'Oh no! Please don't tell me *they* are in the Valley? They are, aren't they? Oh bugger, bugger, bugger. That's it, I might as well go home. Harvey Miller was a bastard, but at least we were playing on the same playing field. These guys aren't just ruthless, they're pig-ignorant – and filthy rich.'

'That does not sound like a good combination.'

'Believe me it's not, it's an alliance forged in Hell. Sylvie Delfosse is an heiress, spoilt rotten and drop-dead gorgeous. Her dad has one of the biggest vineyards in Bordeaux – and he owns a big hotel chain. Rumour has it that Luc – Professeur Delfosse – married her for her money – she was one of his students and he seduced her – bit of a scandal at the time apparently. Anyway, Daddy cut up rough a bit at first, but he came around in the end when it became clear Sylvie was not just totally besotted but a really good palaeontologist. She's one of those that have the knack – just looks at a landscape and plumps straight for the right bit to find the juicy fossils. Gilles – he's a hanger-on, but pretty well connected in his own right, very establishment, has the ear of the French President if you believe what he says. So, what they want, they get. If they don't get, they get mad and things tend to go wrong until they get their way. So, like I say, I might as well pack up and go home.'

'This is not like you, Eliza. I think you need a good meal inside you and then you will feel different.'

'You know, Thomas, you might be right. What's more, I might just break my own expedition rules and have a nice, big glass of wine at lunchtime. Will you join me?'

'If you are to break the rules, then the least I can do is to be your partner in sin – or is that crime? Make mine a *Mosi* and we have a deal.'

It was clear that Lizzie was putting a brave face on things, she looked a little paler than usual, her freckles stood out on her cheekbones, her eyes looked tired and she tapped the table with two fingers whenever her hands were free of cutlery, which was quite a lot of the time.

Thomas said nothing about the imminent arrival at Elephant Camp of the Foreign Legion. Instead he told her the saga of the new headmaster who was supposed to be building latrines and a kitchen for his little girls' school but seemed rather more keen on building his own stature in the community.

'Why don't they go home for their food?'

'Some of them walk for days to get to school, so they have to stay as boarders – but not like the English boarding school of midnight feasts – they have no beds, just grass mats on a concrete floor. And these little ones have to provide their own food and do their own cooking.'

Lizzie's fingers stopped drumming on the table as she pondered a world where children were so keen to learn that they would walk for days to get to school.

'Thomas, can you take me to this school sometime? I sponsor a couple of girls at one of the primary schools, but I've never been inside a school – it's always been arm's length. Maybe it's time I got involved.'

Thomas nodded his approval and then conversation moved on to the slow progress of electrification in the village and the swift impact of the new mobile-phone masts. The fact that the Valley's residents were now connected – signal permitting – to the world of cellphones was both saving and changing lives. In the settlement of Mfuwe a yellow portacabin did a brisk trade selling talk time, and even off-road the occasional bush outside a thatched hut was hung with a sign saying 'top-ups here'.

By the time three o'clock came around, talk had turned again to the palaeo-vultures and Lizzie, having worked through the 'we might as well go home' phase, was well into the 'I'll show the buggers' phase. That was before the vehicle arrived.

Maggie came hurrying out of her office, all smiles, to greet the new arrivals. Thomas was facing in their direction, Lizzie looking out into the bush afternoon, entranced by a couple of young baboons learning to groom each other. Their still-soft hair stood out against the golden light like a halo. Suddenly there was a screaming and chattering as a big male ran into the middle of the group, sending them bounding away. Lizzie looked up, followed Thomas's gaze and took in the scene in an instant.

'So, here they come.' She paused, 'I'm not sure I can take this. They'll ruin everything. I can see it now, they'll buy their way in, go over your head, take over Alex's patch. You know as well as I do there are some people in Lusaka who don't give a damn about what we're doing and will just let it happen – for a price.'

'So, you are giving up without a fight? And what of Dr Sommers in all this? Hmm? Do you want him to give up his years of painstaking labour here in this remote and beautiful Valley? What about his feelings, his career?'

Lizzie looked shamefaced.

'I'm sorry. I'm tired, I'm being selfish and stupid. Maybe I should go home myself, though – it's going to be intolerable with them around and I simply can't compete with their resources – especially now the bone location is out.'

'Is there no way you could work together, befriend them?'

'I've tried before, they regard themselves as monarchs of all they survey. But if you feel like having a go, be my guest, They might respond to you, after all you're the one who has the power to let them work in the park or not.'

'I shall wait for them to come to me – and if they do not, then maybe I shall take up your suggestion. But now, I fear I have to leave you to your own devices. I have an office that needs my attention, an irritating headmaster to meet and then two little girls who need my help with their homework.'

'Oh, Thomas, I am *so* sorry, I'm being thoughtless all round. I've kept you way too long. I really do appreciate it. By the way, I've got a skipping rope each for the girls I'll give you them next time I see you – they're in our chalet and I don't really feel like going back there on my own after last night.'

'That's kind of you, they'll like those and they can wait. Now, I will say goodbye to Maggie and be on my way.'

Lizzie stayed in her chair after Thomas left, wondering how to deal with the latest influx of palaeo-vultures. It was nearing five o'clock by the time she moved, after taking yet more pictures of baboons to add to her extensive collection. Looking at the creatures, she was conscious of just how lucky she was. Her knowledge of these baboons' long-lost cousins in Ethiopia had enabled her to spend several seasons here in South Luangwa with her husband. It had been a fabulous few years. If her luck was about to run out, then so be it, she would resign herself to taking a back seat, avoiding confrontation and to helping Alex as much as she could.

That was before Alex arrived home.

It was nearly dark when the team pulled in, clanking, jolting, chattering, giggling. Then the bar began to come to life, the click of *Mosi* bottle tops landing on the concrete floor, the fizz of frothing Fantas, the smell of insect repellent mingled with sunscreen. Alex stood, a *Mosi* in one hand and Lizzie's shoulder under the other, grinning from ear to ear. The soundtrack was one of a good day, Lizzie could tell. She said nothing, not wanting to prick the bubble of conviviality.

Kate and Amy stood together, leaning on the bar, looking like peas in a pod, medium length brown hair, pale faces and sunburnt noses streaked with dirt, stripy t-shirts showing a little midriff and each holding a thick glass bottle of sweet, unnaturally orange Fanta.

'You should have seen the four giraffes,' Amy exclaimed, 'they just walked out of the trees and stood there, two adults, two babies, just looking at us. It was magic, pure magic.'

It was the new arrivals who pricked the bubble.

'Dr Sommers, Mrs Sommers, *bonjour*, good afternoon. How are you?'

Lizzie said nothing, the smile frozen on her face like bad plastic surgery. All the students went quiet as if to cue.

'Professeur Delfosse, how nice to see you.' Alex's words sounded normal and polite enough, but everyone could tell they did not reflect his mood. 'Lizzie doesn't answer to Mrs Sommers, I'm afraid – she kept her own name when we married – and she's been a professor now for over a year. I could have sworn you knew.' He frowned. 'Didn't you see the paper she wrote earlier this year in *Nature*?'

'I thought perhaps she used *Lamb* so it did not look like she was picking up the scraps which fell from the table of your work, so to say.' Professeur Delfosse examined an old gold ring set with an onyx seal that adorned his right ring finger. 'Lucky for your wife that she was with you when you found that bone, *non*?'

'*Non,* indeed. I was lucky *she* was there – you know bones aren't my expertise and her CV's a lot more impressive than mine – that's why she's a professor and I'm a humble doctor.' Alex took Lizzie's hand, impressed that she had not uttered so much as a squeak.

'Ah, yes,' Delfosse continued, waving one hand around so the smoke from his cigarette created spirals in the air, 'this world of positive discrimination – that is how you say it, yes? So much easier for them to make progress. The women today they have the good fortune, yes?'

A very deep breath was the outward sign that Lizzie's *sang-froid* had completely melted. Alex squeezed her hand and moved the exchange on in as carefree a tone as he could muster.

'Talking of women with fortunes, is Sylvie with you?'

Lizzie was crunching on a large lump of ice which went down the wrong way and she choked. Alex turned to slap her on the back. When he turned back Luc Delfosse was gone.

Zach's eyes were following him as he left.

'Hey, who is that dude?'

'That dude, Zach, is Professor Luc Delfosse. If you want to know how to make it in life without ever using a single scruple, then look and learn. He's got many degrees in the subject.'

'Cool. The man to know.'

Lizzie watched, stunned, as Zach flicked away his roll-up and went after Luc Delfosse.

Chapter 12

The electric light was dimmer than usual when they sat down for dinner and no one was surprised when it went out. The oil lamps, which sometimes seemed romantic, tonight just seemed inadequate.

'Pass me the water, please, Kate.'

Kate passed the water without a word. Lizzie was puzzled, it was not like this crew to be so subdued.

'Are you guys OK? You seem a bit quiet tonight.'

For a few seconds Lizzie thought no one was going to answer, then Martin piped up.

'It's nothing, just those French guys, they've been over at the campsite bar telling everyone how wonderful they are and how their international reputation is second to none. It was a bit frustrating, that's all.'

Leah, the PhD student who had caught Jake's eye, was the only one who seemed impervious to the mood. Her face was flushed, her eyes bright and her lips were slicked with gloss. She made an exaggerated pout and wriggled in her seat as she fixed the dark haired young man across the table in her gaze.

'Zach, you got something hot for me there?'

The two had been flirting since they arrived, but instead of the expected risqué riposte, Zach passed her the squeezy plastic bottle of chilli tomato chutney without a word.

'What's up with you all?' Leah paused to squirt the sauce onto her plate. 'I've had a great day in case you're interested. Spent the first half tracing rock art that you could barely see lying flat on my back on rocky ground that was crawling with ants, then that vet guy Jake turned up and brought this amazing picnic – chicken and bread and wine – cold Spanish wine in a bottle not a box – and even some paw-paw – and we went for a drive – it was just divine.'

She put a forkful of rice in her mouth and continued. 'We went to this spring where there were lots of big black and white birds just sitting around. They had this weird cry. Then if you clapped your hands they all flew up at once and then circled around and landed.'

Zach did not even look up as he replied. 'Gosh that's interesting, Leah. And what did the cheesy old man want in return for that I wonder?'

Alex looked sharply at Zach. Leah looked as if she had been punched. Lizzie scraped back her chair and stood, affecting unconcern.

'That reminds me, I must go and ask Maggie what happened to Vickie. Last I heard she was going to get on a plane to Lusaka this morning and Jake was still sleeping off his hangover. Anyone wants to buy me a drink while I'm gone I wouldn't say no to a large red wine.'

She smiled an arch smile at her husband and started to walk away, but stopped when she heard Martin's voice, loud, almost shouting.

'What's it with you? You're being an absolute bastard, Zach. One minute you're Leah's biggest fan next you're treating her like dirt. So what if she has a wild time with some cheesy old guy? At least she doesn't ... oh, forget it. You know what I'm talking about, so you just watch your back, mate.'

'Oh, shut your stupid face, knob-head, you haven't got a clue, have you? I don't give a damn. And I'm sick of sitting around with a load of dumb arse-lickers like you. I'm going out with those South Africans you didn't like the look of – guess what, they're professional hunters, a bit more exciting than playing cards with a beer and an "ooh look I'm so naughty" roll-up. So you just stay here and suck up to teacher as usual. No one will miss your ugly white mug, that's for sure.'

He threw his chair back at the table and it fell over with a loud bang. Alex walked around to pick up the chair and stood a few moments, looking after the young man, with one hand in his pocket, the other clicking his thumb and middle finger together audibly. Lizzie recognised the signs. Alex was very, very angry.

'OK, I'll get my own glass of wine,' she muttered as she walked towards the table at the far end of the bar, where Maggie sat laughing with one of the guides. Just as she approached the bar the electric light came on. Maggie turned and saw her.

'Lizzie, come and sit down.'

'No thanks, Mags, there's trouble brewing,' she nodded towards the table where the remaining students sat in silence, 'I don't want to miss it. Just wondered if you knew what was happening with Vickie?'

Maggie shook her head.

'That man. Jake got out of bed to put her on a plane to Lusaka and I booked her in with a group heading off to Lower Zambezi – he paid, would you believe? I gather she was pretty tearful when she left. And just guess who went out looking for that PhD student of Alex's today – do you reckon she'll take the bait?'

'Already has – he wined her and dined her and she's instantly cow-eyed. Does Birgit know?'

'She does. Puffy eyes, red nose, lots of tissue in the waste paper basket. I wish she would leave in some ways,' she broke off and turned to Simon, the guide, 'Simon, I don't actually mean that, so don't go telling everyone I want rid of her, I don't, she's just very unhappy.'

'I know madam, we can all see it. That man, ah!'

The staccato Zambian 'ah!' expressed so much: annoyance, exasperation, frustration and agreement.

'Indeed. But all we can do is watch and wait and offer hugs every now and again.' Maggie laid one hand on Simon's arm and made as if to bat her eyelashes at him. 'Not you, Simon darling. She might find that a bit odd.' Maggie never stayed serious for long.

Simon laughed out loud, pushed back his chair and said his farewells, pleading an early morning start with a game drive for seven people. He sang to himself as he meandered out into the night.

'He seems like a nice guy, Mags, does he have a family?'

'No, he lives with his cousin, or maybe it's his brother – but he's a bit of a lady's man, that's why he laughed, an in-joke. Not quite on a par with good old Jake mind, and quite religious too, evangelical Christian. Actually, come to think of it, we haven't had a female guide and a male guide pairing yet – that might be quite good fun.'

'You're a wicked woman! Tell me, out of your great stock of worldly wisdom, what do you think we should do about Leah – anything?'

'I don't see how you can, she's what – 24, 25? She's a grown up and if you try and put her off as sure as eggs are eggs she'll only get stubborn. I'd just leave it, but make sure she's getting on with her work, hmm? A few judicious questions that might make her panic about the time she has left?'

'Good idea. Oh hell, look, Zach's coming back and heading straight for Leah.'

Before anyone could do anything Zach had grabbed her arms and held them against the back of her chair, immobilising her. She struggled, whatever noise she was trying to make muffled by the violent pressure of his mouth on hers. Alex was at their side in an instant.

'That's enough, Zach, just back off.'

As he grabbed Zach by the fleshy part of his arm the young man let out a yelp of pain and pulled back. The shock on his face was almost funny. Alex was rarely aggressive, which made his intervention all the more effective.

'Who the fuck do you think you are – we're adults you know. If I want to—'

'Adult? You? You have to be joking. Apologise. Now!'

'Fuck off.'

Alex stood a moment, quiet but furious.

'Apologise – or pack your bags.'

There was a brief silence.

Alex turned and called, 'Maggie?'

She was on her way over instantly.

'Can I do something for you, Alex?'

'You can get this *boy* on the first plane out of here unless he apologises to me, to Leah and to everyone here within the next twenty seconds.'

Alex looked at his watch and waited.

'Like you can force me to leave,' the boy sneered.

'I suspect there are ways,' said Alex, 'for example, would you like to pay me back for the air fare, the accommodation, the meals?'

Maggie calmly waded in.

'How much money do you have with you, Zach? I think you owe us about 75 dollars on your bar bill, meals – that would be about 25 dollars per day. The air fare back to Lusaka is – ooh – about 200 dollars this time of year, one way, though I suppose you could cadge a lift – it'll take at least 12 hours by road. Oh – and when I think someone might slip off without paying I have an arrangement with the night watchmen – we alert the road blocks, and our police aren't that friendly to people who run off and have no money, so don't even think about it.'

'I don't see why I have to say sorry to anyone.'

Leah piped up.

'Oh really? What about me? I didn't ask you to slobber all over my face.'

'You love it, you're hot for it.'

'Even if I was, you arsehole, that's what rapists say. I choose who I snog and how and when, you don't force your slimy little tongue in my mouth where it's not wanted. Stop being such a wanker and say sorry.'

'Sorry.'

He turned and walked off. Alex gave him a minute then followed.

Leah's spirited fight-back seemed to revitalise the group and within minutes the sound of raucous laughter began to mingle with the sounds of the chef singing, frogs chirruping and the hoarse cough of a distant lion.

Lizzie and Maggie sat at the bar, perched on tall stools, sipping red wine.

'I don't know how they can be friends when they talk to each other like that – am I so middle-aged already that I can't understand the young any more? I teach these little monsters and I had no idea they behaved like this. Zach is just way out of order.'

Maggie thought a moment.

'Is this really new behaviour, or is it just behaviour you haven't seen before? Have you asked any of the others?'

'No, didn't really expect it was going to go this far.' Lizzie looked at her friend. 'You sound as if you think you know what's wrong – assuming there is something – do you?'

'No. But I can hazard a guess. I'm not an expert, but don't you think this might be a drug-induced change of character? I really don't have any experience of it, but I've read the stories – and one of the other kids might have heard something or been offered something. Worth a try – the white-haired boy maybe – or that quiet little girl, I bet she knows what's going on.'

'I don't think I'm going to get anything out of Martin – he seems to be wound up with whatever it is in some way, but Kate? Mm. I could ask her, I'd imagine I could trust her not to say anything.' She sighed. 'It's such a relief to deal with her – she and Amy are such nice girls. Both quiet, both steady. Very different work-wise, though – Kate's creative, emotional, intuitive, Amy's really analytical and scientific.'

'They should get on well together.'

'They do.' Lizzie broke off to yawn. 'Christopher Columbus, I'm whacked. Where's Alex?'

She stood up and looked around.

'He went after Zach – can't have gone far, haven't heard a vehicle. Do you want me to run you over to your hut?'

'I'm not sure I can face it alone – I still feel a bit apprehensive after what happened.'

'Don't forget you've got neighbours in the next chalet now – and I can ask the night-watchman to sit on your porch till Alex gets back if you like?'

'OK. Why not? Then I can do some girlie stuff like painting my toenails before Alex gets in.'

Maggie slipped off her perch and extracted a large bunch of keys from the pocket of her khaki trousers.

Five minutes later Lizzie was back in the comfort of her room, painting her toenails, when the electricity went off again and she began to regret returning alone. She had bravely – or foolishly – decided to leave the night-watchman at his post since she could see the lights on in the chalet just a few metres across the dirt road. Now, in the pitch dark, it seemed like a million miles away.

With nothing much else she could do she slid through the mosquito net and into bed. Not normally one for lying awake worrying, the break-in had left her feeling vulnerable, but it had been a wearing day and before too long she had drifted into sleep, only to be awoken by a 'tap-tap-tap' on the door.

Sitting upright, Lizzie could feel her heart pounding. She pulled a torch from under her pillow, slipped under the mosquito net, padded across to the window and pulled back the curtain. There was a figure standing by the door and Lizzie was shocked to see it was a woman, a white woman. The thudding beat of her heart began to soften and she went and stood behind the door.

'Who is it, what do you want?'

'Lizzie, it is Sylvie, Sylvie Delfosse, I am sorry for this interruption, I regret I am awaking you, please, can I come in, if you and Alex do not mind, I have something I need to tell you.'

Lizzie was astounded. She took another look out of the window to make sure the woman was alone before turning the key in the door and opening it.

'Come in, quickly, it's buggy on the porch and I've got a mosquito coil burning.' She shut the door and turned to look at her visitor.

'Sylvie, what on earth is the matter?' Lizzie realised the woman was shaking, standing stock still and shaking.

'Are you cold, are you ill, is it malaria, can I—'

'It is worse than that. I am so afraid. I need your help Lizzie but Luc must not know. I have to get away, but he will see to it that I do not if he knows I am trying. I have come while he is out – he is seeing some man in Mfuwe about who knows what, God alone knows. '

'Sylvie, come and sit on the bed, I'm sorry, there aren't any chairs. What are you talking about, why are you frightened?' She could see Sylvie looking around. 'I'm sorry, but Alex's not here.' Then they heard the noise of an engine, one that badly needed tuning.

'Oh my God, if Luc comes back and sees me here I am lost. I must go back to my bed. Please say nothing, I will try and find you again. I am sorry.'

With that she ran from the hut and as Lizzie stood by the window she could see her slender form in its pale nightwear running into the next hut along, She was only just in time, just as the door closed the ramshackle vehicle Luc had hired from Gus came to a choking halt outside his wife's hut. He jumped down, looked around, his gaze pausing momentarily on Lizzie's window, or so it seemed to her. She pressed back against the wooden frame, knowing he could not see her in the darkness but cautious nonetheless.

He lit a cigarette and loitered for a while before heading back in. Sylvie was safe, or at least, Lizzie realised, safe in the knowledge that her visit was a secret. Whatever else she was or was not frightened of, it would just have to wait.

Lizzie was not good at waiting. She prowled around the room, frustrated and not a little irritated that Alex was not yet back. The flash of illumination as the electricity suddenly returned had her running to the window to pull across the curtain. As she did so the sound of another vehicle, slightly better tuned, came through the undergrowth.

Alex looked grim.

'I'm sorry I'm so late, that little bugger is lucky I'm not putting him on the next plane.' Alex was throwing off his clothes and only now realised that it was odd that his wife was standing in the middle of the room dressed only in a long t-shirt and no sandals. 'What's wrong? Why didn't you …' He looked at the bed, 'You did get into bed. Are you OK? You're not sick are you?'

He was standing in front of her now, hands either side of her pale face, the cloud of amber hair swept back over her shoulders.

'I'm fine, honest, but I've just had a surprise visit from Sylvie and she sure as hell is not fine. I'm getting back into bed. Hurry up and I'll tell you all about it.'

Within three minutes he was sitting on the bed listening to Lizzie's account of the odd episode.

When she had finished there was nothing more they could say, nothing further they could do and so they switched off the torches they had been using to illuminate their conversation and slid down under the sheet.

'Alex?'

'Mm.'

'You know I have to do something don't you?'

'Yes, but not now.'

'Of course not, silly. But in the morning, can I have another day off?'

'No problem. Now please, go to sleep. I've got to be up at the crack of dawn to see if Zach is fulfilling the conditions of his extended stay.'

'Oh God, Alex, I'm sorry, I didn't ask you.'

'It can wait.'

'But … '

'It *can* wait and it *will* wait. Go to sleep!'

'Alex.'

'What!'

'I'm going to sleep now.'

Alex turned over and fell asleep almost instantly, a reluctant Lizzie following not long after.

Outside, the usual quiet noise was everywhere, the crackle of branches ripped down by hungry elephants, the squeal of a startled baboon, the perennial insect chorus. Beneath it all a sharp ear could have detected the sound of laughter, mirthless laughter, coming from the chalet where Luc Delfosse sat, still smoking, as his wife feigned sleep.

Chapter 13

It was a restless night in Chalet five. Not long before dawn Alex woke from a rare moment of rest to the sound of gentle knocking on the chalet door. Lizzie was still fast asleep beside him. He looked down at her, sad to see her face drawn with the signs of stress. He carefully extracted himself from the bed and the mosquito net and opened the door. It was Moses, the night watchman.

'Sir, madam tells me on the radio to wake you. Can you please go to her office.'

'Do you know what it's about, Moses?'

'No sir, she says do this now-now, so I am thinking this is important?'

'Now-now' topped a scale of urgency which descended to 'now' and 'just now'.

'OK Moses, thanks for telling me. Are there any elephants around?'

'No, sir, there was a big group earlier but they have eaten much and now go back across the river to the Park.'

Moses smiled a beatific smile showing a set of fine, strong white teeth, with just one gap, right in the middle at the front. Before he stepped down from the porch he tightened the string around his waist that held up his threadbare trousers and adjusted his woolly hat. Alex felt one of those pangs that rich white folks so often get when faced with the reality of serious poverty. An accident of birth, that's all it took.

He shut the door on the departing Moses. Lizzie was stirring now and opened bleary green eyes to look at him.

'What time is it? Who was that?'

'It's 5.30 and that was Moses. Maggie wants to see me right away – I'll throw on some clothes and head over. I'll walk – Moses says it's safe.'

Lizzie rolled over and groaned. 'Now what? I can't bear it. And I drank too much wine last night. Can you bring me something back to drink – water or Fanta or something, please?'

Alex, dressed in an ancient white tennis sweater against the cool of the early morning, darted through the mosquito net, kissed her and left in a flash. He ran over to the office, abandoning his usual disciplined, safe and steady pace, trusting that Moses was right and no elephants lurked in the shrubbery. As he approached the open grassy area that signified the main part of the Camp, he could see a little clutch of people standing around the office. One of them was Gus. He was not normally out and about that early and if he was, it would be in the garage. Alex felt the hairs on his arms rise. Something was definitely wrong.

He hurried over to the office, where the silent little group parted to let him through, like a human Red Sea faced with a new Moses.

Maggie turned to face him.

'Sorry to drag you out this early, Alex, we've just discovered we've had another break in – the only thing they went for was all your excavation kit – and I mean all of it. Every last bucket and shovel and even your sieves.'

'You have got to be joking? Who on earth would want all that lot? Well I mean, I can see a farmer might find bits and pieces useful but ...' He stopped dead as the implications began to sink in. 'Has the surveying equipment gone too?'

'Everything. I'm really sorry.'

'Including the unwashed finds, soil samples, everything?'

Maggie nodded.

Alex sought for words to describe the loss, his lips compressed, his fists curled into solid balls, his knuckles white. Eventually he spoke.

'Maggie,' he took a breath, 'where was the night watchman? After the break in to our chalet—?'

'You're not going to believe this.'

'Not drugged, surely not again?'

Maggie nodded, lips pursed. 'Someone bought him a drink. A Coke. Told him it was to help keep him awake.'

'Does he know who it was?' Alex asked, sounding optimistic.

Maggie raised her eyes to heaven.

'A white man,' she said, enunciating very clearly.

'That's all, a white man, nothing else?' Alex was unimpressed.

'I quote, "madam, all white men look the same to me, except for Bwana Gus and Doctor Alex, I see them each day. This man, he is just a white man. I do not know him". Talk about turning the tables, eh? So we're looking for a white man who was here last night – and guess what? As well as you and the other 'ologists' we had a party of American Baptists and a group of bird watchers from Scotland. And before you ask, no, he couldn't tell me what kind of accent – I don't know if you've ever tried to ask a Zambian what accent someone has – blank looks all round – you could be American for all they would know, honestly. It's really frustrating.'

'So in short, all my equipment has gone and the night watchman hasn't a clue who slipped him a Mickey Finn?'

'Correct.'

Alex stood a moment, unable to decide how to react.

'Right. I ought to get back to Lizzie – check she's awake if nothing else. Something else odd happened last night.'

Maggie looked the question.

'I'll tell you later, or Lizzie will. Is there any point in calling the police?'

Maggie shrugged, 'We can do it so you can claim on your insurance, but as for actually finding out who did it and where the stuff is …'

Gus poked his head around the door jamb at this point.

'Sorry to interrupt, Mags, but I thought I might go off for a drive around – you just never know – we have found things dumped before when thieves have taken what they want from their hauls. Like to join me, Alex?'

'Good idea. Can you drive me by our chalet so I can tell Lizzie?'

Gus raised one thumb by way of reply – he was a man of few words, except when the spirit of Islay was upon him – and trotted off to start up the big safari Land Rover.

Gus was a good driver – he needed to be, the 'roads' around Mfuwe were rudimentary. One long stretch of metalled road ran from the airport to the park gate. Just before it reached the park a small spur ran off it for a little distance before petering out. That was where the tracks began that led, in various directions, to Elephant Camp. In the rainy season there had to be plenty of alternatives, as one by one they became impassable, up to the point when the floods rolled in and boats were the only means of transport. It was hard to imagine now. In the open-topped Land Rover specially adapted for game viewing, dust billowed around them as they roared along the pits and peaks of the bush roads, slowing every now and again to check the undergrowth for debris.

'I've got a pretty good idea where the buggers went,' Gus said, 'I picked up a set of tracks behind the kitchen – they're heading towards the Chief's palace so far, but I'm betting they'll turn off at some point. Keep an eye open for one of those trails off to the left with fresh tyre tracks.'

Alex shielded his eyes with his left hand and held on tight with his right – there was no door on the side to hold him in and Gus took no hostages when it came to taking bends.

'There!'

Alex grasped the dashboard with both hands as the vehicle swung off the main track and onto one that was barely visible. Tyre tracks stretched ahead of them into the woods. Gus had been right, the vehicle had veered off the main dirt road well before the turn-off to the Chief's palace.

Gus was slowing down as a split in the track came into view. He ground to a halt beside a tall, graceful *mopane* tree, one of a cluster whose height earned them the name 'cathedral' *mopanes*. Its sparse fronds scarcely troubled the winter sun's passage to the dry earth at their feet.

'We're not going to find anything now.' Gus put one rough, comforting hand out and gripped Alex's arm, briefly, in solidarity. 'I'm sorry Alex, I really thought they might have dumped the rocks and stuff.'

Alex let the 'rocks and stuff' pass, after all Gus was no archaeologist and it hardly mattered whether he called them artefacts now they were gone.

The two sat, briefly silent. Alex felt the immensity of the loss wash over him.

'I just don't believe it,' he said, his voice betraying his utter dejection. 'In all the years I've been coming here – it must be, what, twelve years now that I've been working in Zambia? I mean, we've had our low points. Getting my passport stolen twice hardly rates as fun, not to mention my camp being burnt down back at Mumbwa, but this – why did they have to take everything? Those bags were irreplaceable. Not just the artefacts but the soil samples. And what good will it do them? They'll just find out they're worthless and throw them away. I'm gutted, absolutely gutted.'

'Are they completely worthless?' Gus enquired. 'I mean, I know they're not precious stones or anything, but I'm just wondering why they stole the bags of soil – they're bulky, not to mention heavy, and if they thought something was valuable as opposed to useful like the buckets, wouldn't you think it would be the stones? I know the staff don't really believe what you say half the time, they're convinced you're prospecting for diamonds or emeralds – well that and hunting terrorists for the CIA, of course.'

When he first came to stay at Elephant Camp five years ago the staff had wondered what he was doing there and had decided he was an American spy hunting Bin Laden. The usual joke did not raise the usual smile from Alex.

'I suppose.' Alex roused himself. 'Perhaps they thought we'd found something worthwhile in the mineral line. But what? There's nothing round here. There's the kimberlite pipes – you do get diamonds with that type of geological formation, but no one's ever found much here. I know there was some talk of oil way back in the seventies – and again in the nineties, but the fact that no-one's bothered to follow it up given peak oil and all that suggests there's nothing much there – and anyway, that's all in the North Park, isn't it?'

Gus nodded.

'So far as I know, yes, the North Park's the place – but who knows these days? All this stuff that they need to make new technology work.' He turned the key in the ignition and started to turn around the clumsy vehicle. 'I'm sorry Alex, really sorry. Let's head on back and see if we can rustle up some buckets and spades for you at least.'

It was a quiet return journey. Even the wildlife had gone into hiding, they saw not a single giraffe, nor a single elephant, the only sign of life they encountered a string of weary looking women following each other in straggling line, heads erect under their burden of massive bundles of firewood. It only worsened Alex's mood. What right had he to be depressed? Back home he could light a fire or cook a meal at the touch of a button. He could head back to relative luxury in England any time he wanted. He might have to. Alex stared straight ahead and shifted in his seat as he settled further into a state of bleak despondency.

Chapter 14

Lizzie was standing in the garage when they arrived back, chatting to the head mechanic while he fixed a chair that had been kicked by an elephant.

Gus, in diplomatic mood, left Lizzie and Alex to catch up while he went in search of buckets and spades and anything that might be of use to the archaeologists. Although he had not said much, Lizzie could tell he was both disturbed and hurt by this crime wave. It was not what he expected to happen in his beloved Valley. When Gus's father had brought them here, from what was then Rhodesia, they had all rejoiced in a new kind of paradise. The son of a minister, Lizzie doubted Gus would let the wickedness of a few spoil it for the many. He was a practical man, he would want to do something, something concrete. Watching him wander off, Lizzie saw him stop beside his head mechanic, Lionel – the oldest member of the garage crew. She knew exactly what Gus was up to – soon he and Lionel would be scouring every nook and cranny for useful bits and bobs to make amends for what was lost. She said nothing.

Alex looked dazed, that and dispirited. It alarmed Lizzie. In all the years they had been together she had never seen him so down. The magnitude of the loss was still sinking in. She hugged him tight. One of the cleaners walked by and the two of them sprang apart.

Lizzie braced herself and spoke in what she hoped was something approaching a normal tone.

'Well, there is a tiny bit of good news, Leah's gone for the day, but she said she was leaving some plastic bags and her trowel with the others, so that means with hers and Kate's trowel, plus mine and yours – you've enough to get by on the excavating for the time being.'

Alex looked grateful, but still disheartened. 'I suppose we could do some digging, assuming my site's still intact. But what worries me is the sieving.'

Lizzie floundered now, ' Well, maybe we can have them DHL some mesh in from home, have wooden frames made when they arrive, like we did before, and meanwhile just build up some heaps and make sure we remember which is which till they come. Or we could try and buy some kind of containers on the market to hold the spoil till we can fix something up?' It sounded weak, even to her.

'I don't know,' Alex shrugged, 'perhaps we should give it a rest for a day or two and see if we can get some stuff flown in.'

'Well, you never know. Zach suggested texting Vickie – he seems to have got to know her rather well, given what little we saw of her. He thinks her dad might be able to get some useful stuff out for us, so Leah offered to drive him through Mfuwe to get a signal on his phone – in fact she offered to take him out for the whole day and I thought…'

He forced a smile. 'You thought she might find out what's wrong with him? Good idea. I ought to work out what to do with the rest of the day. I don't think it's worth taking the students out now, but I'm feeling a bit twitchy about the site. I think I'll head out on my own – or with Gus if he'll come – just to set my mind at rest if nothing else. Then tomorrow, I don't know – perhaps we could go and do a recce for sites that would be less labour intensive and where we wouldn't need sieves.'

He sounded dubious, but at least he was trying to be constructive.

'Would you mind if I stayed here?' Lizzie asked as they approached the shade of the bar. 'I'm getting a bit concerned about that body in the cold store. The guy might have been a bastard but he didn't deserve to be murdered – or left to moulder in a cupboard. If it has anything to do with me and that stupid bone I want to know why and if it doesn't then at least I've helped.' She hesitated. 'So – I thought I'd ask Mags if she'd let me poke around the stuff in Harvey Miller's chalet.'

Alex looked sceptical. 'Is that legal?'

'Maybe not. Probably not. But the police aren't exactly rushing to help, are they? And I want to radio Thomas as well, see if he's found anything out about those vehicles – Harvey's and the poachers', he's got them both at his office.' She stopped and looked up at him, the anxiety all too evident in her eyes. 'Alex, one man's been murdered, another man's badly injured and he had three fake passports and a gun and *my name and address* with him in that vehicle. Someone broke into our chalet while we were sleeping and nicked my laptop, they could have killed us. And now all your excavation kit and finds are gone. I just can't sit around and do nothing, even if the police can. I know Thomas is trying to help, but he has a family as well as a day job – he's not omnipotent even if we like to think he is.' She stopped, her hands flailing the air. Her voice was almost inaudible now. 'Alex, I'm scared.'

Alex wrapped his arms around her, closed his eyes and held her tight. 'Be careful,' he whispered, 'please, be careful.'

'OK, you two lovebirds, break it up.'

A series of loud clanking sounds accompanied Gus, returning with buckets and spades, pickaxes and a toolbox.

'Just call me absolutely bloody marvellous, eh?' He dumped the toolbox on the ground and opened it to reveal a rudimentary spirit level, a locally made hammer, some odd-looking tools that could have been trowels, several hanks of rough but strong twine and a spanner, just for good measure. 'This should do you for the time being. Simon here says he'll see what he can do about the sieves,' he slapped the guide on the back, 'his brother has a carpentry shop in Mfuwe. Poor chap spends more time making coffins these days than furniture, doesn't he, Simon, eh?'

Simon nodded agreement and spoke up. 'I am going to the airport this afternoon to pick up some new arrivals. I will stop on the way at my brother's shop, if madam Maggie says this is fine,' he looked sideways at Gus, 'and we will see if we can find a way to make these sieves. I will also speak to my sister, she makes jewellery out of snare wire taken from poachers and sells it to tourists, maybe she can have some good ideas.'

'Thanks Simon,' Alex reached out and shook the man's hand, 'that's really helpful – of course we'll pay your brother and sister for their trouble and for materials, anything you can do would be great.'

Simon waved as he walked away, chewing a stalk of grass and swaying his long, slender body as if in tune with some internal melody. Lizzie watched him go. There was something about the man that made you want to watch him, a tall man with the elegance of a giraffe but something more, something regal, or even priestly. She turned, the others were watching him too. She tapped Gus on the arm.

'Gus, what happened to Harvey Miller's stuff?'

'Haven't a clue. You'll have to ask Mags. Planning on doing a bit of detective work, are you?'

'Yep. Alex's worried it might be illegal but I think it might help the police, what do you reckon?'

He chuckled. 'Makes no bloody difference what I think. *She who must be obeyed* will decide, police or no police. But if you pushed me, then *I* think the person who helped them out with a post-mortem could be trusted to rifle through the poor man's belongings. Go on, ask her. She's in the kitchen, she won't bite!'

Lizzie crackled with sudden energy. Alex's face shone with pride as he watched her almost skip along to the green door beneath the tamarind tree.

Behind the green door in the semi-twilight world of the kitchen, the chef was being uncharacteristically quiet, cowed by the presence of 'madam'. Maggie's half-lens reading glasses sat part way down her nose, anchored on their gilt chain, and Lizzie had to admit she looked formidable. It made her hesitate, ever so briefly, but long enough for Maggie to notice.

'Well don't just stand there, woman, what is it?'

Maggie tugged off her spectacles and left them dangling. Behind her the chef, Innocent, started to measure out the powdery white mealie-meal for the staff's midday meal of '*nshima*'. Looking like a cross between polenta and mashed potato, *nshima* was eaten morning noon and night by most Zambians, accompanied by whatever relish was available: beans stewed for hours over a slow fire, a luxurious chunk of chicken, groundnuts pounded with dried pumpkin leaves or the smelly little dried fish – *kapenta* – that Lizzie hated.

'I was wondering if… whether… would you… Let me start again. Can I look at Harvey Miller's stuff?'

'Don't see why not – no one's claimed any of it – or him for that matter. I've emailed his university to see if there are next of kin who should be informed and they haven't got back to me – they did give me his insurance details, though, so at least I can organise a coffin and a flight when the police let the body go. Having said that, our lazy good for nothing sergeant still hasn't shown up.' She reached out and flicked a large, dead cockroach out of a dark corner.

Lizzie kept her grimace to herself as Maggie carried on.

'Thomas radioed on the private channel, a little while ago, he's going to have another try at getting that sergeant out here. He said he hasn't found out who owns the two vehicles yet – if no one claims them you can bet your boots the police will. Then they'll have no damned excuses left.' She pushed her glasses back on her nose and consulted her watch. 'Oh, God, look at the time! I have to get on, Lizzie – the supply lorry's due soon – we have to work out what we've still got on the shelves before we add the new stuff. And I could really do with getting that store room back – so you just get on and find out whodunnit and then we can get rid of the body. Ask Lucy at reception for Miller's room key – tell her I said you could have it – Chalet nine, by the septic tank.' She peered over her glasses and winked. 'Had to put him in that one, didn't I? A Yank by the septic tank?'

Maggie had a good laugh at her own joke, Lizzie just shook her head as she stepped out into the daylight.

The room was a big one, designed for a family. Lizzie took in her surroundings with interest. New, colourful curtains hung at the mesh windows, the headboards of the beds were carved from local *mukwa* wood and on the main wall was a big, colourful hanging from the Tribal Textiles workshop in Mfuwe. She breathed in slowly, relishing the musky scent emanating from the new furniture. It was one of the things she loved about Zambia, the scent of wood smoke everywhere, greeting her like a guard of honour when she stepped from the plane in Lusaka, lingering in her belongings when she got home, instantly evocative.

The housekeeper had clearly tidied up. Everything was carefully arranged in piles around the room. She could see from the neat array before her that Harvey had not travelled light. It made her wonder how long he had planned to stay, something she had not thought to ask. She could see his document bag, a pile of papers and a hand lens. Her instinct was to go straight for his work, just out of professional curiosity, but instead she picked up his vivid nylon carry-on bag from where it lay, squashed into the space on the floor beneath the bamboo shelves holding his clothes. There was very little inside, a few empty plastic bags, a pair of travel socks for the long haul flights, a sewing kit and a padlock with the keys in it. Lizzie unzipped the side pocket and pushed in her hand. She pulled out a few scraps of paper and a couple of business cards with his Zambian address scrawled on the back. One of the scraps of paper dropped to the polished concrete floor. She bent down to pick it up and as she did so realised that it was a stub of a boarding card. She stared at it for several seconds, before placing it back in the bag.

'What on earth were you doing in Lubumbashi?' she said out loud.

There was a knock on the door.

She went to open it. She found herself unable to speak. It was Luc Delfosse.

'Ah, *Professor* Lamb – so must I call you according to your oh-so protective husband. But, excuse me, is this your chalet?'

'No.'

She felt terse, so she was terse. She had no inclination to waste words on this man.

'Ah, I thought not. I am looking for the chalet of the poor *Professeur* Miller, he has something of mine which I wish to find. May I come in?'

'No, sorry, I am here because I have an official role in the murder enquiry. If you tell me what you are looking for I will keep an eye out for it.'

'If you don't mind, it is a little sensitive, I would rather look for it myself, perhaps I will come back when you have finished.'

'I don't think so, anything found in this room is potentially evidence in a murder enquiry. Now if you would excuse me …'

'But then perhaps you can look for me. I am hoping *Professeur* Miller has kept my article which I sent to him recently, a pre-publication manuscript of our latest report, highly confidential. It is by me and by Sylvie and René, you will recognise our names, *non*?'

'I will bear it in mind. Now, I really must get on.'

She pushed the squeaking door to, almost before he had a chance to move out of the way. Once it had separated them she realised how tense the encounter had made her. Sylvie's anguished state, her talk of terrible things associated with her husband, her sheer fear, had alarmed Lizzie and now she could feel that her pulse rate was up and her breathing shallow. She took a few moments to regain her composure.

She went back to the bag and took another look at the ticket stub. The date of the flight to Lusaka from the Congo was only ten days ago. The man had been there *en route.* She thumbed through the other bits of paper but could not find any more clues to his travel arrangements. She turned to the top of the wobbly shelves where his clothes were piled and riffled through a heap of tatty-looking print-outs. She had nearly reached the end when she found the itinerary. Harvey Miller had left the USA, travelled first to Manchester, then to Brussels, then to Kinshasa before flying on to Lubumbashi, not far from Zambia's Copperbelt, and finally on to Lusaka. What is more, he had broken his trip in Lubumbashi and stayed for nearly two weeks. Lizzie was perplexed.

What on earth was the man doing in the Congo? Friends who used to work there had left years ago, no one had worked there seriously, certainly not out in the field, for ages. She had heard that some intrepid souls were beginning to venture out of Lubumbashi on field trips, but she did not have Harvey down as a brave man. Almost as odd as the stop in Lubumbashi was his choice of a route through Manchester. She knew to her cost, after the last conference she attended, that it was a more expensive way of travelling from the States to England – unless something had changed in the last few months. And once again, he had broken his journey there, it had not been a mere transit stop. He had spent four days in Manchester.

This was all looking decidedly odd. She pulled a notebook out of her own bag and scribbled down the details of the itinerary, then replaced the paper in the heap from which it had come.

Turning her attention to the pile of off-prints of articles from learned journals, she wondered if there really was one by the Gilles and the Delfosses. Fifteen minutes later she was still reading, sitting on one of the room's five single beds, next to the window. It was the best light she could find given the electricity was off, yet again. Her notebook lay open on her lap and a pile of articles grew beside her on the thick, striped Zambian blanket.

Every time she picked up an article she made a note of the journal from which it came and the date it was published. By the time she had reached the end of the heap she had still not found a pre-publication manuscripts or proofs, but there were several articles by the Delfosse and Gilles. They all referred to finds they had made in the Kenyan Rift Valley – all except for one, which referred to 'a survey of fossil-bearing strata' the previous year, in the Democratic Republic of the Congo. As usual the man had exaggerated when he said it was a Delfosse and Gilles article: their names were the last in the long list of collaborators and probably meant they had next to no practical input. As she set it down beside her she stopped to think. Something about it struck her as familiar. Picking up the pile of paper once more, she trawled through the pages till she found the one she wanted.

'Aha! Gotcha,' she voiced her thoughts out loud. '*Mineral extraction technology and exploration, Volume 22.* Key words: Mineral deposits, Lubumbashi, DRC. Well look at that, would you believe it?''

The two articles were based on the same data and the list of authors' names almost identical. The only real difference was the change of subject from 'fossil' to mineral.

'You sneaky little man.' She almost admired the cheek of it. Getting one's work printed twice by using journals in two different fields was one way of boosting your publication record, if a somewhat dishonest one. Then it struck her that the 'mineral' article had, of course, been written well before the 'fossil' one. She checked the date. Nearly a year old already. Setting aside the dubious nature of the duplication, it begged the question: why was the deceased fossil molar expert, Harvey Miller, interested in mere minerals? She sat back and stared out of the window at a clutch of young monkeys chasing each other in and out of the nearest tree, swinging low on its flexible branches and tumbling all over the place like baby clowns.

'Harvey Miller,' she said to herself, as she scanned his room once more. 'What have you been up to?'

His ghost made no reply.

Lizzie looked at her watch. It was nearly time for lunch. She flipped rapidly through the pages of the article till she came to the acknowledgements. At first glance it was all the usual stuff, gratitude for permissions, recognitions for grants and thanks to reviewers, but then she noticed that the last thank you was for a 'donation' from a commercial firm, one she had never heard of. 'Donation' was an unusual word in the context of an academic article and she made a note to look up the 'donor' when she next managed to access the Internet. Lizzie was about to chuck the paper back on the heap when a thought stopped her. Turning to the end, to the pages of references that academics list in support of their written arguments, she scanned through for names beginning with the letter 'M'.

There was one reference to a conference paper given in London by Harvey Miller, 'Australopithecine molars from the DRC and what they tell us about mineral leaching in the tropics'. A rather odd topic for a palaeontologist. But not utterly implausible. Then her finger slid up the page until she got to G, and there it was, Gilles, Delfosse and Delfosse. *Geology and fossil location in Kenya and Tanzania: A field guide*.

Lizzie remembered now. The threesome, all a good bit older than she and Alex, had done a fair bit of surveying in their early days. This book had become a must-have for anyone working in Kenya and Tanzania when they were undergraduates – but she had never used it herself – not just because *Theropithecus darti,* the extinct baboon species she studied, was mainly found in Ethiopia, but because her mentor was himself a geological expert. In fact it was through him that she first heard about the scandals attached to the Delfosse name. He had barely a good word to say for the man – and rarely mentioned Sylvie, other than to sigh and say, 'yes, she showed talent, once upon a time'. Lizzie had always suspected an affair of the heart. But at the time she had paid very little attention, being busy with an 'affair of the heart' all her own. In Ethiopia, fourteen years ago, she had met another PhD student, a certain Alexander Sommers.

Lizzie shuffled the papers into an orderly block and placed them back on top of the shelves. Conscious that she really should be on her way to lunch, she decided nonetheless to have a quick look through Miller's pockets before leaving. She felt a bit uncomfortable about it, but then, she rationalised, someone had to do it and better her than . . . She let the thought tail off in anticipation of the guilt she would experience if she finished that thought.

There was very little of interest in the dead man's pockets. No diary, no little black book with vital messages written in code, no tell-tale love letter from a married woman. Then she came across the GPS in the pocket of an unusually smart-looking jacket. Geography of any kind was definitely not her forte. The woman who could change a Land Rover tyre, calibrate sophisticated laboratory equipment and write complex computer programs had a mental block about using GPS. It was not that she couldn't, she would just find any excuse not to be responsible for it. Even in the remote Ethiopian highlands she would avoid the little yellow gadgets like the plague and always, somehow, managed to get someone else to do it for her. Setting scruples aside, she ripped open the Velcro on the trouser pocket halfway down her left leg and slipped in the GPS. Just as she did so a loud rapping on the door made her start. Guilt again, but more justifiable this time. She hurried over and beyond the creaking door stood a man she had not seen before. His eyes were a grey blur of bloodshot whites. His smile was cheery enough, and his greeting.

'Professor Lamb, good morning, how are you?'

They shook hands in the customary way.

'I am fine, how are you?'

In reality Lizzie was thinking, 'Who are you?', but it would have been rude to ask.

At that point Thomas Nkhoma hove into view.

'Professor Lamb, you have met our good Sergeant I see. He has come to pursue his investigations.' He winked at Lizzie. 'And for lunch.'

'What good timing. I was just on my way to lunch too,' said Lizzie, in what she hoped was a carefree, innocent tone, 'why don't you both join me? You must be hungry after your drive.'

Thomas nodded approvingly behind the policeman's back and, chatting, they all traipsed over to the restaurant, just as soon as Lizzie had locked the chalet door – and put the key into Sergeant Phiri's waiting, outstretched hand.

Lunch was a strained affair, with Sergeant Phiri eating vast quantities, saying very little and smiling a lot in a very disconcerting manner. Lizzie knew she should be circumspect about what she said, but the great lacunae in the conversation made it tempting to blather. Fortunately, Thomas was there to help.

'Sergeant Phiri has recently come to our wonderful Valley from Lusaka, Professor. He had not heard of your great assistance to the police last year, I told him all about how you used your world-renowned brains to work out who was masterminding the smuggling and poaching that shamed our loyal and diligent staff at the Parks office. He agreed with me that your contribution made you a very special person here and that we should accord you the informal title of honorary detective.'

Sergeant Phiri laughed at this, a short burst of sound accompanied by a shower of crumbs from his open mouth. He spluttered.

'Dr Nkhoma tells me a very good story. Hah! I like this story very well, Professor Lamb, we must all be most grateful for your kind help. Me, ah! I would spend all my time finding out more about this terrible business,' he shook his head and clucked a little at this point, 'but as you know, we have no car, we have no computer, even we have no electricity. Can you help us, do you think?'

Lizzie looked at Thomas who nodded, but with a slight frown that signified caution.

'I would be delighted to help you, Sergeant, if you think I can do anything. As you know I am staying here in Elephant Camp, so I am in a good place to see what goes on. If you would like, I can do some investigation – as an honorary detective – and write a little report, not something official maybe, but just for you, so that you may tell your superiors what you have done to solve this terrible crime?'

Sergeant Phiri clasped both hands together and shook them up and down in obvious agreement. Then he picked up the key that lay beside his plate and ceremoniously handed it to Thomas Nkhoma, his intermediary, who in turn handed it, with equal ceremony, to Lizzie.

She thanked them, with a deep bow of the head to each man in turn, accompanied by a clasping of both hands together, implying not just gratitude but subservience.

Then Lizzie ventured a little further, feeling that she might as well clear the field for herself while she could.

'I am wondering if maybe the theft of my laptop, and the theft of my husband's excavation equipment might be connected, so if you are happy for me to do so, I might, perhaps, be able to put in a report concerning all these three incidents if that helps you. I do understand how difficult it is with no vehicle and no computer and such a big, big area to cover alone.'

Sergeant Phiri looked down at his empty plate.

Lizzie signalled to the waiter, Gabriel, who came over in a big hurry. The police were not to be messed with if you lived in the village near the 'station' as he did.

'Gabriel,' Lizzie asked, 'could we all have some tea, and maybe the Sergeant and Thomas might like some cake if there is some available today?'

Gabriel looked worried.

'Ah, madam, we do not have cake, we have only pudding. Innocent has made a fruitie crumble.'

Lizzie could tell Gabriel was nervous by the way he said 'fruitie'. His English was excellent and she could not remember him normally using the 'ie' ending that Zambians so often attached to a word.

Gabriel had taken the broad smiles of the two officials as his order and left before Lizzie had time to speak.

There was a lull in the conversation during which Lizzie realised she had not seen or heard Alex for an hour or two.

'Gentlemen, if you will excuse me a moment, I ought to go and find out what has happened to my husband – if I can't find him then I won't make a very good detective will I?'

Polite laughter followed her as she left and then Lizzie heard the two men's conversation turn to the subject they really enjoyed, politics. She wondered if Sergeant Phiri was a fan of the anti-corruption commission – but then thought that maybe she was being unfair to the man. He had, after all, asked her for nothing but help, yet.

Making her way past the empty office towards the workshops and garage, Lizzie had to squeeze by the refrigerated lorry delivering its precious cargo of butter and milk and meat, shaken and rattled on abysmal roads for the last twelve hours on its way from Lusaka. The engine throbbed in tune with the midday heat, struggling to keep its treasures cool. It was only when she made to pass by the kitchen that she noticed that the door to the cold store was open. As she got nearer one of the kitchen staff came out carrying a mop and bucket and another went in carrying cheese. The body had gone, the store was being pressed back into the service for which it was intended. She hurried, now, into the garage area. There she saw Thomas's vehicle, standing in solitary splendour with its rear door open. Gus came walking around the back with Alex just as she reached it.

'Makeshift hearse,' Gus explained. 'We're wrapping the body up now with some ice, it's on its way to the airport. Jake's helping the police with this end of things – he's had to deal with one or two before and knows the ropes better than anyone else – Simon's brother has made a coffin for it and Thomas is taking the body there for Jake to pick up. It's a bit of an ignominious end for the man isn't it?'

'I suppose so. I presume this means someone has claimed him?' Lizzie was into honorary detective mode not grieving colleague mode.

'It's rather sad actually. His mother is his only living relative. Or the only one who would lay claim to him, anyway. She's nearly 90, Mags said. Poor woman, you'd never expect your child would be the first to go when you'd got to that age would you?'

They all stood a moment in silence, feeling for the elderly Mrs Miller.

Alex put an arm around Lizzie's shoulder.

'Have you eaten?' he enquired.

She nodded.

'I'm sorry I didn't get a chance to warn you,' he continued, 'I saw Thomas, he said he'd sweet-talked the police into sending someone out. Maggie took him off to one side and told him where you were. Given you were rootling around where you shouldn't, he said he'd try to get him to ask for your help, rather than tick you off – appeal to his idle instincts. He thought I should stay out of it.'

'Thanks a bundle. I'm now *unofficially* an *honorary* detective – if that isn't a minefield of bloody nuance, I don't know what is.'

Gus took a few steps back, 'If you two are going to have a row—'

Lizzie's quizzical look stopped him.

'Well, if you're not, can my friend Alex and me go for lunch please, Professor?'

'Oh, stop behaving like schoolkids, you two. Come on – I have a new friend and colleague to introduce you to. You'll like him, but I should warn you he does pick his nose.'

As the three wandered off chatting and laughing, a large bundle wrapped in a blue plastic sheet was being carried round the back of the garage and dumped in the back of Thomas Nkhoma's trusty Land Rover. The door slammed on the mortal remains of Harvey Miller – and not one person was there to pay him any last respects.

Chapter 15

Gus started up his favourite old Land Rover and sped out of the campsite as if an elephant was on his tail.

'Hang onto your hat, old man!' he yelled at Alex over the noise of the engine, 'and watch out for low-hanging branches, don't forget she's got no windscreen.'

Despite being on high alert for thorny branches and speeding insects – which could hit your face like gravel – Alex began to relax as they bumped along through the bush. He was relieved to be leaving it all behind. Amy, Martin and Kate were happy enough, sitting on the grass at the campsite washing what few artefacts remained from the excavations. Zach had gone off with Leah to try and contact Vickie. Lizzie was wrapped up in her own world of mystery and mischief. Gus was in the driving seat – and he had brought his rifle along for the ride. Alex felt the weight of the world begin to shift from his broad shoulders. Someone else was in charge.

He sat hanging on to the dashboard, scanning the bush to either side but seeing nothing. The midday heat was intense. The wildlife had melted into the woodland, exploiting whatever oases of shade they could find amid the stubby trees coppiced by hungry elephants. Gus, never loquacious, seemed to be relishing the chance to be out and about without guests to impress and made no attempt at conversation.

It was less than an hour before they chugged to a halt at the site.

Alex disembarked, stood for a moment then plodded up the slope to the excavation squares. Their carefully laid out grid pattern, a cat's cradle of strings attached to large nails, had been pulled apart, the crude nails thrown together in a heap. Alex ignored the mess. He felt nothing, it was almost as if he had known what he would find. But a scintilla of hope remained. He headed straight for the most important marker on site, the datum, against which every measurement taken on the site was calibrated. It had been pulled out of the ground and thrown aside. There was no way of salvaging the dig.

He looked for Gus and found him wandering around the holes in the ground that used to be the site of a careful excavation. He peered into the nearest pit. The side walls were crumbling in, a great gouge had been dug out of the base and the remains of a fire – burnt wood and ash – had been dumped in the bottom.

Alex slumped onto the log where he usually sat to make his notes or eat his lunch.

'You OK, old chap?'

'I'll be fine, just give me a minute, Gus.'

Gus nodded and walked away.

Alex, even in his miserable state, felt reassured at the sight of the small man, presenting almost a comic figure in his short shorts and long socks, stopping to light his pipe.

He heaved himself up from the log and walked to the top of the small incline that rose above the site. Looking down, his archaeological instincts swam to the surface, obliterating the day's traumas. He gazed at the chunky cobbles scattered around his feet – tools left abandoned by his ancestors, over a million years ago.

Alex raised his head and gazed across the bush, looking through the eyes of a creature that had been there long, long ago. A slight breeze rose. He turned to face it, breathing it in. Here some long-lost ancestor had also stood, scanning the silent landscape for signs of life, the midday sun burning down from a cloudless sky, just as that same sun did now. A ripple of goose bumps ran across his body.

A sudden cough from Gus brought him back to the present.

Alex turned and strode back down the hill to where Gus sat smoking, rifle in one hand, pipe in the other. He spoke with a breath of smoke, the smell of vanilla, foreign, but comforting.

Gus, ever practical, went straight to the point, 'Anything we can do to sort this out?'

'No,' Alex answered, 'we can't salvage anything from this. But at least it was only a test excavation, we hadn't spent weeks on it. And we weren't actually finding much, so we'd probably have given up on it in a few more days. What bothers me, though – well, besides the sheer vandalism – is what's to stop it happening again?

And *why* did they do it? I mean, what the heck have they achieved? I just don't get it.'

'No idea. Can't get into the brain of someone who'd do such a mindless thing. Stealing the nails, hell yes! I remember when the pylons first went up, hah! They came down pretty damn fast when the locals started filching the angle iron members for making bed frames, and even the nuts and bolts were too valuable to leave lying around. But not here, no, they've just left 'em here. And as for the fire – those damn poachers are fire-starters, but you'd never in a million years catch the buggers sitting up on top of a little hill, all nice and visible, lighting a fire and having a smoke. They might just as well say "here I am, come and get me".'

'Did you say having a smoke?' Alex pounced on Gus's casual remark.

'Right there – a cigarette stub in that pit.'

It was the square that Amy and Kate had been excavating. Alex knew that Kate smoked the occasional roll-up, but nobody ever smoked on site. Signs of burning – charcoal, burnt bone, burnt stone – could be vital archaeological evidence and the last thing they wanted was contamination of the site. Even ash, floating from the many fires that crackled through the woodland at this dry time of year was a hazard.

Alex jumped into the pit and picked up the stub. It had no filter but it was definitely a commercial brand, not a roll-up. Pulling a plastic bag – one of a precious few he had found in the back of the Land Rover – from his pocket, he deposited the stub in it and zipped it shut.

Gus gave him a hand as he climbed from the pit and the two men took one more careful look around the site before picking up the nails and stowing them in the vehicle. Just as Alex was about to get back on board, Gus wandered off.

'Aha! Different tyre tracks. See here, those look like Thomas Nkhoma's vehicle – wonky axle – keep telling him he needs to fix that – he's not your vandal though. Now these, they're from a fancy new motor, probably a top of the range Land Cruiser – there's a couple in the Valley. You had any rich visitors out here?'

Alex shook his head.

'It's possible they were tourists from Beacon Ridge,' Gus climbed into the vehicle, 'they get around out here. But if I were you, I'd get whoever's doing the footwork to look out for a brand new Cruiser and check out who's been driving it.'

'I do know,' Alex grabbed the dashboard as they bumped off down the hill, 'that one of the two they've got impounded at Parks HQ's a Land Cruiser, but I don't know how old. And who knows if it's there any more, I'm sure the police will be doing their best to nab it. I suppose you can't blame them.'

Gus snorted.

'Wouldn't mind if they looked after the buggers when they "confiscated" them.'

'I wonder if the game scouts would know anything about what went on here? Do they have patrols out here?'

'Not usually – and like I say, a fire on the hill top? I wonder if they did it by day when no one would see?'

'That's a thought. And if it was white folks, the scouts might even ignore them, they've got used to seeing people doing daft things on my sites.'

'You don't reckon,' Gus ventured, 'it could be Christian fundamentalists do you? The ones who believe God created the world 6,000 years ago with a great big flash and don't believe in evolution?'

'We had a problem with that at Mumbwa, but there's never been a hint of it here. Anyway, we're way off the beaten track out here in the Park. No-one really sees what we're doing. Whoever did it had to have a vehicle and they had to pay to get into the park – unless they're staying inside for some reason, like tourists. No. it's going to be an expensive business for locals, unless they're in here already. And that would mean poachers or lodge workers. Or scouts. Oh, God, I do hope not.'

The mere thought depressed him. The previous year Lizzie had been involved in an awful case involving one of Thomas's scouts – a poacher turned gamekeeper, turned poacher again.

'Are we assuming,' Gus paused a moment to engage four wheel drive for the sandy river bed ahead, 'that it's the same bastards who took your kit from camp?'

Alex jumped down, adjusted the hubs and climbed back in.

'It'd be a pretty odd coincidence otherwise, don't you think?'

'I do. But listen, the *scouts* know what you guys are doing. They've all seen the kind of stuff you dig up. I can't see them doing this. So, what are these guys *really* after?'

'Lizzie would say the bone, I reckon, it's all we have that's valuable – well, in academic terms that is. But I'm not so sure any more. This would be pretty extreme behaviour, even for the fossil-hunting crowd. They are almost all white folks, though – didn't your night watchman say it was a white man who gave him the spiked drink?'

'He did. But that could have been almost anyone, Alex. I know we've got the three French guests and you know they're fossil hunters, but have you met any of the other people we've got in this week? Someone could be here with a group as a kind of disguise, couldn't they?'

'They could, but it's unlikely – and anyway, the Delfosses' ruthless reputation precedes them. They're an obvious choice if we're looking for professional rivalry.'

'OK, let's get back to why, if it's not professional rivalry, what is it? What's to stop someone believing that you *are* finding valuable stuff even if you aren't – they're convinced you're digging up emeralds or gold or something? So they're looking for the gold you're not finding?'

'Yeah, Gus, they could be, but, then, why nick all our kit as well as our samples?'

'To throw you off track – or because they can get cash for the tools anyway? Don't forget, folks are poor around here.'

They had churned their way across the river bed now and Gus pulled on the brake as they reached solid ground. Before Alex jumped down again to adjust the hubs he turned to Gus, exasperated, 'But you said yourself the nuts and bolts from the electricity pylons were valuable enough to be worth nicking – so why leave those great big iron beauties out there on site if it's the same gang?'

They had talked around in several more circles by the time they arrived back at Elephant Camp.

'Hope you don't mind stopping by the campsite,' Gus said as he turned off the main track, 'I've got to give the barman a bit of a pep talk – we haven't had any overland trucks in for a few days and he's inclined to have a lie down and a nap when it's quiet.'

Gus parked up alongside the thatched bar that overlooked the river.

Alex was having a quick look at the artefacts that Kate, Amy and Martin had washed when two more vehicles roared into the campsite. One disgorged Leah and Zach, the other Jake. It was time to leave. Alex was resilient by nature, but right now his work was in tatters and the future looked bleak. He was not up for fun and frivolity.

'Jake – want to join us for dinner – and could you bring the students over with you if you do to save me a trip?'

'Sure, man, that's cool.'

Relieved, Alex jogged off alone along the staff path, heading for the chalet side of the camp. He needed to talk things through with Lizzie. Impatient, his pace faster than usual, he ran over the rickety bridge that crossed an empty ditch and made his way through the bushes, still alert, despite his haste, to the silent menace of elephants. About halfway across there was a slight dip in the ground and here he slowed, looking for the hole, inadequately filled with a rock, where he had twisted his ankle more than once. He stopped dead. A snake's head reared up before him, the grey sliver of a spitting cobra, just feet away. He stopped breathing.

The snake's slim head sank to the ground and it slipped away soundlessly into the undergrowth. Alex exhaled. He put his hand up to his face and adjusted his glasses. There were times when he was glad of them, and this was one. A spitting cobra's trick was to blind you from a distance, to make the biting easier. He set off again, stamping along his way, willing every damn snake in the neighbourhood to hear him coming and flee.

Alex completed the rest of his short trek in safety and now stood framed in the doorway of Maggie's office against the dying sunset.

'Ah, Alex –' Maggie made a show of searching the darkening background for Gus, 'what have you done with that husband of mine?'

'He's chatting with the barman over at the campsite.'

'What's wrong? You look like you've seen a ghost.'

'I've just run into a spitting cobra, put the wind up me a bit. Any idea where Lizzie is?'

'Mm, she's over at the Parks office, Thomas asked her to help with something – to do with the school, I think – but she said she'd be back before dinner.' Maggie shut the lid on her laptop with a snap, 'Well, I've had enough for today – fancy a drink while you're waiting?'

She chucked the black and white cat on the floor and pulled the door to behind her.

Alex was dismayed to find that the French palaeontologists had got there before him, but the dismay was obviously mutual. After the most cursory of greetings the three fossil hunters went to sit outside to catch the dying glimmers of the swift African sunset.

Maggie hauled her short frame up onto the bar stool and sat swinging her sturdy legs as she lit up a cigarette.

'So, how was it?'

Alex paused.

'If you'd told me yesterday what I'd find out there today – I would have cried. But with everything else that's been going on, it kind of puts it all in perspective. Basically it was a mess. Total write-off, utterly wrecked.'

'I had an awful feeling they'd have trashed it. But at least it can't get any worse now they've nicked your kit *and* ruined your site. Can it?'

'Oh yes it can. If we don't get hold of some new kit pretty damn soon we'll have to give up and go home, leaving those bastards' – he nodded his head in the direction of the French fossil hunters – 'to all the bones in the Valley. And frankly, I'm beginning to wish Lizzie had never found that bloody thing. But for God's sake don't tell her I said so.'

'Don't worry.' Maggie paused for a drag on her cigarette, 'But about those three, I think there's something a bit odd about them. They've been sitting around here all day today, drinking coffee. And complaining about it of course. If they're so hot on finding bones why aren't they out there hunting?'

'No permits? I don't know. That wouldn't usually stop them I must admit.' A thought occurred to him. 'Maggie, did Lizzie tell you what happened with Sylvie?'

'No, I haven't really seen her since you left. What was it?'

Alex related the strange story of Sylvie's visit to their chalet by dead of night.

Maggie shivered. 'That's creepy. Have you any idea what it's all about?'

'None at all. Was she ever alone today?'

'No, they've all been hanging around together like they're joined at the hip. They had one visitor, went and sat outside talking to him – and then he drove off with a big grin on his face. Didn't recognise him, didn't look like a local and he was driving a very nice new Land Cruiser.'

'A new one? You don't remember anything else about it do you?' Alex was instantly alert, the subject of Sylvie abandoned.

'I think it was a company car, had some kind of logo on the side – or maybe an NGO vehicle – though it wasn't white.'

They both grinned. It was widely believed that the first thing any NGO did on setting up in Zambia was to buy a brand new, white, four-by-four and have it painted up with the name and the logo of the organisation.

Alex explained about the tracks out on his vandalised site.

'Well,' Maggie tilted her head back and exhaled a long plume of cigarette smoke towards the lacework of spiders' webs under the thatched roof, 'we won't get anywhere by hanging back, will we? I think it's time I had a chat with them. Why don't you go and radio Thomas, find out when he's bringing Lizzie back, I'll go get my slinky black dress on and do my Mata Hari impression.'

Maggie sent Alex on his way and stood a moment planning her campaign. She beckoned Gabriel away from his table-cleaning duties.

'Ask the guys to start the fire *now-now*, Gabriel. When they're on their way come and find me – I'll be with those French people out there and then I want you to come and take orders for some drinks on my tab. Hurry, this is important.'

Gabriel ran, literally, tea towel flapping in his hand, flip-flops slapping against his bare feet. Maggie waited till he had scared up the fire-lighting crew and they had started work, then strolled over to join the guests sitting by the fire-to-be.

'Good evening, I hope you are all having a good time?'

Luc Delfosse and René Gilles stood and reached out to shake Maggie's proffered hand. She nodded at the seated Sylvie, not wishing to make it obvious that she was interested in the woman.

'I haven't had a chance to talk to you yet, I like to greet our guests personally, make sure everything is satisfactory. Do you mind if I join you?'

Luc's expression made it plain he did mind. He shot a glance at Sylvie that was almost animal in its aggression. It shocked Maggie, but she did not let it show.

René, by contrast, was the essence of Gallic charm. He pulled up a chair for Maggie.

Sylvie seemed pleased to see her.

'So, are you going to try one of our famous walking safaris while you are here?' Maggie enquired.

Luc gave a little burst of laughter. 'Sadly, Madame Angus, we are here to work. We have been planning our schedule today and it is difficult with these lazy officials – they take so much time and always, always, there is the need for some dollars. That man who is in charge of your Park, I do not trust him. We contacted him so long ago and still we have no permit. But we can go and drive around and look, even if we cannot work.'

'I noticed you were here all day today – do you have a driver arranged to show you around?'

'We have made our arrangements.'

It was a deflection, Maggie realised, and decided to try the tourist tack again.

'You must let me persuade you into a drive – our night drives are often very exciting – only last week some guests saw a leopard kill and a lion kill in one evening. And then there is our famous Zambian tradition of the walking safari – you leave early in the morning—'

She broke off as Gabriel appeared at her elbow.

'Ah yes, thank you, Gabriel, I will have a large red wine. Madame Delfosse, gentlemen, I do so enjoy the chance to get to know my guests, may I offer you a drink on the house, please, you'd be doing me a favour?'

There was no polite way they could refuse. As Gabriel left with their orders Maggie called after him to bring some freshly roasted groundnuts from the kitchen and she sat back to enjoy herself.

'So, you are from France – whereabouts? I have never been there, it is supposed to be such a beautiful country.'

She looked squarely at Sylvie as she spoke.

'But yes, our country it is both interesting and beautiful. We all live in Bordeaux, where the wine comes from, there the river is wide and the city attractive.'

'Do you all come from that part of the country?'

'No, no, in truth, Luc he is not French, he is from Belgium and René from the north of our country – me I am from Narbonne in the south. We all work there, we are employees of a large academic research organisation that is across the whole country with a big office in Bordeaux.'

'Do you live in the city itself, Madame?'

'Please, call me Sylvie. No, Luc and I, we live in a historic house, a small chateau, in the countryside. Luc also has a small—'

'I also have a family home which I rent out in Belgium, but one day I will sell it. But you were saying, Madame, the famous walking safari.'

It was an adroit redirection of the conversation by the Belgian.

'Yes, as I was saying, they leave very early and take a few hours but there's something truly special about being so close to nature, so vulnerable.'

Luc bowed his head in her direction as she spoke. 'You will forgive me, this sounds dangerous, I am not sure this would be agreeable to me.'

Sylvie shook her head too. 'No, this sounds too hard for me, I like to stay here and watch these lovely animals like giraffe that we see walk around the Camp.'

The fire was warming up nicely, though truth to tell it was already a warm night. Maggie threw back the last mouthful of her drink and, mission accomplished, a conversational relationship established, she made her excuses and left.

Turning she saw that Birgit had brought her supper into the bar to eat. She wondered. Perhaps their only female guide would be more successful in luring these guests out on safari. She stopped to chat briefly to Birgit, suggesting she made overtures to the group by the fire, and left her finishing a plate of lasagne and garlic bread. It galled her that the young woman should be blessed with height, blonde hair and beauty and yet be able to eat like a horse. Maggie reprimanded herself. She had made it to her fifties despite smoking far too much all her life, she had a lovely husband and a wildly interesting life. What need had she of youth and beauty?

Reaching the office she turned to look and saw Birgit laughing with the trio by the fire. She'd had a feeling Luc Delfosse was a sucker for a pretty face – and she was right.

Chapter 16

While Maggie was chatting up the palaeontologists, Alex sat waiting in the office for a response from Thomas on the radio. The skinny black and white cat had draped itself around him as usual, having clawed its way up from the floor using his leg as a ladder. In the humid heat of the early evening a determined mosquito dive-bombed his wrist again and again and Alex signally failed to exterminate it. The whine began to drive him mad. Then finally, the splutter of the radio spat out, 'Elephant Camp, Elephant Camp, Elephant Camp, come in please,' and he was relieved to hear it was Thomas.

'Elephant Camp here, Thomas, are you holding my wife hostage there, over?'

'My dear Doctor Alexander, no ransom would be enough. The professor has her own strong views about returning to you tonight and lest you assume they are of my making I will hand this radio to her now, over.'

'Alex, it's me. I told Thomas you'd pick me up – he's hardly seen his family the last few days. He says I can wait at his house – you know where it is don't you? Over.'

'No problem, and yes I know where it is. I'll be with you in about 20 minutes, as long as there are no wildlife issues on the way. Over and out.'

It was not a trip he relished making. After dark the roads were even more hazardous than usual, the animals perking up for a night of hunting and feeding, their camouflaged bodies all but invisible except in headlights – and by then it was often too late.

Lizzie was waiting when he got there. Thomas's two little girls ran after them as they drove off, arms wildly waving, their little toffee-coloured dog with its curly tail yelping alongside. Soon they were out of sight and Lizzie and Alex alone for once as they drove through the sparse tree cover.

'Maggie said you were at the school, was it a meeting about the new buildings?'

Lizzie groaned.

'It was – and boy did it drag on.' She sighed 'I hope I'm just being a nasty, cynical westerner, but given they've had the money for six months you'd think there'd be something to show for it by now – the latrines at least. I passed a note to Thomas, suggested he ask the headmaster how much interest the money had made so far.'

'I'm not sure I like where this is heading.'

'The headmaster waffled on about how the bank hadn't sent him any statements and how he had gone to the airport to speak to the man in the bank but the bank was closed for lunch – and so on, and so on. Long and short of it, I reckon he's been playing around with the money and that's why the work hasn't started. You know, Alex, it made my blood boil. They have nothing, no computers, no books, no chalk even for the blackboards, but these little ones are *desperate* to learn. When I think about some of the idle little monsters we teach – whining if we don't copy our lecture notes for them or hand out our PowerPoint presentations. One kid I met today has to walk for *two days* to get to school.'

'Liz, it's a different world, you can't compare them, can you, honestly?'

'I know. I'm being unfair, it's just... well anyway, back to the funding, I told Thomas I was worried about it and he's going to do a bit of digging. I think he's a bit embarrassed – kind of wishes he hadn't got me involved.'

'Didn't the charity attach strings to the money?'

'Yes, but construction was supposed to be starting any time and the head said he would need to be able to access the money more easily, so he could pay for materials locally in cash, so they agreed to switch the money into a school account – for which read *headmaster's* account I'm guessing.'

'Well, I hope you're wrong.' Alex checked his watch. 'Look, it's getting late. Oh – and by the way,' they were getting near to the campsite turn off now, 'I invited Jake for dinner.'

Lizzie said nothing. Alex turned to look at her but she was just staring straight ahead. As they passed the campsite one of the safari vehicles lurched their way and they moved aside to let it past. Three tiers of seats rose up behind the driver's seats of these specially adapted vehicles, so that paying guests could get a good view of the passing countryside and hopefully lots of wildlife. Birgit waved at them from the driver's seat. There were only two passengers in the viewing seats and they did not respond to Lizzie and Alex's cheery waves.

'Hey, Alex, that was René Gilles and Luc Delfosse, you know what that means?'

They were moving slowly and the gentle pressure of Alex's foot on the brake brought them to an immediate halt.

'Get to the other side as quickly as possible and find Sylvie?'

He applied his foot heavily to the accelerator pedal and roared around the bend in the main dirt road – at exactly the same time a huge elephant ran out of the scrub and straight into their path. This time Alex stamped his foot on the brake and they braced themselves as a flurry of dust and stones flew up in the air. The elephant let out the most almighty trumpet. It felt as if the ground shook beneath them.

'Oh, God, Alex, can you go back?'

'I don't know if that would be worse, hold on.'

Alex shifted into reverse. The elephant flapped his ears and bellowed his ear-piercing trumpet again. Then he lifted one foot off the ground and took two angry steps forward.

'Alex, reverse, quickly, he's—'

'Hold on, he's distracted by something.'

Lizzie clung with both hands to the sides of her seat, but, sure enough, the great grey head with its small piercing eyes turned to one side, then back, then to one side again, before running across the road and into the cover of the trees, swift as a gazelle and just as silent.

The two humans turned to look at each other.

'Oh my God, I thought we were for it.' Lizzie breathed.

'I haven't told you, I had a close encounter with a spitting cobra today, too.'

'Oh great, no wildlife adventures for ages then along come – oh no, I wish I hadn't said that.'

'Don't be silly, Lizzie,' Alex rebuked her. 'Things don't come in threes, that's just superstitious nonsense.'

Pulling up outside the office back at the main site they scrambled down and Lizzie ran ahead of Alex to the bar. Gabriel stood there poring intently over the large book in which everyone's bar bills were entered, a battery-operated calculator by his left hand. He looked up.

'Madam, this elephant who screams – did you have a traffic accident?' He chuckled to himself.

'Almost. He didn't look before he crossed the road.'

'Some red wine for you, Professor – and for you Doctor?'

Alex had arrived by Lizzie's side having stopped to roll up the windows of the Land Rover against the insects of the night.

'Thanks, Gabriel, but not just now – there's something we have to do first – do you know where Sylvie Delfosse is?'

Gabriel looked puzzled. Lizzie broke in.

'She's the French lady, Gabriel, she and her husband are staying in Chalet three.'

'Ah yes, madam, this lady, she is gone back to that chalet. Her husband drove her there. He says she is not well and cannot go out on the drive with Birgit and him and this other man.' He shook his head. 'She is not a happy person, this lady. I am thinking there must be some big sadness in her life.'

Alex nodded, 'I think you're right, Gabriel, and that's why we need to see her. Now if that man – her husband – comes back before we do, can you try and keep him here – ask him a question about his bar bill or something? Will you do that for us?'

'No problem, sir. I am so stupid it will take many, many minutes to sort out that there is no mistake, by then I am sure you have returned,' he grinned, took out two glasses and the box of South African Pinotage and set them beside the bar bills book, 'then you will find also two nice big glasses of red wine waiting for you.'

'Just one more thing, Gabriel, could you radio the camp site and remind Jake and Leah they're bringing the students over for dinner?'

'No problem, Doctor Alex, it is done already.' He beamed again as Alex and Lizzie ran off.

In silence they drove towards their own chalet, reversed the vehicle and parked it ready for a swift exit.

They both slammed their doors to forewarn Sylvie that someone was approaching. The paltry light bulb gave out very little light, but enough to illuminate the flimsy white curtains which hung across the front window of the room. Just as Lizzie and Alex gained the porch, the light went out. Lizzie looked at Alex and he nodded. She knocked gently on the door.

'Sylvie, it's Lizzie, Alex is with me, can we come in? I know your husband is out, we saw him go.'

There was a pause, during which the light went back on and they heard the key turning in the lock.

'Quickly, *entrez*.'

She locked the door behind them. She was still fully dressed in a chic safari suit, her long hair arranged in an elegant pony tail tied with a silk scarf. There the appearance of leisure and serenity ended. The woman's face was almost haggard.

Lizzie ran to her side and put her arm around her.

'Sylvie, what's wrong – you look so unhappy, what is it?'

Sylvie raised both hands to her face and pulled away from Lizzie's embrace.

'I regret I tell you my worries. I cannot let you share my problems. You must leave before he returns. He can be a devil, and you are kind people. I am so sorry we have not been friends to you, Luc and me. It is Luc, he is so – he is a man who is unreasonable.'

She sat on the bed with a look of total despair. Lizzie looked at Alex, her face fierce with anger. He placed one hand on her arm and said in almost a whisper, 'Let me.'

Then he sat down beside Sylvie on the thin mattress.

'Sylvie, we are safe. We have asked someone to delay Luc if he returns before us. Take your time, tell us what is wrong, we want to help you.'

Lizzie sat to the other side of the woman.

'Alex is right, Sylvie. We want to help you. What is wrong? Please, you can trust us.'

Sylvie stared at her knees for a few seconds then shook her head violently.

'God forgive me, but I must tell someone. He is my husband, but I hate him. It was not always like this. Always he has been a man who can be bad, but always he is so *charmant*, always he comes to me and he is like a child, he says sorry and jokes and soon I love him more than before, but this time. . .' She shuddered.

'He has been meeting these bad people. We came here through Congo – always since I have known him he has some kind of contact there that he does not talk about to me. We stopped in Lubumbashi, he says to go to the university, and yes, we go the university and there we meet this Harvey Miller. But also we meet this other man who I can see is not good, a black man with many gold rings and diamonds in them. Then we meet this man again in Lusaka and here too. Always he is there when we go to a bar – it seems that Luc is arranging to meet him.'

'This man, you say you met him here, is he the problem – or whatever they are talking about? What has this man done?' Alex frowned a warning at Lizzie. She was pushing too hard. 'Sorry,' she mouthed at him, across the desolate woman who sat, unseeing, between them.

Sylvie sighed.

'This man – he has a friend here and we meet them in a bar in Mfuwe – such a dirty, horrible bar, full of men who are drinking too much, men with the eyes that burn with hatred for me, I can see it. These men discuss bad things, they talk about stealing from you, Lizzie, they talk about paying corrupt people for permits to dig in the Park, they talk about frightening you two.'

Tears began to roll down her cheeks and her hands grasped the cloth of her linen trousers.

'This, it is bad, but for me this is not the worst.' She paused again. 'My husband gives much money, in dollars, to one of these men. They all laugh and buy more beers. Then the man who takes the money, he goes to the edge of the bar where a very young girl is laughing and talking to a young man. He takes her hand and drags her over to Luc. Then Luc…' She put her face in her hands again. 'Then my *husband*…' She took another deep breath. 'He takes her hair in his hand and pulls back her head, he pushes his hand up her shirt. She says "no, no, do not do this," but he just laughs. She cannot move because he holds her by the hair. All the men now are looking and laughing. Then he turns to me, he stares at me, his eyes cold. He looks at this little girl's face, she is crying and this monster, my husband, he laughs. He pulls her by her hair till they are outside the door. Then I hear… I hear….'

She broke down and sobbed.

'Sylvie,' Lizzie stroked the woman's convulsed back, 'you don't have to tell us any more, he had sex with this girl, is that it? You *can* get away from him, we can get you somewhere safe before—'

But Sylvie carried on, as if oblivious to the other two.

'I hear the sounds of him, shouting, laughing, noises like an animal, a wild animal. Then he comes back in. Outside I hear this *pauvre petite fille*, she cries, like a child, it hurts to hear her voice. Inside, the men they all still laugh, like devils. And my husband walks to me, stands before me and says loud, for all these men to hear, "she was one hundred times better than you, you cold bitch. Now I am rich I have no need to pretend any more". Then he lights a cigarette and just stands, staring at me. I stand and try to leave but he forces me to sit down again. He pushes a bottle of beer at me and I curse him. He hits me across the face. One of these dirty men comes behind me and puts his arm over my shoulder – I push it off and at this moment René returns and sees what this man is doing, he takes hold of my hand and shouts at Luc and he gets me to the car. I thank God for René – he is my saviour.'

Alex could see tears of shared anguish welling up in Lizzie's eyes as she spoke.

'Sylvie, you poor, poor thing. You *have* to get away from him. Come on – we'll pack some stuff and take you away from here before he gets back.'

Alex stood up, 'Where's your passport, have you got any money?'

'My passport is in the safe in the office with the others, but he has all our money. He has the only credit or debit cards we can use here, he has our traveller's cheques, our satellite phone, everything. What a stupid woman I am, *hein*? To let myself arrive at this situation?'

'Never mind that now,' Lizzie had grabbed a bag and was scanning the shelves holding the couple's belongings. 'Come on, help me. Where are your shoes, underwear, are these your papers? Come on Sylvie, hurry, we don't want to meet him on the way back.'

Within minutes they were knocking on Maggie and Gus's door. A few minutes more and Sylvie was picking at a robust helping of Gus's home-made goulash and Zambian-style cabbage.

Maggie picked up the keys to her vehicle.

'I'd better go brief Moses, he's on night watch so they'll ask him what he saw. And we'll all have to keep to the same story.'

'Well,' suggested Gus, 'none of the staff actually saw the rescue, did they? So we can just say none us saw anything but we heard a vehicle driving off. How about that, nice and simple and no lies involved?'

That evening Moses could be seen muttering to himself like a madman as he made his patrols, rehearsing a sentence which satisfied his strict Christian principles, 'This lady, she must be driven away in a car, I have not seen this car, I only hear this car.'

Lizzie, Alex, Maggie and Gus were not quite so scrupulous, they were happy to lie through their teeth to protect Sylvie.

Chapter 17

Lizzie and Alex hurried back to join the students as soon as Sylvie was calm and secure. They perched on bar stools sipping at red wine while the rest of the group watched elephants tearing branches off a tree on the riverbank in the light of a strong torch.

'You know,' Alex shook his head as he spoke, ' if that bastard had been here when she told us about what he did to that girl, I don't think I could have stopped myself from thumping him. And as for those sleazebags in the bar. Well, I just hope it's not Osca's – if it is then Jake drops about a million points in my estimation.'

'It makes my skin crawl to think about it.' Lizzie shuddered as if to prove the point. 'You just know there's all sorts of diseases lurking in there, waiting for those creeps to spread them around. It's not as if the adults don't know the risks, there's been enough publicity and loads of health education campaigns. But that little girl Sylvie described – it doesn't bear thinking about. She can't have been making a living out of it, surely?'

'I'm going to ask Jake – no, not over dinner don't worry – later, I'll get him alone. Birgit is well out of it. Oh, no, I've just had a thought. Birgit's out with Luc isn't she? You don't suppose – I mean the guy was desperate not to leave Sylvie alone – but he did – do you think it was the lovely Birgit?'

'Oh, God, I hadn't thought of that,' Lizzie paused, frowning, 'but René's with them, she's not on her own with him – now that *would* be worrying. Anyway, we can't do anything about it now. I'm starving, aren't you? And I want to hear what Leah and Zach got up to today.'

Alex signalled to Gabriel that they were ready for dinner to be served.

Kate and Amy were the first to join them at the bar, discussing a monster crocodile they had seen lounging on one of the sandbars in the middle of the Luangwa river.

'There were two men in a dugout canoe,' said Amy. 'They stopped on the other side of the river, on that wide sandy bank. We were really worried the croc would have them for lunch – he was like, really huge, a great big slug of a thing.'

Alex looked at Lizzie.

'Hmm,' he said, his tone expressing little sympathy, 'well they were obviously heading off to do some poaching, so I'm sure they knew the risks. That side is the Park,' he explained, seeing their puzzlement, 'so chances are they were going to examine snares or set out on a poaching trip. Not the brightest thing to do in full view of the campsite, but I have seen it before. By the time anyone can get to them one of them will have slipped off with the canoe and hidden it on the other bank, to make out he's just an honest fisherman.'

'Perhaps the man had a permit?'

'Not in the Park. Anyway, hunting's an expensive business, if you do it legitimately – and that means wealthy foreigners after trophies,' explained Alex.

'But that's awful,' gasped Amy. 'I can understand poor people killing animals to eat – but killing them just for fun – it's horrible!'

'Well, sometimes local people do get food out of it. Depends what kind of group the hunters are with. And what kind of animal. People eat hippos, elephants, antelopes and so on – they call it 'bush meat' and it's really popular – but you won't find anyone sitting down to a meal of lion or leopard – and talking of meals ...'

Trays of steaming plates were heading for their table. A buzz of conversation soon arose with the steam as they wolfed down chicken, beans and rice.

'Mm,' Kate waved her fork around, 'this rice tastes so good – so different from the stuff we get at home.'

'That's because it's local,' explained Lizzie, 'I always buy a bag at Mfuwe airport on my way back home – there's a stall just inside the door, same place they sell the snare wire jewellery.'

'Oh,' Leah broke in, 'Lizzie and Alex, I forgot – we saw Simon's brother's wife in the village – she makes that snare wire jewellery – she said if you're desperate she can actually weave a sieve for you on a frame made by Simon's brother – it will take a lot of her wire but she's willing to do it if you can pay her for the wire. I don't know if it would work – anyway, I said I'd get you to speak to Simon.'

Alex had forgotten all about the loss of the sieves in the frenzy of the last few hours.

'That's nice of her,' he said, 'but it sounds like an awful lot of work, not to mention a waste of materials. Zach, how did you get on, did you get through to Vickie – can her dad help out at all?'

'Oh, God, sorry, I forgot, she told me to check emails, she texted me just before we lost the signal. Back in a sec.'

With that he was gone.

Lucky for him, the office computer was on and everything working. He came back grinning and carrying a sheet of paper.

'You're gonna love this. He's on his way here, via Tanzania. They've got some spare surveying kit that's a couple of years old – he's gonna write it off and replace it with new stuff. He can't get ready-made sieves but he can get the right size mesh so we can have them made here. He's sending buckets, shovels and stuff with the surveying kit. Basically, he'll sort it all. Should be here in about four days' time – he's using his firm's subsidiary in the Copperbelt to import it – kind of thing they do all the time, he says – and he'll make sure it gets to us from there. Boss job, yeah?'

'*Dead* boss! What's it going to cost us?'

'That's the best bit. Says here, "please regard this as sponsorship in kind for my local university". Apparently he's based just outside Liverpool, did you know?'

'No, I didn't,' said Alex. 'That's just fantastic. Is he coming down here himself?'

'Yeah, about the same time as the stuff – he's chartering a plane so he might even bring it himself.'

'Blimey, he must be rolling in it. Did you find out what he actually does?'

Jake raised one hand and coughed, 'If I may, Mr Chairman,' he grinned at Alex, 'Vick's dad is a mining magnate – there's big money in that family, so I wouldn't worry about the expense. She said he might be looking for something particular out in the park – more towards the north, though, I think. Can't remember the name, but it's some mineral they've been getting out of Congo. The operation there's getting tricky, so they're looking for new sources. Wish I could remember the name – whatever – there's so much bloody money in it they can afford to spare no expense prospecting, even a small find would make it worth their while.'

Alex frowned. 'You're not talking about Coltan are you?'

'Could be,' Jake shrugged, 'not my forte, geology. What's it do?'

'It's used in mobile phones. You do find it in other parts of the world – Australia's one of them – but it's in pretty short supply, which makes it very valuable. And inevitably in the Congo that means money for the few, slave labour and a brutal existence for the many.'

A hush descended on the table.

Lizzie's ears pricked up as she heard the sounds of an engine swiftly followed by a man's voice and laughter from someone she presumed was Birgit. Sure enough, the three night-drivers tumbled up into the bar in a burst of chatter and back slapping.

'Birgit,' Luc exclaimed, 'this was a *wonderful* experience, we must do this again. That leopard, he was so superb an animal, a veritable machine for killing, *non? Magnifique!* But we have our fantastic, charming, guide to thank for this. Please, may I buy you a drink?'

Luc had one hand resting on Birgit's shoulder, as he directed the full force of his gaze on her. Lizzie could almost see the sparks fly between the two. Birgit's eyes shone bright in the light of the hurricane lamp before her – as usual there was no electricity – and her delighted smile would have been infectious, thought Lizzie, if only that hand on her shoulder had belonged to a different man, if only she could stop herself thinking of that poor girl crying, alone in the dark outside a sleazy bar full of drunk, lecherous men.

Lizzie took a very deep breath. Now began the real test of their plan. How long would it be before the fury of a thwarted Luc Delfosse was unchained?

Chapter 18

Warm though it was, a small fire burned on the ground outside the little thatched concrete platform where the night watchman sat each night. Moses, in his thick black coat and Dunlops, poked at the few paltry pieces of wood with a long stick and stared out into the whispering shadows.

Alex and Lizzie had stopped, on their way back to their chalet, to check that Moses was still comfortable with the story they had rehearsed. Under the star-spattered Milky Way the three stood together whispering, waiting for a youthful hippo to move to pastures new before they could return to their chalet in safety. Although they were vegetarians who left the water at night to feast on grass, an angry hippo was a dangerous thing. Its massive incisors could dissect a human torso in the wink of a careless eye.

At last Alex turned the key in the lock, reclaiming the relative sanctuary of their bedroom. Lizzie, too weary to push herself through the nightly routine, was in bed in seconds. Alex had begun his own night-time ritual of making ready for morning before it hit him. There would be no morning routine. Everything had changed today, at least for a while. He threw his kit bag down by the door and crawled into bed. They sat, side by side, staring out of the wire mesh window in the dark.

Like clouds slipping across the moon, sleep overtook the tired researchers, slumped against the hard wood of the headboard. They did not hear the car drive up, nor the door slam, nor the opening and closing of the door to the neighbouring chalet, but they heard the shouting of the angry man and the rattling of their doorknob. Alex leapt from bed and slipped on the grass mat as it skidded on the polished concrete floor. Regaining his balance he stood still in the middle of the room and called out.

'Who's there, what do you want?'

Lizzie had pulled her torch from under her pillow and was shining it full on the door.

There was no mistaking the accent.

'Where is my wife? Where is my wife? What have you done? You have no right.'

Alex took his time, pulled on some trousers, some shoes, a t-shirt – and as an afterthought picked up one of the new, clumsy tools from the toolbox Gus had given him, just for good measure.

All the time the angry Belgian was yelling, 'Open this door, come out and be a man, Sommers, I will call the police, I demand to know what you have done with her' and so on, and so on.

Alex turned to make sure Lizzie was ready. She, too, had thrown on some clothes and now she stood, one hand in a pocket, the other holding the torch like a truncheon, behind him. Alex slowly unlocked the door and turned the handle. It was rudely pushed from his grasp, but he was ready and stood his ground.

Luc Delfosse was short, but pugnacious and solid. Anger seethed from every pore. He looked as if he was about to jump at Alex, who held out a restraining palm.

'Luc, whatever it is, we can't help you – go and try the night watchman, or the office. If Sylvie is not in your room, perhaps she is over at the campsite bar or maybe someone has taken her into town. You can rest assured she is not here.'

'Why should I believe you? Let me in.'

'Absolutely not, I have told you she is not here, now go away and leave us alone.'

Delfosse's anger burst forth and he flung himself at Alex, fists pumping back and forth like small battering rams. Alex fell back a couple of steps before recovering his poise and, dropping the makeshift hammer he held in his hand, pushed the man in front of him hard, barely managing to manoeuvre him out of the room. Just as he realised it was not going to be an easy fight, Moses came running up behind his adversary and grabbed him by the arms, pulling the flailing limbs backwards till they met. Alex marvelled at the older man's strength.

'Sir, you run to your car, go find help, I hold this man here, hurry.'

'Lizzie,' Alex turned, but she had already thought it through and was on her way.

'I'll go, Alex, you help Moses, I'll be as quick as I can. And don't let the dirty bugger bite you.'

Even in the heat of the moment, Alex realised, Lizzie was worrying about AIDS. She had a point. He picked up the rudimentary hammer again and stood before Luc with the implement in his hand. The man in front of him snarled like a trapped animal. Alex spoke firmly, quelling the urge to shout.

'I don't want to hear another word. Just shut up till Lizzie gets back.' He was angry, more angry than he had known and welling up inside him was a burning impulse to tell the pathetic creep before him that, yes, they had stolen his wife away, yes he knew where she was and no, he could not see her. He also knew he must not. The little worm started to try new tactics, appealing to the man, the husband, appealing to his love of his wife, making unlikely comparisons between the two of them. Alex did not try to conceal his contempt. That, at least, would give nothing away.

It felt like hours had passed before Lizzie returned with Gus and one of the other security guards in a separate vehicle. Lizzie stood below the verandah, while the scene played itself out. Gus persuaded Luc to accompany him to the office, placated him with a suggestion that he might want to try radioing the police – something the others all knew would be futile – and offered to supply him with bedding and a mosquito net so he could sit up in the bar and wait to see if his wife returned – there, if Alex read the subtext of Gus's diplomatic negotiations correctly, Luc would be provided with a vantage point to calm his suspicions, but, equally, the best of the nightwatchmen could also keep his beady eyes on Luc.

It was gone midnight by the time Gus had departed with his reluctant guest and Moses had returned to his post. Alex and Lizzie re-ran the night's best bit, turning the key in the lock, crawling into bed and snuggling up close before falling asleep. This time no one woke them but the god of light, creeping in slowly to celebrate the dawn.

Yawning madly, Lizzie stumbled around in the grey light that presaged the sunrise. The ibis called its harsh cry, 'Hadada', across the river and she lifted her head to listen.

'Alex, what are we going to do today? More important, what am *I* going to do today?'

'You are going to talk to Maggie, probably see Thomas, get the school kitchen built, solve the murder, put an end to global warming and find the buried treasure that's at the end of every rainbow.'

'OK, so where will you be while I'm sorting out the world?'

'Driving around with the students trying to find something to keep us occupied till Vickie's dad fulfils his far too optimistic promise of parachuting in surveying equipment and everything else we could conceivably need to run an excavation.'

'Don't you like calling it a dig?'

'What?' Alex stopped and looked at her. 'What on earth are you going on about?'

'Well, you just said 'excavation', as if it's better than dig. Is it?'

Sometimes, Alex believed, there were questions without answers, and so often they came from Lizzie's maverick brain when awakened too early in the morning. He ignored it. Lizzie did not seem to notice, nor to mind.

Breakfast began badly.

Luc sat, wrapped in a thick Zambian blanket smoking a cigarette that smelled like rotting vegetation. Next to him sat Birgit.

Lizzie groaned and Alex merely said 'Oh, bugger!' when he saw the arm that rested on Brigit's shoulders and the contented look that transfigured her lovely face from its far too frequent expression of deep misery.

Lizzie stood with both hands clasped around a mug of fragrant Earl Grey tea, the scent of bergamot visibly reviving her jaded spirits.

'Alex,' she had turned her back to Luc and Birgit, 'where's Jake – did he stay the night with Leah?'

Lizzie was not looking at Alex, so when he turned to gauge her expression, instead of her face he saw a mass of pre-Raphaelite curls glowing amber in the early light. She was staring straight ahead in a determined way that he recognised only too well. He groaned. 'Oh no, what now? Lizzie Lamb, what are you up to?'

'Nothing –' she turned to face him and smiled, 'maybe! But did he? Did Jake stay with Leah?'

'I think so – he drove off to the campsite at the same time as she did – in fact I think they were all in his vehicle so they had to go together. Come on, why?'

'None of the others is here yet – let's go get them.' She threw back the last dregs of her tea and set the mug down on the bar with a clunk. 'I want to break up this happy scene, but I don't want to be too obvious. If there's any decency left in Jake I'm going to flush it out – and he's going to prise that slimeball off Birgit.'

'Oh yes. And what about Leah?'

Lizzie paused a moment.

'I'll tell her. I'll tell them both. Did you ask Jake about Osca's last night?'

'No I didn't – I couldn't work up the courage. I don't really want to know, if I'm honest. I like the guy and if he's been hanging out in that kind of place I don't think I could ever feel the same about him again.' He sighed. 'OK, I get the point, we'll do it – but we really ought to ask Sylvie first. It's her secret.'

'All right, we can drop by on our way over there – you drive, I'll run in and explain.'

Alex took a last mouthful of tepid tea. As he put down his mug he caught Lizzie looking daggers at Luc and Brigit and dragged her off before she could say anything. The two couples had been completely ignoring each other, and that was just the way Alex wanted to keep it.

Within two minutes they were at Gus and Maggie's house. A very sleepy and relaxed looking Sylvie was lounging in the garden, wearing peach silk pyjamas, watching the world change colour, chameleon like, as dawn passed over the landscape dragging morning in its wake.

'Sylvie, I'm sorry to bother you so early and sorry to raise this subject with you, but I'm worried about our friend, the guide, Birgit. She took your husband out for a drive last night and it looks like he has fallen for her and I'm afraid she has fallen for him too.'

Sylvie closed her eyes. Lizzie waited. At length Sylvie pulled out a cigarette from the bag beside her chair, lit it, blew out a long trail of smoke and spoke.

'You must tell this woman what you know. She must not be close to him, he is bad. I have suffered, she must not.'

'That's what I came to ask you, I want to tell someone, not her but Jake, the vet who – well never mind, he's a local who has been a lover of Birgit's for years. If he knows, I think he will get her away from him, he might be the only person she would respond to. Do you mind if I tell him and his new girlfriend, Leah, our PhD student?'

'My dear Lizzie, today I am not worrying about him finding me – Gus and Maggie, they will look after me until I can organise to return home. My father he will help, I can speak to him when the telephone is working. Please, do what you think you must, but try not to tell Luc where I am – or that you know anything about it – for your own sake, *hein?*'

Lizzie kissed the woman on both cheeks and they looked into each other's eyes, friends at last after a professional lifetime of hostility.

Alex had the engine running when she rounded the back of the house and jumped in, but in the minute or less it took to get to the campsite turn off they had missed Jake. Lizzie recognised his jalopy jigging off down the road in a halo of dust.

'So what do we do now?' Alex asked as he pulled to a halt.

'I think you should go and pick up the kids – if Leah doesn't mind I can borrow her truck and run after him – he's bound to stop for something in the village, don't you think?'

She had that determined look about her. Alex revved up, drove into the campsite and Lizzie ran straight over to where Leah was zipping up her tent.

'Hey Lizzie, what're you doing here so early?'

'We need to get hold of Jake, urgently, we just missed him. Would you mind if I borrowed your vehicle, I thought maybe I could catch up with him in Mfuwe if he stops there – I mean, he probably will, won't he?'

'Sure. But he's got his phone so why not phone him, if there's a signal, that is?'

Lizzie stood speechless.

'Of course. I keep forgetting – I'm just so used to having just the radio round here – have you got yours there?'

Leah pulled out her phone and within a few seconds Jake had been contacted and Lizzie had persuaded him there was something really urgent going on and that he really had no choice but to come back and help them out. Lizzie gritted her teeth and prayed that he would understand. Now she just had to explain to Leah.

In the bright light of day it was sounding more and more harebrained. She hesitated a moment, watching as Alex drove off to breakfast with Martin, Amy, Kate and Zach.

'Leah,' Lizzie began, 'I have something to tell you and a really big favour to ask of you and Jake. What I'm going to tell you is between you and me, Alex knows, Maggie and Gus know, that's all. It's vital that no one tells Luc Delfosse – or anyone else for that matter – are you OK with that?'

Leah nodded.

'Right. Now Sylvie can tell you the full story one day, but basically Luc Delfosse has got mixed up with some nasty stuff – the worst of it, for Sylvie anyway, God knows about the rest of it, happened just the other night in Mfuwe. It's so sordid I won't repeat it but it involved abusing a young girl and publicly shaming Sylvie in front of a crowd of drunks. He's been more or less keeping her prisoner – last night we got her away from him while Luc was out on a night drive with Birgit. He's furious, but he doesn't know where Sylvie is and we're not telling him – in fact we've told him we don't know anything about it and you absolutely must keep this secret too. Now, the problem is that this morning, it's clear that this total sleazebag has got his hooks into Birgit – he can be charming if he wants and he plainly worked his magic on her last night. We're worried for all sorts of reason – obviously there's a risk he has one or more sexually transmitted diseases, but equally he's a shit and she's a friend who doesn't deserve that.'

'But little Miss Sunshine knows he's a married man, right?' Leah looked, and sounded, just a touch irritated.

'Leah, I know it's a lot to ask and she should really be able to look after herself but, honestly, I think the last couple of years have unsettled her so much she's lost some of her sense of perspective – you know, the whole thing with Jake.'

'So you want him to come along, knight in shining armour and carry her off, is that it? Well thanks, Lizzie. Thanks a lot. And what about me?'

'You know what Jake's like, Leah, and right now he's obviously really taken with you – not to say besotted.'

She stopped for a moment as it hit her for the first time. It was true, Jake had never been quite so open or so normal about a relationship, in her experience.

'In fact,' she continued, 'he really does seem different around you. What I'm asking, I suppose, is for you and him – not just him – to talk to her, peel her away from him, she's got so little self-esteem, I think right now she'd just go along with him for the sake of a morale boost and that's exactly the reverse of what she'll get.'

'I still think you've got a nerve – but if Jake's OK with it, so am I. I don't have any hang-ups about him – if he drops me then fine, I'll live. I'm usually on my own for weeks on end when I'm doing field work so it's kind of nice to have the company, but he's not the only man in the world and I'm under no illusions about him. I do think it's pretty cheeky of you, though.'

'I'm, sorry, I can see how you'd think that. So much has happened, I suppose I've begun to just rush around thinking I have to sort everything and everyone out myself. Forgive me?'

'Forgiven. You've been having a pretty rubbish time yourself. Talking of which,' she made a show of inspecting her nails, 'Zach has something to tell you. I promised not to say anything so don't let on, but it's a pretty big deal so it may take him a while to work up the courage – don't be too hard on him.' She stopped to yawn, deeply. 'God, I'm gagging for a brew, why don't we get on over to breakfast anyway – Jake can join us over there. Come on.'

Grateful – and more than slightly embarrassed – Lizzie gave Leah a hug. They drove over in silence. Lizzie's curiosity was piqued, but Leah was giving nothing more away.

Back at the dining room Luc was nowhere to be seen. Gabriel, busily stirring water into a large jug containing dried milk and destined for cereal, said the Belgian had gone back to his chalet to change. Birgit was also back home, preparing for a trip to the village schools with a Danish couple.

When Jake arrived the whole crew was seated around the usual table. They were intent on eating thick slices of toast cut from heavy home-made loaves, spread with the smoky local honey or chunky Zambian peanut butter, drinking tea or Ricoffy – granules that masqueraded as instant coffee – and listening to Alex tell them about his plans for the day.

Lizzie slipped away from the table and Leah followed her.

'Jake, I'm sorry to drag you back here.'

'No problem,' Jake turned to Leah and his face split into a huge grin, 'missing me already, eh, sweetheart?'

He smacked Leah on the bottom.

'Fuck off, you idiot. Lizzie's got something really shitty to ask you, just listen for once, would you?'

'Charmed, I'm sure. Go on, Professor darling.'

Lizzie took a deep breath. He always managed to needle her, no matter how hard she tried to let it wash over her.

'Jake, can I ask which bars you go to in Mfuwe?'

He looked surprised but answered readily enough.

'Osca's, if I want a laugh and some good music – or to get away from my fellow white men. Otherwise I tend to stick with Wild-Dogs – or go into the park to Beacon Ridge if I'm feeling really fancy, got a top chick to entertain.' He pulled Leah to his side. 'Why, what's it to you?'

She explained about Sylvie's awful experience and his cheeky expression vanished.

'That sounds like High Society, it's a beer den, but it's the pits, a place for piss artists and prostitutes. Diseased going on deceased, most of them. Even some of the really young ones have full blown AIDS – got it from mummy's milk, no point in living anyway, won't accept it and won't take the drugs even if they're free. But this one, it sounds like someone forced himself on an innocent – I've never heard of anything like that before. The bastard's way out of order. Where is the little heap of Belgian shit?'

'Hold on Jake, there's more.'

His face betrayed no further change in emotion as she told him about the last night's adventures.

'You reckon Birgit's falling for this fucker?'

'I'm afraid so.'

Jake turned to Leah.

'Kid, I don't want to mess you around. Contrary to popular opinion I can do the decent thing when called on – sometimes. I'm going to see Birgit, don't take it as meaning I'm two-timing you, OK?'

And with that he walked off up the management staff's private path, heading towards Birgit's little house, hidden in the bushes.

Lizzie looked at Leah. She seemed to be taking it very well.

'Leah, are you OK?'

'Sure, that was nice of him. He didn't have to say anything. Can we get back to the others now?'

Lizzie was astounded. Never in a million years could she have been so cool about such a thing. Sitting back at the table, facing her husband, she pondered the awfulness of the demon, jealousy, she knew only too well how destructive he could be. If there were a pretty girl sitting next to Alex right now and he smiled at her she'd probably feel the smart of an emerald dart – well maybe not, but it would not take much. Leah had just gone up a big notch in her estimation. And so had Jake.

Lizzie looked at her watch. Thomas would be at the office by now and Alex was right about one thing, she had to do something about Harvey Miller. The police showed no signs of returning and besides, her instincts were beginning to twitch. All this talk of the Congo was beginning to sound like more than just coincidence. In all the time she had spent in Zambia, never had she come across so many people who had links with that desperate place.

Once again she slipped away from the table as her husband talked of stratigraphy and soil samples and surface scatters.

Maggie was nowhere to be seen, but the young woman on reception was happy for her to use the radio.

It was not her lucky day. Thomas was not in the office, he had gone to the school, they said, something to do with the new plans. She left a message, which she suspected would not get through, to ask him to radio her when he got in. Then she shook her head, irritated at her own dimness. The telephone. She asked permission and lifted the receiver. The line was bad but at least she had reached Thomas. They arranged to meet mid-morning at the BP petrol station, roughly half way between them, for a chat while Thomas was on his way back to the office. There was no chance of him visiting Elephant Camp – the District Commissioner was paying a rare official visit.

Jake was hanging around outside as she emerged from the already sweltering office.

'Lizzie, I'm worried.'

It was not like him, not like him at all.

'I've tried talking to Birgit, but it's like a switch has flipped in her head. She's on another planet. She says she doesn't care about me any more, that my "sinister" influence has worn off at last, that she rejects every word I say or ever said. Well, that's no bad thing, but basically there's no way she's gonna listen to me warning her off another man, even shit-features himself. All I can say is that she hasn't had time to sleep with him yet – she only met him last night and I can't imagine she'd jump into bed with someone that quick – she's a bit fussy about that sort of thing – personal hygiene's a big issue – oral sex, for example —'

'Jake! For goodness' sake shut up! Too much information.' Infuriated, Lizzie was more embarrassed by the fact that she was blushing than by what the man had said.

Jake's answering chuckle turned into a cough and he pulled out the remnants of a cigar from his shirt pocket, as if seeking medicine. He struck a match on his thumb-nail and lit the wizened stump of tobacco.

'Sorry, I know it's illegal here – the big taboos, oral sex and homosexuality – I just thought you guys would be broad-minded about that kind of thing.' An evil grin punctuated the sentence like a giant full stop.

Lizzie closed her eyes briefly, took a deep breath and restrained herself from screaming at him.

'So,' Jake continued, 'I don't know what I can do to help. My magic charms have worn off. Maybe you should ask Simon if he has an alternative.' There was a wicked gleam in his eye.

'Simon?' Lizzie hesitated, not sure if she was being set up for a joke or if there was something she should know that she did not. 'Why Simon?'

'Oh, I don't know, I'd just heard things about him in the village, you know, lucky in love, good with his hands, well respected, bit of a guru to some of the community – got a fine collection of herbs and such like.'

'Are you telling me he's into traditional medicine or something? Or just implying he'd make a nice boyfriend for Birgit?'

'Either, really,' Jake looked around before continuing, 'I hear he's widely regarded as a bit of a witch,' witchcraft in Zambia being another thing that was illegal, it was wise to be careful when speaking about it, 'or maybe even a shaman. And he's popular with all the ladies, but that could be for purely physical reasons – I understand he's also a big lad!'

'I'll ignore that, but you know, Maggie did hint that Simon and Birgit might get on well together, perhaps it's not so daft as it sounds. The magic thing though, you don't think it actually works do you?'

'Depends what kind of magic we're talking about. If people believe in it, it tends to work. I knew this chief – not far from Lusaka – he was pretty westernised, but this one time I was there he was asked to help find a thief. He had this broken bit of mirror on the ground surrounded by a circle of white pebbles, he had a good look into it then he told his retainer he'd seen the thief. The thief was caught that same night running away, terrified. Now, the chief may have seen nothing for all I know, but everyone heard about it, news spread and everyone believed him, including the thief. That's how it works. And frankly, my dear, even if you don't give a damn, you have to admit that some pretty weird shit happens here.'

'Yes, it does.' Lizzie frowned at the thought. Weird things did happen in Zambia, inexplicable things. She shook the thought from her head.

'Whatever,' she shrugged, 'magic's not really an option, is it? I was convinced you'd persuade her, I don't know what else we can do. Maybe we can't do anything.'

'Listen,' Jake put his hand on her shoulder, 'don't give up, just keep an eye on her. She's not that stupid, just a bit obsessive – I mean the thing with me – there wasn't really anyone else around to take her mind off me, was there? And that's what she needed – just a shame this little turd came along when he did.' He took a last drag on his puny cigar. 'I'm only half-joking about Simon, you know. Have a word with Maggie.' He looked down at his watch. 'Christ, I'm supposed to be at Beacon Ridge. Gotta go, darling, give my love to Alex the Great – and let me know if there's anything at all I can help you with,' he winked, slipped his arm around her waist and growled, 'and I do I mean *anything,* hmmm?'

With a kiss on her cheek he was gone, leaving Lizzie shaking her head but with a smile on her face. It was easy to see why people fell for the guy.

Chapter 19

The celestial thermostat had been turned up while Lizzie was busy machinating and now she was overheating. She peeled off her Liverpool university hoodie and tied it around her waist, then ran her hands through her curls in a hopeless attempt at detangling. A slight cough alerted her to the presence of someone behind her. She turned to see Zach, an unlit roll-up in one hand, lighter in the other, looking nervous.

'Lizzie, I've come to tell you something, to apologise.' He looked around as if to check that no one else was within hearing distance. 'Have you got a minute?'

'Sure, let's sit on the wall.'

They wandered down and perched on the low stone wall overlooking the wide riverbank. Tiny vervet monkeys who had been playing on the wall skittered up into the overhanging tree. A bold one sat in the nearby fork of a branch, one leg crossed over the other, paws behind his head, like a lecturer listening to a student presentation.

'OK, Zach,' ventured Lizzie, 'what's it all about?'

'I had a long talk with Leah yesterday. She made me realise I was being a total arse. Like, I mean, you guys asked me to come out here with you and it's, like, a totally amazing place and I've been behaving like a total jerk.' He put the puny cigarette to his mouth, lit it and took a deep drag.

Lizzie waited patiently, Leah's words of warning in her mind.

'Thing is,' Zach held the slim cigarette between his thumb and second finger, 'I've done something really stupid, really bad. Leah's made me realise I have to own up – but before you shout at me I want you to know I already know what a mess I've made of things and I'll leave if you want me to.'

'What on earth have you been up to? Is it drugs or something?'

He laughed, a brief bitter sound.

'Would that be worse? I don't think so.' He heaved a great sigh. 'There's no easy way to say this, Lizzie. I met up with Harvey Miller in Manchester. I'd met him online – well not met, really, we got into a kind of correspondence – I was doing that essay you set on diet and teeth and I found this article he wrote about Neanderthal molars – I thought it'd be cool if I could get a comment from him so I could cite it – something unique, "Miller, H, personal communication", you know the kind of thing real academics put in their work – I was trying to show off. I was really made up, he was dead friendly, gave me loads of stuff.'

'Yes, I remember. I was impressed, very impressed. You got a first for that, didn't you?'

'Yeah. And now look where it's got me.'

'Out to Zambia?' Lizzie prompted, wondering where this was going. The young man plainly had not yet told all.

'He said he was coming out himself, via DRC, but to keep it to myself. He made out that he was such a big name that you and Alex would be dead chuffed when he turned up – that he would be able to help you with all sorts of stuff you couldn't do yourselves.' Zach could not face her, his eyes were fixed like glue on the smoking cigarette in his left hand. In between drags of the smouldering tobacco he nibbled at his right thumb. He was plainly both nervous and ashamed.

Lizzie bit back her anger. There was no point in venting it on Zach, who, by the sound of it, had been motivated by nothing more heinous than pride. It was Harvey Miller who deserved her wrath, not this silly boy sitting in front of her biting his cuticles.

'Well, he was lying to you, wasn't he? You're not the only one – he makes a habit of persuading impressionable young students to help him. Then he dumps them when they've outlived their usefulness. What did he want you to do for him?'

'He said he was stopping off in Manchester on his way out here and would I go over and spend a night so I could tell him about your plans for the field season. He made out like he wanted to join you at some point to surprise you and was just thinking about the best time. He said he was looking for someone like me to do a PhD with him – that you'd get kudos from it too because his university was about the best in the world.'

Lizzie gritted her teeth and managed – just – to stop herself from interrupting.

Zach shrugged.

'I suppose I should have realised. I was just so flattered that he took me seriously – just an undergraduate, he gave me all that help with just an essay – and him such a big name. Anyway, he put me up for the night in his hotel. We had a smart dinner, he got me pretty drunk and I told him everything I knew. He didn't seem too made up with what I told him – seemed a bit disappointed – and of course that made me want to impress him even more, so I said,' he coughed, 'I said I'd find out the location of the bone for him.'

'But, Zach, I was never going to tell you that – I might have taken you there but … Oh, I get it, he was coming out here and you thought we'd go see the bone site straight away.'

'Right. He gave me a smart new GPS and a wodge of cash – he described it as a "scholarship contribution", like, that made it sound OK – so I agreed to let him know where the bone was, soon as I could. But I never got the chance, did I? Someone nicked your laptop, Harvey's dead and I've been off my head with worry.'

He lifted that head, floppy hair straggling into his brown eyes, wide open and child-like.

'Lizzie, I can't tell you how sorry I am. I feel like I betrayed you, I feel like a total shit. Martin saw me talking to Harvey when he arrived and had a go at me about it. I told him it was none of his business and – I can't believe this – I told him I'd tell you something I know about him – Martin I mean – if he didn't keep it to himself. He said he didn't care if I did, but he'd give me a chance to sort myself out and if I didn't – well, he gave me two days. By then Harvey was dead.'

Lizzie shook her head, but said nothing.

'There – total and complete bastard, the full works. I don't blame you if you want to get rid of me, but if I can stay I promise I'll work like a slave and work really hard back in Liverpool to make you both proud of me, proud of the investment if you like. I know it's a privilege to be here.'

Lizzie opened her mouth to say something but he stopped her.

'I haven't finished yet. Listen, I know I was a real arse to that Thomas guy when he was just being nice to me. I couldn't help myself – it was as if deep down I knew I was doing wrong and it just made me worse. Talking to Leah, she made me realise loads of stuff I should have known before, like you two, you and Alex. You're the business. I suppose I just couldn't quite believe that I was being taught by world experts, at Liverpool. Harvey Miller was someone I knew was a world expert, we had his books in the library, he came from a posh American Ivy League university and he had a fortune to throw around on bribing me, whereas you guys have no money for anything. He seemed – well, more exotic somehow. You get the idea.'

He looked up briefly with a wry grimace on his face.

'I'm digging a hole here, aren't I?'

Lizzie had to smile.

'You know, Zach, you're not the only one. It's a classic reaction – the familiar's never as impressive as the unfamiliar. It's hard to see beyond some of the labels in the academic world, same as the real world. You admire someone's new shoes – then they tell you they got them from Clark's, not Jimmy Choo. You feel different. If you're an academic and you're not Oxbridge or Harvard equivalent, people make assumptions. It's frustrating as hell. But Harvey Miller's last grant was ten grand for one trip to Africa to help someone else with one tiny bit of analysis. I'm not saying money's everything, or that having a specialist expertise isn't as important as what Alex does, but set that against the five hundred grand Alex got to run a five year project all on his own – well, I think it's obvious who's doing the more significant work.'

Lizzie stopped – time to let her hobby horse go.

'Besides which,' she continued, 'even I can do molars at a pinch. Maybe not that well, but I know a woman who can – and she's not at Oxford or Harvard she's at little old Lancaster, so there.' She paused and looked at Zach. He was scratching now at some imagined stain on his trouser leg, avoiding her gaze. 'End of rant. And enough said. It's up to Alex whether you stay or go, but I'll vote for you staying. Go on now, get back to the others and start making up for it.'

'Nice one for that, Lizzie. Sorry I've been such an arse.'

Lizzie sat, thinking, long after he had gone. It was time things started coming together. She felt as if the Gods atop Olympus, sitting around their pool playing the game of mortal chance, were arguing whether to throw her a clue. A cloud passed over the sun like ripples over the Olympian water. She stirred herself from her reverie to face whatever wisdom – or foolery – those idle Gods had let the Fates unleash.

Chapter 20

By the time Alex had left with the students, Lizzie was on her way down the road with Simon. The choice of driver was absolutely fortuitous, all other possible drivers being occupied in the multifarious tasks of running the Camp. It was Lizzie's opportunity – but to do what? Jake's madcap idea of talking to Simon about Birgit was possibly brilliant, possibly disastrous. Should she say something? And if she did, what on earth was she going to say? Simon himself was no help, for a man who was usually garrulous he was being uncharacteristically quiet.

So it was that after Lizzie had been sitting mutely for some time, the game-playing Olympians took the decision out of her mortal hands and put it firmly into those of the wandering Fates.

Bouncing along in the bright winter's morning, the bush showed clear signs of the passing of many elephants – branches torn down or hanging limply, small trees demolished, elephant-width paths snaking off through the undergrowth. Lizzie had plenty of time to look around – to see ominous vultures circling over carrion, pretty impalas twitching nervously in clearings and inscrutable giraffes hesitating in their silent wanderings – because as well as being uncharacteristically quiet, Simon was driving uncharacteristically slowly. Every now and then he would peer intently off to one side until at one point, where the undergrowth thickened significantly, he brought the Land Rover to a complete halt. He pulled on the handbrake with a creak like the distress signal of a small wild animal.

'Prof, can you wait one minute while I find something I need?'

'Of course – as long as I get to the BP station in time to meet Dr Nkhoma.'

He flashed a bright grin at her and jumped down from the Land Rover.

Lizzie frowned against the sun and watched as he stepped carefully over a fallen log and into the undergrowth. Then he crouched and, partially hidden behind the log, seemed to be picking something from the ground. He stood, pulled a small bag from his pocket and pushed something into it, then tied a string around its neck and clambered back on board. He dangled the bag for a moment before stashing it under the dashboard.

'This is a most important thing for me – it helps me find a wife!'

He laughed like a drain at his own statement. Lizzie made a feeble effort to laugh back.

'That's good.' She had no idea what he was talking about. 'What is it, Simon?'

'Special herbs, Professor. These herbs, they take away an illness that is like a bad sadness, this illness, it stops my girlfriend from agreeing to marry me.'

'So it's traditional medicine?' Lizzie was bemused.

'Yes, what you say is right. Some call it magic, but I call it medicine just like *mzungu* medicine. What is the difference? We do not know what is in your white tablets. If you give my friend who has a headache one of these tablets he believes it will work – so he feels better. He takes the same tablet for his aching heart when his wife is unfaithful – and he feels better! But, me, I can read the box. This tablet is not made to cure his aching heart. Now, is my friend lying? No. My friend is believing. So, I believe these little herbs will cure my lonely pain. Next year, when you come, we will see if this traditional medicine has worked.'

He laughed some more and Lizzie sat looking at his handsome face in profile, still bemused.

'Simon, you're an important man, I hear you are popular with girls, you have a good job, you are well educated, I can't imagine you have trouble finding a wife.'

'I find plenty wives, Professor, but the one I want – ah – she is too clever – like you. But she will say yes one day soon. There is also a matter of the marriage settlement. She is not from my tribe, she is a Tonga, they have different customs. She is very tall, very beautiful.'

'Simon,' she began, hesitantly, as the Fates spurred her on, 'have you ever had a *mzungu* girlfriend?'

She had never used that word, *mzungu,* meaning white person, but he had just used it himself, so she risked it.

The silence felt like a black hole. Lizzie wondered if she had gone too far. She was just about to apologise when Simon stopped the car again. He turned to her.

'Professor, I think perhaps some person has told you I like Birgit. She is very pretty. She is a good guide. I think she likes me also. But she has some problem with her spirit, something deep, not just a sadness like me.'

He lapsed into silence again. Lizzie carefully chose her words.

'Do you think this problem with her spirit is because of Jake, Dr Deacon?'

He snorted.

'He is not the problem. I cannot tell you what the problem is. I can only tell you her spirit is not good, she is not a person I want to share my life with. There is no medicine I know that can help.'

'But surely there must be a reason if a person is not well – whether it's in their mind or their body? Does your traditional medicine not have anything that can help, or even any wise advice?' Lizzie had no idea where this was taking her, but felt caught up in something, almost against her will.

'It is not so easy. I do not like to say this, because I think she is your friend – so this is not fine to say, but I feel in my heart that she is not good inside.'

He looked so troubled that Lizzie felt guilty, but still she pursued it.

'Simon, someone told me you had special powers, that you might be a leader in your tribe or a shaman – is this true?'

He looked puzzled.

'I am not a leader in my tribe, I am not a witch either, which some people say, but maybe you have heard some people say that I am a healer. I am not a healer. I know about some traditional medicines, but sometimes I am able to see things other people cannot see, I can see inside hearts if the spirits let me. I have seen inside Birgit's heart, you cannot help her, I cannot help her.' He reached out in a swift, sharp movement and turned the key in the ignition. 'We must go, you will be late.'

The stern expression on Simon's face signalled an end to the matter.

Lizzie sat, as if struck, brimming with anxiety for her friend, for Simon, for who knew what. They were speeding faster now and though they had reached the tarmac the road was far from smooth.

A pick-up truck, almost scraping the ground under its unevenly stacked burden of ragged charcoal bales, was heading towards them on the wrong side of the road, skirting one of the great potholes that could probably have snapped its axle. Simon seemed intent on crashing head on. At the last minute he swerved sharply, drove off the road, narrowly missing a passing cyclist, then bounced back onto the tarmac without even blinking, or so it seemed to a terrified Lizzie clinging for dear life to the dashboard. There was a muffled hooting from the pick-up truck as it vanished into the distance. As they approached the cracked concrete slab that served as a small bridge Lizzie braced herself – and closed her eyes. The bump was enough to lift her out of her seat.

It was with an intense feeling of relief that she saw the battered BP sign looming up ahead. With an even greater sense of relief she saw that Thomas was already standing in the barren compound, leaning against his old green Land Rover, surrounded by small children giggling and chatting. She asked Simon to pick her up half an hour later. He would relish a rare patch of free time in the village with a vehicle – she just hoped it would help him calm down.

As he drove off in a storm of dust she heard Thomas break into song. 'Row, row, row your boat, gently down the stream ...' All the children joined in, little voices loud and tuneful. He waved his arms around, conducting them in singing a round. Tears came to her eyes. She did not know whether to laugh or cry. She edged forward but the moment they spotted her they stopped singing and fell about giggling. Then, with the inevitable cry, '*mzungu, mzungu,*' they came running over hoping for sweets or pens – or a closer look at her hair. One little girl reached up to touch it, enraptured. All of a sudden she became conscious of what she was doing and snapped her hand away as if burnt. The others ran around laughing, holding out their hands and chanting:

'Sweeties, sweeties, pens, pens, how are you, how are you?'

Thomas, who had been mopping his brow with his large white handkerchief, came over to shake hands with Lizzie. The children began to melt away, hovering at a decorous distance, but still fascinated by the white woman's ghost-like skin, freckles and tawny hair.

'Thomas, how are you?'

'Very, very fine my dear, and how are you?'

'I'm fine, well, I was – it's a long story. Do you fancy a Fanta?

Shall we walk down to Captain Marvel's?'

The two grown ups ambled off, followed, pied-piper-like, by a band of dancing children dressed in rags and tatters – snot-smeared, shoeless and just plain nosey.

Inside Captain Marvel's little emporium, surrounded by highly scented bars of dubiously pink soap, by biscuits, eggs and batteries barely visible in the half light, they paid the price of a couple of bottles of the fizzy pop – plus a deposit for the bottle they would return in a few minutes' time – and wandered outside. Leaning against the wooden steps leading up to the shop's colourful concrete frontage, Lizzie gave Thomas a quick run down of events since she had seen him. His frown grew more embedded. When she reached the unsettling episode with Simon he fidgeted as if nervous.

'Lizzie, I am not happy about this. Simon is, well, he's regarded quite widely as a bit of a, well, shaman I suppose you anthropological types would call him. I'm a Catholic as you know, I don't really believe in such things, but even I have to admit he shows a great deal of – what shall we say – insight, hmm? What he said to you about Birgit is most worrying.' He stopped and checked his watch. 'My dear, I am afraid I will have to go, time and tide and District Commissioners wait for no man, not even in landlocked Zambia. I will try to come out to see you at breakfast time tomorrow and review the various crimes we have in our orbit, if that is convenient?'

Lizzie nodded. 'That would be perfect – are you sure?'

'I am sure. Now, I must see if there is any diesel in that pump over there to get me on my way.'

They walked together back to the BP station, the only one in the Valley, proud purveyor of diesel from two weary pumps that stood in not so splendid isolation in a large patch of dusty ground. In the tourist season they ran out of fuel at least once a week, but never to a predictable pattern – it could be any day, any time. And whatever the time of year, if the electricity was off, the pumps simply did not work. Thomas was in luck.

As his back was turned, checking his wallet, Lizzie slipped a bundle of Kwacha into the hand of the attendant. She was not quite quick enough, Thomas interrupted the transaction just before it was complete.

'No, no, Professor, this "corrupt African official" lark is getting out of hand! Come, please take back this money, you do not need to bribe me, Thomas Nkhoma!'

'Thomas, *you* have been out to see *us* I don't know how many times. You've been driving the police around, you're a community asset – so, just think of it as a contribution to the local economy or to the forces of law and order. I won't take no for an answer.'

Thomas reached out two hands and shook hers strenuously.

'My dear, you are most kind. It makes it all the more pressing that I should visit you often, so I accept your generosity. Give my regards to your heroic husband, the great Alexander.' Suddenly his expression changed and he shook his head. 'Please could you also give Maggie some bad news about the school. I am sorry to say, that man has absconded with all our money.'

'Oh, no, Thomas, you're joking? Not all of it?'

'All of it.'

'How could a man who called himself a teacher do such a dreadful thing?'

'Ayee.' He shook his head. 'He seemed a good man, he came with excellent references. Now we learn from his neighbours that he was a man who loved women too well, he had learnt that he had a disease which he called pneumonia, but in reality, I am told, it was TB. Most probably that was also a direct result of the weakness of his system, I suspect he had what some people have come to call 'our disease' of HIV. It saddens my soul to say this, but intellectually I can just about understand why this man did what he did, although I utterly denounce him for his crime. He will spend the money, he will die, he may well give his disease to others in the process and no one will be any better off – except for those happy souls who gave this money, with generosity of spirit, to those who had less than themselves.'

'Thomas, you are too generous. You're a lesson to us all in humility. Look, I'll tell Maggie about it, we'll have a good think about this. There must be something we can do – let's talk about it tomorrow.'

'Bless you, Professor, till tomorrow, then, adieu!'

With a roar his rickety Land Rover took off, skidded up the slope onto the tarmac road and was gone in a puff of smelly grey smoke.

Simon was sitting patiently in the shade of a lonely tree, waiting for his passenger. Lizzie headed towards him with a heavy heart. There were days when Zambia felt like the antidote to all the world's problems, when everyone had all the time in the world, when people were happy to help those in trouble, when life was simple and the future was bright. And then there were the days when corrupt officials fished for bribes, when bureaucracy went mad, when nothing worked and no one bothered to fix it, when it felt like the whole world was doomed to die of AIDS, malaria or just plain poverty. She paced on, each step increasing her resolve not to succumb to gloom and doom. She had no idea how she was going to sort it all out – and equally, no doubt she could – but for the moment, just about everything eluded her. Like looking at the Pleiades and not really seeing them. She braced herself to deal with Simon.

'Hiya, Simon, had a chance to get home?'

'Yes, I delivered my herbs to my aunt. She will keep them for me till my days off. Professor, my sister wants to know if there is any help they can give to you and Doctor Alex – she has found some material she thinks might make a sieve for you. But I told her you have new sieves coming. Am I correct in this, Prof?'

'I hope so. They should be on their way right now.' She paused. 'Simon,' the Fates intervened again, 'I wonder, have we got time to drive by and see your sister so I can thank her?'

'Sure!'

A great big grin greeted this suggestion. For once she had done the right thing on instinct.

Simon's aunt's house, a small round mud hut thatched with the local reeds, was one of a group set a short distance back from the road. Several tall, spindly paw-paw trees stood around the back of the little community, to the front were a couple of flourishing bougainvilleas showing off their vibrant colours. A huge, thin earthenware pot sat on the ground, a large chunk was broken from its lip but it was obviously still in use. The archaeologist's wife could not help but notice the decoration around what was left of the rim. It looked like one they had found placed upside down over a lizard's skull in last year's excavations near the Chief's palace.

Simon waited patiently as Lizzie's attention was diverted. Like all the guides he was familiar with the oddities of the strange couple that came out every year and dug up things that had no value – bits of stone, lumps of charcoal, fragments of broken pottery – things that no one would buy or sell.

'Sorry, Simon, but this pot looks like one we found out at the spring site.'

'Professor, my sister is here.'

A small, graceful young woman stood waiting round the back of the hut where two armchairs had been carefully placed facing a large group of people – friends, family, neighbours – all waiting to see the white woman their relative had talked about. Lizzie's stomach sank, she had no idea what was expected of her.

She walked over to the young woman and offered her hand in greeting, along with the local salutation. There were a few giggles – no doubt her accent was dreadful. But the young woman responded in English and soon the two of them were sitting in the armchairs having a proper conversation, watched by the small audience as if they were in front of a television interview for the BBC or CNN.

Miriam turned out to have been educated to British 'A' level standard thanks to a Scottish woman who had paid for her education. She had then used her creative skills to start a little business, with a small gift to start her off from her sponsor, selling jewellery made from the wire that poachers used to make snares. Lizzie had bought several pieces over the last couple of years and now she found herself chatting easily to the young entrepreneur about the loss of the funds donated to the school.

'Ah, Professor Lizzie, this man, he has done a terrible, terrible thing. We must work hard now to find some money to replace it, but I think this must take a long time. Can you help us?'

'I'll try. I'm seeing Dr Nkhoma tomorrow – I'll talk to him. But that wasn't really what I came to talk about, Miriam, I just wanted to thank you for your kind offer to help us make sieves, it was really nice of you.'

'No problem. I want to help you too. When Simon tells me about these terrible things going on at the Camp, I feel I must do what I can. This is between all of us, we all share in these things, good and bad. Professor—'

'Please, call me Lizzie.'

'Lizzie, we have something else we must tell you. Simon, he told me about the vehicle you saw which is now in the Parks compound. He told me that two men ran from this vehicle, to escape in a boat, and one of these men was leaving much blood. Now, my other brother, you know, is a carpenter, he makes many coffins, plenty people are dying. Because of this he talks to many, many people from all around. He hears that there is a strange man in

Mfuwe, a man from Congo, who is hurt. This man has been seen in one of our not-so-good bars and with another man who lives here, a man who is we think maybe also from Congo. He does not live in the village with others, he has a small place by the river, on the edge of the land owned by that Indian who lives in Chipata and comes here only to fish.'

'This Indian man's land, where is it?'

'I will ask Simon to show you when you return. But be careful, Lizzie, do not go to this place alone. I think that this stranger can be the one who left this blood in the car. He can be very involved with these bad things that are happening here.'

'That's really useful information, Miriam, thank you. Listen, I have to go now, but I will make sure that someone finds out more about this man. And we will stop and buy some of your jewellery before we leave – it is so lovely.'

Miriam bowed her head, accepting the compliment. The instant Lizzie started to walk away a communal murmur arose from the assembled audience, as if the television had been turned off and everyone was discussing what they had seen and heard. The crowd had migrated to the front of the hut by the time they hit the road and there they stood, some of them waving madly, watching the pair zoom out of sight.

Lizzie sat back and relaxed. Simon was driving like a guide again, thank goodness.

'So, Simon, where is this land your sister-in-law was talking about?'

'I cannot show you the place this man lives, it is down by the river and there is only a very rough track – he will hear us coming. But I will show you where the path leaves the road. Prof, Miriam is right, I think these men are bad, I mean really bad. The one who lives here, he is rich by our local standards, his house has electricity. I have seen strange vehicles drive down that road, I see that they come from Congo or Zimbabwe. They only come into town to drink at the place I do not like even to name.'

'You don't by any chance mean High Society?'

'Ah! Professor Lizzie, how do you hear of this place? You must not talk about this, it is full of wicked people. It is better not to know about this place.'

Lizzie was quite taken aback by the violence of his reaction. One thing was for certain, Luc Delfosse had obviously fallen in with his own kind. She gave mental thanks for the fact that Jake was not among them – he might irritate the hell out of her but she liked him and – as today's events had proved – a genuine heart beat beneath that cool dude facade.

The tarmac road was about to peter out, she could see the great drop approaching where they would turn right and head down towards the river. They jolted down over the mini precipice and bounced along the dirt road for three or four minutes before the Land Rover slowed almost to a halt. Even before Simon pointed it out, she could see the rough track darting off into the bush.

'This is the road to that man's house.'

'Can you see the place from anywhere else?'

'Not unless you are a scout, or in an aeroplane, the river bends here and on the other side is the park – a part of the park where there is no road – only people on foot will see it, so that must be scouts on patrol – or poachers. I think they do not wish to be seen.'

'Mm, sounds like it. I wonder why he hasn't been to claim the car – it must be costing him a lot of money?'

'Perhaps he has much money, enough so he can deny it is his and maybe pay the police and miss the chance to be accused of a crime in the Park?'

'But how would he be so rich? And why live here?'

Shrugging, Simon started to drive off again.

'Maybe he has found something here in Luangwa. Or maybe he sells drugs that are smuggled. He can be many things I think, and hide here quite well. Perhaps even he is a spy. But maybe he has made a lot of money in Congo – from mining, or from cattle.'

'Cattle?'

'I am reading – maybe in the Economist, some magazine left by a guest – some of the big troubles in the far north-east come because the land for cattle is so valuable, this is their new gold.'

Lizzie found it hard to believe that, in a land brutalised by conflict and exploitation, mere cattle could be worth a life of crime.

'You're talking about the area near Rwanda – Burundi, Uganda? Are you saying that cattle are so important that people kill for land to graze them?'

'I think this is what this article is saying, if I am reading it right. Right or correct?'

'Correctly,' Lizzie corrected. 'But to get back to Zambia – surely north-eastern Congo is too far away to have an effect here?'

'You can say yes and be wrong – these men have many ways to make money. But I can imagine they are interested more in minerals than land for cows. Everyone now wants a cellphone, if this mineral that they put in the phone is so hard to find and so many people kill for it, then surely it is worth plenty of dollars?'

'I think you're right, I can't really see the cattle thing bringing someone down here.'

Lizzie grabbed the dashboard with both hands as they swung into the turn-off for the main part of the camp. As usual, there was no door on the passenger side.

'That was a really helpful trip,' Lizzie turned to Simon as they came to a full stop, 'and I enjoyed meeting your sister. If you hear anything else about that man, let me know. Dr Nkhoma's coming over in the morning, I'll try and email him before then, he may be able to find out a bit more about him.'

Passing by the office, Lizzie could hear that Maggie was in, long before she reached the half-door. Knocking first, she stepped in to find her on the phone. Miming to her to wait, Maggie continued her call, confirming the flight details for two people heading down from Lusaka. Finally she put down the receiver.

'One more chalet taken, thank the Lord. I was beginning to worry that they weren't coming after all. Zach asked me to give you this, honey – don't know what it is but he was quite insistent I should give it to you as soon as I saw you. And how the devil are you, anyway?'

'Oh, I'm fine – interesting little trip out with Simon. But first, some bad news I'm afraid. The money for the school – the headmaster ran off with it.'

'The little bugger! I don't believe it. I do believe it. Christ! That man. If I ever get my hands on him. May he roast in Hell. Is that the worst news – no murders today? No? My goodness, your magic must be wearing off, old lady!'

'Hey, thanks Maggie – that makes me feel so much better, roll up and see the woman who's a murder magnet. Um, did they get off safely, the diggers?'

'Do you see them? Do you hear them? Yes, angel, they got off safely and your sweet little Alex looked *so* happy to be doing something. He has got lovely eyes behind those glasses, hasn't he? Deep. And he's always so calm about things – I bet he's a coiled spring isn't he?' She laughed out loud then shook her head. 'It's a crying shame about all his kit – and the site. But you never know – silver linings and all that, he might find an amazing new place to dig. No doubt full of tsetses and mambas but that won't stop him. Come on, let's go grab a coffee and you can tell me about the rest of your trip.'

It was more than an hour before Lizzie managed to find time to read the note.

> Dear Lizzie
> Sorry but I forgot to tell you something else – not on purpose!!!!!!!!!!
> That dude Delvo, he came through DRC on his way here and when he was there he met Harvey Molar – H sent me an email from Lubumbashi – I went and checked it this morning to make sure I remembered it right – he said some Belgians he met 'at the school' (which means the uni, American-style, yeah?, 'cos he went on to say they met the Prof in the Earth Sciences dept) offered him a lift 'cos they were driving down – he said (this is copied off the email) 'I checked their transport – it had no aircon, nice new white 4x4 but no aircon, can you believe it? So I'll stay on the flight but meet up with them again in Lusaka before I fly down to Mfuwe. Never know, they might be useful'.
> Well, I don't know if that's useful but maybe you can check to see if that 4x4 we found abandoned had aircon or not...
> Laters!!!!!!!!!!
> And cheers again for being so cool about it all, I'm working hard, honest!!!!!!
> Good boy Zach ☺

She smiled. Silver linings indeed, Maggie was right even if in the wrong context. The day was improving. Lizzie looked at her watch, time to do some work and sort through her emails. For some reason, the thought made her nervous. She brushed the feeling away and set to work.

Chapter 21

Lizzie estimated that she had at least an hour to start work on an article she had promised to an American scholarly journal. Her data stick was securely zipped in a pocket in her bag and Alex's laptop sat in Maggie's office, where it had, she hoped, been charging up. First, though, there was the irritation of wading through the wretched inbox. It made life so much easier, in many ways, but so much more stressful in others, now they could access their emails in the Valley. She took a deep breath and squared up to the computer. If everything was working, she could email Thomas, too. At least that would be a good thing.

The laptop was charged up and the electricity lines fully functioning – so far the Fates continued to smile on Lizzie. She logged into her university email account via the satellite link and groaned as over 200 messages were added to the already stuffed mailbox. Her head felt heavy with the heat. Flicking down through them, trying to see which, if any were urgent, her fingers slithered over the keys and she wondered for the umpteenth time why Maggie hadn't sited the office somewhere cooler. Sweat was dripping down the back of her neck where the bulk of her hair lay insulating her nicely.

All of a sudden she stopped, stock still. Her fingers hovered above the keyboard as if freeze-framed. Her eyes were glued to the screen. She could feel the blood pulsing in her neck. After a second she stood and stepped out of the door to where Maggie stood smoking.

'Mags.'

'Yes, darling?' She frowned as she saw a Lizzie who was even paler than usual, freckles standing out like beacons in her white face. 'Are you all right?'

'Can you come and look at this? Please?'

Maggie frowned and stubbed out the cigarette stub carefully before following her in. The older woman peered over the younger's head through her half-rimmed glasses.

'What am I looking at?'

'See this one?' Lizzie pointed at the subject line.

'If you get this I'm probably dead!!!' Maggie read. 'Christ almighty! Who's the joker who sent you...oh shit, Harvey Miller. That's not funny. Have you opened it?'

Lizzie shook her head.

'No, I couldn't, I needed moral support. I'm still scared. But here goes.' Lizzie double clicked on the message and they both waited, the air between them bristling with tension, for the message to appear.

Hey Lizzie, I'll get straight to it – you saw the subject – this ain't the time for pleasantries – not that we do them anyway, huh? I asked a friend to send this on to you if I didn't contact him by a certain time – just in case something serious was wrong. I probably read too much Agatha Christie as a boy.

Cards on the table kid. I set this up because I know they'll be after me, I've done some bad stuff and you could say it's justice catching up with me at last – I know you don't think highly of me and you're not the only one. But I'm not a total shit. Listen, this is important, if they don't know where the bone is yet for God's sake tell them, your life is more precious than some f—ing fossil.

And since I don't have to stick around and live with the consequences, I may as well admit it, you're about the best there is kid - no bull. Maybe you're not as hot on humans as you think but you kick ass with them 'boons. And tell young Zach the grass ain't always greener... but I guess he knows that by now too. For what it's worth - nah, he'll find out for himself!

One final thing, if they are after something besides the bone, as I now suspect, watch that pretty ass and tell Alex to get himself armed up - those guys don't play softball. You'll have realised by now that Luc Delfosse is a heap of dung, so don't let him get too close to you or anyone you care about - and he's pretty damn bad but he's not the worst of them, don't trust anyone (nothing beats a good old cliché eh?). Be careful, you're not paranoid, they are after you.

I hope I'll just be grossly embarrassed when I see you again if you got this and I'm still breathing, if not... well 'Say a little prayer for me' as the lady sang. We all need some heavenly insurance come the end.

Yours in scholarly appreciation,

Molar Man (yeah of course I knew, it coulda been a lot worse – over and out)

Maggie put her hand on Lizzie's shoulder and leant on it, hard.

'Lizzie, I never thought you'd hear me say this, but I'm scared. What the hell is going on – what did that guy get into and why in God's name didn't he tell us more? This is worse than useless. What time is it?'

'Why? Sorry, it's nearly midday.'

'Come on, by the time we get to the bar it will be noon and time for a lunchtime drink. I need gin.'

'I'll catch you up – better just scroll through the rest and make sure there's no other hand grenades in there.'

'Gin too?'

'You bet. With tonic please – or bitter lemon if there's none.'

Lizzie scrolled down through the pages of her Webmail system out of sheer habit, but she was not seeing anything. She reached down and scratched the head of the cat who had just returned from who knew where. She felt like she should do something, but what? Then she thought of Thomas, scrolled back up to the shocking email and forwarded it to him. She began to log off but some application or other was taking ages to close. As she sat, twisting a long strand of copper hair round and round her index finger, waiting for the click from her laptop that signalled its temporary oblivion, the radio crackled into life.

'Elephant Camp, Elephant Camp, this is Parks HQ, do you read me?'

Lizzie leapt from her seat and picked up the handset. With a pained mewl the cat ran from the room.

'Thomas, it's Lizzie here did you get my message? Over.'

'Indeed. That is partly why I am calling – the other is to tell you that the police are here, they are taking away the vehicles. Starting with the nice new one.'

So much for asking him about the aircon in the vehicle, it would have to wait.

'There's nothing I can do today regarding your recent email,' Thomas continued, 'unless you want to share it with my guests here? Over.'

'Thank you Thomas, we will look after it ourselves for now, what do you suggest, over?'

'Bearing in mind we are on the public channel, I recommend extreme caution. Tell Gus immediately. On no account must you go out alone, or even with one member of staff. Stay there and when Alex gets back I agree with what your correspondent said about equipping himself. Maybe I can persuade a scout to come out for the night if you can help with the cost – radio me in about an hour if you want me to try – Gus may have a better idea. I hope you get my meaning. You must be careful. I will be there as early as I can tomorrow, so save me some bacon and eggs. I am sorry, Professor dear, but I must go, there are papers to sign – I am not letting these things go without some official signatures. Take care of yourselves. Over'

'All understood, Thomas, and you take care too. Over and out.'

Lizzie stood, fists clenched, tense as a high diver ready to jump. Thomas was advising her to barricade herself in. That meant she was in real danger. But as for Alex 'equipping himself' with a gun, even if Gus had one to spare, she knew Alex had never used one. Maybe now would be a good time to learn.

The computer whined, clicked and died. She padded over to the bar where Maggie was smoking, yet again.

'I've just realised,' said Lizzie, 'I've seen you smoke about five cigarettes in about the last five minutes.'

Maggie grimaced. 'I know, it's the stress, I'm really going to try to stop, as soon as – well, when it feels like a good time. Don't nag me. Here, bottoms up.'

Lizzie lifted the glass cloudy with gin and bitter lemon, something she never drank at home. It hit the spot.

'Thomas just radioed,' she told Maggie, 'I forwarded the email to him and he got back straight away. He's got the police there, but we agreed not to tell them.' She was twirling her hair again. 'You know, I usually find Thomas really reassuring, but this time he made me feel even more worried. He said to ask Gus if we should try and get an armed scout out for the night to protect us – what do you think?'

Maggie tilted her head back and blew a long stream of smoke

up towards a tree squirrel giggling in the thatch.

'I'll ask Gus how many guns he can raise. We've got one each at the house and he can probably call on a couple of mates. I'd rather have friends than just any old scout – there's no guarantee whoever's available is reliable.' She shook her head. 'I know you lot are fond of Isaiah – and I wouldn't question him for a second, but there are some of those guys that you know damn well can be bought. Don't tell Thomas I said that. He knows, of course, but he has to make a show of confidence.' Maggie took a sip of her gin. 'And I think you and Alex should move up to the guest cottage next to us for the duration. You'll like it – nice verandah overlooking the river – fantastic sunsets, a dinky shower room and a little place for making tea. But the biggest plus is we can look after you two and Sylvie all in one place, near as dammit.'

A worrying thought was creeping into Lizzie's super-alert mind.

'Mags, what about the students? Shouldn't we do something about them?'

Maggie groaned. Then she tapped her cigarette lighter loudly on the bar. Gabriel looked up from his book.

'Madam?'

'Gabriel, be an angel and run fetch Gus – tell him from me that *whatever* he's doing *this* is more important, OK?'

Gabriel jumped from his stool and ran from the bar. It was clear that Maggie was serious.

The barman returned with his boss at an unnatural brisk trot.

Lizzie realised now she should have printed out the email. As she told Gus about the subject line she felt that awful sinking feeling again. This was deadly – literally deadly – serious.

Gus pulled out his pipe and sucked on it, empty though it was, whilst she spoke, then tapped it on the bar and began to fill it as he thought about what she had said.

'I think Maggie's right,' he said, at last. 'First thing we do is get you guys moved up to our place, I'm not even sure you should stay in the cottage, nice though it is, let's talk about that when Alex gets back. It's a toss up as to who's most vulnerable, you two or Sylvie – but at least there's two of you – and one's a man.' He turned to Maggie, who had snorted at the last remark, 'You may snort away, my darling, but even you have to admit that a demented, idiot-male of the species is more likely to feel threatened by another male than a female – we're talking brute psychology here.'

Maggie opened her mouth to speak, but Gus was having none of it. Waving away the words before they formed he carried on, 'For the time being I'll take you back to the house and get out my elephant gun. No point in half measures.' He grinned. 'Maggie, why don't you Skype our Valley mates and see if you can rustle up a couple of guys with guns for the evening. We'll work out a better plan tomorrow when we've had a chance to get a few more brains on the case. Did Thomas say anything about coming over himself?'

'Tomorrow before breakfast,' replied Lizzie.

'Good, we'll make sure we're safe tonight and take it from there. Now, about these students. They're not the prime target – sorry Liz – so I reckon they'd be safe enough here, but if you're worried then we could move them to another lodge or campsite – or – hang on, there's only five of them – they're used to roughing it aren't they?' Lizzie nodded and Gus continued, 'Good ol' Jake has a nice big place, why not see if he can put them up? He must have a couple of spare beds and they've got their mats for camping anyway. Given they're all officially adults I think you have to lay your cards on the table – give them the options, their choice. But worth seeing if Jake's open to the idea – he owes us plenty for all the time we've spent mopping up after him with Birgit.'

Lizzie nodded. 'I reckon they'd all jump at the chance – not because they'll be worried but because it'd be an adventure. Leah won't need much persuading.'

Another snort escaped Maggie, 'And I doubt the spare bed thing will be an issue for her.'

They all smiled, briefly.

'Right, are you ready Lizzie? I'll go get the gun first then come back and take you over to your room to pick up your stuff. Stay here and don't leave her alone, Mags. Gabriel, don't let Lizzie out of your sight.'

It was the first acknowledgement from Gus that the barman was listening to each and every word they spoke. He had been with them for many years. Lizzie hoped to goodness that he was beyond reproach.

Gus dumped out the contents of his pipe in the 'ashtray', an earthenware pot that wobbled on its irregular bottom on the irregular bar. His square hand grasped his wife's shoulder, briefly, in a rare public display of affection – and he trotted off again.

In less than a couple of minutes they heard the engine turn and the Land Rover ricocheted off down the potholed track to the house.

Lunch was a glum interlude in a distressing day. Lizzie forced herself to eat a few forkfuls of a stodgy pie then sent back the bulk of it untouched, carefully cutting off the leftovers from the small portion she had sampled – it would make a decent meal for someone who needed it more than she did. As soon as they had finished, Gus drove her over to the chalet and she shoved all their belongings, with no concern for the niceties of folding or rolling that Alex was so good at, into their two sailcloth bags and, having heaved the whole lot into the car, they headed off in silence to the little guest house. Maggie had convinced Gus that, with the extra crew she had rustled up with the promise of steak and beer, they would be safe enough there – and still retain a little privacy. Secretly, Lizzie was more grateful for the distance between herself and Sylvie than the privacy. They may have been reconciled, but they had nothing in common bar work, and that was the last thing on her mind.

Sylvie, however, had no such antipathy. For the rest of the afternoon they sat chatting about their strange world of ancient bones and, despite her reservations, Lizzie was surprised to find she enjoyed the distraction.

'You know, Lizzie,' Sylvie said, 'we all wanted to find more of your bone. Me, I wanted to see the site, maybe find some other bits of the skeleton, also René, but that man,' she refused to name her husband, 'he wanted to find it for the ground. The soil I mean. This work we have done in the Congo, it shows we have only to find some bone like this one and we find perhaps the right kind of ground for some special minerals, maybe even these Coltan minerals. So, this is why he is so aggressive about this. That man is a devil for money, always it is the money. That is why he marries me. I was a fool. My father, he was right.'

'But, Sylvie, you're supposed to be really good at finding fossils – everyone says you have an instinct – why did he not just drive around with you? Surely with some good geological maps—'

'Pff. He is not one to take time. If he can do this quicker with some danger, he takes the danger.'

Lizzie's relaxed state began to fray around the edges.

'And what do you think he will do now that he has lost you and knows where the bone is? Do you think it was him, he, who stole the excavation kit and trashed the site?'

'He would not do this himself, he is too full of pomp – is this a word? He is too much of the good opinion of himself to do dirty work. These men he has met in Lusaka and here in Mfuwe, wicked men, perhaps it is them who does this for him.'

'Remind me, what were they like – the one here, for example, could you tell if he was local, did he look like the men here? I think you said you thought he might be from the Congo, is that right?'

'This one in the bar, he has much hair, he speaks very good French, this is unusual here, yes?'

'Yes. The official language is English. But the hair too – well, you've seen for yourself, most men have very short hair here. You don't know anything else about him, do you?'

'No, but René – he may know. Is he still here? You have not spoken of him.' Sylvie took a deep drag on her cigarette. 'And tell me, what has happened with your friend and that man? I do not want to know in my heart but my head it must ask.'

'I haven't seen René to be honest – not for – not since you left Luc. And as for Birgit, I'm afraid she seems to have been bewitched by him – she won't listen to anyone, but today she has been with a Danish family all day and she should be doing a night drive into the park tonight, so with any luck she won't see him again till tomorrow. But I don't see how we can stop two grown adults having a relationship if they choose to. Jake has tried, that was really my best hope.'

They both lapsed into silence.

'Good evening, all, settling in for the sunset?'

Alex materialised around the corner of the house. Lizzie ran over to hug him. Alex held her tight for all too brief a moment, then took her hand and walked with her to the semi-circle of chairs set facing the river where Sylvie sat, tactfully ignoring them. Now she turned and smiled at the couple.

'*Bonsoir* Alex, *ça va*? Did you have a good day?'

'Hi, Sylvie, not bad actually. We did quite a long drive into the park given how late we started, I think we've found a site, believe it or not, just one of those lucky chances. We stopped for lunch and one of the girls went off for a pee, she came back saying she thought there might be something worth looking at – and there was – stone tools just lying around. Really old stuff, choppers. They're on the surface so I'm not sure if it's a real possibility for a serious excavation – but that's what we have to find out. I think we might need to stay out there, though, it's quite a long way. I'll have to check with Thomas, see if he'll let us camp for two or three nights and whether he can spare a good scout. But what about you two?'

Sylvie spoke first.

'I am fine, but poor Lizzie has had a very bad day today.' She stood and smoothed out her wrinkled but somehow still elegant white linen trousers. 'I will find a bottle of wine, this will help us talk, *non*? I will come back very soon.'

With that she swished into the house, leaving Lizzie, in her tatty combats, dusty t-shirt and sturdy boots, feeling grubby, shabby and in serious need of a makeover. Alex sensed it straight away.

'Come here, gorgeous.'

Lizzie laughed. 'Yeah, right! Look at me!'

'Aha! That's a good sign. Gloom, doom but still enough spirit for vanity! I saw the email. Maggie showed me. She also told me about the gin, I'm surprised you're not under the table.'

They stood close together, taking comfort in the brief magic of intimacy. The tinkle of glasses on a tray alerted them to Sylvie's return. She placed the tray on a wonky tin table that had seen better days and poured three glasses of white wine. They clinked glasses in silence, awed by the majesty of the scene before them. No matter how many sunsets they saw, the Luangwa had the power to enthral anew every day. The sky above them was almost black now, the river aflame under a horizon glowing peach, pink, crimson, gold. Clouds formed dark striations, blending slowly into the darkness as the sun dipped swiftly behind the distant ridge of the escarpment.

They sat. The mosquitoes had already begun to emerge. Lizzie pulled a baggy shirt off the back of her chair and put it on, rolling down the sleeves to cover her arms. Alex too adjusted his shirt and fastened it at the cuffs. Sylvie took out another cigarette and lit it.

'Do they help with the mosquitoes?' Lizzie ventured into the void. Conversation seemed to have vanished with the sun. Sylvie's reply passed her by, but at least Alex and she were chatting now, filling the space between them.

The comment on the cigarette had sparked a thought. All those cigarette stubs they had been finding were exotic brands she was sure. Sylvie's cigarette packet was the kind the students called Blue Peter – Peter Stuyvesant in a blue packet – it smelt like a normal cigarette unlike those that Luc smoked. She wondered.

'Sylvie,' she interpolated, 'sorry to interrupt, but do you happen to know what kind of cigarettes Luc smokes?'

Sylvie laughed. 'He is obsessed with French cigarettes, we both smoke Gitanes when we can but sad to say they are now made in the *Pays Bas*. Me, I was smoking the ones we call *blondes* but Luc prefers the ones in the yellow paper made of *maïs* – this is corn, yes? They are hard to find.'

Lizzie could almost feel the adrenaline racing around her veins. She tried to keep the excitement out of her voice. 'Yellow? Gosh, I've never heard of them – have you got one, I'd be interested to see it?'

'*Ah non*! I leave them and the *blondes* in our room – this is why I now smoke these. Luc thinks the *blondes* are weak and so for women, he prefers the strong *brunes* if he cannot get the *maïs,* René likes these too. But he will smoke them if he has no other French cigarettes so, *malheureusement*, they are lost to me now. But I talk too much – why did you ask me, is there some reason?'

Lizzie wished she had thought of a more tactful way of broaching the subject. Sylvie did not need any more worries and she had no desire to upset the woman further by explaining why she was suddenly so interested in Luc's smoking preferences.

Just as she was about to resort to talking about Jake and his filthy cigar-smoking habit, Maggie arrived with company.

'On the booze already? Is that white?' she picked up the bottle, 'I'll get some red. Lizzie, Alex, have you met Piet and André before?'

The two were almost caricatures of a certain type of safari guide: khaki shirt and short shorts, ragged blonde hair, deep suntans and plimsolls with no socks. The two men reached out rough hands and shook those proffered by Lizzie and Alex. Sylvie stood.

'Ah, Sylvie,' Maggie added, 'sorry, love, didn't see you at first. Now, what can I get you boys?'

No one was surprised to hear the double order of beer: one Castle, one Mosi.

'So,' said one of the two – Lizzie had not matched the names to the faces – 'you're the guys who've sparked our crime wave, eh? Well, we've got our rifles and we're ready for the bastards.' He rubbed his ear. 'I do enjoy hunting.'

'Steady now, Piet,' cautioned his mate, 'hunting humans is illegal, even if they are thieving, robbing, murdering bastards. We'll just give 'em a big fright then hand them over to our gentlemen of the law for a long spell in hell. Can't think of a much worse way to spend your life than festering in a Zambian prison.'

Maggie returned clanking with chilled beers and another bottle of wine.

'I've spoken to Jake, by the way, radioed him. He's only too pleased to offer Leah a bed for the night and the others are welcome to camp out in his house or his garden – whichever they fancy. He's even got a shed but they'd have to share that with sick animals – wouldn't be my first choice, I must say. I had a word with the kids over at the camp site. Leah thought about it a bit and said she'd go over to Jake's, the two girls and Martin are going too, taking their tents. Zach wants to stay so I spoke to the night watchman over there and told him to stay awake and keep an eye on him. When I left he had started a fire big enough to frighten a whole bloody herd of buffalos, so he should last the night.'

Alex leant back in his chair and stretched, the fabric creaking ominously.

'That's a weight off my mind, Mags, you're a hero. One question, where's everyone eating tonight?'

'Leah and that lot are going to eat at Wild-Dogs with Jake, I thought the rest of us'd all eat here if that's OK. I've promised Piet and André steaks, and told Zach we'll get him picked up and taken back later. How does that sound?'

'Perfect.' Alex looked happier already. 'Lizzie, shall we go and settle in – give these people time to sort themselves out?'

The two sloped off to the little hut silhouetted against the night sky. Lizzie almost felt guilty. No students – except for Zach – no notes to catch up on, no responsibility. It was almost like being on holiday. The two of them giggled like schoolchildren as they squeezed red wine into two chipped tumblers from the box they found by the sink. A packet of fruit chutney crisps sat beside the box, on top of a note from Maggie.

'Happy honeymoon, lovebirds! Enjoy it while you can!'

They slumped onto the little sofa facing the moonlit river, fully prepared to do as they were told – until the spell broke, as, so inevitably, it would.

Chapter 22

It was a riotous evening. Piet and André had brought with them the Zambian equivalent of a boom box – boasting the brand name 'Philibs'. As the night waned there was much strutting of stuff and Piet's interpretation of Queen's *Bohemian Rhapsody* was a wonder to behold. From the outside it must have looked as if some weird, wild ritual was underway. But the night passed safely, despite – or perhaps because of – the hedonistic activity. Morning ambled in, as desultory as the students who finally appeared at breakfast looking tired but happy. Zach, despite his proximity, was the last to arrive. Lizzie watched as he spread his toast with peanut butter.

'Don't look at me like that, Lizzie,' he said, 'I'm good. It's all fine.'

'Who says I was looking at you – I was waiting for the peanut butter.'

He grinned and handed her the sticky pot.

Alex cleared his throat, 'Right, you lot, listen up, we've got work to do.'

There were groans all round. Lizzie looked at him, puzzled. What could they do, with no site to work on, no kit, all the finds already washed and access to the new site yet to be agreed with Thomas?

'To be more accurate,' continued Alex, 'you have work to do, a special task. You've all seen the schools around here – pretty basic by our standards. Well, a charity back home raised seven grand to build long-drop loos and a kitchen hut for one of them – the one Thomas's little girls go to. Well, guess what, the headmaster ran off with the funds – so I said we'd help. I want a fully thought-through plan by lunchtime. You need to raise the funds by Christmas.'

The silence was broken only by the distant sound of the chef, singing God's praises in his clear, pure voice.

'Right,' Alex clapped his hands, 'off you go! See you back here for lunch.'

The students looked bewildered. Eventually they picked up their belongings and shambled off down to the riverbank path, still speechless.

'Alex,' Lizzie said, poking him in the ribs, 'that was lovely of you. But what are *we* going to do?'

'Don't poke me or I'll tickle you. I thought Thomas was coming over?'

'Oh, gosh, yes.' She checked her watch. 'Come on, we've just got time to brush our teeth before he arrives.'

They set off towards the path, but stopped in their tracks as they heard Gabriel's urgent voice, rising above the 'slap, slap' of feet running in cheap plastic tropicals – flip-flops.

'Doctor Alex, Professor Lizzie! Sergeant Phiri is on his way here, very soon. Madam says to tell you Bwana Gus is a very big expert in how our police in Zambia work, so if you want you must ask him to sit with you when you talk to this man.' He shook his head vigorously, 'Me, I think this is a good idea. This man is not a bad man, but he is still a policeman and – eh! I have said it.'

'Where is Gus?' asked Lizzie.

'He is in his garage. I can run to find him for you.'

'Brilliant, we'll head back to the breakfast table. Could we have some more tea – and if there's any more bread...?' Lizzie wheedled.

Gabriel laughed. 'I will bring toast.' And off he ran.

They had barely finished their extra slices of crumbly brown toast when Sergeant Phiri arrived. Lizzie raised her eyebrows when she saw what he was driving.

'That looks familiar. What do you reckon, the one that Harvey Miller left behind?'

'Looks suspiciously like it.'

Sergeant Phiri ambled towards them, in his hand a black nylon briefcase, emblazoned with the logo of a well-known cigarette, which swung to the rhythm of the policeman's walk.

'Professor, how are you?'

'I am fine, how are you? Sergeant, have you met my husband, Doctor Sommers?'

Polite rituals over, Alex ushered the Sergeant over to a trio of squat wooden chairs set around a squat wooden table.

Phiri sat back, his eyes focused on Lizzie.

'So, Professor, we have work to do. Have you any news for me?'

'I don't really know where to begin.' Lizzie admitted. 'I was waiting for Thomas – Dr Nkhoma – we were going to run through things together. Do you mind?'

Phiri nodded silently, still focusing on Lizzie, tapping his fingers on the chair arm.

'I see you have a new vehicle,' Lizzie ventured, 'is this by any chance the one that Professor Miller was driving?'

Sergeant Phiri stared at her through eyes that did not blink. The tapping stopped. Lizzie squirmed as the silence continued for what seemed like a very long time. Then the Sergeant chuckled.

'You know, Professor, a policeman in Mfuwe has a *very* difficult job. This is a *very* big place, *many* miles, *many* dangerous animals. We have no car. Now, tell me, Professor, how do we investigate crime when we cannot leave our small office near the airport?' He settled further into his seat with a smile. 'Yes, this is Professor Miller's car. Myself, I think it is better for me to visit the scene of the crimes in this car than to sit in my office waiting for the crime to solve itself.'

'I didn't mean to criticise you, Sergeant,' a nervous Lizzie waved her hands around, 'there was a reason I wanted to know. I am sure you try very hard to do your job – in very difficult circumstances.'

Again the policeman sat back and scrutinised Lizzie for some seconds before speaking. Lizzie began to regret saying anything about the vehicle. At last he broke his silence.

'We are corrupt.' He raised one hand as if in atonement. 'This is what most people say and they can be correct, to some degree. We take money when it is offered, we stop cars and fine them when maybe it is not strictly necessary. But tell me, Professor, how would you find it doing your job if you had no pay for several months? Yes, we can sometimes take money when we should not. Some of my colleagues are living very well this way. I am not one of them. I take only what I need to do my job, to feed my family, and I trust in God for the rest. God is my judge, He will say on judgement day, "Ah! This man! He did what he could, we will forgive him some small sins". So now, Professor, I have put my cards on this fine table, maybe you can share with me your thoughts about these many terrible crimes and feel that we can work together?'

'Of course – I really didn't intend to criticise. I can't imagine how we would cope in England if none of our policemen were paid for months on end – there would be riots. We must order you some breakfast. Which reminds me, Alex,' she turned to her husband, 'would you mind going to the office and radioing to see if Thomas has set off yet? And could you see if you can get into my emails and print out that message I got from Molar man?'

Alex looked surprised, but complied. He was heading for the office as Gus was coming to join them.

'Sergeant,' Gus barked, removing his empty pipe from his mouth and placing it in his breast pocket. 'Nice new vehicle. Make sure you keep it properly maintained, eh? Always ready to lend a hand, you know. Need to keep the officers of the law on the road.'

He sat and beckoned to Gabriel.

Lizzie leant forward.

'Sergeant, this vehicle, does it have air conditioning?'

'Sadly, no, it is a very fine vehicle in all respects but this respect is lacking. But we beggars must not be choosers, as you say in England. How is England? Do you have snow often? Do the elephant get cold?'

It was one of those recurring conversations.

'We don't have elephants, we don't have giraffes or lions or even hippos.'

'Eh!' He shook his head. 'No elephant. You are most fortunate. But, to go back to this vehicle. It has an interesting history. This vehicle has been bought by a man with a foreign name in DRC and imported illegally. These Zambian number plates are not legal. So, in fact, we are allowed to confiscate this vehicle, it is not in the end an act of corruption. The name I have written down, do you recognise this name perhaps?'

He showed them a scrap of cheap ruled paper torn from an exercise book, the words written in large round letters using blue biro.

Lizzie shook her head. 'Looks French, a man's name.'

Gus frowned.

'It's not one of the people staying here, that much I can tell you. Someone told me the guy who lives off the dirt track down by the river – on the edge of the land that Mr Kumar from Chipata owns – is Congolese. That would fit, wouldn't it? He's the only person round here I can think of – and presumably whoever bought this vehicle isn't local.

Lizzie turned to the policeman who was picking his teeth with a matchstick.

'Sergeant, do you know if Harvey Miller was driving it, or was he being driven? I remember that first day I saw him, he had a driver. We know he turned down a free trip from Lusaka in a vehicle without air conditioning, so it wouldn't make any sense for him to hire one himself without and drive it down from Lusaka, would it? Maybe it's that vehicle, though. And maybe he hired it here, or it belonged to a friend or something?'

Gabriel had been standing quietly to one side and cleared his throat loudly now.

'Ah, Gabriel,' said Gus, 'Some refreshment for Sergeant Phiri. Toast, maybe some sausage, an omelette? How does that sound?'

It obviously sounded good, judging by the single silent but beaming nod.

'And Gabriel, I think we will be receiving Dr Nkhoma soon, too, so please warn chef.'

At this point Alex returned holding a piece of paper.

'Here you are, Lizzie, the email. Thomas left nearly twenty minutes ago so he should be here any minute.'

Lizzie gave him a brilliant smile and turned again to the policeman.

'Here Sergeant, take a look at this. I received this yesterday. Now you will see why I was asking about air conditioning.'

The Sergeant took his time, chewing all the while on his matchstick.

He slipped the paper down onto the coffee table and scratched his head.

'We will wait till Dr Nkhoma is here and then perhaps we can assemble all the evidence in order. We must clear our heads. My head is not clear.'

With that he stood and wandered off towards the bar. There he bought a packet of cigarettes and proceeded to smoke one, standing at the counter, chatting to Gabriel. Gus shrugged his shoulders at Lizzie and Alex and they all sat back in their chairs, waiting, as if in suspended animation. An Africa interlude.

Gus went through the ritual of filling his pipe, tamping it down and lighting it, making the gentle sucking sounds of a habitual pipe smoker. The scent of tobacco mixed with vanilla filled the air. Tea arrived and was poured. One more cup was drunk before Thomas's noisy Land Rover ruptured the unnatural silence.

Away across the dusty grass the chef laughed, a cleaner ran from reception giggling and even the vervet monkeys chattered and scattered as Thomas progressed, trailing mirth. Sergeant Phiri was infected, too, laughter echoed around the bar and there was much shaking of hands, patting of arms and frequent exclamations before the two men finally stood before the patient tea- drinkers.

By this time Gabriel had laid a table for the newcomers' breakfast, to which they all now adjourned.

'Well, gentlemen,' began Lizzie, 'I've written up a kind of summary of where I think we are, so why don't I run through it all while you two eat?'

She sat at the head of the table and imagined herself, just for a moment, back in Liverpool, in her cold basement office, surrounded by nervous 18-year-olds. It was an oddly reassuring thought.

'Right. First, let's list everything that's happened and see if we think they're all connected or not. The first and major incident: the murder of Harvey Miller by garrotting, either in his vehicle or after being forcibly dragged from it by a person unknown. We can assume one person, I think, because Isaiah had a good look around and he seemed to think it was one person. Thomas, would you agree?'

He nodded.

'Next, the theft of my laptop. It sounds quite innocent by comparison, but it really spooked me – we could have been murdered in our bed. So, he must have had a very light step for such big feet. We saw footprints but they were all gone by mid-morning thanks to the groundsman's watering and a heavy footed elephant. And of course the night watchman getting drugged, that was obviously planned well in advance. I did wonder whether Harvey had arranged it before he died, but on reflection I don't really think so. Especially given what happened afterwards – news travels so fast here anyway so if you knew the man who paid you to do a job was dead why do it? – well unless someone else took over, or you knew what you were looking for and thought you could sell it to someone else. Hmm. I hadn't thought of that. Anyway. Back to the list.'

Lizzie took a deep breath and studied her notes a moment before continuing.

'Is the theft connected with Harvey's murder? Possibly, I would say. We were both interested in the bone and that was what he said he was here for. Though of course there is that email – Thomas, the one I forwarded to you yesterday – which suggests there may be more to it than that. And now we know he has been looking for fossils in DRC, or at the very least putting his name to articles about it.' She stopped to sip some tea. 'Moving on to the theft of Alex's excavation kit, which also involved another night watchman drugged by a white person – a man, the night watchman said – is that connected? Not sure, but also possibly, if it's all bone related.' She frowned and looked again at her notes. 'Sorry, I've just realised I'm not doing this strictly chronologically. Before we get to the kit being stolen there's the abandoned vehicle – the one that I think I saw the Belgians in earlier that same day – with the blood and the other stuff in the glove compartment. By the way, where is that stuff?' She looked at Thomas.

'I have it locked in my safe at work with a guard on the door. Three passports, one sheet of paper containing your address here and a gun. Please continue with this vivid, one might say lively, reconstruction of events, Professor.' His twinkle was the only sign he was amused at her presentation. In her anxious state it passed Lizzie by, but not Alex, who quickly hid a smile in yet another cup of tea. Sergeant Phiri had plainly taken note of the comments about passports, paper and gun and his stare was now fixed on Thomas, instead of Lizzie, as he chewed.

'Fine,' continued Lizzie. 'So, the kit? Well maybe it's linked to Harvey in some way, for the same reason, the bone, etcetera. And the site vandalism, ditto. And my bone site – sorry, that should have come much earlier in the list – that was messed up, which fits. Now Luc Delfosse and Sylvie – let's just call them the Belgians, it's not accurate, but never mind. Nothing's really happened there, certainly nothing criminal between man and wife, except he's awful and cruel to her but it's presumably all part of the whole set up – but of course there is what Harvey says about Delfosse in the email, which makes him sound very suspicious and capable of really awful things. Is that it? I should have written this up as a flow diagram. Oh, I forgot to mention that I found the papers about mineral exploitation in Harvey Miller's— '

She stopped dead and blushed as she realised that not only had she forgotten to mention that she had found the articles in the dead man's bedroom, she had forgotten all about the GPS that she had pocketed. She reached for her duffel bag.

'Actually, I have a confession to make, I took this GPS from his room and I completely forgot. Would someone like to take a look at it.'

She made an attempt at a wide-eyed innocent look and succeeded only in looking like she had seen something terrifying in the undergrowth on the riverbank. Everyone turned to look and turned back puzzled.

Alex shook his head, reached out and took the little gadget from her.

Thomas broke the ensuing silence.

'Alex, Lizzie, if I may, I have made a few notes of my own. Perhaps we can see if they reinforce the good Professor's eloquently stated summary of our situation.'

Lizzie's face registered dismay as she realised that Thomas was being kind rather than accurate.

Thomas held a sheet of paper at arm's length and began to declaim.

Alex frowned over the GPS.

Sergeant Phiri yawned.

'I have made a list of the aforementioned incidents, cross referenced by basic theme, namely: one, Congo connection; two, Belgian palaeontologists; three, Professor Eliza Lamb and/or her fossil bone. The cross-referencing indicates that all six incidents cross refer to two categories, namely, one, the Belgians and two, Eliza and the bone. But not all have the Congo connection. Thus, the murder of Harvey Miller, the theft of Lizzie's laptop and drugging of the night watchman, the finding of the abandoned vehicle, the theft of Alexander's equipment, the vandalism to his site and the disturbance to the site where the bone was found may all be connected in one way or another to Lizzie and the bone or the Belgians, if we agree that the abandoned vehicle was the one in which Lizzie saw the Belgians earlier that same day.'

Thomas cleared his throat, took a sip of tepid tea and continued.

'I have taken this list-making and cross-referencing one step further, moreover, and tentatively identified a select group of individuals who are central to this little drama, viz, Harvey Miller, the

Belgians, Lizzie, Alex, the invisible injured man and/or the abandoned vehicle's driver. Which is not to say that the group is our only pool of *dramatis personae*, but merely a starting point for our deliberations. Now, my friends, here comes the interesting part, if we cross-refer these people amongst themselves, as to who knows whom or had contact of some kind, the greatest congruity comes in the category of the Belgians. This little exercise is clearly lacking in objectivity and scientific rigour, but I think it tells us something, it tells us that we should look carefully at whatever these Belgian and French people have been doing, especially but *not exclusively* with regard to Lizzie's bone.'

A grunt came from the representative of the law.

'Most clear, Dr Nkhoma. Did I hear that you have found passports in this car you have found empty with blood, this car which is now in our compound at the police post?'

'Ah! You are so right! Did I neglect to tell you this? *Mea culpa,* Sergeant, please forgive me. In my safe at our headquarters I have three very fine passports, each in the same name, each with the same picture, each from a different sovereign nation, one from Zimbabwe, one from Libya and one from the so-say *Democratic* Republic of Congo. In addition I have in my safe's keeping a small hand gun with a silencer. The other item found in the vehicle was a sheet of paper – it was taken from an academic article and listed the address of the workplace of our dear Professor at Liverpool University in England, but written by hand on this paper was also the address of her temporary home here at Elephant Camp in Mfuwe. I am happy to keep these items in the official safe or to give them to you if you have a more secure repository? I am not aware whether you have such a thing as a strong box at the police post?'

'We have no such thing, Dr Nkhoma. I am happy that you keep these things safe. Let us say that they might be more safe there than with me – and my colleagues. It is good that you have not yet told others of these things and it may be that this is the good way to continue, with diplomacy. You are all doing a fine job. Now, my honorary colleague, Professor Lamb, please write a report for me about what Dr Nkhoma has said, in very simple words for my boss whose understanding of your language is small, and make sure to include what information Doctor Sommers finds inside that machine he looks at so strongly, but maybe not the details of what has been found in this car we talk about here. Me, I must leave here and visit the school of my daughters and son, where many dollars have been lost in a most unhappy way.'

Alex looked up. 'So, your children are at the school whose headmaster ran off with the money? Is there any chance of finding him – or the cash?'

Sergeant Phiri looked down at the polished concrete floor beneath his feet. He sighed and raised his head.

'My friends, this man has the powers of a witch, he has flown by night to who knows where. He can be on the escarpment, he can be in Lusaka, he can even be in England. He is full of bad magic. We will not see those dollars in Mfuwe again. I must make an official visit and, if God wishes, then maybe some kind person can send more money – it is in His hands now.'

With that emphatic and fatalistic statement he stood, picked up his shiny cellphone and hitched up his trousers revealing sockless, bony ankles disappearing into glossy, caramel-coloured shoes. The Sergeant reached out, shook hands with Lizzie and Alex then walked off to his nice new car, flanked by Thomas and Gus.

Lizzie perched on the arm of Alex's chair and peered down at the little images on the screen of the GPS.

'What've you got? Where's he been?'

'I'm not sure, there are several tracks with coordinates I don't recognise. Some are close to the northern border of the Copperbelt so they're probably Congo. At first sight, I'd say,' Alex stopped peering at the little screen and turned to face Lizzie, 'I'd say whoever owns this GPS has been making tracks not just in the Congo but way up in north Africa, possibly Libya. I need a map or Google Earth. And here, look. Cute names he's given them all – things like "Ur" "Cu" "Au" "oil" and "Col" – doesn't take a genius to work out what those little tags could signify does it?'

'Crikey. Uranium, copper, gold, oil – and presumably Coltan. That's scary. I mean, I know we suspected it, but it didn't seem real. This, it's like – well, it's like finding out you really are pregnant or you really have got a grey hair.'

'Lizzie! Honestly! This is serious, it could be a motive for murder. These coordinates could be new mineral finds – and they look like they're in some pretty dangerous places, it's not something you'd just leave lying around, is it? In fact, I'm wondering if it *was* left lying around, or whether it has a more important role in this little tragedy. What I'm wondering is, who *does* this actually belong to? Was this GPS borrowed – or even stolen – from someone else? I mean, if it's Harvey's, then how come it's got these tracks in North Africa?'

'Well it was definitely in his bedroom. But that's not to say … hang on, you know, the lovely Luc Delfosse did come knocking when I was going through Harvey's stuff, made out he was after the proofs of a paper they had written together, but there were no proofs at all. I did find published papers with their names on, two published within the last year in fact. And, you know, they were about fossil finds and mineral locations.' She rolled a long strand of hair around and around the fingers of her right hand. 'Hmm. I wonder if you're right? Maybe we could ask Sylvie. Then again, I really don't want to trouble her any more than I have to, poor thing.'

'Oh come on, Lizzie, she can handle it, we *are* dealing with a murder you know.' Alex looked at his watch. 'Not to mention the total ruination of my career if Vickie's dad doesn't produce the goods pretty damn soon.'

'Sorry, love, I suppose you're right. I'll speak to Sylvie when we get back to Maggie's tonight. God, I'm tired. Is it lunchtime yet? I wonder how those kids are getting on? That was a bit off the wall, getting them to work up a fundraising plan.'

Alex slipped his arm around her shoulders. 'I know, pretty damn inventive I thought for the spur of the moment – and I did think it might earn me Brownie points with teacher.'

'Definitely.' She leant forward to kiss him, picked up the GPS from the table and carefully buttoned it into the breast pocket of her shirt.

When Thomas returned they told him what they had learnt from the GPS and Alex hurried off to check the coordinates for North Africa on the Internet in Maggie's office. By the time he got back Lizzie and Thomas were deep in earnest conversation.

'Sorry to interrupt you two,' he said as he sank into the brightly-patterned cushions, 'The electricity's off, so no satellite *ergo* no Internet, but I've checked the coordinates using Maggie's old school atlas as a rough guide – we're talking someone who's been active in Libya, in the DRC near the border with the Zambian Copperbelt but also somewhere not far from Rwanda where all that trouble was that flared up last year. We are talking seriously dodgy here. We need to find out whose GPS this was.'

Thomas turned to Lizzie.

'Professor, you found this in Harvey Miller's bedroom – where exactly was it, can you recall?'

'It was in one of his pockets, in the pocket of a jacket that looked like a jacket he might have travelled in, a little smarter than you would wear in the bush but not so smart as to be the kind of thing you would wear to an occasion. Come to think of it, given what we've found on here is pretty sensitive, you'd think he'd have hidden it away somewhere. Most tourists think their belongings are all going to get nicked by the staff – Maggie says she often has to put the most ridiculous things in the safe.'

'I don't really see how we can tell now. There's no case for it, no marks on it, no – hang on a minute, I haven't been through the whole menu. Let me just have another look, I may have missed something.' Alex held out his hand and Lizzie placed the GPS in it.

They sat and watched as he scrutinised the small gadget packed with vital information.

'OK, so here's one thing, the dates these tracks were set. When was Harvey in Manchester?'

Lizzie pulled out her notebook.

'He spent two weeks in Lubumbashi before he arrived here, and before that he was two days in Kinshasa, three in Brussels and before that was Manchester.'

'That confirms it, if this was his then he certainly wasn't using it himself – unless he was in two places at once. The Libyan tracks were set when he would have been in Manchester, the one that I think is probably near Rwanda was while he was in Brussels, so either it's not his or he lent it to someone.'

'Or,' Thomas ventured, 'the jacket in which you found this little machine was not Professor Miller's property. Did it look like something he would wear, Lizzie? You said it was smarter than the clothes one would wear in the bush?'

Lizzie hesitated, all too aware that she and Alex were wearing scruffy, old clothes deeply ingrained with bush dust, whereas Thomas sat opposite her, immaculately turned out as usual in dark trousers, polished black leather lace-up shoes, a sparkling white shirt and striped tie.

'Smarter than the clothes we would wear, yes, but don't forget he had been staying in Manchester and Brussels on the way here. Actually, thinking about it, you're right, it doesn't ring true. I mean we dress better than this at home,' she blushed, embarrassed by what she felt that statement said to Thomas about their attitude to *his* home, 'because of course we're not digging holes in the ground like we are here – but I've seen Harvey at conferences and he always looks the same whatever he's doing. Pretty much, anyway.'

She was spared further sartorial discomfort by the rattling and clattering that signalled the arrival of a Land Rover. They all turned to look as the doors clanged shut and Maggie shepherded a slender man with dark hair round to the bar. Lizzie looked at Alex who raised his eyebrows.

'Do you think he looks like Vickie?' she asked.

There was no need to reply. Maggie and he were heading straight for them now carrying cold drinks. The sun was beating down from a cloudless sky as it neared midday, warming the air despite the obscuring thatch. There was not even a hint of a breeze.

'What a fine sight!' boomed Maggie. 'Three of my favourite people all together at once. Edward Monk, may I introduce Professor Lizzie Lamb, Dr Thomas Nkhoma and last, but by no means least, the happy puppy you've brought the sticks for, Doctor Alexander Sommers.'

Edward Monk was a lean man who looked like he lived on his nerves. His fingers played with a string of worry beads and his left heel tapped the ground quietly in its canvas lace-up while the ball of his foot stayed attached to the floor. His clothes were of a business-traveller-does-Africa style, probably something like Rohan, guessed Lizzie, khaki and creaseless at any rate. When he spoke it was in a quiet but strong voice, as if condensed to create maximum effect for minimum effort.

'I hired a private plane to bring the stuff down, the weight allowance you get on those commercial flights is pathetic – I can't imagine the hunters use them much?'

He directed the question at Maggie, but Thomas answered.

'Frankly, Mr Monk, we do not make much of a fuss about this, I for one am rather glad of anything that puts obstacles in the way of the destructive tourist. It may be legal, but as far as I am concerned it is far from ethical to preserve game on the one hand and shoot it on the other.'

'Oh, don't get me wrong,' Monk displayed a fine set of suspiciously regular white teeth, 'I totally agree. I hate the whole macho gun-toting business – but I guess there are those who say the money is more important than the ethics. I thought the proceeds got shared around the locals?'

'To some extent, yes. I am afraid wherever there is a way to make more money, humans will exploit loopholes. But we are digressing, I think my friend Doctor Sommers is itching to find out what you have brought.'

Alex nodded, 'I am, but it's nearly lunchtime and I'm sure your private plane didn't do lasagne and garlic bread, Edward. And the students will be here in a few minutes. I presume we'll need some help carting stuff around?'

'You will,' grinned Edward. 'I've got a crate of smaller items like trowels and buckets. And hard hats. I've also brought some of our old surveying equipment – top of the range, just outdated. And then of course there's the ground-penetrating radar. How does that sound?'

Alex looked stunned. Lizzie just grinned like the cat who had eaten the cream.

'I hardly know where to begin, Edward,' Alex almost stuttered, 'it's like Christmas. Gosh, I've never had the chance to use ground penetrating radar here. I don't know if it will work, but I don't see why not, especially on sites like the one at the hot springs where we have lots of different occupation levels not too far down and not too compacted. What do you think?'

'I can't see why not, either. If you've no objections, I'd like to join you out there – help you get used to the kit and have fun at the same time – you never know, might even find something to keep me here a bit longer.'

'Great,' Alex beamed, 'we'd appreciate some knowledgeable company, wouldn't we, Lizzie?'

'Absolutely,' she confirmed, 'and I've got loads of questions for you. Vickie said you thought there might be something commercially valuable here in the Luangwa Valley – what do you think you might find? Everyone always says there should be diamonds and I know there are kimberlite pipes in the park but I thought they were unproductive – or not commercially viable anyway?'

'I'd be moderately surprised if there was anything in the park that was worth the effort of extraction. I'm just interested, really. And it's good to be somewhere that's dangerous because of the wildlife not the politics for a change. It's a cut-throat world, mining – I spend a lot of my time with crooks and villains. It's hard to keep your integrity. I won't say I always do, but I try.'

Lizzie looked at the man, noticing the intense brown eyes, with growing respect but also a little apprehension. He noticed, and smiled at her before continuing.

'I should explain – we want profits first and foremost, but not at any price. It makes good business sense to do it properly – and I'm not just spouting stuff out of the annual report, it's the voice of bitter experience speaking. You must find that in your work too, Alex, you reap what you sow – in Zambia anyway, maybe not in DRC. You can't always plan for conflict zones – never know what might happen.'

The worry beads clicked as he spoke.

'Anyway,' he continued, 'I'm trying to get good commercial operations set up on both sides of the border with DRC – make sure that each country gets its share, that workers get properly paid, that working conditions are at least adequate. That way you don't have this abysmal spectacle you see in the Sunday papers back home – poor people, little kids, scrabbling with their bare hands for toxic deposits that they have to pay some dangerous middleman to exploit in the first place. People get angry about the Americans setting up there, talk about exploitation, but frankly, you should see the mess some of the Indians and Chinese have made – now the going's getting a bit tough they're beginning to cut and run, leaving it for poor old Congo to sort out.'

The worry beads were in a frenzy of movement between his thumb and fingers now and he suddenly laughed, stopped and looked around at the solemn faces around the table. 'Sorry, it gets me riled up, I'm afraid. Did someone say something about lunch? I could eat a horse.'

'Be careful what you wish for,' said Lizzie. 'It ain't horse but it's probably about that size. Come on.'

Nearing their table, Lizzie was disappointed to see that Luc Delfosse and René Gilles were there before them, smoking and drinking beer, heads together, deep in conversation, oblivious to the world around them. Lizzie peered as intently as she could at Luc's cigarette and either it was one of the yellow-wrapped corn-paper Gitanes that Sylvie had mentioned or she had been unintentionally looking at the sun. She was about to nudge Alex and mention the cigarette when Luc looked up and an expression of shock swept across his square, pugnacious face. His chair slid back with a screech and he marched forward. Lizzie thought for a moment that he was about to hit her and froze where she stood, but she was not his goal.

'Monk! What the hell are you doing here?'

'Well, how nice to see you, *Professeur* Delfosse. It's been a while. Shame you didn't get that stake in the Big Hill after all that wheeling and dealing. Did I hear that your operations are under investigation again? Or am I thinking about last year, or was it the year before – time passes so quickly in Lubumbashi, doesn't it?'

Lizzie pulled out a pen and notepad and scribbled down three words for later investigation with Edward: Big, Hill and Lubumbashi. Anything connected with the ugly little toad Delfosse was potentially suspect.

'Never mind my business,' Luc stabbed at the air with a nicotine-stained finger, 'I am a highly regarded, world-class academic researcher in France. I am stuck here in this Camp because a fat, corrupt African official is working for your British friends. But I will not be stopped. So you – you just keep out your big English nose. I warn you—'

'Warn me! That's rich. I'm here on holiday, Luc, I'm also doing this highly regarded English academic a good turn because some bastard stole all his excavation kit – not the kind of thing that should happen to a genuinely world-class researcher. Then, I suppose you wouldn't recognise a real intellect from an insignificant piece of rotten garbage like yourself, would you, even with a *very* big nose?'

René had joined Luc now and was holding him by one arm and muttering in his ear. Luc, plainly furious, listened against his will. He shrugged off the hand but returned to his seat and pointedly turned his back to the little group. At that moment Birgit came around the back of the bar. Her glance swept past her one-time friend and she pulled up the chair next to Luc and sat without a word or a smile.

The midday sun beat down upon the desiccated ground, the air was clear and still, the natural world lay languid in the heat, but the icy finger of menace reached out and sent a shiver shooting down Lizzie's spine.

Chapter 23

Dozens of baboons, digging for tubers in the dusty soil of the sun-bleached riverbank, scattered before the youngsters tromping towards lunch. Squeals were struck from the floor as the students dragged out heavy wooden chairs and a babble of high-pitched voices rose roofwards with the cigarette smoke. Zach had just begun describing an ingenious fundraising scheme, using online social networking sites, when the brash clatter of a helicopter shattered the midday calm. Everyone, including Gabriel behind the bar, instantly abandoned what they were doing and ran out to look at the source of the noise.

Just above the trees, their dry leaves rattling in the artificial wind, a man clutching a rifle leaned out of the throbbing whirligig, precariously perched half in, half out, with one foot braced against the leg of the machine. Jake Deacon's trademark hair was tidied back in a pony tail with a dull baseball-cap rammed down over his head, his clothing an uncharacteristically bland blur of camouflage colours. Lizzie noted his rather more characteristic something-of-a-leer grin. The 'copter began to veer away and within seconds had vanished from view, if not from earshot.

'The flying vet pays a flying visit,' frowned Maggie, 'that's not like him – he usually stays out of our way when he's darting.' She turned to Lizzie. 'Must mean there's something really big stuck in a snare somewhere nearby. Either that or he's trying to impress someone.'

'Like who?'

Alex tapped her arm and nodded in the direction of a tall, slim figure, her helmet of blonde hair glistening in the sun, striding off down the staff path.

'Oh dear. Birgit. She's not speaking to me. I think she knows we sent Jake to talk to her. He probably told her, knowing him. Oh, honestly, I'm tired of all this silliness. Why can't everyone just grow up?'

Thomas cleared his throat, theatrically. They all turned to face him.

'Maggie,' he enquired, 'tell me, is one able to communicate with our friend in the gyratory machine?'

'They're probably on radio, but I've never tried it. Why?'

'I have an idea. My friends, bear with me. If Maggie can help me, I may be able to acquire some useful information.'

He put one hand on Maggie's shoulder as they turned and walked off, chatting, towards the office.

Lizzie bit back her annoyance, itching to know what Thomas was up to, having no option but to wait. Frustrated, she was reduced to pacing to and fro under the big tamarind tree, watched by curious little grey faces perched up in its branches, while Alex headed back to the table with Edward and the students. At least that was good news – discussing the school's needs with a rich, well-connected businessman was likely to be constructive, if not downright lucrative.

She had stopped pacing and was standing, staring out at the river, wondering if she was ever going to get back to hunting for more of the extinct baboons' bones she had been after when this whole mess began, when Thomas and Maggie returned.

'He's wasted on the Parks,' said Maggie, 'he should be running New Scotland Yard.'

'Come on, Thomas,' Lizzie was terse, her patience at breaking point, 'what have you been up to?'

The response took everyone by surprise. Thomas puffed out his chest, put his feet a pace apart, spread his arms wide – and burst into song.

'When the foe-man bares his steel, Tarantara! tarantara!

We uncomfortable feel, Tarantara!

And we find the wisest thing, Tarantara! tarantara!

Is to slap our chests and sing, Tarantara! tarantara!'

It was a short but impressive performance.

'Well, my friends,' a breathing space, accompanied by Thomas wiping his forehead with a clean white handkerchief, 'I hope the reference was not lost on you?'

'I haven't a clue what's going on. What *was* that?' asked Amy.

'That was the policemen's chorus from the Pirates of Penzance, an operetta by Gilbert and Sullivan. I did so enjoy them at Cambridge, though I had to keep it quiet – my fellow graduates derided them as *bourgeois.* But I digress, as usual. Professor, I have been in touch with our aerobatic veterinarian and he is *en route* to take some nice digital photographs for us of the living accommodation of the man who may or may not be French, Belgian or Congolese, the same man who lives down by the water and who makes us quite rightly nervous of going down to the woods today lest we get a big surprise – one which is not benign like a teddy bear's picnic.'

'Thomas,' said Lizzie, shaking her head, 'you wear me out. I can almost imagine a reverse colonisation with you invading England and teaching us all about stiff upper lips and cricket and Gilbert and Sullivan.'

'It would be a pleasure. Though my cricketing skills are far inferior to my interpretation of your musical heritage. Shall we retire to the luncheon table where we may also drink hot tea to cool us down?'

Lizzie really did feel dazed. Thomas was like a toy box, you never knew what was going to come spilling out. He made her feel as if she was in the midst of one of those old French farces, where people keep coming and going by different doors missing each other, but seen by the audience. She was missing things, that she knew. Lizzie sat, subdued, as everyone chattered and egged each other on with more and better and wilder ideas for raising money. At last the arrival of lasagne reduced the noise to a manageable level.

'Lizzie,' Alex said, between mouthfuls of pasta and salad, 'you know I said I'd found a site and we'd have to camp, how do you feel about setting off tomorrow?'

Lizzie felt slightly sick at the thought and pushed away her plate, the salad all eaten and the pasta barely touched.

'I'm not sure. Right now it feels rather scary and a bit daunting.' She shrugged. 'It's a lot to organise – food, equipment, water. But if you think we can do it, let's go for it.'

Alex put his hand on hers. 'I was thinking, I could go alone, leave you here with Maggie and Gus. I don't want you to feel you have to come, I know you hate camping with students.'

'I don't hate it, I just don't like it very much. I hate digging a hole to go to the loo, there's never enough vegetation around these places. Then there are the insects and scorpions and snakes.' She shrugged. 'Other than that it's great fun.'

She looked at Alex with an expression that said, 'I'm sorry, I can't help it.'

'You don't have to come,' Alex said. 'And I know what you're going to say, you'll worry – but I'll have a scout and Edward said he would come, he's good with guns, apparently. I don't like the idea of leaving you behind with all this madness going on, but you and Thomas seem to be getting somewhere at last. You've got that look in your eyes – and you haven't mentioned *Theropithecus* in days, that's always a sign.'

Lizzie grimaced. 'Funny you should say that, I was thinking about the bones when I was waiting for Thomas – but it wasn't like, wow, I must get out on the trail again, it was more, damn those bloody bones for getting me into this mess. But I ought to get on with it, my work ought to come first.'

'Why? You're not on a deadline or a grant. You're here because you want to be – OK, and because you want to find more *Theropithecus* – but you don't *have* to do it. And surely it's more important you find out who the hell murdered Harvey Miller – not to mention who nicked my stuff and ruined the site? Thomas is good, he's got all the local insights and the contacts – but he's got a day job. And a family. You've got the luxury of time *and* independence. He needs you.'

Lizzie sat very still, very quiet. Then she shook her head.

'I wish it didn't have to be like this. I don't want to let you go out there on your own, but you're right. I'd be more useful staying here and helping Thomas. Sergeant Phiri's not as useless as I thought he'd be, but there's no way he's going to sort this out alone.'

'Listen. I'll ask Thomas if we can get a scout and permission to camp. If he says yes we'll do it as quickly as we possibly can, just a test dig to see what's there, OK?'

Lizzie nodded, sad, but relieved. Alex was right. She needed space to think, time to discuss things properly with Thomas – and Sergeant Phiri.

Alex grasped her hand under the table, squeezed it, then turned to Thomas and began the arduous process of leaving.

An hour later and it was all agreed: Thomas would provide a scout, possibly Isaiah, for a three-night camping trip and Edward would join them – bringing a rifle for which he miraculously seemed to have a permit. The students were buzzing with adrenaline at the news, more than ready for adventure after the enforced quietude of dig-less days.

Lizzie went back to the little cottage alone, ostensibly to make some notes. She felt and looked despondent. She had her pad of paper, her pen and her peace and quiet, but she was not sure she wanted it any more. Sitting on the verandah, her thoughts turned to Jake. A mental picture of the vet, leaning out of that helicopter wearing a boring baseball cap and unusually dull clothes, popped up in her brain. He had looked so like Harvey Miller, it was disconcerting. An uncomfortable memory came back to her: she saw Birgit's expression change at the moment they realised the body they had found was not Jake, but Harvey. It had seemed beyond mere relief, more like joy.

Birgit had been behaving so strangely this trip. Last year and the year before they had become friends, or so she thought, and now ... Now the young woman had taken up with a creepy married man, was that the top and bottom of it? Had she changed her view of Birgit just because she had rotten taste in men? She sighed and shook her head to bring herself out of the pointless inner debate. But then Simon's words popped into her head, 'I feel in my heart that she is not good inside.' She was not the only one who had her doubts about Birgit.

The sun was almost two hours from setting and the day was hot. She stepped off the verandah and listened for noise coming from the campsite. She could hear nothing. If it was quiet she could slip into the tiny pool for a little while, float away her tensions and dry off before sundown. She went back into the room, pulled on her swimsuit and wiggled her feet into Kenyan leather sandals. Pulling the door to behind her, she locked up carefully before heading down the little path running through the bushes which would bring her out at the back of the campsite. It was as quiet as she could have wished. A man in the purple shirt of the bar staff sat behind the counter reading a thick, dog-eared paperback left by a guest. Another in bright blue overalls and worn tropicals was rhythmically brushing the concrete floor, his Sisyphean task to clear it of lizard droppings, cigarette stubs and tufts of thatch dislodged by tree squirrels.

Lizzie dragged a heavy wooden lounger out from the benign shade of the thatch into the hostile sun. She threw down her towel and tiptoed over on the sizzling patchwork of concrete to sit on the edge of the pool, dangling her legs in the warm water. She felt the tension dissolving. Way across the river, on the opposite bank, she could just make out a large group of elephants dusting themselves with sand. She edged into the water and, wafting her arms gently from side to side, floated her troubles away.

By the time a random child in lime-green water-wings splashed in to interrupt her solitary soaking, Lizzie was ready to emerge and climbed up the chrome ladder, back onto the scorching crazy paving. She flopped on her lounger and lay back on the knobbly old cushion to dry off naturally, indulging in a few rare, brief minutes of unprotected sunbathing before she either applied her factor 60 sun screen or retreated into the shade.

It was too good to last. She screamed when a shower of cold water landed on her bare belly and sat up with a start to discover Jake Deacon standing over her with a smirk on his face.

'You bastard!' she hissed.

'Sorry – I couldn't resist, never was very good with temptation. Here let me—'

'Don't you dare.'

Lizzie was up out of her lounger in a flash, grabbing the towel from his hands.

'Honestly, Jake, you drive me nuts. I get five minutes peace and quiet and what do you do? Ruin it.'

'I bet you were a Catholic, weren't you? Remember the old fashioned Catechism? No, neither do I, really. But I remember my granddad repeating it, trying to make me learn it, "Who made me? God made me? Why did God make me?" and before he could get to the next bit I would really piss him off by yelling, "to be a pain in the neck". That's my role in life, the little demon with a tiny pitchfork, pricking you in the sensitive bits.'

'You do a bloody good job of it.'

'Fancy a drink? Go on, my treat, then we can look at dirty pictures together.'

Lizzie, who had been drying off her ankles, looked up, interested.

'Pictures? The ones you've just taken?'

'The very same,' he rejoined, 'so, white wine? *Mosi?* Sprite? Africoco? Come on, name your poison.'

'I haven't heard that one for a while, Jake, sounds like something else your granddad would say. I'll have a Schweppes lemonade, thanks. And a glass, please.'

'Your wish is my command.' He bowed with a smirk.

Lizzie shook her head in mock exasperation as he sauntered over to the bar. Shading her eyes with her hand she watched him, taking note of his clothes. He had changed since his flight, he was back in floppy green shorts, a loud, baggy floral shirt and ancient leather sandals that looked like they'd spent a lifetime under Gandhi. Unlike Gandhi his thick hair fell in waves from his hatless head, loose and suspiciously evenly streaked with blonde. He looked nothing like Harvey Miller now. It was probably just a red herring, Lizzie decided, but one worth keeping on the list. She looked around and realised she had not brought her pad with her.

She pulled the lounger back into the shade, alongside another. If she stayed in the sun she would have to put on sunscreen and she was not about to give Jake the satisfaction of offering to help apply it – or of watching her do it herself, for that matter.

The vet came back carrying a tray loaded with glasses, bottles and fruit chutney crisps.

Jake lit up an unusually fresh looking cigar and leant back on his lounger.

'Great view from up there. Shame I can't fly it myself, I'd be in voyeur heaven. You look so cute from a bird's perspective you know.'

Lizzie was ready for it this time and did not even blush.

'I noticed Birgit was there too, she hasn't spoken to me since we tried to put her off Luc Delfosse. Did you tell her that Alex and I spoke to you about it?'

'I didn't need to, she guessed. Give her time, she'll come around, she's in a place I don't understand and I don't think she's interested in anyone else right now. She does have her dark side you know, she gets all introspective – not my forte, deep and meaningful.'

Lizzie said nothing, just narrowed her eyes and looked at him.

'What?' he said.

'I don't really believe you – I think there are depths to rival the deepest ocean behind those bloodshot eyes of yours.'

'If that's what turns you on, princess, I'm Mr Deep. Plumb my depths. Please, baby, please!'

'Oh shut up,' she laughed, 'where are those pictures, you idiot?'

He handed her the camera, took a deep drag on his cigar, then blew the smoke in a steady stream up towards an excited tree squirrel squeaking in the rafters.

Lizzie squinted at the small screen of the camera.

They sat in silence.

'This one,' asked Lizzie, 'where was this – the same place?'

Jake leant over her. 'It's an outbuilding near his main house. He's got a pretty fancy place by local standards, a bit like the chalets here but bigger, brick built to about three or four feet, then mostly wood, bamboo and screens under thatch. I reckon he must have at least four rooms in there, or one mighty big one – and as for that outbuilding, I shudder to think what goes on in there. Look,' he zoomed in on the picture, 'loads of rubbish lying around – can't make out exactly what, need to put it up on a laptop and get a better look. What do you think?'

'Looks suspiciously like excavation kit to me. But I'll suspend judgement till I see it on a bigger screen. Did you see any sign of the man himself?'

'Yeah! Great thing with this beauty, they hear the noise and come running to look before they realise how low you are – he took a few seconds to realise I had a camera. I got one shot but he was a bit quick so it's not very good, scroll down a few more.'

'Oh yes, you can just make out he has dreadlocks. Never seen that around here before – well not long ones anyway.'

'There are a few incomers with them – but he's definitely not someone I recognise – I'm guessing he keeps a low profile. So, what next? Does it help at all? Thomas was pretty excited by the idea of snapping the guy's pad but he didn't say why.'

'I don't know what Thomas had in mind,' said Lizzie, hesitantly, 'but, whatever, now we can see there's a real out-of-towner living nearby – he could be one of our runaways from that abandoned vehicle. Not the injured one, he's probably holed up nursing his wounds. So maybe he's our driver. What do you reckon?'

'I think we need to take a closer look. He's seen me anyway, so I could drop by and tell him I'm looking for a wounded animal, couldn't find it in the open, think it's taken shelter somewhere. His grounds are quite thickly wooded, but it looks like he's got electric fencing directly around his house and that little patch of garden – see,' he pointed to the small screen, 'to keep the ellies out, I presume. Thomas could come with me for company, or protection.'

'Too dodgy. If he's got guns he might just use them – and you never know, there may be other people indoors. Anyway, what would we gain?'

'We'd be able to tell what all the crap around the place is – whether it's Alex's kit or something else – or just rubbish. I dunno, I just have this itchy feeling that there's something going on there we need to know about.'

'I know what you mean, but if he is one of the baddies then he probably wouldn't hesitate to have a pop at you. He might be the man who killed Harvey.'

'I guess. Might be best to leave it for now. Tell you what, I'll see if I can get out with a scout patrol over the other side – take my telephoto lens with me.'

'That might be a better idea. Less chance of him taking a shot at you both. I'd hate to see anything happen to Thomas, those two little girls and his poor wife – I'm amazed she recovered so well from the little boy's death.'

'No choice really, was there? And thanks for your concern, Professor, I love you too.'

'Well obviously I don't want you to get shot either – oh, stop it, Jake,' she snapped at him as he puckered up his lips in a mimed kiss, 'can't you be serious for more than a minute at a time? Don't answer that. Look, elephants crossing the river down there. I think I'd better get back to our little cottage – Alex'll be back soon. He's going out to do a test excavation on a new site tomorrow – he'll be gone a few days. Are you around?'

'If you're lonely, princess, I'm your man.'

'Not quite what I meant, just wondered if you might have time to help if necessary, so I'll take that as a yes. Seeing Leah tonight?'

'No. She's too busy, she says. I'll have dinner here then pop by Osca's or Wild-Dogs – fancy joining me?'

'Not tonight.'

'Oh yeah, lover boy's leaving tomorrow. Nookie time. So how about tomorrow night?'

'Maybe. Ask me again tomorrow. Second thoughts, why not, it could be useful.'

'Useful wasn't exactly what I had in mind, but it's a start. I'll be in touch. *Ciao bella*, take care of that lovely body – and I'll see you later.'

Lizzie hurried on her way, leaving Jake to watch the heavens mutate in glorious technicolour as the Gods turned out the celestial light for another night. She had left it almost too late. The sky was darkening rapidly, she could hear the hippos' humourless chortling as they made their way landwards for the night's grazing. Mindful of the contrasting, almost silent way the elephant migrated through the undergrowth at dusk, she picked her way quickly through the bushes, keeping an eye out for the least sign of movement. Sniffing the air she detected an odour like sweaty horses. So, it was true, Alex could smell them coming. Even without the smell she had known, instinctively, there were elephants around. She just prayed they weren't behind the next bush.

By the time she reached the relative safety of their homely cottage Lizzie was twice as tense as when she had left for her relaxing soak in the pool. Standing on the verandah, looking out at the river glistening like a slick of black treacle drizzled across the landscape, Lizzie realised she was not just anxious, she was downright scared. And for the next three nights she would be scared – and on her own.

Chapter 24

Lizzie was curled up on the bed, fast asleep, when Alex returned to the little cottage to pack his own belongings for the trip. He reached out to touch her slender arm, sprinkled with the sun's golden gift of freckles.

'Lizzie,' he spoke softly, and she stirred. Lizzie opened her eyes.

Alex sat on the edge of the bed.

'Lizzie, you left the door open. Promise me you won't do that again?'

'Oh shit, you are joking? I intended to lock it, I must have forgotten.' She shook herself awake. 'You know, I think I might see if Maggie has a spare sofa in the main house. I have to be honest, I'm feeling a wee bit worried about being here on my own.'

'Only a wee bit? I'm beginning to think you should come with us after all. I'll be worried sick all the time, thinking about you forgetting to lock doors and look after yourself properly.'

'Don't be silly,' Lizzie slid off the bed and stretched, 'I'm much better at looking after me than you think – especially when no one else is around to do it for me. Come on, get your packing done and I'll buy you a big glass of wine and you can relax.'

It was an unspoken pact, 'we'll both accept that we don't like this and pretend it is all absolutely normal'. It was easier that way.

As Alex closed the door on the packed bag and turned the key, Lizzie shut her eyes and shook her head. It had only been four nights ago that someone had crept into their room and stolen her laptop. And that door had been locked.

Jumping into the Land Rover they headed for the bar. They were early, dinner was nowhere near ready and the students still over at the campsite. Lizzie organised the promised glasses of wine and the two of them strolled out to the little wall above the riverbank where they sat, drinking in the sounds of the night with their generous glasses of boxed South African red, looking up at a night sky brilliant with stars.

'We're lucky, aren't we?' Lizzie said, at last.

'We are.' Alex took a sip of his wine. 'Especially me. But why now in particular?'

'I don't know, so many reasons. We're alive for a start. We don't hate each other like Sylvie and Luc, we're not sad gits like Harvey Miller was, I'm not destined to fall in love with all the wrong men like Birgit, you've got a big grant to do stuff you really enjoy – and I have the luxury of being able to come with you and fit in my own passion for dead and buried baboon bones. It's a lot to be grateful for, don't you think?'

'Mm. How does René Gilles fit into your picture of perfection?'

'What? Oh bugger.'

Sure enough, the Frenchman was heading towards them with a purposeful look on his face.

'Good evening, Professor, Doctor, please, I do not wish to interrupt. I simply ask if you can tell me anything about Sylvie? I think Luc is now forgetting to be interested, but me, I worry for her – is she well? Do you know where she is?'

'She's fine, René,' answered Lizzie, 'but she asked us not to tell anyone where she is – she did ask about you though, last I heard, so I will tell her you asked after her when I see her again.'

'Please, do that for me. Perhaps you can also give her this small gift from me, I know she likes to smoke the *blondes* – they are a special cigarette in France – I have found this carton in Luc's room, he will not miss them. She will not enjoy the local ones, this I know from the past, in Congo.'

He hesitated.

'If I may, I want to say sorry for how Luc is. We cannot be what we are not. He is a man who is sad in some ways, his life has been not too easy, but he is better than he seems. *Voilà*, I have said what I must – I will leave you to drink in peace. Oh – one thing more – did you know that we have some more colleagues here in Mfuwe now? They are from America, they stay at the lodge a long way out in the Park, Chimbwe I think it is. That bone, it is like a magnet, *non*? But I wonder why they choose this place so far from where you find the fossil jaw?'

'I don't know.' Lizzie's voice was flat and dull. 'I'm sure they have some reason. Never mind. It's just a bone.'

'You are correct in this, it is just a bone, an important bone, but not the *san gréal*, the holy grail. I feel we become like a film of Indiana Jones, it is all too much a drama.'

'I quite agree. But you know what palaeontologists are like, René, and without being unkind, Sylvie and Luc are not exactly shining examples of good behaviour.'

'You are right. There may be reasons … but now is not the time. One day perhaps I will explain a little more, but not now. I must go before Luc arrives back – please tell Sylvie that if there is anything I can do, she must ask. I am here. Good bye.'

With that he turned his back on them and walked away, leaving the carton of *Gitanes* on the little wall.

'More vultures.' Lizzie's words were only just audible. 'Alex, I can't bear it.'

Alex reached out for his wife and pulled her towards him. He wrapped both arms around her and hugged tight, feeling her breathing, deeply, as she struggled to stay calm. After a few seconds her breaths came more normally and she let out a deep sigh. Alex unclasped his arms and took her face in his hands, looking into her eyes for signs of tears.

'I'm sorry, it's just that – coming on top of you going away and everything. It'll be alright,' she said, with an attempt at a smile, 'and anyway, it was only a matter of time. But at least there's one small blessing to come out of the theft of that wretched laptop – no one at Chimbwe can give away the location of the bone because that's already out there. All they could do is tell them where else we looked and that's no use to them, is it? It's like eliminating a few little straws in a haystack. Come on, let's drink to the Americans.'

She picked up her glass, waited for Alex to lift his and they clinked glasses and drank deep before sitting back down on their crumbling brick perch.

'Alex, I was just thinking about those articles I found in Harvey's room, about minerals and fossils found in similar places. They never actually made the connection explicitly in writing, but it was implied. And it's logical if you think about it – if you find bones of a certain type and you almost always find minerals associated with them, then if you find one you find the other. I found that wretched bone, they expect to find minerals. I asked Sylvie if she thought Luc had done the damage to your site and she said he wouldn't dirty his own hands but might have hired someone to do it for him. One of the guys in that sleazy bar perhaps. But I still find it hard to believe he'd go to those lengths.' She frowned. 'Do *you* think that's what Luc and co were really up to? Just looking for minerals? Nothing to do with palaeontology? And if so, what about Harvey?'

'I'm not sure about Harvey, he wasn't exactly living a playboy lifestyle, was he? Maybe he'd only just begun to twig what was going on. But as for the Belgians – if it was going to make them money you can bet they'd be up to their necks – look at their lifestyle – properties here, there and everywhere – not a solitary suburban semi, like us.'

'That's a bit unfair, it's a jolly nice semi with lots of Edwardian features and a very pretty garden.'

'You know what I mean, Eliza. It's very nice, but it's not a watermill, is it?'

'Alex,' Lizzie ignored him and carried on with her speculation, 'if there's something about the minerals the Delfosses were looking at that makes them likely bedmates with fossils, and if Harvey was writing about mineral leaching and molars – which he was – then it's not just another connection, there's a chance Edward might be able to help us predict where *we* might find more bones. I bet that's what Harvey was up to. I don't really see him chasing mineral rights – he was genuinely obsessed with fossils, whatever you might say about his disgusting habits – he had a good brain, he was just a sleazebag.'

She took another sip of her wine as Alex waited, patiently, for her train of thought to reach its destination.

'Money. That's the key. Yes. Now I think about it, there was a donation from a commercial company mentioned in the acknowledgements to one of the articles I picked up in Harvey's room. I didn't recognise it, but I bet your Edward would know who they are.'

'All right, let's ask Edward if he knows anything about it. Did you make a note of the name?'

'I did and what's more I might even have it with me.'

Lizzie pulled out her pad from a large sailcloth duffel bag that had seen better days and flipped through the pages.

'Here it is, BelCoMin, that's all it said. And lo, what timing, here comes Edward.' Lizzie jumped up and waved at the approaching figure. 'Edward, just the man we want to see. Would you like a drink?'

'If that's your way of bribing me, then yes. I'll have a G&T please.'

Alex picked up their two empty glasses and was about to make his way to the bar when Gabriel signalled he was coming over. Orders duly taken, they pulled up three of the canvas loungers and sat in a row, Edward in the middle, with their feet propped up on the little wall where Lizzie and Alex had been sitting.

'So,' said Edward, 'what's all this about? How can I help?'

'It's quite a long story,' began Lizzie, 'so unless you can help us with the key thing then I won't bore you with it. Have you heard of a company called BelCoMin?'

'You'd better tell me that long story. BelCoMin is our most serious competitor – they're in all the worst places, like us except more so. They're small enough to be flexible, like us, and privately owned, like us. When you have no scruples that makes for a pretty unholy concoction. Is that enough to be going on with?'

'It's a damn fine start. OK, here's a very short version of a long story. You know about the murder, you know about the thefts and the vandalism. We think they may all be connected. One of the key links is the two French people and a Belgian who are after more of what everyone calls 'my' bone – a jaw of *Homo rudolfensis,* a very rare early human. You haven't met Sylvie because she's in hiding to get away from her horrid husband Luc Delfosse – you do know him, obviously, since he had a go at you when you arrived. Their other colleague is called René Gilles. They write about stuff in the Congo, Kenya and Tanzania – minerals and bones. The dead man, Harvey Miller, had their articles in his possession and had written one himself about fossil molars in the Congo and how mineral leaching affected them. He came out here via Congo – DRC, I mean. So did they. Now he's dead. One of the articles listed BelCoMin as having given them money. Now, that's unusual, we don't really get people giving us dosh in our field. Not normal people anyway and not commercial companies, unless it's help in kind like mechanical diggers and so forth. So, I can tell you lots more, but that's it, in a nutshell.'

'Right,' Edward leant forward and looked at each of them in turn. 'First of all, I want you to know that there can be some pretty nasty people in this business and you'll just have to trust me that I'm not one of them. We try to steer clear of things like human rights violations and avoidable pollution – I'm not saying I'm an angel and sometimes your agents on the ground aren't saints and you have to turn a bit of a blind eye, but, like I said before, having a few scruples makes sound business sense – if you're in it for the long term. Fines can destroy you, so can international blacklisting. Now, your lovely BelCoMin has probably the worst reputation around. No one's ever managed to pin anything on them, but that's because their bribes are just so bloody huge. They milk corrupt officials all over the world – we're not just talking poor old Africa here, far from it. You'd be amazed how easy it is to grease palms in the rich west if you know how – and more importantly, if you know who. We're talking Washington, Geneva, Beijing, London, Rome, Paris – and Brussels.'

Edward stopped for a sip of his gin.

'Brussels has many blind spots. One of them is BelCoMin. It slips under the radar quite deftly. It's Belgian in origin, has offices in Brussels, but for tax purposes claims its HQ is somewhere like Andorra or Monaco – I forget exactly where. Its roots are colonial. Changed its name of course – Belgian Congo Mining and Mineral Exploitation Company was too literal for today's tastes and I guess they thought BelCoMin sounded nice and innocuous. But there's nothing innocuous about it. They pay the worst prices, health and safety is non-existent, they avoid taxes, treat people like scum and to cap it all, they hired mercenaries at one stage to set two warring groups at each others' throats in northern Congo.'

'What a bunch of bastards.' Lizzie was on the edge of her seat, her wine untouched. 'Is there more?'

'There are a couple of other things. Remember I mentioned the Big Hill in Lubumbashi?'

'I do,' Lizzie pointed to her pad, 'in fact I wrote it down so I'd remember to ask you about it. What is it?'

'It's essentially a big slag heap from old mineral extractions. There are lots of these old mining dumps in Africa and it hasn't taken people long to pick up on the fact that reasonable quantities of valuable minerals can still be extracted from the tailings using modern technologies. Enough to make it worthwhile. This particular heap's got Coltan, cobalt and copper in it and there was fierce competition to get involved in exploiting it. Your little friend Delfosse – well, he was doing the front-man job of wheeling and dealing, but it was his wife who was actually on the board of BelCoMin. She was there to give it some academic credibility. Someone told me the wife's father had a stake in it and that's why she was the named one – but anyway, they must have greased all the wrong palms this time because they got nowhere, not even short-listed – some American firm won the main contract and they're sharing it with a DRC government-owned enterprise. All pukka. You don't need to know more than that – but, basically, the Delfosse name became associated with some pretty shady goings-on several years back and my sources tell me they're still poking around the world's dumps looking to make a quick buck.'

'Lovely. Just what we need.' Lizzie turned to make sure that René was no longer within earshot. 'So Luc and Sylvie are both involved in this scurrilous company – what about René Gilles?'

'Don't recognise the name – but I can look him up. If he's here he's probably involved.'

'I agree. Hell, this is awful – as if palaeontologists didn't have a bad enough reputation. Fossil hunting pales into insignificance. Edward, you said Sylvie *was* on the board – is she still, do you know?'

'I don't, but again, I can check for you – in fact anything you need to know about the world of mining and mineral processing, just ask – I'm hooked into all the networks, got all the right subscriptions to online information services – plus some covert sources. Don't ask, just trust me – no animals were harmed in the making of my company!' Edward grinned.

Lizzie warmed to him despite her misgivings about his business.

'How long will it take you to check – I'd really like to know before you go off into the bush. Any chance?'

'I'll do it right now. Got a fab new gizmo gives me instant satellite access to my network. Don't go away.'

With that Edward was gone.

Alex moved into his empty seat and reached out for Lizzie's hand.

'I'm proud of you. You're on the trail now, I can feel it. But, be careful, won't you? Whatever they're after it's obvious those guys will stop at nothing. Yes, I know, it's a cliché. But *if* what Edward says is true, then don't forget they're ruthless enough to start wars – so one little redhead won't stop them in their tracks.'

'I am not a redhead, it's burnished copper. And of course I'll be careful. They scare me, this lot. But they're not in familiar territory here, that's the one really big thing I've got on my side. I know people who know people. Oh, I forgot to tell you, I saw the pics that Jake took – he came over to the campsite. There is a guy in that house who looks Congolese – or at least not local. Jake's going to see if he can go out on patrol with some Parks scouts on the opposite bank and take his telephoto lens. He wanted to pop round and see the guy but I suggested that might be a tad dangerous. One of the pics showed a load of what looked like rubbish strewn around but we wondered if it might be your kit.'

'Thanks, as a professional I always choose to work with rubbish.'

'Don't be silly, I'm not being offensive, it just looked like that from the picture. Anyway, I said I would go out with Jake tomorrow night – I think he's trying to show Leah he can be cool too – she blew him out for tonight, too busy. Got to admire the girl.'

'Girl? How old—'

'Oh, shut up, I just knew you'd say that. She's over 18 so she's a young woman, OK? Why do I do it? I harp on about it myself and then fall into the trap. Anyway, you're distracting me. Jake said he'd take me to Osca's so I thought it might be useful research. Do you think I might dare drop into High Society too for a gander?'

'Lizzie, don't you dare. Promise me?'

'No, I won't,' she said, plainly annoyed. 'What if it helps us find the killer? I mean, if I'm with Jake they're not going to drag me off and rape me, are they? And as long as I'm sober I'll be fine.'

'I'll talk to Jake,' Alex muttered.

'No you will not! I'm not a child.'

A laugh came from behind and they turned to see Edward bearing down on them.

'Never too old to talk like a teenager, eh? Vickie used to say that to me all the time. Now, would you like the good news or the bad news?'

Lizzie turned to Alex, he looked up at Edward and spoke for them both.

'Bad.'

'René Gilles is up to his neck. No criminal convictions, but plenty of rumour and enough well-founded speculation to damn him. He's not even with a university any more, his last one kicked him out – can't find out what for. Could be an affair with a student, could be falsifying results – no one will tell. Looks like someone paid handsomely to cover it up. He's part of a little operation called PalaeoCom

– directors René, Luc and Sylvie, non-exec Chairman Sylvie's dad. It's supposedly a vehicle for their research funds, but where those funds come from is another matter. My source couldn't follow the trail beyond a charitable trust based in the Cayman Islands. It's a registered charity and its business is combining – wait for it – research into fossils with mineral exploration. Supposedly purely educational, not for profit. Believe that, you'll believe anything.'

'Well, it could be worse,' Alex sounded quite relieved, 'and it sounds like Sylvie's father is the money man. So what's the good news?'

'Good news? Well, Sylvie's no longer on BelCoMin's board. Does that count?'

'It's better than nothing,' muttered Lizzie. 'I'm going to have to probe her tactfully about this stuff, see if she'll let something drop by accident. I guess even though he's been such a shit she must have some loyalties to Luc, not to mention her dear old dad, plus there's always the chance she benefited from it anyway.'

'I think you can take that as read. Let's be honest, no one sits on boards for nothing, do they? Especially if they're companies with crap reputations.' Edward was plainly not a man to mince words.

The rattle and clank of a noisy vehicle approaching put an end to their conversation. It signalled the arrival of the students – and Jake. Raucous cries and hoots of laughter floated across the still night air.

Lizzie, Alex and Edward struggled out of their low-slung chairs and wandered over to the chirpy bunch at the bar.

Leah was looking wild, her hair gelled into spikes, her eyes black with liner and her lips cherry red. Jake was completely incapable of keeping his eyes – or his hands – off her. The rest of them were fired up by the prospect of the next day's trip and eager to take advantage of the bar, their last chance for several days. Edward's generosity spilled out into drinks and soon the whole crowd was gathered around the newly lit camp fire – superfluous but cheerful on a warm winter's night – toasting Vickie's dad with beer, wine and Amarula.

Lizzie touched Alex's arm to gain his attention and whispered in his ear, 'Look over there, Birgit. I need to make it up with her, what do you think, tackle her now?'

Alex watched the guide stop outside the kitchen and turn towards them, as if she sensed they were talking about her.

'Good idea, hurry before she vanishes.'

Lizzie ran off, leaving Alex to re-immerse himself in the chattering troupe around the fire.

Lizzie realised she had no idea what she was going to say. She stopped right in front of Birgit and neither of them spoke.

Finally, Lizzie opened her mouth and words came out, not quite the ones she would have chosen.

'I'm worried about you, Birgit. What's going on?'

Birgit looked startled.

'I don't know what you mean. Why should you be worried, I am an adult.'

Lizzie laughed, then realised Birgit would not know why.

'Sorry, it's just that I just said that to someone now and was accused of being a teenager. I'm not suggesting ... Look, let's sit down and have a proper talk. I'm worried about you because of Luc Delfosse, because of Jake, because of all sorts of things. Are you all right?'

'I'm fine. My love life is none of your concern. I do not care for Jake any more, so you need not worry about that. I have met a man, a real man. Yes, he is married, but I don't think he will be married for long. You have no idea what this is like – love at first sight. It is something you cannot control, you just know. He has some money, he is going to find somewhere – here or somewhere else in Zambia, or some other African country if we cannot find the right place here, where I can work as a guide, where we can live together.'

'Birgit, you've only known him a couple of days! What do you know about his past? That man is not what you think.'

'Not what I think? Tell me, Lizzie, what do I think?'

'I'm sorry, but really – how much *do* you know about him? Where did he get this money he's promising – he's an academic, how come he has money? I don't.'

'I am not prepared to talk about this any more. This relationship may come to nothing, as you rightly point out we have only just met. So if it comes to nothing you can laugh all you like. But I am going to give it a chance.'

With that Birgit walked off.

She had disappeared from view and Lizzie was about to return to the bar when Simon emerged from the side of the kitchen.

'I am sorry, I did not mean to listen. Professor, there is one other thing I must tell you. My friend's sister she cleans rooms here, she says Birgit made friends with another man before this one you do not like. This man looked like Jake Deacon, she thought it was him, but no, she sees he is older and he smells strange. This man, he stays all night with Birgit, this man is the dead man now.'

The words forming in her brain never made it to her lips – a good thing as they would have upset the religious Simon. She thanked him, then took her time returning to the bar, where she decided to break her two-drink rule. She lifted the brimming glass poured by Gabriel, took a gulp of the wine and put it down carefully on the bar. She had lost a friend. The question was, had she ever really known her? She thought back to that dreadful moment when she first saw the dead body, pecked by vultures, gashed and gory. Could she trust anything she had seen or heard? Was all this talk of Coltan and copper and cobalt just a diversion, was the motive for Harvey's murder that most basic of human instincts after all?

Birgit had lied. She had been pleased when she 'realised' the dead man was Harvey Miller. Was that the sane reaction of a woman who had shared her bed with him, possibly the night before? Lizzie felt sick. It was a dreadful thought, but even her own reactions dismayed her. Was she happier accepting a world where three apparently civilised human beings had ruthlessly exploited vulnerable people, incited violence and defrauded governments, rather than believing a one-time friend had slipped from the realms of sanity into the madness of murder?

This profound moment was the one Jake chose to creep up behind her and whisper in her ear.

'Cheer up sweetheart, I'm all yours tomorrow night. That ought to put the smile back on your pretty little face.'

Lizzie turned to look at him and he realised, instantly, that she was not in the mood for flirtation.

'Hey, what's wrong, Prof? You look dreadful. Has something happened?'

'Jake, listen, you know Birgit better than anyone. I need you to tell me, no joking, I mean *really* seriously, do you think she is at all – well – mad?'

Jake stood staring at her for several seconds. Lizzie stared back.

She blinked, then spoke.

'I think you're saying yes. Am I right?'

'She's not absolutely barking, at least I don't think she hears voices and stuff, but she's not what you might call well-adjusted. Listen,' Jake pulled out a cigar stub and rolled it around between his finger and thumb, 'don't get me wrong, I don't like to bad mouth anyone I've shagged, but I put up with a lot for the action in the sack. I know you don't want to hear this so I won't make too much of it, but it was good, the sex. She knew it and she used it. I realised after a while she was probably a bit off the rails – obsessive compulsive at the very least, possibly bipolar. A very difficult bunny to stroke. If I knew then what I know now I wouldn't have touched her with a barge-pole, sex or no sex. I've been keeping my hand in every now and again for obvious reasons – I'm just a man when all's said and done – but also to keep her on a relatively even keel. Which may have been a mistake.'

'But you went along with the whole "nasty Jake, I'm really hurt, he's a bastard" thing – why?'

'It was easier that way – and probably not bad for my reputation, let's be honest.'

'You idiot! Listen, I really need to understand, are you saying you genuinely think she might have serious behavioural problems?'

'Serious. I mean like weird central. And while we're talking about weird behaviour, let me tell you that her concern for animals doesn't extend to humane killing – I once found a dead baby monkey on her verandah. I asked what had happened to it. She said she had smothered it, said she couldn't face using an axe or a knife but that it had drunk some bleach from the cleaner's bowl. Stupid story. It hadn't. She knew it and I knew it – and she knew I knew it. Monkeys don't drink stuff that smells that weird and I'm not blind. Plus. Here's the thing. I picked it up to check it was dead when she went in to fix a drink. It had been strangled, not smothered. I might even go so far as to use the term garrotted for the second time in a week.'

'Do you realise what you're saying?'

'I do. But part of the reason I'm being straight with you is that I think it's highly unlikely.' He lit his cigar stub and took a drag. 'God, but I'm being calm. Don't you just admire my composure under pressure?'

Lizzie brushed his attempt at light-heartedness aside, impatiently, 'You're telling me that this woman that I thought I knew can strangle an innocent young animal. Don't you think it's within the bounds of possibility that she could have gone a wee bit further and killed a human being?'

'Listen, if she did garrotte Harvey Miller then there'd have to be a reason. I'm going to tell you something I haven't told anyone else except Gus – so don't pass it on. I've been getting death threats, letters in the post, from someone who knows a hell of a lot about my intimate lifestyle. And I mean *intimate*. I told Gus as insurance, just in case anything happens. Now, even though I'm sure as dammit they're from Miss Scandinavia's poison pen, I don't really think she means it, they're just another part of her weirdness. I mean, she ain't done anything – I'm still here. And she's had her chances. Why would she go for this Miller guy – I mean, it's not as if she'd been shagging him, is it?'

Lizzie looked him in the eyes.

'Oh yes, Jake, I'm very much afraid she had.'

Chapter 25

Back at their cottage, Alex packed his bags as Lizzie recounted Jake's startling exposé of Birgit. It did not do anything to ease their anxiety at the imminent parting of their ways. They slipped into bed early, only to pass a restless night. A playful wind arose, blowing the dry leaves in the bushes till they crackled. Every now and then, some small creature walked around the walls of their bedroom, snuffling, crunching the vegetation underfoot, sounding more like T-Rex in the amplifying quiet of the night. Once an hour the *ad hoc* and seriously sober night watchmen, Piet and Andre, made a circuit of the hut, their sizeable feet making proportionate amounts of noise and their rifles at the ready. At one point a leopard coughed gruffly. When dawn began its stealthy theft of night the sleeping couple was far from rested.

Alex lugged his bundles out to the waiting Land Rover while Lizzie, struggling with her wet hair, stood staring out to the opposite bank across the river.

'Jake said he'd be going out on patrol as soon as he could swing it,' she said, almost to herself, 'I wonder if he made it last night? Given Leah had turned him down.'

'Right. I'm ready. Shall we?' Alex was oblivious, focused on his short but critical field trip.

It was the moment they had both been dreading. Lizzie made a show of locking the door and gave him a big, insincere grin. They both clambered aboard and drove off to breakfast without a word. Now their goodbyes had been said, the locking of that door meant the expedition was underway and Lizzie turned her mind to concentrating on the grim task that lay ahead.

By the time the students had arrived, stuffed their hungry bellies with toast and washed it down with strong tea and insipid Ricoffy, Alex was getting twitchy. Edward arrived last at the feast but was ready first, standing in the weak rays of the dawning sun, fiddling with his satellite phone, waiting patiently as the mayhem of loading food and water happened all around him. They were heading out in two vehicles, having the double luxury of a cook who could conjure banquets from seemingly thin air as well as drive their second vehicle.

The water barrel was the last, but arguably most important item to be loaded into the cook's unwieldy-looking van and as the final set of doors slammed on Martin, the last human in, Lizzie's anxiety reached its peak. She stood and waved until a billowing cloud of dust obscured them from view. The sense of desolation was like a wave of suffocating air. Marching over to the bar she forced herself to smile at Gabriel, chat about the man's family – and made herself another mug of Earl Grey while the electricity held and the kettle could still be relied upon to produce hot water.

It was a relief to see Maggie bustling over from her tiny office.

'Good morning, Lizzie, ready for battle? Thomas has been on the phone already. Sergeant Phiri's in Mfuwe, apparently. He stayed with a cousin last night and now he's waiting for a lift up here.'

'What happened to that nice new vehicle Sergeant Phiri confiscated?'

'Ran out of diesel. There's none at the BP station today – tanker's not due in till tomorrow. Thomas has a full tank – some nice English woman apparently filled it up for him the other day – and he needs to go to the airport too, so could bring Phiri here and drop him back at base. But I was thinking, you're probably feeling a bit stir-crazy, I have a parcel to pick up at the airport, so why don't we go and meet them in Mfuwe, take them all to the airport, then we could sit in the café and have a cold drink, drop the good sergeant back at his concrete box when we're finished, drop Thomas back at Parks HQ and, hey presto, be back home by lunchtime.'

'Good plan. I've got an email to send first, then give me five minutes to pick up my pad and pen and I'll be with you – where's your car?'

'Back at the house – I'm off to deal with the kitchen staff now, so you send your email and I'll see you there in fifteen minutes. If you have time, pop in and say hi to Sylvie – she's been very quiet – don't want her getting into a depression.'

With that Maggie trotted off towards the kitchen, Lizzie to the office. It was still early in the day but already it was hot. Lizzie groaned when the scrawny black and white cat arrived, jumped up and draped itself around the middle of her back.

Trawling through Google to find her friend Jess's Bordeaux University email address, she composed what she hoped was a reasonably discreet email, probing her for information about the Delfosses. There was no time for a more thoughtful missive, the electricity could go off at any moment and besides, she wanted a few minutes with Sylvie. She asked Jess to keep the request to herself but tell her anything she knew about the couple's involvement in mineral rights in the DRC – or indeed anywhere else in the world. She added as an afterthought a similar query about René Gilles. No harm fishing for more than one catch at a time, she reckoned.

Back at her cottage, Lizzie changed into one of the smarter shirts she had with her, hung a pair of silver earrings from her lobes, slipped a malachite bracelet onto her wrist and gave her lips a slick of gloss. Just as she was about to leave she remembered the cigarettes René had given her for Sylvie and pulled them out of her duffel bag. Then she stepped out into the sunshine, locked the door behind her, tried the handle just to make sure, and strode off up the little slope to Maggie's house.

The cosmetic touches had made her feel good as she left her temporary home but when she arrived in Maggie's garden and saw Sylvie, looking even more chic than usual, her morale plummeted.

'Honestly, Sylvie, you look so – so *soignée* – there's no English word for it. How do you do it out here? That suit is lovely – what is it made of?'

'This? You are too kind, it is an old thing – a vintage Chanel I buy in one of those London charity shops. I love the feel of raw silk on my skin – and it does not make creases. But you, you look *gamine*, so fresh. And you are going out? That sounds so good, freedom. Me, I am a little tired of this place, I think maybe it is time for me to return to my home, but I wait to hear from my father. He is thinking maybe to fly his private jet here – but then he is a little worried about the small airport in Mfuwe. Perhaps he will just organise tickets. I must be patient a little longer. Maggie and Gus, they are so kind and this scene of the river in front of me – so beautiful, *non*?'

'It is. Never get tired of it. Here,' she held out the cigarettes, 'maybe these will help. René gave them to me for you – he wanted us to tell him where you are and I told him no, he asked me to pass on his best wishes.'

'Wonderful, *blondes,* I can abandon these atrocious Zambian Blue packs.'

Lizzie smiled, distracted. The cigarettes were preying on her mind. René and Luc supposedly liked the same kind, the yellow ones, but she had not seen René smoking them, only Luc – and René had not said anything when she discussed Sylvie's preference for the *blondes* with him. The stubs had only been found at the disturbed sites, they proved nothing, they had not established any real link between the murder of Harvey Miller and the vandalism, or the thefts, but still it niggled her. She made a mental note to check the ones that Thomas was holding as evidence next time they met, to make sure that she was right, that they were *maïs*, not just ingrained with dust from the bush. She pushed the thought to the back of her mind and returned to what Edward had said about Sylvie being on the board of BelCoMin. Time was running out, but Lizzie decided to wait, at least till she had heard back from her friend at the University of Bordeaux. With a bit more time and some inside information, then she would tackle Sylvie about BelCoMin – and about René.

'I wish we could offer you a trip out,' Lizzie said in what she hoped was a bright, breezy, tone, 'but I'm afraid I really must poke my nose into the murder investigation. I'm meeting the top Parks man and we're picking up the police sergeant. We need to find out what's going on before more bad things happen.'

'Ah, you are now the sleuth, is that how you say it? A difficult word to pronounce. Lizzie,' she touched Lizzie's bare forearm, her hand cool and soft with – Lizzie could not help but notice – long, manicured nails, 'you must ask me if you need to know things about Luc or me – there are many things I can tell you. Perhaps I can help a little. Maybe when you return we can have the cup of tea and I can tell you all about our work in Congo? You will be interested about some of it, but maybe not my father's business there, that I find even myself tedious.'

Here she paused and gave Lizzie a look which was possibly meant to be sisterly. But Lizzie was spooked at the sudden change of conversational tack and she felt the wave of goose-bumps ripple across her arms. It was as if Sylvie been listening in on her thoughts. She tried not to show her unease.

'Business, but how does that tie in with your academic work?' Lizzie ventured.

Sylvie continued.

'We spend some interesting time looking for fossils – I pay for this pleasure with pretending to interest myself in minerals – it is not too hard to make this pretence when one gets such exciting fossils in the end. My father, you know he also works in Congo – it is our family history. I do not like it but it pays my father for his lifestyle. He spends too much. I am like the parent, I discipline him! Stop spending, papa, I say, you do not need to make more money if you spend less.' She stopped to light another cigarette.

'Luc, he too is mad for money, my father asked me to be on his board, it is a mining company called BelCoMin. I was not happy to do this. Luc, he pushes me and pushes me and eventually I say yes, if I can spend my own time to find fossils, so he says yes, but happily I have stopped that. I have enough money now to leave it – we set up a small trust to fund this work I like – for me and René it is the fossils that are important. I do not find the business world agreeable and some of the things they have to do are not really human – is that the word? *Ah non*, humane, I think you say. Ask your Mr Monk, he will tell you. But listen,' she paused and raised both elegant hands, 'Maggie she calls, you must leave. Enjoy your *petit voyage*, Lizzie. *A bientôt*!'

The call was a relief. Lizzie had found herself wondering what on earth to say to Sylvie. It was eerie, as if the woman had been inside her head.

Maggie's car, whilst still that bush essential, a four-by-four, was more glamorous than the usual bone-shakers, luxuriating in leather seats, a CD player and air conditioning. Lizzie slithered in and sank back into upholstered luxury.

'Maggie,' she asked, 'do you like Sylvie?'

'Yes, of course. Well, I say yes, I mean, she seems very nice but a bit, I don't know, a bit too considerate, too enthusiastic. Too bloody well turned-out. I do wonder if she's maybe a bit manic under that suave exterior. But then with the life she's had – who knows. Why, what did she say to upset you?'

'Nothing, nothing at all, rather the reverse, she was very nice and very helpful and I came away feeling like she had seen right through me. It was a bit unnerving. How do people do it?'

'They gossip without your noticing, that's how. She spends half her time talking to the staff, the other half peering through binoculars at the campsite and watching animals across the river in the park. She probably knows more about what's going on than we do. She's lonely, sweetie, that's all. But I do think it's time we got her out of here, Luc's not a dope, he'll realise where she is sooner or later, or someone will let it slip accidentally – and I don't want any more trouble.'

'I don't think there'll be any, to be honest. I think he's so besotted with Birgit – and vice versa. Oh God, I had the most awful conversation with her. She hates me. And she's gone all weird. Jake reckons she's always been weird. Borderline mentally ill. And did you know she had slept with Harvey Miller?'

Maggie hesitated, her face a picture of disappointed humanity. 'Oh, Lord. It's still happening then.'

'You mean you knew?'

'I didn't know about Harvey Miller, no. But she's been through a bad patch before. You know, we get some pretty odd people choosing to live here, misfits in one way or another, usually quite pleasant and straightforward, just – well, different. But some of them are troubled, they come to escape something and if it's themselves, chances are they can't. Still, I always imagine that being out here, living with nature, will soothe people's souls. With Birgit, it was fine at the beginning, when she'd just arrived. She did all her exams and passed first time with flying colours, she was a great guide. Then she met Jake. I thought it was his influence. She started behaving oddly. Or maybe I just noticed for the first time. Perhaps I'd been hiding it from myself.'

Maggie looked quickly sideways at Lizzie before turning her attention back to the dusty bush road.

'You were here last summer,' she continued, 'she was still with Jake early on and everything was fine then – well, more or less. She got more and more distracted, to the point where I had to speak to her and tell her to get her mind back on her job. Then Jake started drinking more and coming round here less and I thought it was just his usual gigolo-like way of dropping her because he was tired of her. Then I noticed she had a few flings on the side with guests and they weren't what you might call happy when they left. Now call me old-fashioned, but if a guy comes out here and gets amazing wildlife, good food and hot sex, you'd think he might leave feeling he'd had the holiday of a lifetime, that I'd have lots of satisfied customers, but –'

'Maggie! You weren't turning a blind eye just because you thought she was making your customers happy, were you?'

'Lizzie! What kind of person do you think I am? Of course not – I'm just telling you what I thought was going on.' Maggie looked outraged.

'I'm sorry, it just sounded so strange coming from you – I didn't really – oh never mind, I'm sorry, honest, carry on.' Lizzie clasped Maggie's arm.

'Well, I didn't let it carry on. I told her in no uncertain terms that it had to stop. We had a big row about it and she said she was going to leave. But then her behaviour switched back to what I thought was normal. It's only been the last month or so that's she's started behaving erratically again.'

'So she's been behaving oddly since the start of the season? She was OK when there were no new arrivals, but now there are lots of new people passing through. Does that seem like just a coincidence?'

'When you put it like that, it sounds obvious. But to be fair, I didn't notice any bed-hopping, I thought she was being really mopey, I thought she was still messed up about Jake. I mean, he does appear every now and again.'

Lizzie nodded, 'Yes, he said he feels he has to keep her sweet.'

'Streuth, she must be one hell of an actress. She had me fooled. You're really telling me that Jake's the one who's caught up in the relationship from hell?'

''Fraid so. I presume Gus told you about the death threats?'

Maggie nodded.

'Well,' Lizzie continued, 'he thinks they've definitely been coming from her. Says they reveal an intimate knowledge of his lifestyle – I didn't ask any more, he's told me more than enough already. He thinks she's benignly mad. But when I told him about Harvey, he admitted there was more.' Lizzie related the unsettling story of the baby monkey.

'Oh, God, Lizzie,' said Maggie, 'we have to do something. If there's any chance – Christ, that poor man Delfosse.'

Lizzie snorted. 'Steady on, Mags, not so poor and not so nice. OK, he doesn't deserve garrotting in his sleep, maybe.'

'Too right. But, Lizzie, if you're suggesting Birgit killed Harvey Miller – no, I'm sorry, I just don't buy it. There must be some other explanation. How come she was out there on the walking safari and found him? Wouldn't she choose to go a different route instead of leading you right to him?'

'Maybe she wanted him found, maybe she thought he'd have been well and truly picked over by then? We know there's a leopard living around there somewhere, she could blame him. You know how quickly the vultures zoom in on dead meat. Watch out Mags!'

They stopped abruptly as a huge male elephant stepped into the road in front of them and flapped his ears. Maggie sat calmly revving the engine.

'He drove out there. How did she get back to camp after she killed him?' Maggie asked in a quiet voice, staring hard at the lone elephant in her path as if willing him to walk away.

'She's a guide, she knows her bushcraft, she walked back. We'd walked out there, after all.'

'True. That's my boy, off you go, big fella.' She drove off slowly as the hulking beast slunk into the undergrowth and vanished from sight.

'Anyway,' Lizzie resumed, 'I don't necessarily think it was Birgit, it's just she's suddenly seeming like a possible when before I'd never have connected her with Harvey Miller. Honestly, Maggie, I mean, how gross can you get, it'd be like sleeping with a slimy weasel.'

'You do have a turn of phrase, don't you? Look, we're nearly there now, let's wait till we all get comfortable at the café before we carry on with this, I'm feeling the need for some caffeine. Let's just listen to what our great policeman has to say shall we? He might have some news for us, you never know.'

Thomas was nearly ready when they arrived. Lizzie spent a few minutes diplomatically shaking hands with people she had met before, asking after families and discussing Liverpool's chances of making it to the finals of the European cup again. She had long ago given up the struggle to avoid the so-called 'beautiful game', it was in everyone's blood, or so it seemed.

Lizzie insisted on Thomas taking the front seat when they drove off and Thomas, in turn, insisted on Sergeant Phiri taking the front seat when they picked him up from the BP station. They found him sitting in the shade of the nearest tree, chatting to a very small boy holding a white chicken upside down by its legs. It turned out to have been a negotiation, rather than a chat and the chicken was now in the back of the vehicle, its legs securely tied and placed in a basket Maggie happened to have with her. It would no doubt make a good meal – or two – for the policeman and his extended family. Tying its legs seemed to have rendered it silent, too, there was not a peep out of it all the way to the airport.

It always surprised Lizzie that it took so long to get to the airport, but the forty-five minutes passed quickly as Thomas and Phiri debated, first, the merits of the chilli pepper fence – one of the many weird and wonderful ways of trying to keep elephants off their precious small crops, next the new Internet 'café' – Internet but no café – funded by a generous Japanese donor and finally, how *Chipolopolo,* aka the Copper Bullets, the Zambian national football team, could climb back up from its position at ninety-two in the international rankings.

Maggie parked close to one of the two entrances to the little airport. They all clambered down and while Maggie went off to collect her post, the others wandered over, at a leisurely pace, to the thatched building that housed the café. They all ordered soft drinks and sat outside in the mid-morning warmth, listening to a small plane taxiing around on the runway.

'So, honorary Detective,' began Sergeant Phiri, staring at Lizzie in undisguised fascination, 'tell me about the progress you have made in our investigation.'

'I am not sure where to begin, Sergeant, things are getting very complicated, I must say.' Lizzie waffled on for a few more seconds giving her brain a chance to decide what to say.

'I believe,' she finally said, 'that we have a variety of options as to motive and a variety of suspects. I think that we have two main options for motive: one, that old favourite, passion, human passion, the other mammon, good old money, represented by minerals. At the moment, I think we have one suspect who may be motivated by passion, a young woman, the other possible criminal is a man who is motivated by greed. I am not in a position to prove anything yet, I am afraid, but we are certainly getting nearer to the truth. Or at least, I think we are.'

She smiled at the policeman and he failed to respond. Her heart sank. She turned to Thomas.

'One thing I do want to pursue is cigarettes. Thomas, I believe you have some stubs that were found in various locations? I have some interesting information about cigarettes that may be useful.'

Thomas cleared his throat and at last spoke up.

'That may prove interesting, certainly. But first, let me tell you one of the reasons we came here today, to the airport, is that here we may find extra evidence to substantiate one or more of our pathways of suspicion. Indeed,' continued Thomas, in a pompous tone that sounded unnatural to Lizzie, 'I made contact with the immigration department yesterday. I have asked our good Mr Sakala if he can find any record of the names we see on those three passports that we found in the abandoned vehicle. It may be that this man is the one who is living in isolation.'

'Very good, Dr Nkhoma, very good. I can see we have more than one honorary detective in this lucky town. I must be careful for my job.' At this Phiri showed his perfect teeth in a long drawn out laugh at his own joke.

Maggie arrived back carrying a small parcel. Lizzie jumped up and walked across the dry stubble that masqueraded as grass to buy more soft drinks for them all at the bar. Thomas joined her.

'I am sorry that I was not more enthusiastic about the cigarettes, Professor, I'm afraid we have a small problem. Our best belovèd police sergeant took the stubs away. He also took the passports, but my clever daughter had already scanned the useful pages into the computer in my office. The stubs, alas, are gone with the wind.'

'Are you suggesting there's some hanky-panky going on?'

'Probably just the usual petty venality. But I am a little concerned that all our evidence has evaporated. The cars, the passports, the cigarette stubs and yes, before you ask, the gun. These are all, sadly, things which someone may find useful, even the cigarette stubs which contained more than a little remaining tobacco, certainly enough to be worth making into new cigarettes and smoking. I will try tapping into my juvenile networks, like a more benevolent Fagin, to see if I can find news of these things. Children see much that we do not. But at least I can tell you what the cigarettes looked like, which is important because they were surprisingly yellow, not like the ones we are used to in Zambia—'

'Yellow,' Lizzie broke in, 'you're sure, not just odd but definitely yellow? That's what I thought too, I just thought I might have been imagining it, that's why I wanted to see them again. One of the Belgians must have been at Alex's site and the bone site. Unless someone else has this special type of Gitanes that the Delfosses have with them.'

'Perhaps it is both of them?'

Lizzie sighed. 'No, just one of them. Each has a favourite type, but I can't seem to get to the bottom of who likes which kind. There are 'blondes' and these yellow ones called 'maïs', the French for maize, but they have completely confused me now. Or René and Sylvie have. Which suggests one of them is doing it on purpose. Or both of them. René or Sylvie, oh my goodness...'

'Yes, I wondered if you had made that leap yet. It is most exciting, dear Professor, but I am worried because my word is not evidence. We have nothing left with which to mount a case in court – certainly not one which would satisfy the law in your country. But we must not give up. If we can accumulate enough evidence from other sources and keep it to ourselves – then maybe we can eventually sort this out.'

'Were you serious about immigration helping?'

'Yes. I already know the answers to my questions, but my friend Mr Sakala is from my church and will be circumspect in his dispensation of what we know. We must perform a short drama for an audience of one policeman when we return to the table.'

At that moment Mr Sakala arrived and hurried to join them at the bar. A small, round man, he was dressed in a smart suit and carried a neat briefcase. He and Lizzie went through the usual polite rituals of introduction and the immigration official accepted her offer of a soft drink, choosing Lizzie's own favourite, Grenadilla. As the two of them sipped at their fizzy pop, Thomas kept an eye on the policeman seated at the table.

'Dr Nkhoma tells me you are a great help to him in our troubles,' said Mr Sakala. 'I will not say this in front of Sergeant Phiri, for reasons which will become clear, but I think the passports you have lost are quite important.'

He turned his head towards the table like a nervous bird, as if to check that he was not overheard.

'They are for a real individual, but of course one man should not have three nationalities. This man is really from DRC. He is not a criminal, however, he is in a category I cannot find described – it seems to be something like a diplomatic category, but not from an embassy or consulate.'

He coughed and looked at his neat feet in their black, lace-up shoes.

'I am just a lowly cog in our big machine of immigration, but I have a relative in Lubumbashi who has better knowledge than I, who has very, very good contacts. He tells me – and I must ask you to be very careful with this knowledge – he tells me that this man is almost certainly an agent of a foreign power. If the Sergeant suspects this, he may put this man's life in danger, whether he wishes to or not. This man is most probably working under the cover of an alias. If he is working with criminals, as I suspect, they will not hesitate to kill him if he is found to be a traitor to them.'

'Mr Sakala, this is both good and bad news,' said Thomas, holding his friend's hand, the way Zambian men sometimes do when talking. 'Now, we should perhaps join our guest. Perhaps we can agree to tell the Sergeant a little story. God will forgive us a little deception if it is to save a man's life. I will bear the burden of the lie. I will tell him you have found that these passports are false, which is not entirely untrue, and do not belong to this man living on the edge of the bush which may be what you could call a little white lie.'

Mr Sakala nodded his bald head, putting Lizzie in mind of Buddha. He was a very serene man, she decided, just the kind of man needed in a tough job like immigration.

Sergeant Phiri looked less than thrilled to see Mr Sakala. The two men shook hands in a perfunctory manner and neither said a word. Maggie raised her eyebrows at Lizzie and with a jaunty smile broke the silence.

'So, Mr Sakala, how is business? Do we have plenty of rich tourists desperate to stay beyond their permits?'

The serene man nodded.

'We have some, Madam Angus. I think you know who these people mostly are.'

There was a twinkle to his serenity now as he glanced at Lizzie. Lizzie blushed. Twice now she had forgotten to extend her tourist visa until a couple of days after it expired and it was only thanks to the kindness of the local immigration officials that she had not been expelled.

'But more importantly,' continued the serene official, 'I think you are interested in the man who lives beyond the end of the main road, off the dirt road which leads to Elephant Camp, down the track by the river. I have investigated this man and find he is here legally. He is from DRC and as far as I know he has committed no crimes. I am sorry to disappoint you and bring you to this blind end.'

'The passports, they are false, therefore?' Thomas enquired, brightly.

'They are false,' agreed Mr Sakala.

'So they are not the passports of our suspect.' Thomas gave his friend from the church no time to incriminate himself with a lie, however white. 'Good. This helps us to move on. It has been a very helpful trip. Thank you, my friend.' Thomas bowed his head slightly towards the Buddha of the immigration service.

Maggie looked at her watch.

'Heavens above, we need to get back or we'll miss lunch. Lizzie, are you ready? Sergeant, can we drop you back at your post? Thomas – we'll take you back of course.'

The Sergeant stood slowly and hoiked up his loudly checked trousers by their cheap plastic belt. 'I can go back to my post now, yes, and be happy that we are moving this investigation towards a conclusion. My boss, who has all the evidence that you have gathered so far in *his* possession,' here he paused, underlining his obvious meaning, 'will no doubt be surprised and happy. We may one day find out who did these terrible things at Elephant Camp.'

The sergeant shook his head as if to deny his words. Thomas clapped him on the back in mute sympathy and after making their farewells to the immigration officer they all headed back to the luxury of Maggie's vehicle. Lizzie hung back, slightly, and made a special point of shaking Mr Sakala's hand and thanking him for his help.

'I am happy to be of service, Professor. Let me know if I can do anything further for you, we all want to find out who killed this man. It is not good for our little town. And I look forward to stamping your passport, in due course. You will not leave it too late, this time, will you?' He flashed her a big grin and scampered off to work.

Maggie revved up and drove off with a roar, raising a shower of grit from the car park as she turned into the road. It took only a few seconds to reach the police post. A reluctant-looking Sergeant Phiri clambered down from the front seat to be replaced by Thomas. There was no sign of the nice new, confiscated four-by-fours and no sign of any other officers on site. Lizzie watched Phiri shuffle into the dingy concrete box, the wretched chicken dangling from his hand, his shoulders hunched, looking more like a convict than a policeman, and she felt a dart of sympathy. Even stray animals had better facilities back in England. Now that really did make her angry.

Maggie turned back onto the road and slid a CD into action. The melodic voice of Danny acted like honeyed sunshine on Lizzie's mood.

'Thomas,' she leant forward from the back to make herself heard, 'this guy who we now reckon is a spy of some kind, did Jake ask you if he could go out on patrol with your guys to check out his house from across the river?'

'He went out first thing this morning. Now we know who the man is, perhaps we could risk a visit if we do need to find out more.'

'Excuse me,' Maggie's voice broke across Danny like a large wave crashing over a container ship in a storm, 'I know I'm just the chauffeur, but I do have ears. What's this about a spy – or am I too low down the food chain to deserve an explanation?'

'Oh, Mags, I'm sorry!' Lizzie put her hand on her friend's shoulder. 'I forgot you weren't there. The immigration man said the guy on the edge of the bush around Ellie Camp is from DRC, but he's got some kind of diplomatic status which we guess equals spy. So the passports themselves are false but kind-of officially false. We decided not to give Phiri the full story just in case. The spy might be endangered if anyone knew, if he'd been hanging out with the bad guys as part of his work. And Jake said he might go out on patrol with the Parks scouts on the other side of the river and see if he could get some better shots of the place with his telephoto lens. That's all, honest!'

'You're forgiven. Thomas, won't Jake be back by now?'

Thomas looked at his watch.

'He may well be waiting for us. We shall see.'

One of those natural lulls in conversation settled over them now as they rolled ever closer to Parks HQ. Sure enough, when they turned in, Jake was sitting on the steps of Thomas's office, smoking. He squeezed the cigar stub between his thumb and forefinger, popped it in the pocket of his sober khaki shirt, designed to blend in when on patrol, and ambled over to greet them.

'Morning, troops, have I got news for you!'

He pulled out his camera from its protective bag and clicked it on. Lizzie took it from him and stared at the little screen. She gasped as she realised what she was seeing.

'Oh my God, it's Luc Delfosse!'

Chapter 26

They were late for lunch. Lizzie had almost, but not quite, become angry with Maggie by the time they left the HQ. It had seemed such a trivial reason to leave, feeding greedy, rich tourists, but Maggie had made it clear that the welfare of her guests was her responsibility and Thomas, while patient, managed to convey the message that he had work to do. Lizzie resigned herself with bad grace to the reality of everyone else's working life. As they neared the lodge, the uncomfortable realisation dawned on her that she had really been procrastinating, delaying the inevitable. Tonight she would have to face her first ever night alone at Elephant Camp.

As they neared camp Danny ran out of songs and Maggie turned off the CD player.

'Lizzie, how would you feel about sleeping in the small spare room while Alex is away? It's full of junk but we can put a spare bed in there, no problem.'

'That would be fantastic. I was worrying – I mean, Piet and Andre have been fantastic, but …'

'Mmm. They have. But they're not getting the chance to offer to keep you company in that cottage! And they have jobs and homes to go to. I did hear their wives were glad to see the back of them for a couple of nights, though.'

'So, is anyone else coming over?'

'No, honey, Gus is on guard duty tonight. Don't worry, he's a damn fine shot and observant with it.'

'I'm sure he is, I didn't mean to suggest – it's just I thought he might be a bit tired, it's been going on a while now and you two must be dead worried.'

'We are. But we KBO.'

'KBO?'

'Keep Buggering On – Winston Churchill used to say it apparently.'

'Great. I'll adopt it.' Lizzie squirmed a little in her seat. 'Look, do you mind if I go off and sit somewhere and have a think when we get back? I'm feeling a bit confused about everything at the moment.'

'Not at all, but why don't you sit in the restaurant where we can at least keep an eye on you, eh?'

So, Maggie went back to her office while Lizzie sloped off and sat, one leg crossed over the other, thinking, round and round and round in circles. She needed a pen and paper. She stood and walked back over to the office where she took some scrap paper out of the bin and borrowed a pencil.

'What do we know?' she wrote.

Then she sat and chewed the pencil, oblivious to the fact that it had come ready-chewed by who knew whom.

She ended up doing her usual exercise, two columns of jottings in no particular order that – in the end – were worse than useless but had somehow managed to unscramble her brain. In particular, a note about René reminded her she ought to check her emails to see if she had a reply from Jess.

Maggie had vanished and Simon was sitting at the computer when she got there. Frustrated in her mission she wandered out and stood gazing into the trees, watching monkeys at play. The Camp's dog, Jimmy, came over and nuzzled her legs.

'Hello, smelly,' she said as she bent to scratch his mongrel head. He sank down onto her left foot, his warm body a doggy version of a peace, happiness and security blanket.

Simon came out of the office to join her.

'I am sorry to keep you from your work, Lizzie, I have finished. How are things with you?'

'Not bad, Simon. And you, how goes the hunt for Mrs Simon?'

A broad grin spread across his face.

'I have a wife-to-be, the medicine has worked before even I took it.'

A call from Gus had him running off, still grinning.

Lizzie hurried over to the office, reassured by both the comfort of the hot dog and the happy news from Simon. Life went on. Trite, but true.

Her in-box was full enough to have received a university warning. Near the top of the massive list of new messages was one from her friend.

Lizzie, good to hear.

I'm in a hurry so this is brief. Don't trust Gilles, he got sacked for something trivial but the real story was corruption. It was something to do with a dodgy firm he got involved with – the two Delfosses were implicated – as you've probably already guessed they're best avoided too. I did hear that Luc is more sinned against than sinning but that was from a young woman who studied with him and you can't believe everything you hear. René has lost all academic credibility, he's been following Sylvie and Luc around for years and the lifestyle's gone to his head – they've paid for him to travel with them everywhere and he rarely leaves their sides – or should I say hers – he's plainly besotted with her. René makes out he's related to someone in government but I think that's a load of tosh, they just pay for favours. Finally, there was talk that Sylvie and Luc had got mixed up in some odd sexual goings on – orgies or something – so don't go round theirs for dinner on your own, my girl.

Sorry, not much help, but suggest you steer well clear. No good smells round that lot. By the way, your bone is making news again – some Yanks are saying they've found another part of the skull – how did they worm their way into your patch, Lizzie? I'm really sorry, what a disappointment for you. Don't let the bastards grind you down.

Lots of love Jess

She was still sitting in the stuffy little room, tears rolling down her face, when Jake arrived some half an hour later.

'Hey, princess,' called the vet as he approached, 'you're not dressed, where's the tiara?'

Then he made it through the door and his tone changed.

'Christ, Lizzie, what's happened? Is Alex OK?'

Lizzie unfurled herself from the chair and stood. As she did so the tears came flooding out and she sobbed like a child. Jake put one arm round her shoulders and wiped at her tears with his free hand.

'Hey now, it's never as bad as you think. Come on, tell Uncle Jake, what's up?'

He removed his arm from her shoulders, took her hand and dragged her towards the bar. There he pushed her into a chair and left her wiping her nose with a paper napkin as he went to order. He returned with a large gin and tonic.

'Drink up and tell me all about it, you can trust me, I'm a doctor.'

'So was Mengele,' Lizzie sniffed.

'That's my girl, that's more like it. Now. What's up?'

'It's not much really, I think it's just that coming on top of everything else. Oh hell, some Americans have found another bit of bone like the one I found, but it's a bit of skull.'

'Is that better than a jaw?'

'Depends how much they've got. It's just that they've done it and I never even knew they were here.'

'Where was it published? Did Thomas know they were here?'

'Both good questions – no idea where it was published or when. And if Thomas doesn't know, then they're in trouble. Unless they got their permit from someone in Lusaka on the way down here, of course. Oh why did it have to happen now, when Alex is away?'

'Because God knew it would give me a foot in the door, darling! Seriously, are we still on for tonight? I've got it all planned, dinner at mine, drinks at Wild-Dogs, a hasty peek into the den of iniquity and then – fireworks, shooting stars, trains rushing through tunnels Alfred Hitchcock style? What do you reckon?'

Lizzie was smiling by now.

'A spare bed on my own at Maggie's house springs to mind. Thanks, Jake, you're a tonic. I know it's only a bone but…'

'I do understand. But wait till you find out some more, eh? It could be a mistake.'

'It could. And besides which there's a few little trivial things like murder that are a bit more pressing.' She sniffed. 'That picture you took, Luc Delfosse, what the hell was he doing there, calmly chatting to that man?'

'Let's talk about it tonight. Listen, I don't want to set off too late, why don't you go and wash your face and put on your glad rags and I'll check in with Leah. Then we can head out and start the night early, what you say?'

'Sounds great. Give me – what, half an hour?'

'Perfect. See you at the campsite bar, yeah?'

He sauntered off without a backward glance.

Lizzie sat a little longer, still feeling sorry for herself, but better. She believed what she had said, the bone was trivial by comparison. It was just that everything felt worse when Alex was not there to reassure her. Sometimes she wondered if she would even be a professor if he had not been there urging her on, boosting her self esteem. He was the one with a real passion for his work, but maybe that made him less ambitious. She was driven by feelings of inadequacy, he by thirst for knowledge.

Gabriel interrupted her brown study.

'Madam, there is a radio call for you, now-now.'

Two nows. Urgent. She ran, thinking of Alex and all the terrible things that might have happened to him.

Simon was holding the radio receiver and smiling, so it could not be bad news, she assumed.

He whispered 'Doctor Alex,' and left, a man of tact.

'Lizzie speaking, over.'

'Liz, it's Alex, we're in range for a minute so thought I'd try you. Listen, it's looking good, better than I thought, so we're just going to do a quick test pit and come back some other time. We'll stay one night then come back, OK? Over.'

'Brilliant, that's really good news. One thing, did you know the Americans have found a bit of *rudolfensis* skull? Jess emailed. Have you heard anything? Over.'

'Not a murmur. Look, I have to go, don't let it get you down – there's something I've seen that should cheer you up, trust me. Take care Lizzie, and be good. Listen, got to go, sooner it's done the sooner I'm back. Take care. Over and out.'

The silence was like a slap in the face. She thought back to what he had said and massaged her imaginary welt with reassuring memories. Something to cheer her up, he said. That sounded hopeful. Maybe he'd seen a site with bones. Maybe the site he was digging had bones. She looked at her watch and realised with a jolt she had only ten minutes left to get ready and meet Jake. At least he would find her happier, if not more relaxed. Lizzie had a feeling that the metaphorical storm that had been brewing for the last few days was about to produce some thunder and lightning. Her nerve endings were tingling with anticipation. An uncomfortable thought pushed its way to the surface. Was any of it down to spending an evening alone with Jake? She quashed the thought firmly. That was one problem she definitely did not need.

Back at her room she found that all her belongings had been moved and ran quickly over to Maggie's house. There she had to dodge the polite conversation of Sylvie and Gus and head straight for the bathroom. She selected clothes from her very limited wardrobe that were good enough for polite company but should not make Jake think she had dressed for him, a side-effect of that uncomfortable thought she had suppressed. As she emerged from the bathroom, washed, dressed, wearing lip gloss with her hair down, Gus started to chuckle.

'What?' Lizzie snapped.

'Oops, sorry,' Gus responded, 'just thought you looked rather smart for a change. Going somewhere nice, are we?'

'Gus, I've got clean clothes on and a bit of lip gloss, it's not as if—'

'I'm teasing, Alex isn't here to do it so I'm just fighting his corner. You take care with that charmer. I'll send out the search parties if you're not back by eleven and if it's later than that you're grounded, young lady.'

Lizzie laughed and kissed him on the cheek. Sylvie's expression was enigmatic. If Lizzie didn't see her as a goddess of chic sophistication she might have been tempted to think there was a little envy in her appraisal. But Lizzie could not see or appreciate her self. Only those around her could see the sparkling eyes, the luminous skin, the ready smile, all framed by billowing waves of tawny hair. The netball team captain on a night out.

She ran out of the house and towards the camp site, then slowed, realising she was risking life and limb. Dusk was falling like dust in the air. It was the elephant hour of the day, the time they liked to wander through from the riverbank to the woodland, on their way to who knew what. She reached the campsite slowly, but safely, to find Jake sitting at the bar with Leah.

Jake failed to remark upon her appearance, to Lizzie's relief. She perched herself on a stool.

'Hi, Leah, sure you don't want to come with us?'

'I'm washing my hair, thanks, Lizzie, if you know what I mean?'

'Not entirely, but I won't push you. I heard from Alex, he's only staying one night, it sounds like the site's already looking good – he's going to dig one test pit then come back and make plans for a proper excavation. So that's good news.'

'Great. What about you, you've been stuck here for days, aren't you itching to find more bones?'

'Don't! I had some bad news. Friend in Bordeaux told me some Americans have found a skull fragment. Didn't say any more and so of course I'm on tenterhooks – not to mention being totally pissed off. But – hey, I can't do anything till Alex gets back.'

'Listen, princess,' Jake looked at his watch, 'hate to interrupt, but we'd best get off while the going's good. Sure you're not interested, sweetheart?'

He had moved his caress to Leah's backside as usual. She brushed it off as usual and grinned in reply.

'Thanks, but maybe another night. See you tomorrow, guys, be careful and have fun.'

With that she wandered off, the pert bum provocative in her tight white jeans.

'Christ, but she's hot.' Jake was riveted.

'Come on, sex bomb.' Lizzie nudged his elbow and started towards his wreck of a pick-up.

Mfuwe in the dark was a different place. The scruffiness was airbrushed, the poverty packed away, the lights so few and far between that they merely leant a cheerful glow to the village. Driving past the poorer shops that lined the road – concrete shells, mere facades emptied of their paltry goods each night – stray bursts of music came and went. Jake turned the wheel, drove off the tarmac road and bumped down a dirt track.

'I thought we'd go to Wild-Dogs for dinner instead of mine, my cook's off sick again – I think I've got another AIDs casualty on my hands. And the food's probably better here anyway.'

Lizzie had to admit she was both a little relieved and a little disappointed. Relieved because she was, if she were honest, just a little apprehensive about being alone with Jake; disappointed because she loved to see a person's home environment, it helped her piece together the jigsaw puzzle that was each human being.

Dinner was a fun affair. Piet the temporary guard was one of the owners and came and joined them. They ate steak, drank cold *Mosi* and cheap red wine and laughed like drains.

Then Luc Delfosse came in.

Lizzie froze.

The few other diners also lapsed into silence. It must have been something in the way Lizzie stared and Luc stomped across the concrete floor.

'Professor Lamb, I am sure you do not wish me to join you, but can I talk with you for one moment?'

Lizzie looked at Jake who shrugged and laid down his fork.

'I'll go pick up another beer. Keep it snappy, mate, and no funny business, I'm watching you.'

Jake walked over to the bar and perched on a bar stool, eyes fixed on the two palaeontologists. Lizzie folded her arms and sat back in her chair.

'Well?' she said. 'You have your moment, go on.'

'I see you are angry, this is not surprising. I will be concise. You think I am a criminal, but I am not the murderer you seek. Ah – I know these things without being told,' Lizzie had glanced at Jake, and Luc had noticed, 'there is no spy in your camp. It does not need a genius to see that you are looking for a person who can be a murderer and who is also a person mad for fossils. I am not all you think. Others are not what you think. René and Sylvie are not what you think. I suggest you ask her about her work with her father, a mining company called BelCoMin. She may say nothing, in which case ask your friend Mr Monk. I am sure he can find out what you need to know. I am not the person you seek, Professor. Be careful with my dear wife. You will find she has dangerous contacts.'

'Don't you mean you have dangerous contacts? We know you have been in the company of a man who hides away down by the river, a man who comes from the Congo, who has false passports and bad friends. We have a picture of you there, surrounded by stolen property. So now what do you say about who is dangerous?'

Lizzie regretted it the instant she had uttered it. What made her tell the man the only useful bit of information she had?

Luc Delfosse stared at her.

'In English I think you say that appearances can deceive. Go to this man and ask him to tell you why I was there. Ask him who he is working with and what he is doing. Tell him I sent you. But for God's sake do not tell anyone else that you have seen me there, other people will be in danger.' He looked at his watch. 'I must go, I am meeting your friend Birgit. She is a lovely woman, not rich like Sylvie, but rich in life. I have the money I need now, I can say goodbye to my wife with pleasure. I will leave here as soon as I can be sure Sylvie is no longer a problem. She is mad. Money is her god, she is forever on his crusade.' He paused. 'But you do not believe me, I can see. Ask the man by the river. Tell him Luc sent you. He will be my witness.'

He broke off and laughed.

'Yes, tell him Luc sent you. I will be interested to hear how he responds. Give him my *very best* regards.'

With that he rose and walked away.

Lizzie realised everyone in the bar had been listening and her stomach sank. She just prayed that no one else had understood what they were talking about. She looked around at the assembled guests. She did not recognise anyone and the relief was immense. She looked at Jake who signalled an offer of a drink. She nodded, vehemently.

'So, princess,' he said as he slid into the bench opposite her, 'now the whole world knows what you're up to and who's the lynchpin of your evidence. You fancy a trip to see this geezer on the way home tonight?'

'I suppose we better had, hadn't we?' She looked worried and whispered, 'Have you got a gun, Jake?'

He nodded and held up forked fingers indicating he had two.

'Drink up quick, my pretty, that man's already on the road, if you're worried about what he might do, he's got a lead on us already.'

She threw back her wine. He threw back his beer, stubbed out his cigar and put the nub in his pocket. They almost ran to the car. Jake unlocked a box in the back of the cab and handed her a small gun. He took out a rifle for himself.

'Just wave it at him, the safety catch is on. This is how you take it off – but only do that if I'm out of action and we're desperate. There's a knack to these things, you might not have it.'

In the dark everything seemed to take so much longer. The first time they drove past the turning, missed it, and had to turn around and drive back. At least the wildlife was cooperating and nothing on four legs hindered their progress. The track was not well graded, great lumps of stone stuck up from its surface and they plunged down from them into craters formed in the last wet season and never filled in. Try as they might there was no way they could get there without making noise and Jake eventually abandoned caution and drove as fast as he could without breaking an axle.

Lizzie hung on for all she was worth to the seat belt that failed to extend from the side of the cab. In her other hand the gun hung from her hand at the end of a stiffly extended arm, pointed at the floor. It was not something she was used to carrying and despite Jake's reassurance that the safety catch was on she did not trust it.

She thought of Alex and what he would say if he could see what she was doing. She put the gun in the glove compartment, reached out her hand to Jake and touched his knee.

'Hello, only one night and you're missing it already?'

'Oh, shut up, Jake. Listen, do you think we should get someone else to do this? Don't you think it's a bit dangerous?'

'Yes, and yes, but who and when? Don't worry, darling, we'll terrify the bollocks off the guy, you wait and see.'

Lizzie shut her eyes and prayed, it was the only thing left to do that she thought might make any difference now.

Sounds that usually seemed so exotic, so exciting, so colourful, now felt merely sinister. The screech of an owl evoked a soul in torment, the hyena's whoop a cry of the damned, the lion's bark pure blood lust. Lizzie opened her eyes again and looking through the window sought solace in the stars above. None came, the vastness of the Milky Way simply reinforced their vulnerability.

The bush had begun to break up and an open space loomed ahead. The electric fence that surrounded the house and the grounds around it was interrupted by a gate, which stood open before them. Jake slowed almost to a halt and bent low over the wheel, squinting at the house in the darkness.

'Lizzie, I'm not liking this, no one goes to these lengths and leaves a gate open. And there's no light at all. I reckon the bugger's scarpered. But we'd best keep alert, it might be a ruse. I'll drive up as close as I can. When I stop, get out and stay behind the vehicle, I'll edge my way over to the house.'

He pulled up. Lizzie took out the gun, opened her door as if it was booby-trapped, slithered off the seat and settled on the ground. Her head was pounding and her stomach felt like acid had been poured into it. She regretted that last gulp of wine.

Jake, surprisingly light-footed in his decrepit sandals, was nearly at the door when she dared to peep around the corner of the vehicle.

He stopped and felt in his pocket, from which he pulled a torch. Lizzie was, yet again, surprised how well prepared the guy was. She stood, feeling her whole body shake with a little tremor at each beat of her heart. Adrenaline really worked.

She almost gasped when the light suddenly flooded the hut ahead of her. Then she heard a stream of profanities and Jake made a quick exit.

'We're too bloody late, the poor guy's crawling with insects already. Blood everywhere. Listen, can you find your way from here to Elephant Camp easily? I think I ought to stay here and we ought to get help – someone has to stand guard tonight so the police can see this tomorrow. I don't like sending you off alone but I can't see an alternative – can you?'

'Only if there's a radio. Or your phone works.'

'Tried the phone already – no signal. Wait there, I'll check for a radio.'

He vanished into the hut again and after a few seconds that felt like an hour she heard the tell-tale crackle of the lifeline of the Valley. Just a few seconds later and it was done.

Jake flipped down the back flap of the pick-up truck and they climbed up and sat facing the direction the rescuers would come. Jake put an arm around her and she huddled up close. It was no time for useless decorum, human contact was what she needed.

'I called Gus,' Jake muttered, 'no reply from the police of course. He's going to drive by Thomas's house and see if he can rouse a couple of game scouts to stand guard overnight.'

'That's a good idea – but I hope he doesn't bring Thomas, his family needs him at home, not out here and in danger. Those little girls, they're so adorable, those pretty little frocks and frilly white socks they wear.'

'Ahh, sweet.' He paused. 'Lizzie, it's not like me to be serious, I know, but pretend for a moment I'm your big brother. Are you planning to have kids, you and Alex? I mean – it's none of my business but . . .'

His voice tailed off into the night, having nowhere else to go.

Lizzie sighed a deep sigh.

'We don't know, is the honest answer. It's one of those side-effects of the great feminist revolution. I can choose whether or not to try for a baby and I can have a career but I can't choose to ignore my biology. I'm quite happy as we are, but who knows how I'll feel in twenty years time if I don't – it goes round and round in my head.'

'Listen, I'm no role model I know, but if your main worry is whether you'll feel something's missing in twenty years time, don't you think that suggests you're not up for it? In twenty years time you could be missing plenty of other things – in fact you could be dead if this ridiculous scenario pans out the wrong way. Don't get me wrong, I actually do like kids, just don't want any of my own, but you know, most people like you who choose to have them do it because they really, really want kids. Doesn't sound to me like you do.'

Lizzie sat silent. It felt like a penny had dropped.

'You know, Jake, no one has ever said that to me before – odd, isn't it? And now you have, well, I think you might be right. I think I —'

Just at that moment the sound of a vehicle reached them. Jake withdrew his arm and they both jumped down from their perch.

A few seconds later they saw the beams of headlights coming down the track, a few seconds more and they had company. 'Thomas,' cried Lizzie, 'You shouldn't have come!'

Jake nudged her and whispered, 'Say something nice, quick, or he'll be upset.'

'I mean,' Lizzie blundered on, flustered, 'I'm glad you're here, I just, no, never mind, I'm glad you're here, that's all.'

Gus came over and gave Lizzie a big hug. He took a good look at her then spoke quietly, 'Are you all right? Why don't you sit in the vehicle while Thomas and I have a good look round?'

She nodded and went straight for the front seat of Gus's vehicle. It was as if she were surrounded by family and it felt good. Thomas came and stood beside the open door and filled her in on their plans.

'Two of my scouts are on their way in a Parks' vehicle, Isaiah has gone to rouse one of our other men – whom I have to hope we can trust. They will stay here tonight. But Gus and I agreed we need to have a look around straight away in case there is anyone out there in the bush, maybe even our injured man, who knows. So, I'll ask Jake to stay guard while we scout around, is that all right with you, my dear?'

Lizzie merely nodded. At the arrival of the cavalry her trusty adrenaline had retreated, she was now barely able to think, let alone speak. She sat, drained, as Jake stood smoking, a small cigar in his right hand, the rifle still in his left.

Feeling began to return to her body. She frowned as her brain resumed its normal cacophonic activity. It had been such a relief, not to think, but now one troublesome thought kept pushing itself to the front of the crowd. Her groan was audible. Jake threw his cigar to the ground, stubbed it out carefully and paced over.

'You OK, princess?'

'No. I have to see the body.'

'Oh no you don't, it's a god-awful mess and there's no need. It's absolutely bloody obvious what happened.'

'Jake, you know I have to, if there's a need for an expert witness it's got to be me.' Jake made to interrupt her but she ignored him, 'Yes, I know you're a medical doctor by training but it's been years since you did any real forensics on humans whereas I did a refresher course less than a year ago. I'm not saying you're not the more expert eye, just I can't ignore my expertise and if it comes to legal proceedings I want to be prepared.'

'Fine. Take your point. I'll come with you. Here, you take the torch.'

They stood before the open door.

'Better not go in again, at least not till the scouts have had a look,' Jake said. 'You can see the body from here.'

It was indeed a bloody mess.

Lizzie scanned the area round the body with Jake's torch.

'Look,' she whispered, subdued in the presence, again, of violent death, 'a cigarette stub. It's been the coda running through this piece – cigarette stubs at the site that was vandalised, at the bone site, now here. We never thought to look at Harvey Miller's murder scene. I bet Isaiah would have noticed. Remind me to ask him.'

'Yes, ma'am!'

She smiled. Trust Jake to lighten things up even when they were standing in front of a gory mess.

'Come on, Professor,' he spoke firmly now, and put his arm around her shoulders once again, 'back to the car for you. I should be standing guard, not standing with my back to the potential enemy.'

He was right. She climbed back into the back of the pick-up and leant against the side. She looked up at the starry sky and thought of Alex. He was looking at those same stars, probably assuming she was safely tucked up in bed. A thought occurred to her. Thomas had sent Isaiah for help, that meant he was not with Alex. She picked at the skin beside her thumbnail, hoping whoever they had with them was trustworthy. But there was nothing she could do about that now. With an effort of will she turned her thoughts back to the murder. The cigarette stub she had seen might or might not be yellow, she couldn't tell in the light of the torch. René had taken the *blondes* for Sylvie so no matter who she believed, that meant Luc had the *maïs*. It was evidence of some kind – not conclusive, he could have been there any time – but if the scouts were able to reconstruct the scene and Luc had been there at the time of the murder then it looked really, really bad for him. And if Luc was involved, what did that say about Birgit? But then, if Luc was involved, why send them down here to see the mess?

Lizzie needed Alex, but in his absence, Jake would have to do. She jumped down again and wandered over to talk it through with the 'next best thing in the circumstances'. Jake would not have been flattered.

Chapter 27

Lizzie woke early, too early. Not even a glimmer of sun had reached the ink-black sky and the fish eagles were still in their palm-tree eyries. She sat on the edge of the bed, listening to the sounds of the bush. It made her realise how unnaturally quiet the western world could be. She thought of that book, *Silent Spring*. The end would come one day when the birds were silenced and the bees were gone and the flowers no longer bloomed. Humans would get their wish: a quiet life. Or a quiet death. She sighed. No time for that now. She listened carefully, alert to the tell-tale whine of mosquitoes. Nothing. She pulled back the net and padded over on bare feet to the little door into the corridor. She slipped along to the bathroom, rinsed her tired eyes and sprinkled some water in her hair to bring it back to life. She hesitated before flushing the loo then realised she could hear movement in the kitchen. Someone was up and running water.

It was Gus. Bless him. He had been there when Thomas found the papers under the dead man's bed, there when she arranged to meet him at Parks HQ soon after dawn, still there when she left. He could hardly have had any sleep and yet here he was, smiling, holding out a mug of tea.

'Alex is back today, isn't he?'

'Yes, thank God,' Lizzie breathed over her steaming tea. 'It's been a nightmare. I just hope nothing else happens.' She closed her eyes, just for a second. 'You know, you talk glibly of death, of murder even, but you never really know what it feels like to be confronted with it till it happens. And even then, with Harvey Miller it was weird because we thought it was a natural death at first, in the sense that we thought it was an animal kill. But this, it's just awful. So brutal, so much blood. And if Thomas is right and the guy was a spy – well, he was probably doing something important. It's so frightening. I mean, whoever's doing this, they're here with us, aren't they?' She shuddered.

Gus put one big hand on her shoulder for a couple of seconds and sighed.

'We've never lived through anything like it. It's at times like these that you realise there are down-sides to living in a remote wildlife paradise. We need your British CID. But thank God for you and Thomas, eh? Come on, eat something before you go.'

He plonked a plate down in front of her and she found she was surprisingly hungry. A large omelette quickly vanished, with a slice of dense brown bread, washed down by mellow Malawi tea.

Lizzie checked her watch. Time to go. Gus gave her a big hug.

She left the sanctuary of the house as if dragging a heavy weight. It was a day like no other and a burden she had no choice but to bear.

Gus had insisted she take Maggie's car. As she sat in the leather embrace of the driving seat she was grateful, it helped make the journey less of an ordeal. She noticed the Danny CD was on the passenger seat and pushed it in. His voice would keep her company and might even lift her spirits.

Driving into the Parks compound she saw Thomas waiting. Even he was showing the strain, his face looking grey, his smile a little less broad. He helped her out of the big vehicle and they quickly made for the shelter of his office. There he had the papers. They sat, side by side, carefully checking through the pages. The poor man, whose unmasking had been partly their fault, had kept a careful paper trail. It looked as if the criminals he had been tracking were, after all, interested in one simple thing: not ivory, not gold, not Coltan, just money. Plain, ordinary, dirty, money.

'See here,' Thomas pointed to a record of a flight into Libya, 'he followed whoever it was – let's call them Mammon – into each of these countries at regular intervals over the last three years. Libya, DRC and Zimbabwe. Wherever Mammon goes it looks like there's a mineral interest of some kind. Except just recently in Zimbabwe where there's nothing that looks like mining interests, but there's some activity at the border that could be smuggling.'

'So,' Lizzie interrupted, 'when you say it's not minerals but money...?'

'It seems as if the reason they were involved with the mining concessions was not to trade in the goods directly, but to exploit the locals. They set up what you might call a franchise activity. They negotiated concessions using local agents, under cover of so-called local businesses which they set up with thieves and criminals. Then they set up local management, a kind of holding company, with their own security – mercenaries of a kind, many South Africans and some from Europe, Russia and so on. Then the poor workers who risk their lives had to pay go-betweens in the local subsidiary companies for the privilege of working and those companies then pay the holding companies which pay Mammon. The local managements are responsible for the whole of the risky side and just pay Mammon for having set it all up. They can't run it without them – the paperwork shows clearly that the locals are expected to operate within certain guidelines that look like they are legally binding, but the ultimate owners – BelCoMin – can wash their hands of it all if their stooges on the ground behave illegally. They must have some excellent lawyers, I think, in Monaco or Lichtenstein or wherever this sorry organisation is based.'

'Have I got this right?' Lizzie looked puzzled as well as tired, 'Mammon gets to cream off the money, but has none of the hassle of exporting dubious materials from dubious places. They have to pay the security guys who run their so-called holding companies – men who they must be able to trust – but after that, it's just sheer profit for them and if anything goes wrong they just smile, wash their hands and move on? Is that the top and bottom of it?'

'Very neatly put, Professor. It is possible the customers for the minerals are also part of this network, and maybe get a favourable price – it wouldn't surprise me. And the whole foundation rests on bribery, I am guessing.'

'Great. So, the big question is, who is Mammon? Are we looking for one person?'

'Ultimately, yes. One clever, devious person who it seems is happy to kill on a whim or at the slightest whiff of danger. A very, very dangerous person. A person who might even as we speak be eating toast with honey and sipping breakfast tea at Elephant Camp.'

'That cigarette stub, it was a yellow one, wasn't it?'

'It was, and if what Sylvie told you is right that means Luc was there, but there's no way of knowing when it was left there and we're not blessed with a twenty-first century DNA testing facility here in rural Zambia so it would take many weeks to get any evidence of that kind. And anyway, even if no one steals the stub, something will happen to it and we will get no evidence from that, I can assure you. I know this world too well, I am sad to say.'

'Thomas, did you glean any other clues about Mammon that would help pin it down, male, female, nationality, colour?'

'Francophone, that is all I can tell you. So, Belgian, French, Congolese, Cameroonian… I could go on through many more African states, but I think we both suspect that we know the answer already, do we not?'

Lizzie nodded. Her sombre mood was deepening, sharpened by fear. All of the potential suspects were freely roaming around. And they could do nothing.

'OK, Thomas, what can we use from these papers to help us confirm or reject our suspicions?'

Thomas handed her a rather crumpled looking sheet of paper.

'Here, this details the dates when Mammon was in Libya, Zimbabwe and DRC. In all these places one's passport will be stamped. Can you find any way to obtain the passport?'

'Maggie takes everyone's passports when they arrive and keeps them in the safe. She only hands them back when they leave. I'll radio her—'

'It may be better to telephone, that way no prying ears – if there are such things, I am not sure ears can be so active, so let us say instead, lest anyone overhear.'

Lizzie was happy to hear Thomas in more characteristic form. And he was right.

The satellite link was working and she made it through on first attempt. Maggie would wait for her return and they would check the passport together.

'Excellent.' Thomas took her hand. 'You must be careful that no one sees you doing this exercise. Would you like me to come back with you?'

Thomas looked anxious. Lizzie knew he should really stay behind and hold the fort. Police were on their way from Chipata, the nearest big town, to pick up the body and the evidence, but for now it was his responsibility. Until they had the murderer behind bars there was no telling whether there were accomplices abroad – possibly even in the Parks HQ – who might act alone to damage their evidence. She could tell he wanted to get back to the dead man's house and stand guard with his men. Money was a powerful tool, it might sway even the most loyal of workers, especially those who really were not paid very much for doing a pretty dangerous job.

Lizzie took a deep breath and smiled.

'I'll be fine, Thomas. I know you need to stay here really. Once I get back Gus and Piet and André will be there to look after me. Those guys have been fantastic. I'll radio through as soon as I have an answer – I'll work out some way of telling you that won't be obvious to everyone out there. In one way I just hope to God it is him, then we can do something. It's not knowing that's so bad, looking at everyone with suspicion. It's frightening how we respond under pressure, isn't it?'

'*You* respond like a human being with a conscience, that is what we must all try to do. Be careful, my dear. And may God be with you.'

Thomas walked out to the car and saw her off, waving until he was lost to view.

Lizzie was nervous. The sun was higher in the sky now, it was late morning, time for coffee and biscuits. The banality of evil, someone had once said to her, was the most frightening thing about it. When Thomas had said that the murderer could be sipping tea and eating toast it almost made her feel sick. And now it was morning coffee time. A wry smile almost made it to her lips as she thought of Ricoffy. It barely bore a passing resemblance to coffee, serve the murdering bastard right if he was drinking it.

Wary of being seen, lest she get drawn into a conversation she just could not imagine handling, Lizzie parked the vehicle outside Maggie's house rather than driving to the reception area, then carefully picked her way along a rarely used and overgrown path to the office side of the site.

Lizzie scuttled into Maggie's office in a hurry, as if someone were watching. No one was, but it had become a habit over the last couple of days, behaving as if she was under constant surveillance. Maggie closed the door behind her and pulled the wooden shutters to across the little window. Lizzie heard a mosquito, but she was so preoccupied with what Maggie was doing that she felt it sink its thirsty proboscis into her arm not once but twice before she snapped into action and slapped at it. She missed. Maggie watched it land on her desk, on a piece of white paper, and dealt it a deadly blow. Blood spattered the paper, Lizzie's blood.

'The little bugger! It bit me twice. How long does it take to get malaria?'

'What are you taking?'

'Doxicycline.'

'It's as good as anything else – keep your fingers crossed – and watch out for the symptoms. Doxicycline tends to mask them – if you get a bad headache that doesn't go away I'll take you down to the clinic.'

'What, the one near the BP station?' Lizzie's face betrayed her shock.

'Don't worry, it's hygienic and they have Coartem – that's what you need – kills it before it gets into your system to stay. Anyway, chances are you won't.' Maggie sighed. 'We're putting it off aren't we?'

Lizzie nodded.

Maggie opened the wooden door to a tall cabinet. Inside, next to the rifle whose possible implications Lizzie tried to ignore, was a small safe, built into the inner wall of the office which divided Maggie's side from the reception desk. The wall was more robust than it looked, Lizzie could see now.

Maggie unlocked the thick metal door and pulled out a canvas bag. From it she took a trio of passports. She handed them to Lizzie.

'I don't know what I want to see, so you can look and tell me if he really is our madman,' wheezed Maggie, her breath coming shorter as she became anxious, something Lizzie had not heard before. She looked at her friend in consternation but was met by a firm jaw and pursed lips. She laid the piece of paper which listed Mammon's travel dates on the desk where she could see it. Then she looked down at the passports in her hand, two French, one Congolese. Lizzie went straight for the odd one out.

'Congo, eh? So the little creep isn't even Belgian.' She thumbed through its pages, then thumbed through them more slowly, then turned each page deliberately in turn till she came to the end for the third time.

'It's not him. He wasn't in Libya, he wasn't in Zimbabwe. He was in DRC, but that's all. Oh shit, Mags, it's not him. So who the hell is it?'

Maggie reached out and took the redundant passport off Lizzie. 'You've got a choice of two. Go on, you can't stop now.'

Lizzie held a passport in each hand and arbitrarily chose the one in her left.

'This one's René's. Here goes.'

She flipped through the passport, then flipped again, stopping towards the end. 'It's only just over a year old so we can't check all the dates. But he was there, he was in Libya. He was in Zim. They check out exactly as far as it goes. Oh God. I can't believe it. Tell me I'm wrong.'

She handed the open passport to Maggie who blew out a stream of smoke as she spoke.

She looked down at the document in her hand, open to show a series of visas stamped across the pages, dates clearly legible.

'Sorry, kid, the evidence is right there in front of you. I don't know what you're going to do about it now, mind.' She looked up at Lizzie. 'What are you going to do?'

'I'm going to tell Thomas and get him to talk to Sergeant Phiri. And I'm going to carry on as if nothing has happened. So are you. Above all, I'm not going to say anything to Sylvie unless René does something I think might endanger her. He obviously adores her – it's just so hard to see how he can ... But then whoever has been doing this stuff has to be a bit barking don't they?'

'They do. Totally woofers. Come on, let's put this stuff away and you can call Thomas. And we can open those shutters and get some bloody air back in this room. I feel like I've been in a Turkish bath. Do they still have Turkish baths in the UK? Never mind, forget I asked.'

Lizzie shook her head. It was all too much. She was not sure whether Turkish baths did exist any more, in that far country she called home. She was not sure if they ever really had. She was not sure she knew what one actually was. In fact, she was not sure of anything.

She called Thomas. He took it all on board quite calmly and confirmed that he would drive to the police station to see the Sergeant rather than using the open airwaves.

Music filtered through the anxiety numbing her brain. The radio was playing a song she recognised from an Eagles album in her mum's old vinyl collection. *Lyin' eyes*. It was a good line, but they were wrong, it was all too easy for some people to hide them.

Maggie locked up the safe, threw back the shutters and flung open the door. They walked across to the bar laughing and chattering like little girls with new toys. It was an act. In reality, clouds had come in to cover the sun. One of the people with whom they were sharing their daily lives was at the very least a liar, if not a murderer.

That line about lying eyes had stuck in Lizzie's head. It circled her brain like a bee buzzing round a lavender bush on a hot July day, stirring up her thoughts. She frowned, willing the words to go away, willing the tune to go away, willing the thoughts to go away. But the thoughts kept on coming.

'Maggie.' she said, at last.

'Yes, darling, what is it?'

'We need to go back in the sweat box.'

Maggie stood stock still, a cold *Mosi* dripping with condensation clasped in her left hand, a cigarette burning in the right. She hesitated, scrutinised her friend's tired face, put down the *Mosi* then turned and set off back to the office without a word. Lizzie followed behind in silence, like a convict *en route* to a cell.

Maggie stopped by the door.

'Do I need to go through the whole rigmarole again?'

Lizzie nodded.

Maggie closed the shutters, locked the door, opened the safe and took out the canvas bag once more. She held the passports in her hand, looked down at them and held out the one she knew Lizzie wanted. It became real at that moment. What their hearts did not want to know, what their heads should have told them long, long ago.

Lizzie took the passport from Maggie and opened it, flipping through each of the well-worn pages, checking the stamps, the colourful, the monochrome, the terse and the elaborate. They accused Sylvie Delfosse. The evidence was there in graphic form. She had been in Libya, in Congo, in Zimbabwe. The dates worked. All the dates, going back years.

'I can't believe it. She's been in every hell hole in the world by the looks of it. She's been there when René hasn't. There are dates in there when she's been there without him just this year. How could she? What made her … I can't deal with this. Maggie, how are we going to … I don't know what to do.'

'Did I tell you she's booked on a flight this afternoon? Her dad organised it. She's staying at the Pamodzi in Lusaka tonight and flying directly to London tomorrow. If she leaves the Valley we're stuffed, without evidence and with daddy's money behind her we've no chance of getting her bang to rights.' She took a deep drag on a cigarette. 'She's got it all planned out. She must be expecting us to go for Luc, she won't know about the evidence from our poor little spy. She may not have got blood on her hands but she sure as hell set it all up. I have *never* met anyone so cold and calculating in all my life.'

'You're right. Cold, calculating and so very, very good at empathy. I think,' Lizzie stopped and sat on the desk, 'I think she must be a psychopath. We're going to have to be extremely careful. She's super-intelligent, intuitive and ruthless. People think psychopaths have magical powers sometimes, they're so perceptive – she'll understand our behaviour better than we do ourselves. Any little signs we give off that indicate a change of heart or reaction will be like traffic signals for her. And true psychopaths are not just totally devious, they can be utterly plausible. She may well convince us we're wrong before this is over. I only wish we were.'

'Lizzie, what made you come back and look?'

'It was the Eagles, that song about lying eyes on the radio. I kept hearing it in my head, it was going on and on but never got to the end, always got stuck at the same point. It was driving me nuts because I didn't know all the words. I thought, why did I just remember that bit when it was a whole song? And then, I don't know why, but hearing the music I kind of saw this image of your hand holding two passports and thought, why did I choose René's passport? It was only part of the story. And what would have happened if I'd chosen Sylvie's, would I have looked at it? Those bloody cigarettes, all this time I kept making excuses in my head for why they could have been at the sites, if they were hers.'

Lizzie chewed at a bit of skin on the side of her thumb.

'Then I realised I'd been purposely blocking her out from the murder, despite the fact that we knew she was on the board of BelCoMin, just because she had said she was bullied into it by Luc. We wouldn't have listened to Luc if he'd said the same thing. And she totally fooled me with that little drama, the love-lorn wife running away from her brutal husband – I mean, come on, daddy's filthy rich and she's not exactly a timid beastie. She could have left him any time she wanted.'

She stood up.

'I'm a failure of a feminist. I didn't want to think it might be her,'

Lizzie continued. 'I didn't realise I had been making excuses for her, convincing myself she was manipulated or bullied or cowed into doing what Luc wanted. Then I thought, Harvey Miller said Luc wasn't the worst of them. I thought he meant the bastards who work in the Congo in general, I didn't think he might mean the worst of the Delfosses. She's betrayed everything I care about, Maggie, humanity, trust, civilisation – women. How could she?'

'You said it yourself – a psychopath. Even if she had all the material advantages she could have been abused, or maybe her folks were warped. We won't know till we sort it out – and we have a way to go yet, honey.'

'I know,' sighed Lizzie, 'We have to carry on as normal till we can get hold of Thomas and Sergeant Phiri.'

Maggie shook her head in disbelief, 'That poor man down by the river, he was just doing his job and look what she did to him, what Sylvie did to him. And for what? That woman and her money. I hope she spends the rest of her life in a Zambian jail with no one to feed her. Oh hell, let's get out of here and get on with it. Come on, there's a beer going warm out there with my name on it. You want me to be normal, I want to drink beer.'

As the two of them strolled, chatting, back to the bar, Lizzie realised how hard it was going to be to conceal her fears from Sylvie, if she saw her. As Alex was always saying, she didn't have a poker face. They had to get some kind of evidence, find some way of arresting her, stop her leaving the Valley. Lizzie looked at her watch. It was time for lunch. By three o'clock the safari Land Rover would be waiting and Sylvie's luggage would be loaded on it. By four o'clock she would be at the airport. By six o'clock she would be lounging around the bar at the Pamodzi Hotel in Lusaka and by nine the next morning, assuming the computers weren't down, British Airways would have flown her far, far away from any danger of being arrested for anything, anything at all, ever.

Chapter 28

It was unusual for Lizzie to drink beer, even more so to drink it at lunchtime. She thought for a few seconds before ordering a *Mosi*, paranoid that even this small change in her normal behaviour might suggest deception, but then she realised it was ridiculous, she had drunk beers often enough before on this trip for it to be a perfectly natural rather than aberrant choice. And anyway, there was no one around to see. The golden liquid trickled down her throat, the icy bottle in her hand was acting like a tranquiliser. Maggie, always a natural at everything, was chatting with Gabriel, whose laugh, loud and long, burst forth at regular intervals. Lizzie simply could not join in. She realised she had just hours to work out a way to stop a murderer leaving the Valley and escaping any hope of punishment for her crimes. It was like that wretched song again, she thought, going round and round her head, never getting to the end because she did not know the words.

Unbeknown to Lizzie, the answer to her circular problem was bearing down the dirt road towards Elephant Camp at a speed best left to the level tarmac of the Great North Road. The first she knew of it was a rattle and screech as Thomas and Jake drew up beside each other at the reception. They each moved with a speed that was equally alien to both of them.

Lizzie quickly checked the surroundings. Even with her smart binoculars, Sylvie – assuming she was at the house – would not be able to see who was sitting with her or what was going on. Lizzie was still far from relaxed, but the realisation made her slightly less tense. That and the sight of Jake sporting a large sticking plaster on his chin. It was hard to look at him without staring at it.

'Yes, I cut myself shaving,' he muttered, 'just have your laugh and then pay attention. Thomas and I have been checking out the stuff at the dead guy's house. It's definitely Alex's kit. We assumed the dead guy must have been involved in nicking it as part of his cover, blending in with local criminals, like the one he was working with – the one who got injured, the poacher Isaiah tracked out in the bush that day with you lot. Still haven't found any trace of him. But as for the kit, it looks like it was a set-up. We've got a witness, we've got evidence that Sylvie was directly involved in disposing of the stolen goods at his place.'

'Fantastic,' Lizzie leant forward, eager in anticipation, 'come on – who is it?'

'Not who.' Jake breathed on the nails of his right hand and rubbed them on his vivid lime green shirt in the traditional western gesture of showing off, 'Our witness didn't actually see the frame-up, but she got an electronic visual record. I hate to mention the name in polite company but Birgit, she who must absolutely not be obeyed, was out there on patrol with the anti-poaching squad, she had her big camera with her and she took a long distance snap of our mate's place. Several in fact. There was a lion and two young apparently and while taking shots of them she got this unexpected bounty. She was in the village, I came across her at the market on her own, looking pretty down, and I just had to speak to her. She said she wanted to work something out and I thought – oh-oh screwball time, and was all ready to jump ship —'

'Jake,' Lizzie was impatient, 'can you cut to the chase and leave out the "how I saved the world" bit?'

'Certainly, your loveliness. She'd showed Luc these pictures and he swore her to secrecy, told her Sylvie would probably kill her if she heard, told her the woman had a weird ability to know what was going on. Spies everywhere. Luc told Birgit he'd been planning to leave Sylvie for nearly a year. He's been helping the DRC government try to get evidence against her that would be strong enough to bring down her whole house of cards – apparently it's quite an operation. He was frightened that because she'd dumped him she would probably kill him and he'd been trying to work out an escape route with the guy who got splattered last night. But Birgit thought we still had Luc in the frame for the first murder and was convinced it would get Luc out of trouble if she made sure Sylvie – and René – got implicated in the theft. Enter your local vet. I've printed them out big on my PC – it's working for once – and so we've got her for the theft, if nothing else.'

'Can I see?'

Thomas handed the print-outs to Lizzie.

She scrutinised them in silence.

'You mean we've got René. She's just standing around isn't she. She's one clever woman.'

'There's another,' Jake leant over, 'here.'

'Aha, you're right, she's actually handling the stuff. OK, so we can reckon this would help get her arrested for theft, what about murder?'

Jake looked to Thomas.

'Lizzie, I hate to be the spectre at the feast,' Thomas spoke up, 'but why have you assumed the murderer is Sylvie and not René? Where is your evidence?'

Lizzie looked at Maggie.

'We – Maggie and I – we just know, don't we?'

Maggie nodded.

Lizzie sighed.

'That's not good enough, I know. We were hoping something concrete would come up. But what you've got there, surely that's enough to stop her from leaving this afternoon?'

'I hope so.' Thomas shook his head, his expression at odds with his words. 'I will have to report to my favourite policeman yet again. I hope the BP station is luxuriating in a sufficiency of fuel or we will not make it in time. Jake – are you willing to accompany me in case of difficulties?'

Jake nodded, stood, hitched up his baggy shorts then reached into a shirt pocket for a cigar and a box of matches.

The two left in as much of a hurry as they had arrived.

Lizzie looked thoroughly disconsolate. Then her expression changed.

'Maggie, if you were Sylvie, and you realised Luc had escaped being blamed but you wanted René blamed and not yourself, what would you do?'

'I'd make sure I was around, being friendly and nice, and that René left in a hurry looking suspicious, then had an accident. Crikey. Where is he, Lizzie? That man's in danger, isn't he? Oh hell. Gus, we need Gus.'

Maggie dropped her cigarette in the ashtray, jumped out of her chair and ran to the bar.

'Gabriel, find bwana Gus, now-now!'

Gabriel was like greased lightning.

Seconds later he was back, trailing Gus.

Maggie spoke quietly to Gus who ran off to the nearest vehicle, jumped on board and drove off. By then Lizzie was standing next to Maggie.

'Where's he going?'

'He's heading for the house, I'm going to drive over to the campsite and you're going to stay here with Gabriel. Gabriel – make sure Lizzie is safe, the woman from France is dangerous, be careful.'

With that she left in a hurry.

Gabriel stood behind the bar, polishing glasses with a tea towel, looking for all the world as if nothing unusual had happened. Lizzie could tell, however, that he was on guard. His eyes never looked at the glasses, his hands kept on rubbing the same ones again and again and the number left standing on the bar, shinier and shinier, never increased.

Despite the heat of the day Lizzie began to feel cold. It started at shoulder height and spread down her arms, down her back and up into her hair, which, had there not been so much of it, would have stood on end. The vulnerability of her situation was dawning on her.

Gabriel put down his tea towel and started to walk out from behind the bar. Lizzie turned towards the direction of his gaze. Sylvie was walking towards her, a beatific smile on her lovely face. She was dressed, unusually, in pink, instead of her normal neutral shades of ivory, beige and white. Her trousers were wide and made of something soft and light, her top low, revealing her cleavage, draping her torso like a classical statue.

Both Lizzie and Gabriel were spellbound. It was as if a vision had walked out of a dream and into real life. It was Sylvie who spoke first.

'Dear Lizzie, so very clever, so very pale, so very English. What an ugly pair of trousers, and this dirty t-shirt, even clean this colour is not for you, it shouts with your hair. You have no idea of how to make yourself beautiful. But I do not give you the lessons. I leave soon for the airport. Perhaps you can help me with my bag, Gabriel?'

Gabriel looked at Lizzie.

'Gabriel is helping me, Sylvie, I am afraid he is not free. Maybe you can ask someone in the garage?'

'Ah, non, je suis désolée, mais non.'

With that she pulled a small, shiny, deadly weapon from her pocket. Lizzie had never seen a small gun before and the sheer beauty of the specimen before her made it all the more sinister. Lizzie's thoughts were so humdrum, it was as if there were two realities: the one in which she was faced with a mad woman with a gun that could kill her at any moment, the other in which she stood, watching, as if in a documentary, commenting on what she saw before her. That reality stayed in control. She wondered what to do, yes, but more than that she wondered at her own calmness. She had never considered how someone must feel when faced with a gun, it was such a cliché of television drama, of so many films. And just trust Sylvie to have a gun with a pearl handle, she thought. Lizzie could glimpse the shiny white decoration through the fingers furled around the pistol. Sylvie's nails, she noticed, matched her outfit perfectly.

'Of course,' Lizzie said out loud, 'your nails. No one in our world has nails like that. How could anyone dig with perfect nails?'

'Oh my dear, what are men for? I have René, who may still have a use, although his best use is now accomplished. He is so good with the garrotte – it works well on small animals – and also on ugly American palaeontologists. That man Miller, he was clever as well as disgusting, he learnt things that it is not healthy to know about me and my business activities. He had realised what we were doing with the fossils was just a cover.'

She gave a little shrug.

'Then, I tolerated the idiot Luc for longer than he was useful. Men always do what I ask. My father, even. They all must go in the end. So sad. But not yet René. I find him agreeable enough in bed. And he will say whatever I ask of him. Once I am out of this mediocre place I can decide what to do about him. But for now, I am leaving.'

'Tell me, how did you do it, Sylvie? How did you get that stolen kit down there? Oh, of course, that was before you engineered your removal from Luc – you did engineer it, well, didn't you? None of that stuff with Luc and the young girl at the bar happened, did it?'

Sylvie merely smirked.

Lizzie was getting angry now. 'And the murder, how did you do it? I know damn well you made that happen. Was it little René again, can he beat people to a pulp for you too? Is that it?' She fumed as Sylvie calmly watched her temper rise. 'I wondered why you didn't get your daddy to fly you out straight away, but you had other things to finish didn't you? You had to get rid of that man because he knew who the real criminal was. He knew you were the one setting up the companies, evading the taxes, corrupting the officials, exploiting the poor people who had the misfortune to be born into those rotten lives in those pathetic hell holes. And all for what, more bloody money?'

'Your Duchess of Windsor said one can never be too rich or too thin, Lizzie, but you would not know about that, *hein*? You are not rich and I would not say you are thin. Poor Alex. But then he is a little dull, so much the archaeologist, even with those large eyes and all that wonderful long dark hair.'

Lizzie snorted.

'Give me a break, Sylvie. You really are scraping the barrel. But I really want to know, come on, how did you get that man killed?'

'Oh, you are so childish, Lizzie. I pay a man to do everything: one steals your laptop and drugs your night watchman – he was good, very good, a man from my firm in the Congo. He made a game of it for me, taking his time, making himself a friend of that useless old man and frightening you by entering your room at night and leaving you safe and sound. A local man steals Alex's kit – the night watchman was just a sleepy man – we did not drug him, it was his excuse. You should be more careful who you trust.'

She was enjoying this, Lizzie realised, showing off.

'Now, the sites, that was more fun, we did that ourselves. It was so good to see the saint Alex's work ruined.'

'And did you beat the man down by the river to a pulp Sylvie, come on, was it you, or did some other poor, foolish male sell his soul for that one?'

Sylvie let out a yelp of laughter.

'Lizzie, Lizzie, you do not think straight. How are you a professor? No, I do not get blood on my hands, not with these nails, as you say. Besides, by then I am in *purdah* with Maggie and Gus. And why make René do it and risk the danger of AIDS when there is an ugly, stupid, poor man who is probably dying anyway to do it for us. We pay him just a bag of bush-meat and a few dollars. What is more amusing than to turn one of your oh-so holy Thomas's game scouts into an assassin? Yes,' Sylvie laughed at the evident dismay on Lizzie's face, 'I hear this expression "poacher turned gamekeeper" – I hear that many of these men are poachers who are made to become gamekeepers or to go to prison. How easy, then, for me to pay this man to kill for me when he earns so little money and has so little loyalty?'

Lizzie had not finished.

'OK, I have to admit you're pretty damn clever, but, Sylvie, what made you *do* all this dreadful stuff in the first place? I mean, you're rich, you used to be such a brilliant palaeontologist, I honestly thought you were here because you're interested in bones, a palaeontologist to the core, from the heart even?'

'I have no heart, you should understand this now, Professor. I am born without this inconvenient organ. How does it feel, to be a Professor, to have such a big heart but to be so very poor? I came here for the bones, it is true, I love them, as far as I can love anything. And I was hoping to take away your little bit of glory, find more. It was to be fun, a holiday from making money.' She shrugged her shoulders. 'I enjoy the game. I trained this idiot man from my company – a fool who then steals a car from that spy and goes out poaching with someone he has just met and who is even more the fool and is attacked by an elephant – but I trained him to steal your laptop, to let you know I have found your site, to steal your husband's things. It is an enormous, wonderful game for me to play with human beings instead of chess pieces. You see, I can do anything because I have money, so much you can only dream of these amounts.'

Her expression suddenly changed, the smile vanished and in its place a quick frown like a cloud scudding over the sun. Her voice grew harsh.

'Yes, this is what I have, little Lizzie. I have money, I have intelligence – I have everything. I can click my fingers and order men to do what I want and I can pay the policeman you think might arrest me and go free. Do not attempt to stop me now, or I will kill you. I think you understand this.'

Sylvie turned to see her lover walking towards her, a sycophantic smile on his bland face.

'Ah, René, at last. Let us go before these other people return. Lizzie, Gabriel will come with us. If you come after us we will kill him. If you radio the airport to stop us we will kill him – and anyway, I have already paid the people at the airport, they are mine. They are just men, *tu sais*? This game can be so easy. If we leave safely, your Gabriel, he will be safe. You understand?'

'I understand. Gabriel, I am so sorry.'

'Madam Lizzie, do not fear for me, God looks at even the smallest of creatures, he will take care of me.'

Sylvie laughed out loud.

'Imbecile. There is no God. *Et bien, René – on y va?*'

He nodded.

'I do not hope to see you again, Professor. Now, remember, do not try to stop me or this man is dead, his life is yours until I leave Mfuwe with René.'

She backed off towards the waiting vehicle, a smart new four-by-four, keeping Lizzie in her vision, the gun still in her hand but her arm hanging slack against her side, so confident was she in her own invulnerability.

René pushed Gabriel into the passenger seat then walked around and took the wheel. Sylvie sat in the back, one languid hand lying on Gabriel's shoulder, the gun visible through the window. They drove off, Sylvie languidly waving with her other hand, like royalty.

'Shit, shit, shit.' Lizzie swore.

She did not know what to do. She ran for the office. There was no moral dilemma to face about radioing the airport – Sylvie had seemed remarkably unconcerned and now she knew why. The radio handset had been smashed, the telephone had been smashed, there was no way of contacting the airport, or the police, even if she dared. Even if she had a mobile and even if there was a signal she had no idea what their numbers might be. She looked at her watch.

She guessed that Maggie would return within a matter of minutes, either because she had failed to find René and Sylvie or because she had seen – or heard – them leave. There was nothing to do but wait.

Sure enough, after what seemed like eternity, but was in fact about three minutes, Maggie was back.

The two of them drove like maniacs across to the campsite. Gus, Maggie and Lizzie stood, huddled, wondering what on earth to do for the best.

'Parks HQ,' Lizzie almost yelled, 'it's not far, we can go there and radio the airport or the police station. Come on.'

They jumped into Gus's vehicle and screeched into the dirt road leaving a dust-storm in their wake. Rounding a bend they saw a huge elephant standing right in the middle of the road, looking their way. Gus yelled, 'Hang on' and swerved off the track, careering through the bushes, terrifying Lizzie who shut her eyes as she clung to the side of the Land Rover. By the time they were back on the road her fingers were numb.

It took them less then fifteen minutes. Lizzie ran into the office and faced Thomas's smiling deputy. It was almost uncanny, the way the radio crackled out just at that moment.

'Parks HQ, Parks HQ, Parks HQ, do you read me? This is Sylvie Delfosse, is Professor Lamb there yet, over?'

It was followed by a burst of laughter.

Lizzie felt like crying. She turned to Maggie.

'Maggie, if we use the closed channel can we reach the police or the airport without them hearing us?'

'If they don't know what the channel is, yes, and given where we are we should be safe.'

Lizzie looked at the bemused man in front of her.

'I'm sorry, this is really urgent, I need to radio the airport on your own channel, can you set it up for me?'

'No problem, here you are Professor.'

Lizzie held the receiver and started the call.

'Mfuwe airport, do you read me? This is Parks HQ, come in please.'

She repeated it four times.

'Ah, Professor,' the Parks officer shook his head to and fro, 'these guys, they never answer our radio calls. We always call them on the main channel first to make sure they answer.'

Maggie held up her hands in despair.

Lizzie tried three more times to no avail.

She was walking through the door when the Parks official spoke, slowly, in his deep and measured tone.

'Professor, do you have a cellphone you can use? I know the telephone number of a friend at the airport.'

Maggie burst out laughing.

'I still can't get used to having those bloody things round here,' she said, 'have you got one?'

Lizzie shook her head.

The nice man with the mellow voice cleared his throat.

'First, maybe you must speak to Dr Nkhoma?'

Lizzie nodded.

He dialled and handed her the phone.

'Thomas, where are you? You are joking?' She turned to Maggie, 'He's had a puncture, Jake's gone on without him.' She spoke again to Thomas. 'Do you have Jake's number, Thomas? No? Not to worry. Sylvie's on her way to the airport with René and they've taken Gabriel as a hostage – she's got a gun pointed at him so don't even think about intervening from the side of the road, no. I'll try to get Jake's number and see if he can sort something out at the airport. We're worried that she's bought the airport though, she says she's bribed them, is your Mr Sakala there? Where is that? Great, bye, be careful.'

'Nothing is simple. We'll have to find Mr Sakala. Thomas doesn't have Jake's number – the vet Jake Deacon – do you?'

The official shook his head. Lizzie made to hand back the phone.

He raised one hand and said 'Ah, no. Please, Professor, borrow this thing until you have this problem solved.'

She thanked him profusely.

'Now, do you know where Mr Sakala lives? Thomas said it is—'

'It is most easy for me to come with you, Professor, please drive me up to the main road.'

It was a mere four minutes before they arrived at Mr Sakala's 'house'. Lizzie stared at the place. He had met them wearing a suit, a white shirt and a tie, carrying a briefcase, his shoes as bright as a button. What stood before her was a mud hut, a good-sized mud hut, admittedly, but a hut nonetheless. Mr Sakala came out, smiling.

His wife stood in the background looking anxious but inquisitive.

Lizzie explained her dilemma.

'If this woman has paid to bribe someone then I am afraid I cannot help, I am just in immigration, if there is someone corrupt at the airport then I will have no influence. I am so sorry. But is there not anyone else you can telephone? Where is your husband, the good doctor? Is he not with you?'

'Mr Sakala, you are possibly brilliant. I had not thought of that. We must go, please give my greetings to your wife and say I am sorry for not stopping. Thank you!'

Lizzie pulled out the borrowed phone again and racked her brain for Alex's number. She had no idea what it was.

Maggie pulled a piece of paper from her bag, like a magician, and said, 'Is this what you're looking for? He gave it to me in case there was some kind of emergency with you. He was worried.'

Lizzie kissed her on the cheek and grabbed the paper.

Seconds later she got through. It was as if the gods were at long last smiling on them.

'Alex, it's me, no time for a chat, listen, Sylvie's our murderer and she's on her way to the airport with René. They've got Gabriel and a gun and threaten to kill him if we try to stop them. She thinks you are out of the way so won't expect you to be there. Where are you?'

She listened biting her lip. A smile broke across her face as she replied.

'Great, that means you should be able to get there before her. I don't know what you can do, and for God's sake be careful, she says she's bribed them at the airport, maybe a mention of the President will do it – you are meeting him next week aren't you, nudge, nudge, wink, wink? Spot on, good luck and *don't do anything silly*, she'll kill you soon as look at you. Love you too, bye, bye...'

Lizzie's elation was vanished in an instant.

'Maggie, I've just sent my husband and four students to meet a mad woman with a gun. What the hell was I thinking of? I'm going to ring him back.'

The gods, fickle as ever had changed their minds. Try as she might Lizzie could not get through.

'Professor?'

It was a tentative enquiry from the almost forgotten provider of the mobile phone.

'I'm so sorry,' Lizzie gasped, 'I'd forgotten you were there.'

The man smiled.

'I am here. I think I must ring my friend at the airport now.'

Lizzie stared blankly then remembered that was how the whole mobile phone thing had started.

'But Mr Sakala said it was no use if they had been bribed. Can your friend help without being in danger?'

'My friend is a most important man. He is a mechanic. He is the man who says, "no, this plane he is not good to fly" and then this plane he cannot fly. I am thinking this is a most useful friend to have at this minute.'

The gods were rubbing their hands with glee, they were really enjoying the game of 'surprise the mortals'. This time Lizzie could not restrain herself and did indeed hug the poor man who looked a little startled but not upset.

Lizzie handed him the phone.

'There is a white French woman and a white man with her who are trying to leave the airport, she has a barman, Gabriel, from Elephant Camp with her and a gun, she is dangerous. She says she will kill the barman if anyone tries to stop her. She says she has bribed the airport authorities so that no one can stop her. We need to get her arrested by the police before she can leave Mfuwe.'

'I understand.'

With that he walked away and soon they could hear him deep in animated conversation. There was nothing they could do but listen.

He came back looking glum.

'My friend says he has been asked already to check the plane and has said it is fine. He cannot do anything now as they are all forbidden to enter the airfield again. The plane and the pilot are ready. I am sorry, I cannot do any more.'

'Thank you for trying. You never know, there might still be something. At least your friend knows the situation. OK,' Lizzie scratched her head unconsciously as she spoke, 'Jake or Sergeant Phiri – they're our last hope. I know, let's drive to the anti-poaching unit and see if anyone is there – they'll know Jake's number I bet.'

No words were spoken, everyone just leapt for the vehicle.

They screeched to a halt outside the closed door. Lizzie's spirits fell briefly but soared as she saw Birgit emerging from the box-like building.

'Birgit, quick, it's a matter of life and death, what's Jake's mobile number?'

'His what?'

'Cellphone, his cellphone number.'

Birgit pulled out her bag and her own cellphone and scrolled through the numbers.

'In fact can I use your phone, Birgit, this kind man has already let us use his twice?'

Birgit handed the phone over, 'Just press the button, it's ready to go,' she said in a dull, flat voice.

'Oh sod it!' Lizzie stamped her foot in frustration raising a small puff of orange dust. 'I had a signal and now it's just vanished.'

'I have a signal, Professor,' the saviour of the day from Parks HQ passed his phone to her as he spoke, 'maybe it is the battery.'

Once more Lizzie dialled Jake and this time he responded.

'Jake.' She explained the details again. 'Where are you – can you do anything without getting yourself or Gabriel killed do you think? I rang Alex and he's on his way too with the students. I know, stupid thing to do but it's done and I can't get through to him now, he must be in a bad signal spot. OK, thanks. Be careful.'

'Well,' Lizzie said as she handed over the phone one more time, 'I've no idea what's going to happen now, but Alex and Jake are on the case and there's one man at the airport who knows what's going on but probably can't do anything. Now we just get on the road and pray. Jake's going to try and pick up a policeman on the way. Let's go.'

It was a good job Gus had brought the safari vehicle. The motley crew climbed aboard. As they drove off Lizzie turned back to look at Birgit and saw a figure emerge from the building behind her: Luc Delfosse. He saw her and waved. She waved back. She might not like the man, but he had told the truth.

Gus drove as quickly as he could with an open vehicle full of people. Along the way they came across Thomas standing by the side of the road with a gaggle of children around him as usual. He ran over and climbed on board. They zoomed off to much giggling and waving from the little ones, running in the wake of the Land Rover until it vanished with the road into a section bordered with long grass.

'I have some news,' Thomas yelled in Lizzie's ear from the back seat, wind rushing through their hair, flies intermittently smacking them on the face. 'My young friends from the school have found a laptop, they think it might be yours. It is not quite the gun or the passports, but at least it is something.'

Lizzie turned, held up her thumb and gave the brightest smile she could manage. It seemed almost trivial now. She decided there and then to give it to the school, they deserved it.

No one spoke for the rest of the trip, the tension growing with each minute that passed. It felt, Lizzie thought, like a desperate race against time to catch a plane, but magnified a hundred times.

Half an hour later they pulled up outside the airport. Jake's vehicle was there, Alex's vehicle was there, but no one was to be seen, no one at all. It was like a ghost airport. Then the sound of an engine starting up rattled into the still heat of the day and Lizzie could stand it no more, she jumped to the ground and ran for the airport building, swiftly pursued by the man from the Parks, then Thomas, Gus and finally Maggie, puffing along behind.

They scattered around the small building. The little bank was closed, the post office was closed, the stall selling hot bread and fizzy pop was closed. The only remaining space that could be closed with doors was the Tribal Textiles shop around the corner. That had glass doors. Lizzie came to a sudden halt a few metres away as she saw the man standing guard with a gun. She held up both hands – it came naturally, not something she had ever learned to do, she found herself wondering if it was a learnt behaviour from watching films or a natural instinct. Then reality intruded.

She turned and ran back, stopping the others before they turned the corner and became visible to the gun man.

'Listen, there's a man with a gun – everyone's locked up in the Tribal Textiles shop – Gabriel's with them, thank God. I don't think the guy really knows what he's doing – I reckon he was just paid to stand guard – he didn't even try to stop me running away.'

At that moment Maggie came rushing up and grabbed Lizzie by the arm.

'Listen' she hissed, 'listen.'

They all obeyed.

Lizzie looked puzzled, 'What am I listening to?' she asked.

'Nothing! You can't hear anything because the plane's engine has stopped. It's just stopped in the middle of the runway. That engineer who couldn't do anything told his friend who does the refuelling and he pretended to refuel. If the pilot tried to set off with what he has in the tank he'd drop from the sky like a stone before he got half a mile. Well done –', she frowned at the man from the Parks with the heaven-sent cellphone, 'what is your name?'

'My name it is Levey, Mrs Angus.'

'Levey, that was brilliant. I don't know what we do now, but at least they're not going anywhere. So, Thomas, what about this gunman?'

'Why don't I try persuasion. Wait here please.'

With that he walked off and no one tried to stop him because no one had a clue what else to do.

Sure enough, just a few minutes later, the gunman was to be found sitting on the floor, knees up to his chin, back against the wall, gun at his feet, grinning like a Cheshire cat. Thomas stood to one side laughing and the door of Tribal Textiles stood open. The students still sat on the ground chatting, but Gabriel, Edward, Jake and Alex had come out to join the posse.

'Hang on,' said Lizzie in a peremptory voice, 'what happened to the police?'

'No one there, darling,' answered Jake.

'I'm going to see if anyone's come back since you called. Come on, Alex, drive!'

He ran with his wife and they jumped into the waiting vehicle and sped off across the gritty car park.

In seconds they were at the police station. Lizzie jumped down and ran inside. Less than a minute later she was followed by a dazed looking Sergeant Phiri out to the vehicle.

'I've told him what happened,' Lizzie yelled from the back seat. 'He's got his gun.'

Back at the airport it was as if an odd sort of picnic was happening. The students, seemingly unconcerned, sat around chatting with Gabriel, Levey and the gunman-cum-guard about their ambitious plans for rebuilding the local school, while Edward, Thomas, Jake and Gus kept watch on the plane sitting out on the tarmac in not-so-splendid isolation.

They were busy discussing with Sergeant Phiri what to do when the next surprise hit. Everyone sitting on the floor suddenly fell silent as they saw Birgit and Luc enter the building behind the men standing with Lizzie. Lizzie, standing with her back to them, noticed the sudden silence straight away and turned.

'Birgit, Luc, what on earth are you doing here?'

'Luc has come to sort out his problem with his wife.' Birgit's smile looked far from happy.

'Birgit is right, I helped to make this mess, where is she?'

'She's in that plane out on the runway that has no fuel. She's with René and she has a gun.' Lizzie's exposition of the situation was clear, if brief.

'Very well,' said Luc, 'I will go to her. Can someone lend to me a gun for my protection?'

'I'm not sure...' began Lizzie.

Thomas put one hand on her arm.

'Lizzie, I think we should give this man his chance to make amends. Here, take this one.' He pointed to the one lying at the feet of the erstwhile guard.

'Is it loaded?' asked Luc.

The guard nodded.

Luc kissed Birgit quickly and strode from the glass doors through which arrivals normally walked, past the little flower beds and their pebble designs of welcome, to the tarmac runway.

They all stood now, watching, as the little man calmly began to pace out the distance to the plane.

Before he could reach the four-seater a man came running from the side of the track to meet him. Luc hesitated, listened and then stood waiting as the man ran off again. Lizzie almost laughed at what she saw next, two men in baggy blue overalls and flapping orange visibility vests pushing the steps out towards the plane. Of course, Sylvie was hardly likely to lower the steps for him.

Luc stood waiting for the men to manoeuvre the steps into place.

Lizzie was not the only one to gasp as the unmistakable sound of a shot spat into the still, stifling air.

Luc hesitated. The plane's door opened and the pilot got out. Then René got out. A few moments later the three of them walked back across the tarmac.

'Where's Sylvie?' Birgit's flat, blunt question to no one expected no answer.

It was as if a chill had suddenly passed through the humid airport.

Birgit put one hand over her mouth as she saw Luc push René, stumbling, over the threshold.

'The woman is dead. He says she killed herself. The pilot says René killed her. The bitch has escaped justice, damn her. But you are all safe. Birgit, we must go. There is nothing more for either of us here.'

With that the two of them strode away, hand in hand.

Lizzie turned to Sergeant Phiri.

'Sergeant, don't you need to question them?'

He shrugged. 'Why? Is he the murderer we looked for, is he the thief? Is she?'

Lizzie shook her head.

'So, we do not need this man or this woman. We need the woman who is dead on this little aeroplane and we need the man who was with her – and we can also talk to this pilot, but there is no hurry for that, he will not run away. You can take him with you for safe keeping if you wish. So, we have what we need. And you, honorary detective, are in at the kill again. We salute you, Professor. But now you can leave us to do the paperwork.' He coughed, before speaking again in a lower pitch. 'If, however, you can manage some small paragraphs for me then this would be extremely helpful.'

'No problem, Sergeant,' Lizzie said, nodding. 'I'll get them to you as soon as I can.'

He grinned a broad grin, 'Excellent. There is no hurry. Our jail is quite empty so there is no rush for the space, this man will be all alone in our detention. Though perhaps hungry. Heh, heh, heh.'

René was not happy. He tried to argue his way out of his predicament, he tried to pay his way out of it, but that was a very big mistake, trying to bribe the Sergeant in front of other people. He found the policeman's baton whipping his bare legs and then handcuffs were applied with an expert touch. Lizzie almost felt sorry for him as she watched him walk away to the accompaniment of more swift blows on his bare calves.

Thomas was, by then, talking to the pilot.

'Ah, Dr Nkhoma, it was terrible, terrible. This woman she would not believe there was no fuel. She threatened to kill me. She put this gun to my head. This man shouted at her in French, I do not know what he said. She turned to him and shouted back, he grabbed the gun and shot her. It was terrible, terrible. I am shocked. I am shocked.'

The poor man plainly was shocked and, as wide-eyed and silent members of the airport staff began to emerge from the nooks and crannies where they had been hiding, Thomas shepherded the pilot off to the thatched café for a bracing cup of tea, Zambian style, with at least four sugars.

Chapter 29

It really was a good thing Gus had brought the safari vehicle. When they returned to it after drinking gallons of tea, they found Sergeant Phiri sitting in the first tier of the viewing seats, picking his teeth, while a frustrated looking René squirmed, hatless under the hot sun, in the passenger seat in front of him. Phiri was able to look down on the man's balding, rapidly reddening head and his baton lay ready for action on his lap. When he saw the others walking towards him a broad grin cracked open his face. It was no doubt beneath his dignity to walk the few hundred metres to the police station with his prisoner when a perfectly good motorised vehicle was available to chauffeur them instead.

Gus dropped the policeman and his catch off first, then Maggie insisted on leaving Gabriel for a break at his family home down the road past the airport, despite his protestations that he was 'very fine'. Thomas was next out – they deposited him to wait by his useless Land Rover, Jake having gone ahead to fetch him some diesel. Edward and the pilot were chatting at the back, sharing tales of derring-do. It was like being on a school bus for a very bizarre school, Lizzie thought to herself. The real students, unusually subdued, were in the vehicle behind them, driven by a rather tired Alex, chugging along with its load of buckets and trowels, dusty bags of soil and newly excavated stone tools.

She was unable to pin down exactly how things returned to normal after that, the day became a haze of sun and tea and food and wine and laughter. After a leisurely lunch Thomas vanished back to his world of poaching patrols and tourist protection, happy to see that justice – of sorts – had been done, or at the very least that injustice had not been tolerated.

By half past four in the afternoon Lizzie was sitting on her own, watching the river glistening in the sun, sneaking past a fat crocodile camouflaged on a sand bar, when Birgit came and sat beside her.

'Lizzie, I am leaving Elephant Camp now. Luc has found a place in Tunisia that we can go, he can work and I can look for work. I want to say goodbye to you, to thank you for trying to do what you think is right for me. I know you can't understand it and there is so much you don't know, my life has not been easy, I find myself drawn to men of a certain type. Luc is a lot like me, I think he is good at heart and he understands my problems – I will be happy with him. I feel it. You and I, we can never be real friends after all this, I know, and I guess Jake has told you some things that would make it impossible anyway. I have left a note for him with Maggie, but when you see him, tell him I came and said sorry to you, that I am sorry for what I did to him. He will know what I mean.'

She looked sad. She stood and turned to walk away.

'Birgit,' Lizzie called after her, 'be careful. I hope it all works out for you, I really do. Good luck.' She stood and hugged her former friend and the two exchanged rueful smiles.

Lizzie sighed as Birgit vanished down the path to what had once been her home at the Camp. The world had changed so much in how long – could it really only be a week since Harvey Miller died? She rubbed tired eyes and picked up her bag. Time to rejoin the real world. She wandered over to the campsite bar where a few hours with the students would soon bring her back down to earth. Two open bottles of sweet South African fizzy wine, the nearest thing to champagne that could be found, stood on the bar. She gracefully turned down her share and instead plumped for a large gin and tonic, the twin of the one that Alex was drinking. She slid her arm around her husband's waist and leant her head on his shoulder, weary but happy. Then she heard her name called across the crowded bar.

'Lizzie!'

Zach looked extremely cheerful, Lizzie noticed as he beckoned to her. She made her way to his side across the gaggle of students augmented by youngsters from an overland truck which had arrived that afternoon.

'We're celebrating,' grinned Zach. 'This dude has come up with a sweet scheme to get the school rebuilt. Martin, Kate, Amy and me, we all do holiday jobs for him and he pays us half the going rate and half goes to the school fund – what do you think? Boss, or what?'

The others had gathered around now. Lizzie scanned their happy young faces and turned to the partial philanthropist.

'Edward, this sounds suspiciously like a bad deal for you – or are you employing them as slave labour?'

He laughed.

'Remember that little thing called the minimum wage? Most of them would only get that anyway, so this way I pay kids who are semi-qualified in a relevant subject to do stuff that I'd have to pay someone else a fortune for. They get a decent deal, good experience, the pleasure of my company – and Vickie's,' with this he winked at Zach, 'from time to time and the school gets the rest. Seems fair to me.'

'Whoo – hooh!'

The hoots went up all round as they raised their beer bottles and assorted glasses and danced to the reggae on the bar's iPod. They had all, obviously had a few drinks. Lizzie left them to it and nodded as Alex pointed towards their motorised chariot. No point trying to get at the details now, or find out just how much they thought they would raise this way. She suspected Edward was going to put his own hand into his deep pockets and stump up a bit more than he was letting on. A businessman with money who was based near to the university and was interested in archaeology. She grinned as she imagined telling their colleagues. They would be spitting!

Later that night, sitting in bed in the dark, luxuriating in the simplicity of the room, Lizzie listened to the sound track of the bush with a profound sensation of relief.

'Alex,' she snuggled close to him. 'I'm really looking forward to getting back to work now. Do you think we could do some bone hunting soon? When you've had a chance to sort out what you're doing next? I can't let those damn Americans stop me, not when I've got this far. If they've found more *rudolfensis* then that means I can too, and I bloody well will, I'll show them.'

Alex was so slow to respond that Lizzie sat forward, concerned, and turned to look at him in the moonlight flooding through the mesh-covered window frame. Alex hunched his shoulders, grimaced and spoke.

'Don't kill me, please don't kill me.'

'What? What are you talking about. Alex. . . ?'

'I forgot to tell you, I checked your emails for you, there was one from Jess, she got it wrong, it was a skull fragment they'd found in Zimbabwe, not Zambia and it wasn't even *rudolfensis*, she read it too quickly and just assumed.'

'I don't believe it! Alexander Sommers! How could you forget to tell me something as important as that?'

'I'm sorry, really I am. It has been quite a day, you know.'

'I know.' She twirled her fingers around in a long strand of hair, tawny in the moonlight. 'All right, I forgive you, just this once. But only because you found me a new boney site.' She sighed. 'I can't wait to see it.'

They sat in silence a little longer then Alex spoke.

'Lizzie?'

'Mm?'

'The baby thing. I think I've reached a conclusion. Do you want to talk about it now?'

'Not really.' She let out a deep sigh. 'But now you've mentioned it. What with all this death and destruction you'd think I'd be rushing to procreate to make up for it wouldn't you? But – listen, don't get annoyed – I talked to Jake about it when we were waiting for Thomas, after we found that horrible mess of a body. He said something really sensible. He made me realise that I'm worrying about whether I will regret not having children, way down the line. What I'm *not* thinking is, I really want to have children, but maybe I shouldn't, for whatever reasons. So, if you assume that you should only have children if it comes naturally or you're religious or you really want them. . .'

Her voice tailed off. Alex shook his head.

'You are funny, I assumed you really wanted babies, but you thought I didn't, so you didn't want to push me. I had a chat too – with Thomas. One of the sensible things *he* said was, if we did change our minds and it was too late to have children of our own we could always adopt an unwanted child and make the world a happier place. I thought it was a nice way of putting it.'

There was a pause. Neither of them could think of anything else to say.

'Shall we go to sleep?' a weary Lizzie whispered. The last drop of wakefulness had drained from her tired body.

'Lizzie, what did happen to the cigarette stubs? And who do you think she paid—'

'Alex! Stop it. If you're going to start asking me all the details I'm going to put my ear plugs in. It doesn't matter who nicked the cigarette stubs – or why. As far as I'm concerned I've done my bit. Sylvie was the real criminal and she's dead. René was a murdering bastard and he's worse than dead, he's in a Zambian jail. Luc is surprisingly innocent and he's off to Tunisia with Birgit. Thomas will have to find out who his rotten scout is. That's it, over. I'm not going to answer any more questions. Good night.'

Without another word she lay down her drowsy head and slept.

It was nearly six o'clock when Alex awoke and turned to look at Lizzie, her hair strewn around her like a swathe of rich fabric. She opened bleary eyes and looked up at him.

'Alex,' she whispered, 'the baby thing, there's no such thing as a conclusion, is there?'

He shook his head.

'It's just going to have to be resolved by fate,' Alex said. 'Meanwhile, I've got four surrogate offspring out there ready and raring to go. Are you coming with us? I thought we'd go out and try Edward's new ground-penetrating radar kit.'

Lizzie yawned loudly.

'That sounds really, really dull, but I'll do anything for a nice, peaceful trip out into the wild and dangerous bush.'

Right on cue they were almost physically shaken by the eardrum-shattering trumpet of an elephant, obviously somewhere very nearby. Lizzie shuddered.

'I take that back. I'd like a nice, quiet day shopping, followed by a nice cup of tea and a nice toasted teacake.'

'No you wouldn't.'

Lizzie smiled, shut her eyes and pulled up the white cotton sheet.

END